In the Presence of Angels

A Novel

Book One in the Saint Michael Trilogy

Michael L. Sherer

PublishAmerica

Baltimore

First printing

ISBN: 1-4137-4854-6
PUBLISHED BY PUBLISHAMERICA, LLLP
www.publishamerica.com
Baltimore

Printed in the United States of America

Dedicated to the founders, faculty, staff and students of St. Paul Luther College and Seminary, St. Paul, Minnesota, and to their counterparts in the schools which succeeded them — Wartburg Theological Seminary, Dubuque, Iowa, and Wartburg College, Waverly, Iowa. Their lives touched and enriched those of thousands more.

Soli Deo Gloria

Chapter 1

Adam Engelhardt studied the quiet interior of the print shop, assured himself that everything was in its place, and then turned off the lights. He pulled the heavy wooden door shut behind him, with authority, so that the glass insert shuddered and the welcome bell banged on the inside, against the door frame. From his coat pocket he pulled out the skeleton key that would secure the building. The bolt sounded a familiar thunk as it moved into the lock position.

The print shop owner slid one hand into the inside pocket of his coat, assuring himself that the envelope was still there. He stepped from the curb, walked briskly across Bloomington Avenue, and turned toward the corner. Two blocks west brought him to Anderson Avenue, where he headed north, along the east side of the street. The boulevard trees created strange shapes in the darkening gloom. From somewhere overhead an acorn came hurtling down, a lost meal for some clumsy squirrel.

It was only four minutes from the print shop to the Engelhardt residence. The spacious two-story frame house, with its twin dormers, fireplace chimney on one side, and oval-windowed front door, gave evidence that a family of means lived here. Adam had purchased the comfortable residence at a savings. There was no other way he and his family of four could have made the purchase six years earlier, when his business was just getting a footing.

Dry leaves swirled around the edges of the long wooden front porch, then lodged in the corners. The wind was picking up. *With temperatures dropping, the night could turn unpleasant,* he thought, reaching for the brass door handle. That wouldn't scare off any of the expected guests this evening, he realized. Except, perhaps, old Mrs. Stellhorn. No, chill weather wouldn't keep Mrs. Stellhorn away either.

It was Frieda Stellhorn who had prompted Adam to write the letter to Ohio, which brought the reply now tucked inside his coat. It was its arrival, in this morning's mail, that had led him to urge Elsa to host the meeting in their home this evening.

Adam climbed three steps, crossed the porch and opened the solid oak front door. Barely noticing the etched glass insert he had once admired, he hurried inside, out of the chill. He liked the feel of this place. The house was solidly built. Had the previous owner, a local surgeon, not died so unexpectedly, his widow would never have sold it. But her family was living in Eau Claire, and Minneapolis was too far away for an old woman living alone in a big city.

The agreeable aroma of stew wafted through the dining room. Sliding out of his coat, he found the proper hook inside the hall closet, then retrieved the envelope. Crossing the hardwood floor, he laid it on the fireplace mantel. He waited for Elsa's predictable shout. It came as if on cue, in words he silently mouthed as he heard them: "Wash your hands, Adam. Get all the ink off. I don't want it on my tablecloth."

How does it happen, he asked himself, *that a woman vows to obey her husband, but when it comes right down to it, he does most of the obeying?* He wasn't sure, and he wasn't about to make an issue of it. Nor was he inclined to remind his wife that he'd already washed up at the shop, and that this second scrubbing was redundant. They'd had this conversation many times before. He had never prevailed.

As he stood in the downstairs lavatory, squeezing the lather through his fingers, he reflected on how much joy Elsa had brought into his life. He marveled that she had agreed so readily, in the early summer of 1922, to take a train trip with him and two teenage boys, from Galion, Ohio, to St. Paul, Minnesota. They'd come to visit their church's outpost college, St. Paul Luther, near the banks of Lake Phalen, so that Adam could say he'd given the place a look, before sending his boys off to Capital University instead.

Their self-guided tour of the two cities, on the streetcar system, had brought them down Bloomington Avenue, to the discovery that an ailing printing house was about to close and could be had, inventory and customers, for a song. Adam's father, Abraham, had offered him a junior partnership in the family printing business in Galion, Ohio, but it would have been twenty years or more before he could have taken over. By then he'd be on the edge of retirement. This way, he could start out on his own. And, in a city like Minneapolis, the customer base would be limited only by his own lack of ambition.

Ambition was one thing Adam Engelhardt was not lacking. The day he and Elsa walked through the shop, still cluttered from the last work day when the previous owner had collapsed, at his desk, from a stroke, it was clear to him that this was his opportunity. And, it was clear to Elsa that there would be no talking him out of it.

To his surprise, she didn't put up much of an argument. On the train trip home, he'd asked his wife if she might consider living in Minnesota. To his astonishment, she'd warmed to the idea. Like Adam, she'd been born and raised in central Ohio. But she was ready for something new.

When he'd suggested to his two sons that they might consider attending St. Paul Luther instead of Capital, they'd been unexpectedly enthusiastic. The older boy had said, "Dad, that would be incredible. That college is only two blocks from a really big lake!" While Capital was a four-year school, St. Paul Luther offered only two years of college instruction. But the University of Minnesota was nearby, and both boys could finish there.

So, here they were, German Lutherans from Ohio, living in the middle of Minnesota. And now, in the fall of 1927, Adam and Elsa's two sons were happily enrolled in college — David in his first year at St. Paul Luther and Jonathan a junior at the university. And Engelhardt Printing was making so much money that Adam had already had to hire two assistants.

AS ELSA LADLED out his stew, Adam said, "You reached all of them then?"

"They're all coming. All five couples. And also Mrs. Stellhorn."

"That should make for interesting conversation," Adam said, stroking his chin between his forefinger and his thumb. "Five couples in their twenties. You and I in our late thirties. And one seventy-five-year-old lady."

"You can't possibly *not* invite Mrs. Stellhorn," Elsa said. "This whole thing was her idea in the first place."

"I wouldn't think of not inviting her," Adam replied. "But, as I say, it's going to make for some really interesting conversation."

"I like Mrs. Stellhorn," Elsa replied, beginning to clear away the dishes.

"Of course. What's not to like? She's the salt of the earth. But just a tiny bit stubborn. I wonder who's really going to run this meeting?"

"It's your living room. You are."

"Yes, dear," he replied. She was right. It was his living room. But nobody ever really knew quite what to expect when Frieda Stellhorn started talking

BY SEVEN THIRTY the living room was full. Adam had helped Elsa move all the chairs from the dining room table, so that thirteen people could all have somewhere to sit. Adam was not superstitious, but the idea of bringing together thirteen people made him a little uneasy. But then he remembered, Jesus and the Twelve had been a group of thirteen. So, why was it an unlucky number? Was it because of Judas? He wasn't sure.

Adam had thought he'd begin the meeting by reading the letter, but Frieda

Stellhorn decided she would start instead. She leaned forward in Adam's upholstered rocking chair — she'd been the first to arrive, perhaps sensing the penalty for tardiness might be a hard dining room chair — and gripped the padded arms. Her white curls framed her thin face, and her equally-thin voice seemed to crackle as she took charge.

"It's wonderful to see all you boys together again." To a seventy-five-year-old, men in their mid-twenties obviously seemed like boys. "And, except for Adam here, all of you are Saint Paul Luther boys." Adam had gone to Capital University. His father had seen to that. But all the others, Ohio transplants like himself, had completed two years at the small Ohio Synod school on St. Paul's east side.

Frieda continued, "And here we all are, living in south Minneapolis, with no place to worship." She looked around the room. Nobody was saying anything. From their expressions, nobody was agreeing — or disagreeing. The men, except for Adam, were all college classmates, and had all kept in close touch, since they were all now married and living near one another. All of them knew Frieda. One couldn't *not* know her. For the last ten years, since retiring from her job with the Minneapolis public library, she'd made regular trips on the streetcar, from south Minneapolis to the college. She'd helped out wherever she could. And, on a campus with too little money to do much more than the basics, she was a godsend.

A transplant from Canton, Ohio, and a lifelong member of the Lutheran Joint Synod of Ohio and Other States, Frieda was upfront, abrasive, opinionated and in-your-face. But she was your best friend when you needed one, and when she grasped your two cheeks with her thumbs and curled index fingers, pulling you close and peering into your eyes, you knew she was on your side — even if she disagreed with almost everything you had to say.

"Now, you boys all know," she continued, as if no other women were present, "that Adam Engelhardt wrote a letter on our behalf. We're asking the Ohio Synod to send us a pastor so we can have our own congregation, here in south Minneapolis."

Well, Adam thought, at least he'd written on *Frieda's* behalf. She hadn't really consulted anyone, except Adam, and that was only because she was convinced that the leadership of the church would pay more attention to a letter from a man. Adam knew that Frieda had first consulted with the seminary president at St. Paul Luther, but he had told her to write to Synod headquarters instead.

"Read the letter, Adam," she commanded.

Adam pulled the folded sheet of paper from the envelope, flattened it carefully, and began to read. As he did so, he tried to catch the expressions of others around the circle, especially Frieda. " ... glad that there is interest in south Minneapolis for a new Ohio Synod congregation ... cannot encourage your endeavors at this time ... no available funds ... consider joining one of the several German Lutheran congregations already in your area ... Kindest regards ..."

The other men in the room listened wide-eyed, looking furtively from Adam to Frieda and back again. Frieda's gaze never left Adam. As he folded the letter, she blurted out, "Astonishing! Our church wants to grow. We offer them an opportunity and what do they do? *Nothing!*"

Freddie Stumpf tried stifling a smirk, but was not entirely successful. On the way to the meeting, he'd admitted to his wife, Myrtle, who sat next to him on the couch, that he wouldn't miss this meeting for anything, if for no other reason than to see what kind of performance Frieda Stellhorn would offer up. Myrtle saw his expression and quickly pinched his arm. His face turned sober.

But the performance wasn't over. Frieda fairly erupted, declaring, "Let the record show that on this twenty-ninth day of September, in the Year of Our Lord Nineteen-hundred and twenty-seven, the Joint Synod of Ohio and Other States has officially made a *fool* of itself!"

Now there were chuckles and smirks all around. Andy Scheidt tried to save the moment when he interjected, "Well, you know, Frieda, it's true. There are quite a few other German congregations around here."

"Where are you attending?" Frieda demanded.

"Holy Trinity, on Thirty-first."

"United Lutheran! Way too liberal!" she shot back.

Andy shrugged. Frieda was loyal to the Ohio Synod and there was no getting past it. He decided not to offer a defense for his errant worship ways.

"There are the Missouri Synod congregations," offered Jake Bauer.

"And Wisconsin Synod," added George Kleinhans, wanting to get his oar in.

They might as well have poured gasoline on a bonfire. "*Purity cults!*" Frieda retorted savagely. "Offer them the right hand of fellowship and they spit in it!"

Everybody knew Frieda would respond this way, because everybody had heard this speech before. But the men all loved hearing her recite the litany, and so far they'd gotten their money's worth.

Frieda turned to Willie Langholz. "And where have *you* been attending?"

She might as well have been the Grand Inquisitor.

Willie replied, sheepishly, "Well, we tried the Norwegian and the Swedish churches. But it's the language thing, of course. So we've been going to a … well …"

The words caught in his throat, so his wife, Georgianna, finished the sentence: " … a Methodist congregation."

"Good God in *heaven!*" Frieda exploded. "Why did we sacrifice to build that college over at Phalen Park anyway? So you could all become infidels?"

Adam had heard enough. And he realized the discomfort level in the room had become palpable. He finally took charge. "I've had most of today, since this letter arrived this morning, to think about all of this. With all due respect to Frieda and her optimism about what the Synod might or might not do, I suspected all along we might not get too far down the road with this proposition."

He looked at Frieda. She was pursing her lips. He plowed ahead. "We all know that the Ohio Synod congregation in north Minneapolis, Our Savior's, is too far away for us to attend. But I think there might be an alternative to consider, at least for the short term."

All eyes were locked on him. Avoiding Frieda's gaze, but looking from one to the next of the others present, he said, "In the earliest church, until there were pastors available, Christians met in people's homes. They probably took turns leading worship. Why couldn't *we* do that?"

"That wouldn't be a real church," Frieda snapped. "If it was a *real* church, we could get a third-year student from St. Paul Luther Seminary to come over and help us get organized. But they aren't going to do that for a bunch of people in a living room!"

Adam surprised himself with his directness. He replied, "Frieda, who was in charge at Philippi, and Corinth, and Ephesus?"

"Paul was."

"Three places at once?"

She pondered it. "He trained other people."

"Did he make them go to seminary?"

The room fell silent. The ticking of the Regulator clock in the hallway sounded unusually loud to Adam. But he waited for a reply. What he got from Frieda was unexpected.

"So, would everyone here be willing to take a turn hosting a living-room church?"

The men all looked at their wives, all of whom nodded in the affirmative.

"There used to be extra hymnals at the college," said Jake. "Some of the covers were getting worn. They might give them to us, for a living-room church."

"Who would preach?" Andy asked.

"We men would take turns," Adam volunteered.

"We would?" said Willie, incredulous.

"Just like when we used to take turns at college chapel," said Freddie. "No big thing."

"Those talks only lasted about six minutes," said Willie.

"And that's a problem?" Jake interjected.

For the first time in the evening, there was open laughter.

"We'll have to call it something," said Frieda. "It may be a living-room church, but it's still a church. And a church needs a name."

Everyone looked at everyone else. Then, for the first time, Elsa spoke up. She said, "Today was my grandfather's birthday, God rest his soul. September 29 is the day to remember St. Michael, the Archangel. That's how he got his name. I don't think there are any 'St. Michael' Lutheran Churches in Minneapolis."

It was her living room. Nobody was going to challenge Elsa. But nobody said anything either. One thing was certain to Adam. He was not going to let Frieda settle the issue. "I second it," he said, as though a motion had been offered.

"Then let's vote," said George, raising his hand. "All in favor?"

All the hands went up.

Chapter 2

George Kleinhans had finished his two-year term at St. Paul Luther College unsure what career to pursue. A friend had suggested he consider selling real estate, something about which he knew next to nothing. But a visit with the agent who had sold his parents their small south Minneapolis home convinced him he might make a good salesman. Within a month of finishing his studies, he was affiliated with a south Minneapolis real estate agency.

One day in mid-October, George noticed a crudely-lettered sign in front of a house on Anderson Avenue. It announced "House for Sale." The red paint used to letter the board had run down, making the placard look even more unprofessional. George studied the house, a one-story frame bungalow with a small front porch and an adjoining vacant lot. It was a corner property, not far from where George's friends, Adam and Elsa Engelhardt, lived.

His curiosity got the better of him. He went to the door and knocked. There was no answer, but he thought he saw the frayed lace curtain move slightly at the living room window. Convinced someone was inside, he knocked again. He waited for what seemed to him to have been a very long time. As he turned to leave, the door opened.

"Yeah?" The man on the other side of the door was thin, almost emaciated. He was unshaven and his clothing was dirty and disheveled. George couldn't tell exactly how old he was but guessed mid-forties.

"I saw your sign."

"What sign?"

"On your lawn. It says your house is for sale."

"Oh. *That* sign." The man seemed not to be fully in charge of his faculties.

"Why are you selling your house?"

"Hafta. Need the money."

"Bills?"

"You could say that."

"How much are you asking?"

"How much can you pay?"

George stifled a laugh. He said, "You know, that's not a very sound way to conduct business. You need to have a firm price. Then, when someone makes you an offer, you can decide if it's fair or not."

"I don't know nothin' about how that works," the pathetic-looking homeowner replied. It was obvious to George that he was intoxicated. He considered reminding him that Prohibition was in force, but decided not to bring it up. "Would you be willing to ... you know ... show me around? Maybe I'd be interested in buying the place."

The man studied him with bleary eyes, then opened the door wider and stepped aside. George walked through the door, and was met with an incredible scene. There was trash everywhere. Old newspapers littered the furniture. The dining room table was a forest of empty liquor bottles.

George saw that the floors and woodwork were in good condition. It was a solid house and would probably draw a decent price. But not with all the debris cluttering up the place. He felt sorry for the homeowner, who was clearly drinking himself into poverty. He said, "Do you own this house outright, or are you paying a mortgage?"

"I own it. But I can't pay the taxes. So I have to sell."

"That would be a shame. Are the taxes current now?"

"Nope. This here's what I owe." Somehow he found the right piece of paper from the clutter on a desk in the living room and handed it over. George studied the form. The name Elroy Simmons appeared on the document. George said, "This isn't so very much, Elroy. You should be able to pay this."

"Can't. No money. I lost my job."

Small wonder, George thought. He asked, "Who has the deed to your house?" He felt as if he was rapidly becoming this homeowner's financial advisor. In spite of his disgust over the way the man had allowed his affairs to deteriorate, he felt pity for him. The Scripture verse "Am I my brother's keeper?" crept into his consciousness.

The man disappeared into another room and returned with two more documents. One was the deed to the property. The other was a property insurance form. It showed the coverage had lapsed more than two years before.

George couldn't believe he was saying what next came out of his mouth. "I'll tell you what. You give me the deed to take care of for you. It probably shouldn't be kept inside your house, anyway. And, in exchange for taking care of the deed, I'll pay your taxes."

"Why would you do that?"

"Because, if you ever decide you really *do* have to sell this house, I want to have the right to buy it before you offer it to anybody else. Does that sound fair?"

Simmons shrugged. "Well, I suppose. Why not?"

They shook hands on it. George carefully folded the property deed and tax statement together, and tucked them inside his jacket pocket. He said, "Elroy, do you live alone?"

"Always have."

"Where's your family?"

"I'm an only child. My parents died a while back."

"Do you have anybody — you know, relatives, friends — to look in on you?"

"My business is my business. I'm not what you'd call a neighborly person. I'm just a stubborn old bachelor."

"When did you start drinking?"

"When I lost my job. "

"Why did you lose your job?"

"Drinking too much."

George stifled a laugh, but only with great difficulty. He promised Elroy he'd check in on him from time to time. On his way back to the street, he pulled the "House for Sale" sign out of the ground and carried it around to the alley, where he propped it against the rear wall of an old shed at the back of the property.

EIGHT DAYS before Thanksgiving, Eleanor Melrose Morgan-Houseman lost her long battle with failing health. The following Monday they took her remains to Lakewood Cemetery, the hearse moving slowly along Hennepin Avenue. The funeral procession was a Who's Who of Minneapolis' upper crust. Standing nearest the open grave were the surviving spouse, multi-millionaire Michael Morgan-Houseman, his four-year-old son, Michael, Jr., and the young boy's nanny, Annabelle.

The forty-year-old stockbroker stared into the opening which was soon to receive the casket. He remembered how his wife had begged for more children, but he had refused her. Now he felt vindicated.

He reflected on the twelve years of their married life, and how much of it he'd spent sequestered in his downtown office, neglecting his wife and the son he had finally deigned to give her. He found it easy to rationalize what she had always called his neglect of their relationship. He had, after all, provided her comforts even beyond what her considerable dowry could have afforded. He had President Calvin Coolidge and Wall Street to thank for that, along with his own diligence and success as broker. He now managed the accounts of some of the wealthiest tycoons in Minneapolis.

His burgeoning bank accounts had been fueled by the incredible stock market surge, which gave no sign of slowing down. As 1927 drew to a close, his ambition, along with his penchant for taking risks in a market that seemed to have no ceiling, had made him extremely wealthy in his own right. No longer had he needed to depend for status upon his wife's inherited wealth.

He mulled, but only briefly, the consequences of his self-professed agnosticism. Eleanor had long urged him to take up membership in one of the city's fashionable congregations, at least for the sake of appearances, and perhaps also to improve his business. But he'd gotten all the business he needed by befriending the movers and shakers who frequented the Minneapolis Club. And, besides, he'd needed his Sundays to consolidate the successes he'd created during the regular work week. There had simply been no time for religion. And, in response to Eleanor's concern that one of them might die without the services of a clergyman, he'd reminded her that there were always clergy ready to do the bidding of wealthy men.

He looked with satisfaction at the robed Episcopal clergyman conducting the graveside service and thought to himself, *You see, Eleanor, you needn't have worried.*

But he *was* worried, at least a little. His young son would have to learn to live without a mother. Of course, there was Annabelle. She had become more than a mother to the youngster, while Eleanor had spent most of her time going to receptions, luncheons and benefits with other women in her social class.

Three days after the graveside service, Morgan-Houseman sat in the parlor of his brown brick mansion on Franklin Avenue. The rain, which had begun at mid morning, was rapidly turning to snow. Outside his window the automobiles and delivery vans were slowing to a crawl, and the palatial homes on the other side of the street were more and more difficult to make out.

The businessman drained his fourth glass of brandy and set it down. He studied the flames dancing in the fireplace and tried in vain to make himself more comfortable in his overstuffed chair. He stood up and began to pace. It was Thanksgiving day, but the traditional meal had been canceled. Annabelle had fed his son and taken him away for his nap. He himself had eaten nothing, contenting himself with downing one glass of the forbidden beverage after another.

Perhaps it was the alcohol that was causing his melancholy at this moment. The gloom he saw outside his window had somehow invaded his soul. He could not seem to shake it. Why was it that, standing at Eleanor's grave, he had felt nothing of regret, yet now, unaccountably, he was almost morbid with grief? Was it a delayed reaction? Was it the onset of contrition, due to his own neglect of Eleanor? Was it the sudden realization that he was, in fact alone, and all his money could not bring her back?

Morgan-Houseman did not know, and he hadn't the slightest clue as to how he might find out. Suddenly, he wished it was Friday. At least then he could busy himself at his desk downtown. What was the point of closing all the stores and offices on a perfectly good work day? All it did was give people like himself an idle day to sit and brood. And lose a day's earnings.

The framed portrait of his son, painted only a month before, occupied a central place on the mantel above the fireplace. He studied it with pride and affection. He took satisfaction knowing that he had an heir, and that the family name would continue. But, he realized, he was a stranger to the boy. He resolved to change that. He would spend more time with the lad, before the year's end. When, exactly, he wasn't sure. But he would try to find the time.

And he made a second resolution. In case anything should happen to himself, as it had to Eleanor, he would want the boy to be provided for. Why hadn't he established a trust for him? What was holding him back? He could create a rough draft, and later take it to an attorney. That was something he could begin this very day, here in the comfort of his own parlor. He went to the writing desk, rummaged around for writing paper and a pen, and busily set to work.

A THICK WHITE BLANKET of snow lay like ermine on the lawns of the great houses lining Franklin Avenue. The covering crowned the shrubbery surrounding the elegant brown brick residence where young Michael Morgan-Houseman looked down from his second-level playroom window. He was fascinated with the sight. The bright mid-morning sunlight made the landscape sparkle, as if someone had scattered diamond chips everywhere.

He thought about the ride his nanny, Annabelle, had taken him on the day before. Their chauffeur, Wesley, had driven them in the family's new white Packard, down Park Avenue, all the way to 42nd Street. Michael had enjoyed the sound of fresh snow crunching beneath the car's tires. On the way back, they'd paused at the Franklin Avenue intersection, to wait for the streetcar to pass. The youngster had squealed with delight each time the trolley's bell rang out.

How far could you ride on the streetcar, he wondered. Would it cross the

Mississippi River? Would it go all the way to the big round tower with the roof that looked like a witch's hat? Wesley had taken his mother and him on a ride not so many months before, in the Packard, all the way to the big round tower. It had been summer then. The three of them had had a picnic in the park on the hill.

He turned away from the window. He missed his mother. But he knew he would miss Nanny Annabelle a lot more, if anything should ever happen to her. His mother had loved him a lot, he realized, but she had never been home very much. Nanny Annabelle seemed like his real mother. She was always there when he needed something. She made his meals for him, and played with him, and taught him how to tell time, and put him down for his naps, and tucked him into bed at night.

He ran from the room and raced down the hallway, to the top of the banister. Looking down, into the spacious entryway, he shouted, "Nanny Annabelle! Nanny Annabelle! Where are you?"

Annabelle appeared in the vestibule below. Standing at the foot of the stairs, she said, in her pretend-angry voice, "Michael, I've told you not to shout in the house, unless the house is on fire or there's a burglar in your room. Is the house on fire?"

"No, Nanny Annabelle."

"Is there a burglar?"

"No."

"Then use your indoors voice, please."

"But if I use my indoors voice, you won't be able to hear me."

Annabelle grinned in spite of herself. She extended her arms, as if to hug the little boy at the top of the stairs. She commanded, "Come down here, you little minx."

Michael didn't know what a minx was, but every time Annabelle said it, he got a warm and cozy feeling inside. He raced down the stairs and into his nanny's arms. She gathered him up and whirled around and around with him. "Master Michael, what in the world are we going to do with you?" she asked, hugging him so close he found it hard to breathe.

"Why do we have to do anything with me?" he asked.

She set him down and, taking his hand, led him toward the kitchen. "It's just something that grown-ups say," she said, her voice sounding musical.

"Why do adults say things like that?"

"Master Michael, you have far too many questions for your own good. How would you like a morning treat?"

Usually, after Nanny Annabelle called him a minx, there would be a treat. He enjoyed feeling her lift him and set him onto his tall chair, and then push him in, close against the kitchen table. As she poured steaming cups of hot chocolate for both of them, he said, "Nanny Annabelle, when can we ride on the streetcar?"

She set his cup before him and said, "Now drink little tiny sips at first. The chocolate is very hot. You don't want to burn your mouth."

He picked up the cup and sipped as carefully as he could. He set it down and repeated his question. "When can we ride on the streetcar?"

Annabelle responded with an earnest gaze. She said, "People like us don't ride on streetcars, Master Michael."

"But why don't we?"

"We have a wonderful automobile for taking rides. And Wesley will take us wherever we want to go."

"But the Packard doesn't have a bell on it," he protested.

"It has a horn."

"But Wesley never honks it."

"You only honk a horn to tell people to get out of the way. It's not polite to honk a horn if you don't need to."

"But the streetcar clangs its bell all the way down the street."

"That's what the streetcar does. It tells people it's coming. And to get off the tracks."

"Nanny Annabelle, how long until my birthday?"

"A long time. Not until next August."

"I only want one thing for my birthday. A ride on the streetcar."

Chapter 3

The bell banged against the shop door. Adam looked up from his ledger. A tall young man, perhaps in his mid-twenties, stepped inside, bringing the chill wind of February with him. Removing his winter hat and gloves, he approached the counter. Beneath his warm coat, a pale white dress shirt gave contrast to a dark suit coat and tie. He ran the fingers of one hand through dark, wavy hair, trying unsuccessfully to make it look presentable. Equally dark eyebrows set off a pair of intense brown eyes.

The stranger placed his hands on the countertop and took turns tapping each of his fingers on the smooth wooden surface, as if playing a piano. It was clear to Adam this young man was brimming with energy and needed to get rid of some of it.

"How may I help you?"

"I'm looking for a quality printer. I've heard good things about this place."

"Thank you," Adam replied, wondering exactly where he'd heard them.

"I'll tell you what," the young man said, "I need to have some announcements printed. I want them to look very nice. Fine paper. Matching envelopes. Is that something you can do?"

Adam's eyes sparkled. He loved customers like this. "Come with me," he said, lifting the hinged gate that served as an extension of the customer counter.

The stranger followed the proprietor to the far end of the single large room, past a linotype machine, three hand presses, and shelves of printing stock. At a large wooden work table, which doubled as his desk, Adam pulled out one of two weathered old captain's chairs for his guest and then took the other himself.

The visitor looked around the tidy shop, amazed that so much furniture, equipment, paper, ink and miscellany could be contained in such a space, and be kept in such good order. Personal biases and experience brought the thought to his mind, *I'm dealing with a German.* All doubt evaporated when he glanced beyond Adam, to a printed sheet, framed in a fine wooden border. He silently read the elegantly lettered German script:

Oeffne, Gott, meine augen und mein herz, fur dein erscheinen. Ich sehe wie du mich liebst. Du bist da.

The German he'd been forced to learn, unwillingly, as a child growing up, served him well enough to translate the words: "Open, O God, my eyes and my heart for your coming. I see your love for me. You are present to me."

Then, as if coming out of a trance, he focused on Adam and extended his right hand. The shopkeeper was amazed at the young man's powerful a grip. "Daniel Wilhelm Jonas," he announced, pronouncing the W like a V and the J like a Y.

"Adam Engelhardt. I'm pleased to make your acquaintance."

"The ... ahh ... the sentiment there in the frame. I like it very much."

"An elderly woman, a good friend, told me she learned that growing up in Canton, Ohio. She's taken to reciting it every time we meet for worship. It's become a sort of invocation, a kind of liturgical ritual, I suppose."

Daniel's head was spinning. He said, "Ohio! I'm from Fremont. I have friends in Canton. This woman, does she have a name?"

Adam chuckled silently. "Indeed. Her name is Frieda Stellhorn."

"Stellhorn! A big name in the Ohio Synod."

"You're familiar with the Joint Synod of Ohio?"

"*Familiar!* My dear Mr. Engelhardt, I grew up in Grace Lutheran Church, a daughter congregation of St. John Lutheran. Both are crown jewels of the Synod." He paused, but only long enough to catch his breath. "The more important question may be, just how do you, a south Minneapolis shopkeeper in the midst of all these Scandinavians, know about the Joint Synod of Ohio?"

"You should have guessed, reading my window sign, that Engelhardt isn't exactly Scandinavian."

"Yes. Of course. But Ohio?"

"Peace Lutheran Church in Galion. My father is an elder there."

"Which still doesn't explain how you got to Minnesota."

"It's a long story. Perhaps we should save it for another time."

"Yes. You're right. My printing project. We should talk about that."

"Exactly what's the occasion for which you need the invitations?"

"My graduation. In three months' time. From St. Paul Luther Seminary."

Adam eyed Daniel with puzzlement. "You're attending a seminary on the east side of St. Paul, and you come to a south Minneapolis printer? Aren't there any over there on Payne Avenue — or Arcade?"

Daniel laughed softly. "I don't live on campus. I have an apartment not so far from here."

Adam said, "My two boys both attended St. Paul Luther College. One's still there. Perhaps you know them."

"Well, the seminary men don't mix much with underclassmen. But it's not a very big campus." He thought for a moment. "I knew a Jon Engelhardt. He was a second-year college boy last year, I believe." Adam nodded. "And ... well ... I haven't met the other one."

"David. He's a first-year student. David lives on campus. The school expects it. And so do his mother and I. If the college department offered four years, Jon would still be there as well. But, since he could only get two, he's finishing at the University of Minnesota. David will no doubt do the same."

Daniel said, "They wanted me to live on campus, too. I had a dickens of a time getting permission not to. But my dear friend, Rosetta, the love of my life, whom I've known since childhood, and who went through Capital University in my class, took a clerical position here in Minneapolis. With the Pillsbury Company. I want to be near her, so, naturally, I had to enroll at St. Paul Luther Seminary."

He paused, as if to catch his breath, but only momentarily. "I convinced the president to allow me to live in Minneapolis so I could spend more time with Rosetta. Then, last spring, I asked her to be my wife — after graduation, of course. She consented, but said not until I had a position with an income sufficient to take care of her." He sighed, studied the pattern of the wood grain on the table top, and then said, "It's complicated my life, taking the streetcar to classes every day. But I knew I'd never survive three long years living an entire city away from her. And besides, how do I know some young dandy might not come along in the meantime and sweep her off her feet? I couldn't take a chance on that."

Adam smiled knowingly. He'd felt similarly about his chances with Elsa, and she'd only lived six blocks from him in Galion. She'd made him wait eighteen months before they had married. It had been the longest year and a half of his life, wracked with fears of other suitors beating his time with her. As she had assured him after the wedding, his paranoia had been no more than that. But he could not have been persuaded so beforehand.

Daniel returned to the business at hand, explaining exactly what he had in mind. Adam brought samples for his customer to examine, and explained how the pricing worked. When the seminarian seemed to wince at the estimated total, Adam said, "Given your situation, and on the basis of our cordial conversation, I'll only charge you half."

Daniel's eyes widened. Suddenly he broke into a broad smile. "Mr.

Engelhardt, you're an incredibly good friend. All the more incredible, considering I've only known you for twenty minutes!"

"Call me Adam. And just keep one thing in mind. I'm only cutting my price to you on the condition that you don't go all around the neighborhood telling people what I've done. I'd be out of business in a month if everyone started expecting such favors."

"My lips are sealed."

"If you don't mind my asking, where will the church be sending you after graduation?"

"Well, as you no doubt know, Lutheran pastors-in-training don't go anywhere without a divine call. A congregation has to offer me a position. And, well, so far things don't look too hopeful."

"Seminary men can't get calls these days?"

"Oh, there are calls available. But Rosetta has a good job now. She thinks she may want to keep it for a while, after we marry. And there are no openings for Ohio Synod pastors nearby."

"If you had your choice, where would you go?"

"It's not appropriate to second-guess the Holy Spirit," Daniel said solemnly. But his countenance quickly changed. A grin began at the corners of his mouth, and then spread. With a mischievous twinkle, he said, "My home congregation has decided to construct a wonderful new building. It will look like a medieval cloister. My parents wrote and said some members think they're selling out to the Roman Catholics. But it will be an astonishing witness to faith in Fremont, Ohio. I would truly love to serve that congregation."

He paused and studied the table top again. "Of course, that will never happen. Congregations almost never call former members. And they probably shouldn't. Besides, seminarians don't start out in cathedral-sized churches. They go to tiny little places where nobody else wants to go. That's more likely my future."

Adam thought about what he'd heard. Then, as if changing the subject, he said, "As a pastor-in-training, do you lead Sunday worship?"

"Yes. If I'm asked."

"How often are you asked?"

"Not often. The other senior men and I take turns, when the opportunities come."

"Have you ever worshiped with a living-room congregation?"

"I beg your pardon?"

"Our church, the one where my wife Elsa and I worship, is a living-room church. We take turns meeting in different people's homes."

Daniel's eyes narrowed. Adam couldn't tell whether it was a look of uncertainty, amazement, or disdain. He guessed perhaps a bit of all three. He continued, "We begin with Frieda Stellhorn speaking her German invocation. Then we follow the liturgy from the Ohio Synod hymnal."

"You have copies of that? Then you're practically a regular congregation!"

"We have the English language version. Frieda would be okay with German, but the rest of us are trying to behave like real Americans." He looked at Daniel, who offered a knowing nod. German-heritage Minnesotans had suffered unfairly during the Kaiser-bashing hysteria a dozen years before. Many had changed the spellings of their last names, trying to make them sound English, more acceptable to their super-patriotic neighbors.

Adam continued, "We use the order of service, and the hymns. Sometimes there's a piano. Sometimes there isn't. We just plow through."

Daniel was fascinated. He leaned forward, eager for more details.

"The six men in our group — including me — we all take turns with the message. We don't actually call it a sermon. We're all theologically untrained, you know." He studied Daniel's expression, which he could not read. He went on, trying not to sound as though he was apologizing. "What we offer is more like little talks. But it works well. It's all from the heart."

Daniel spoke in a mysterious whisper, with a voice one might use upon finally having located the holy grail. "You're all the way back to the Book of Acts. The first church did what you're doing."

Adam seemed not to have heard. He said, "But, there's a problem with the Sacrament."

"The Eucharist?"

"Yes. Holy Communion. We don't know how to arrange for it. None of us think it's proper for *us* to offer it."

Technically and officially, Daniel realized, they'd need to have the church authorize a celebrant. "And, so, how have you solved that problem?"

Adam looked pensive. "We haven't."

Daniel nodded thoughtfully. He ran his tongue along his lower lip, as if looking for a solution.

Adam was wrinkling his face, as if debating whether to say the next thing. Suddenly he asked, "Does the seminary permit a student like yourself to administer the Sacrament?"

Daniel replied, "I'm not sure. I don't think so. Of course, they might make an exception and deputize someone — in an exceptional situation."

Adam appeared resigned to the fact that there was no solution. But Daniel suddenly brightened and said, "On the other hand, you're not an officially-organized congregation, are you?"

"Well, no. Not really."

"So, then, technically, no rules would be broken if, say, a theologically-trained young man happened to show up and preside at the Sacrament, from time to time."

"What would the seminary faculty say?"

"What if the seminary faculty didn't know?"

Adam looked at Daniel with a confused expression. What was he suggesting?

"As it turns out," Daniel continued, "I'm about to graduate from the seminary, but there's a good chance I can't leave town, at least for a year or so. Rosetta wants to keep working at least that long. And there are no calls on the horizon for me here. So, where does that leave me?"

Adam didn't know the answer.

"It leaves me to fend for myself. I'm going to have to become a tentmaker."

"I beg your pardon?"

"The Apostle Paul, remember? He had no church to pay his wages. So he sewed tents for a living. And led the church community in addition."

"*That's* what you're planning to do?"

"It's one option. Believe me, I've been mulling this ever since I came to Minneapolis. The problem is, I don't know how I could convince Rosetta to go along with it. She thinks I'm going to have a church of my own, one that pays me a pastor's wage. I may end up having to become a day laborer somewhere, just to earn my rent."

Adam stroked his chin thoughtfully. He asked, "How are you at driving nails?"

"Carpentry?"

"Yes. Exactly."

"I'm very good at it, if I may say so."

"Our Lord was a carpenter," Adam said.

Daniel nodded, affirming the obvious.

"In our living-room church, we have a young man … well, he's twenty-four, which is fourteen years younger than I am, so that seems young to me."

"That's my age," Daniel interrupted.

"Anyway, this young man builds houses for people. I think he needs more help." Daniel's eyes were full of expectation. Adam said, "Perhaps you could hammer nails for him, and also preside at the Sacrament in our living-room church."

Daniel was nodding vigorously. It was hard for Adam to tell whether he was giving assent, or simply indicating that he understood the proposition.

"It might be a possibility, anyway," Adam continued. "Would you like me to explore it with our group?"

"The Spirit works in mysterious ways," said Daniel, reaching across the table and laying his hand on Adam's. "Yes. Please. Explore it."

"And," Adam continued, seeming to make it up as he went along, "perhaps you could even offer the message for our gathering, at least now and then."

"That's one of the reasons they send us to seminary," Daniel said. "I'd hate to have learned a skill and then let it go all rusty from lack of use."

"I think this may turn out to have been a very profitable conversation," said Adam, pushing back his chair and getting up.

"Bless you, Adam Engelhardt," said Daniel, standing. He grasped the printer's hand with a grip so eager that Adam wondered whether he would ever again have full use of his five fingers.

Chapter 4

Molly Lundgren walked slowly along Marquette Avenue, the gloom of early evening settling into her soul. She stared uncomprehending into the store windows, seeing nothing. A chill gust of wind raced down the avenue, causing her to shudder. Her eyes came to rest on a poster plastered onto the front window of a deserted shop. It proclaimed, "Liquor destroys lives! Remember, Prohibition is now the law. Put Demon Rum in its Place."

Molly was convinced it wasn't only liquor that destroyed lives. She rather suspected her own was on the brink of ruin. But she had no clear idea what to do about it. Another cold blast assaulted her, tugging at her cloth coat. She pulled the lapels close together and stayed as close to the storefronts as possible. Slowly, she made her way to the end of the block. She was in no particular hurry to get home, but she realized she might freeze to death if she didn't get moving.

Arriving at the intersection where the streetcar would soon arrive, she reflected on her remarkable fortunes since her seventeenth birthday. The third of six children raised in a pious Swedish Lutheran family in Litchfield, Minnesota, she had come to Minneapolis to enroll in business college. Upon completion of her one-year course, she had secured a secretarial position in a prosperous brokerage firm in the center of the city. She wasn't sure whether it had been her fetching good looks — her blue eyes, curly blonde hair and demure smile — that had resulted, after only two years, in her rapid rise through the ranks, to the position of executive secretary for the owner of the firm. She preferred to believe it was her skill and efficiency.

It had been a wonderful success story. Her high school classmates, most of whom were still in Litchfield, could not believe how well she had done. But nobody in Litchfield had any idea about the dark side of her success. Nor would she ever be able to tell any of them. Certainly not her parents.

But, if her closest friends could not be trusted with her secret, then who could?

The streetcar arrived. She boarded and settled into a seat for the short ride to her boarding house. Out the window, in the descending gloom, she caught sight of the rising form of the new Foshay Tower, soon to become the city's lone skyscraper. She wondered where she would be in two years, when the sleek stone spire was due to be completed.

As the streetcar neared her corner, she made a decision. She would talk to her roommate. She would tell her everything. She realized that if she didn't, she might soon go crazy.

The trolley arrived at her corner. Standing in front of the wooden apartment house, she considered, but only briefly, waiting for the next streetcar and getting back on. She could ride to the end of the line, something she'd never done before. But what would she do then? Sooner or later, she would have to go home.

She trudged up the wooden stairs to the second floor apartment and let herself in. Her roommate had already eaten and was relaxing on the sofa, casually turning the pages of the daily *Tribune*. She looked up when Molly walked in and said, "You're late."

"I was window shopping."

"That's not like you."

"Well, I was in the mood to window-shop."

"But of all nights! It's March! And it's cold out there!"

Molly felt resentment rising. But she controlled her feelings. She didn't want this to degenerate into an argument. Not tonight. She hung up her coat and came into the small living room. Dropping into the rocker, she sighed heavily and brushed her curls back from her eyes.

Her roommate folded the newspaper and laid it aside. She said, "That was a pretty deep sigh. What's behind it?"

"Oh, I don't know."

"Sure you do. Would you like to tell me?"

Molly almost said no. But it would have been a lie, and she knew it. She sighed again, and then started slowly. "I ... well ... I have a kind of situation. It's not good."

"What sort of 'situation'?"

"With my boss."

"Oh, no. You're not losing your job, are you?"

"No, no. It's pretty much the opposite."

"So ... what exactly is going on?"

Molly sighed still again. Then she said, "If I tell you this, you have to promise not to judge me. And you have to promise not to tell anyone. Ever."

"Molly, this is making me really nervous. Just tell me."

"He … well … he's decided to change the terms of my employment."

"Like …?"

"Like … like this: if I want to keep my job, I have to give him what he wants."

"Molly, that's what *my* boss expects. That's not unreasonable."

"It is if it's sexual."

"*What!*"

Molly pursed her lips, then pressed them tightly together. She folded and unfolded and refolded her hands. Tears began forming in the corners of her eyes. She nodded. "A month ago he told me he has …" The words were caught in her throat. She forced herself to go on. "He told me he has needs, and that only I can satisfy them. He told me if I cooperated, I'd get a nice raise." She paused, sniffed, and pulled a handkerchief from her purse. She said, "And, if I don't, I'll have no future with the firm."

"Then you have to quit."

"But I need the job."

"Not that badly, you don't. Molly, he could ruin your life."

"If I lose this job, I'll never get another one."

"Why not?"

"Because he won't give me a decent reference. In fact, he says he'll destroy my career."

"That slimy creep. How can he get away with that?"

"He has a lot of influence in this city."

"So, what will you do?"

"What *can* I do? Give him what he wants." There was a significant pause. "And hope I don't get pregnant."

THE SNOW BEGAN TO FALL sometime before dawn. As the city awoke, there was already a thick, wet blanket covering everything. Traffic was reduced to a crawl. By mid-day, with brisk winds complicating the situation, the schools were letting out. The blizzard intensified from hour to hour. Adam Engelhardt held out longer than other businessmen along Bloomington Avenue, but by three o'clock he decided to call it a day. It was with difficulty that he shoved open the front door to his shop, creating a snowy arc on the front step. He trudged across the street, heading for Anderson Avenue, his feet sinking knee-deep in the drifts.

By suppertime the entire metropolitan area was shut down. Nothing was moving. Minnesotans, accustomed to such wintery assaults, hunkered down for a long siege. As the last of the sun faded, just before suppertime, the wind began to pick up. Large drifts began to accumulate against buildings, some up to the windowsills. The streets began to resemble frozen oceans.

Anyone who was still awake at two o'clock the following morning would have seen the storm finally begin to abate. But unless they lived on Anderson Avenue, a half block north of the Engelhardt residence, they would not have been aware that the bungalow at the corner of Anderson and Caldwell had begun to glow unnaturally. Nor would they have seen the flames when, around a quarter of three, they roared through the interior of the compact dwelling, burst the windows, and sent a conflagration of burning ash and cinder roaring toward the heavens. If anyone had seen the blaze, and had tried to summon the fire department, their alarm would have been in vain.

The following morning, as the city began to dig out, the near neighbors realized that Elroy Simmon's house had completely disappeared, reduced to a heap of blackened timbers and singed shingles. Nobody could be sure, but there was every reason to believe that Elroy had been inside when the fire began and had surely died in the flames.

Another day went by before George Kleinhans was able to find his way to the site of the holocaust. He stood on the drifted front walkway and marveled how the heat of the blaze had melted all the snow around the circumference of the building, exposing last summer's grass for up to a foot away from the house. It had been providential that it was a corner lot, and that there was a vacant lot next door. Those two realities had, doubtless, prevented the fire from jumping from one property to the next.

He studied the pit, once the basement, into which the charred debris had collapsed. He felt a sickness in his stomach. He tried to imagine what might have happened. He pictured Elroy, intoxicated, falling asleep with a burning cigarette in his hand. He envisioned it falling to the floor, igniting a stack of old newspapers. If Elroy really had been in the house, would he have been aware of what was happening?

George walked through the deep snow to the back of the property. The old wooden shed was still standing. Something caught his eye. Leaning against the side wall, now half buried in a drift, was a battered board. Lettered crudely on its surface, in red paint, was the message, "House for Sale."

SEATED AT THE PIANO in the corner of Fred and Myrtle Stumpf's living room, Frances Bauer played the introduction to hymn 504. The tiny congregation began to sing:

Savior, teach me, day by day, love's sweet lesson to obey;
Sweeter lesson cannot be, loving him who first loved me.

Daniel Jonas looked around the room. His newly-inherited flock sang and worshiped with such fervor, he found it hard to absorb it all. He realized that every single person in this room was here because he or she truly wanted to be. How many other congregations could make such a claim?

With a childlike heart of love, at thy bidding may I move;
Prompt to serve and follow thee, loving him who first loved me.

He reflected on the sentimental nature of the hymn they were singing. It would not have been his first choice, but Frances was at the piano this Sunday morning, and he had taken to allowing the accompanist to choose the closing hymn each week. This was one of her favorites.

Teach me all thy steps to trace, strong to follow in thy grace;
Learning how to love from thee; loving him who first loved me.

Repetition, Daniel realized, was not exactly the hallmark of a strong hymn text. But the words carried an important message. Maybe if he, himself, could learn to apply their instruction to his own behavior, he'd become a little less judgmental. Maybe.

Love in loving finds employ, in obedience all her joy;
Ever new that joy will be, loving him who first loved me.

Only one more stanza. Then he'd introduce the subject that had been weighing on him for the past month. He hoped he could do it without causing rancor among these devout living-room saints, who had been so hospitable to him.

Thus may I rejoice to show that I feel the love I owe;
Singing, till thy face I see, of his love who first loved me.

The room fell silent. Daniel waited as the hymn books went shut and all eyes turned toward him. Still seated, he raised his hand and pronounced the benediction. At the declaration of the trinitarian formula, he made the sign of the cross. Nobody traced the sign upon themselves. One day, perhaps, he would suggest that to them.

In the split second between the silence following the benediction and the moment when the room would ordinarily dissolve into happy chaos, the young pastor-in-training spoke. "Friends, one more thing …" Polly Kleinhans was halfway out of her chair. She had agreed to help Myrtle serve the coffee, and was ready to head for the kitchen. But she sat down again. Everyone was looking with curiosity at Daniel.

"There's something I've been wanting to share with you."

"Oh, no," said Will Langholz, his brow furrowed. "They've offered you a call to a real church. You're leaving us, aren't you?"

Daniel smiled. "No. Nothing like that."

"Then what?" asked George Kleinhans. "Are you getting tired of us already?"

George's wife, Polly, elbowed him and said, "Just let the pastor speak."

Daniel appreciated being called "pastor," even though he realized it was premature. He said, "How could I get tired of you? You're like my family." He felt as though the eyes of the members of his tiny flock were boring right through him. He tried to gather his thoughts, attempted to slow his racing heart, and said, "I … I have a concern about our … about our future together."

Adam Engelhardt sat straight up and leaned forward in his chair. Where was this leading, he wondered. Daniel continued, "You know, much as I really love this intimate arrangement we have, I wonder if we're ever expecting to grow ourselves … you know … into a larger community."

"What you're saying is, there's no room for visitors, or new members, in a crowded living room like this," said Jacob Bauer. "We've thought about that, Pastor. We don't want to keep doing this forever. Is that what's on your mind?"

Daniel was surprised with Jacob's directness, and how well he'd read him. "Yes. Yes, that's it exactly."

"Do you have a suggestion for us?" Jacob probed.

"Well, no, not exactly. Except that, if we really want to reach other people in our neighborhood, and I'm sure there must be other people who might want to join us, we need to think about finding somewhere with more space."

"A real church building, right?" chimed in Frieda Stellhorn. Everybody knew Frieda had always wanted that in the first place.

Daniel nodded. But before he could speak again, George Kleinhans said, "I agree. This congregation needs its own building. And I have an idea." Now everybody's eyes were on George. The young real estate salesman said, "You all know about the big fire last month, over on Anderson Avenue and Caldwell Street. There's that double lot, and the foundation, with all the trash and debris that fell into it when the house burned down. Well, to make a long story short, I seem to have ended up owning that property. And I don't plan to build a house on it. And I don't really want to pay taxes on it either. I'd like to donate it to the congregation. We could build a nice little chapel, right on the foundation that's already there."

Fred Stumpf broke in. "This is pretty amazing, really."

"What?" asked Andy Scheidt. "The fact that George has property he's ready to give us for a church building?"

"Well, yes, that. But listen. You all know I work for a construction company. And you know the economy is really, really good right now. They're building new stores and commercial buildings all up and down Lake Street. The fellow I work for just got a contract to tear down two frame buildings and replace them with a nice new brick one. He told me a month ago that, if I could find anybody to take the buildings down, they could have the used lumber. Otherwise, he wants to petition the city for the fire department to come in and burn it down, just to clear the property."

There were murmurs all around the room. Adam asked, "How soon would that have to happen? I mean, salvaging the lumber?"

"Spring's coming. When it's nice enough out to do construction again, they'll be moving ahead. I'd say there's about a month, maybe six weeks, when we could get the lumber out of there. After that, they may just torch it."

"How much work … I mean, how many men, would it take?" asked Adam.

"I'd say all six of us, working Saturdays and evenings, could get it done in about three weeks. Maybe less."

"Wouldn't we have to get a permit to build something?" Jacob asked.

"I get permits to build houses every month or so," said Andy. "Just leave that to me. And my hired hand here would probably help us with the project, so that would make seven sets of hands, not just six."

He turned and looked at Daniel, who was trying to absorb the fact that, within ten minutes he had gone from being called "Pastor" to "hired hand." But he nodded vigorously at the suggestion and said, "Absolutely. I'm ready. Let's do it."

Chapter 5

"Please, Rosetta. Please!"

"Daniel, you're begging."

"I am. I admit it. I'd do it on my knees if it would help."

"Daniel, I'm just not sure. I'm really not ready for this."

"But I have a good job now. I'm working for Mr. Scheidt. It's enough to support you. Not in luxury, but I never promised you that. "

"How long will Mr. Scheidt keep you on?"

"Indefinitely. Permanently, if he likes my work. He says he does. And he told me that if I get full-time pastoral work, he'll let me go without complaint."

"But Daniel, you're living above a print shop."

"That was Mr. Engelhardt's idea. He's giving me the rooms rent-free. And Andy and I …"

"Andy?"

"Andreas. Mr. Scheidt. He and I spent a month of weekends fixing it up during the winter. It's cozy, but it's nice. You and I could live there."

"Daniel, a proper pastor should not live above a print shop."

"It saves me having to pay rent. That's why I can afford to marry you now."

Rosetta brushed her dark, wavy hair back from her face. Her cute dimples disappeared when she was troubled. They were invisible now. She sighed heavily and said, "I don't know, Daniel. I told my friends and family I was planning to marry a Lutheran pastor. But a tent-making minister, working for a carpenter and living over a store …"

"Our Lord was a carpenter, Rosetta."

"Our Lord got himself crucified."

Daniel was silent. He pursed his lips, returning a defeated look.

Rosetta said, "I'm sorry, Daniel. That wasn't fair."

"*Here's* what isn't fair," Daniel replied, looking earnestly at his intended. "You promised that, if I finished my seminary training and secured a pastoral position, and was able to earn a salary sufficient to take care of both of us, you would marry me."

She looked cautiously at him.

"Rosetta, I've done all of those things. Except for seminary graduation. But I've only one month to go, and it's a certainty I'll graduate with my class. I realize what I'm proposing isn't exactly according to what you expected. But it isn't exactly as I expected either. Still, I've done what you asked of me. I even came to Minnesota to be near you."

"Daniel, I'm just not feeling good about this. I'm just *not*."

"And, on top of everything, I think I'm having a faith crisis."

She looked alarmed. "What do you mean?"

"I think I may be losing faith in you. Because you seem not to have much faith in me."

DANIEL JONAS AND ROSETTA SIEGEL were married on a Sunday in June at Grace Lutheran Church in Fremont, Ohio. It was an enormous affair, since both the bride and the groom had grown up in the large congregation. Their friends came from everywhere to attend the solemn service and the festivities which followed.

In answer to the unending stream of questions, from family and guests, about Daniel's new congregation, Rosetta simply said, "It's brand new. It's in Minneapolis. He's going to do very well there, I'm sure."

The couple accepted a ride with friends, to Sandusky, where they boarded a Lake Erie cruise boat for a breezy ride to Detroit. There they spent their honeymoon at a quiet inn. After five days, they boarded a train for Chicago, and then changed for Minneapolis.

Andy Scheidt met the pastor and his new bride at the Milwaukee Road station and loaded them and their luggage into his new Ford automobile. It was mid-summer 1928, and Andy was prospering enough to have purchased the fine black sedan for cash. He realized his economic success was enhanced in no small part by St. Michael congregation's new tentmaker pastor, who worked so industriously beside him, now two hours a day, six days a week.

Seated next to Daniel in the back seat, Rosetta said, "I'm really scared. I hope we're doing the right thing. I don't even know if these people will like me."

"It's no problem," Daniel said seriously. "If they don't like you, we'll just go back to Fremont and I'll work in my father's lumber yard."

She gave him a wry smile and said, "Sure we will. And what would you do with three years of wasted seminary training?"

"I'll preach to the crows, and the chipmunks, and the mice, like Francis of Asissi," he replied, leaning close and brushing a soft kiss onto her cheek.

"Be serious," she said, trying to sound stern. "You're a pastor now."

In front of Engelhardt Printing on Bloomington Avenue, members of the living-room congregation waited expectantly on the sidewalk. As Andy Scheidt's car pulled up to the curb, they began to unroll a long, long paper banner, which they held high above their heads. The carefully lettered message read:

Welcome Pastor Daniel and Rosetta. We love you.

Daniel looked with astonishment. He circled his arm around his bride and hugged her so hard she gasped. He looked into her eyes, and saw that tears of gratitude were streaming down her face.

ON THE LAST SUNDAY OF JUNE, 1928, the members of the Lutheran Church of St. Michael and All Angels dedicated their spartan frame chapel. It was painted white and had plastered interior walls. Three rectangular, clear-glass windows on either side brought large squares of light into the bright interior. A Presbyterian congregation had donated the pews, altar (really a "sacrament table"), pulpit and lectern. The furniture had been stored for two years in the back of a half-empty warehouse, after the Presbyterians had moved into a larger and newly-furnished building.

Frieda Stellhorn had pulled strings with a friend in Columbus, Ohio, who knew someone at the Lutheran Book Concern. It turned out that, with the coming merger of the Ohio and Iowa synods, the publishing house in Columbus was ready to begin selling a new worship book for use in the new "American Lutheran Church," and had plenty of copies of the now-nearly-obsolete Ohio Synod *Evangelical Lutheran Hymnal* in storage. Frieda got 100 of them for the cost of shipping, which she paid herself.

The little congregation felt like they were rattling around in the new building, which, at six to a pew, could easily seat 120 people. But in his sermon, Daniel announced, "We are no longer a living-room congregation. We are now a community church. Let the word go out from this place, that the Church of St. Michael and All Angels is ready to welcome all who want to come here."

He studied his small flock, noting a handful of strange faces. As if speaking to them, he said, "I see that some of our friends and neighbors have discovered us already. To you, we say, please come back and worship with us again. It doesn't matter if you weren't part of the living-room church for nine months. It was just an accident that we began that way. None of us who helped to get this congregation started are any better than any of you. We are all called to be God's angels and acolytes."

Regulars and visitors alike seemed caught off guard. What was the preacher talking about? Daniel continued, "This congregation was organized last September 29. That's the day on which the church remembers St. Michael and All Angels." He studied the congregation. Elsa Engelhardt, whose idea it had been to name the congregation for the warrior angel, sat a little straighter in her pew. She knew pride was a sin, but she couldn't help feeling a surge of it right now.

Daniel continued, "How many of you believe in angels?" The members looked at each other, wondering if they should raise a hand, or even if anybody agreed with the proposition. No hands went up. Daniel said, "Don't any of you believe in yourselves?" He looked out on a sea of puzzled faces. "All of us are angels in Michael's army. We truly are." He noticed a scowl creeping into Jacob Bauer's face. "You don't believe me, do you, Jacob?"

Jacob's eyes became large. He looked furtively around, wondering if people were staring at him. They were. Daniel said, "Well, let's not all pick on Jacob, now. Nobody raised their hand when I asked if you believed in angels. But think about this. The Greek word for angel is 'angelos.' It means messenger. So angels are really messengers. Remember when the Angel Gabriel came to Mary and told her she would be the mother of Jesus? What was Gabriel doing?" He paused, as if waiting for a response. But these were Lutherans, so none came.

"We all know the answer. Gabriel was bringing Mary a message. That's what messengers do. And when Michael chased Satan out of heaven, that was a message too. The message was, 'If you don't want to be on God's team, then you need to get out of the way.'"

He paused. The congregation was right with him. Suddenly he surprised himself by saying, "Pick up your hymnal." Elsa Engelhardt blinked. Was it time to sing already? If so, she'd need to get back to the piano bench in a hurry. But Daniel wasn't at the end of his message. He said, "Look at the title. Read it with me, out loud."

Like schoolchildren, the congregation recited together, "Evangelical Lutheran Hymnal."

Said Daniel, "Now look at the word 'Evangelical.' Do you see another word tucked away inside it?" He looked across the congregation and caught sight of Georgianna Langholz, confidently nodding her head. He said, "Georgianna, tell us."

Without hesitation, the grocery clerk's wife replied, "Angel."

"Exactly. The church is evangelical because it's full of angels. Evangelical means 'sharing a good message.' So that makes us a church full of message-makers. That's what angels are — messengers. And that's what we're going to do here at St. Michael and All Angels Church. We're going to share good-news messages, all around our neighborhood."

Daniel thought he detected uncertainty on his listeners' faces. He said, "I know what you're thinking. Angels are supposed to have wings. Well, there's nothing in the New Testament that says so. That's a romantic idea that's completely unprovable. So, if your wings haven't sprouted yet, don't assume you're off the hook. You and I are angels, and God has a message for us to tell. The message is simple — God loves us whether we expect him to or not. Even when we're sure we don't deserve it, God loves us. In spite of everything we may do, God loves us. And, if that isn't good news, I don't know what is."

Most of the congregation was nodding now. He'd made his point. They seemed convinced. He continued, "So, now we know we're all angels. But we're also acolytes. What does that mean?"

Frieda Stellhorn studied the candles burning on the altar. Back in Canton, Ohio, the acolytes were the young men who lit them and put them out. But they'd never allowed girls to do it, so she wondered where the pastor was headed.

Daniel said, "An acolyte is someone who serves. Some people think an acolyte is an altar boy, or a candle lighter. That's part of it. But an acolyte is anyone who provides service to God. So, if you helped build this chapel, you're an acolyte. If you've taken your turn preparing and delivering the Sunday message, back when we were a living-room church, you're an acolyte. If you play the piano for worship, you're an acolyte."

The congregation was getting it. "But you're also an acolyte if you set the table for Holy Communion, or wash the vessels afterward, or put the hymn numbers on the board, or sweep the floors in this building, or teach a class, or usher and help with receiving the offering."

It was time to bring things to a close. Daniel said, "So that's who we are. We're acolytes, people who serve inside the church family. And we're angels, people who share good news out in the neighborhood. Are we ready for that?" The question was rhetorical, but he waited for a response. When none came, he said, "I know we are."

AT THE CHURCH DOOR the members thanked their pastor for his message. Having heard Daniel speak from a pulpit for the very first time,

Frieda Stellhorn offered what was, for her, a high compliment. She said, "Well, I have to say, young man, you're a lot better at this than I thought you'd be."

As she stood near the front pew, waiting to thank Elsa Engelhardt for her piano prelude and postlude, Rosetta Jonas became aware of someone lingering nearby. She turned to discover, to her surprise, that Molly Lundgren was standing there. She looked tired, and older than Rosetta remembered her.

"I heard you were moving into your new chapel today," Molly said, smiling.

"How did you know?"

"I came to the print shop after you returned from your wedding trip. I wanted to welcome you back to Minneapolis. You were out that day. Mr. Engelhardt told me about the service today. So I decided to come."

"Adam Engelhardt didn't mention you'd been to the print shop."

"Oh, it wasn't him. It was *young* Mr. Engelhardt. David, I think he said his name was."

"College boys," said Rosetta with poorly-concealed disdain. "I guess you can't trust them with a simple message."

"Don't be too hard on him. He was really busy with customers. He didn't write it down or anything. I think he just forgot."

"That's no excuse," Rosetta said.

"Well, he seemed like a nice young man. I'll give him the benefit of the doubt. Anyway, I wanted to say hello to you."

Rosetta took Molly by the arm and pulled her to one side, away from the hearing of others. She said, "How are you, Molly? I mean, how are you really?"

Molly sighed and looked down. "Nothing has changed. Except, since you've moved out, I've left the rooming house. I have a very nice apartment now, on Park Avenue."

"Can you afford that?"

Molly looked uncertainly around her. She almost whispered, "With what I'm getting paid now, yes, easily. But it wouldn't matter anyway."

"What do you mean?"

"My boss has started paying my rent."

"Why on earth would he do that?"

"He says it's a benefit I deserve for quality work. But that's not really the reason."

Rosetta looked carefully at her former roommate and suspected what she would hear next.

Molly said, "I think he feels he has a right, now, to come and go whenever he wants to. And he does. He keeps a key to my place."

"Oh, Molly!" said Rosetta, in a whispered rebuke. "You have to get out of that job."

"How would I get another one?"

"Times are good. There have to be other jobs available."

"Not when your employer has influence. He says he'll destroy my reputation."

Rosetta thought, *as if he hasn't done it already.*

Chapter 6

Among the handful of visitors at the first worship service in the new chapel were a young policeman and his wife. Sam and Susan Warner had lived in the neighborhood for three years but had never found a church they really liked. This one was different. As they walked the four blocks from St. Michael Chapel to their home, they discussed what they had experienced.

Sam said, "That pastor Jonas really knows how to deliver a sermon."

"He seemed really … I don't know exactly what … personal, I guess I should say. I've never heard another pastor talk to the members like he was their friend. Maybe that's what it is."

"All I know is, I want to go back there."

At work the next morning, Sam mentioned the service to a couple of co-workers. He asked, "Where do you fellows go to church?" Neither went anywhere. He said, "Well, if you're looking for a place, you really ought to come and hear this minister. I think you'd like him."

The same afternoon, Susan went to coffee with her neighbor, Ellen Shaw. The two had become good friends over the past two years, and looked forward to their Monday afternoon chats. Today Ellen was in a sour mood. She confessed, "Allan is making so much money now, down at the furniture store, I hardly see him any more. If business gets any better, I'm afraid it just may destroy our marriage."

Susan listened sympathetically. She said, "Have you talked to your pastor?"

"We haven't been to church for five years. The last church we went to, the minister kept beating us over the head with how nothing we did was ever quite good enough. He kept telling us to give God more, more, more. I always felt like I went away from there on flat tires."

"You know, Sam and I visited in a cute little church yesterday. We're looking for a place to belong. We think this might just be it. You want to come with us next time?"

Ellen wrinkled her forehead, then shrugged. She said, "Let me think about it."

The following Sunday there were three new families in church, all people whom the Warners had invited — the Warners, who weren't even members!

It was just the beginning. People who heard the young Lutheran pastor speak felt an immediate connection. His messages consistently focused on the power and promises of God, and reminded them to be the messengers God wanted them to be. The message members and visitors began sharing with their friends and acquaintances was simple and direct: "St. Michael and All Angels is a friendly little church, with a pastor whose sermons are heartfelt — and which will change the way you think and live."

Within six weeks the chapel on the corner of Anderson and Caldwell was nearly half full on Sunday mornings.

JONATHAN ENGELHARDT looked at his mother, across the dining room table. "Mom, it's great to be eating your food again," he said. He trimmed off a thin slice of roast beef and popped it into his mouth.

"Does that mean your Aunt Louisa wasn't feeding you very well in Columbus?" Adam asked his older son.

"She was feeding me just fine. But there's just no cooking like Mom's cooking."

Jon's younger brother, David, set down his water glass and said, "Sounds like you're really keen on working with Uncle Adolph."

"It was the perfect summer job — for me, anyway. Uncle Adolph has three clothing stores now. Business is booming. I really learned a lot about sales and store management."

Jonathan made no effort to conceal his enthusiasm. His father listened with appreciation. His brother-in-law had obviously treated his son well during his summer internship in Ohio's capital city. He said, "You'll graduate from the university next spring. Do you plan to go back to work with your uncle?"

"Uncle Adolph says I can have a job with his company. But he says he doesn't want me to get stuck just doing that."

"What do you mean?" Elsa asked her son.

"He thinks I should get a master's degree in business. At Ohio State. I could live with him and Aunt Louisa while I do my studies. And after that, who knows? Maybe I could sign on with Uncle Adolph. Or maybe start my own business."

"You're sure you want to do graduate study?" Adam prodded. He himself had not pursued anything beyond four years of college, and he was doing just fine.

Jon laid down his steak knife and looked at his father. "My business administration advisor at the university has suggested the same thing."

"Has he, now?"

"Yes. He says I've got what it takes."

"Well, I don't doubt that," said Adam. "I just wonder if it's all that necessary."

"Dad, your parents weren't all that sure you should even go to college. Because they didn't. It's only natural you'd feel that way."

"Just so you don't get some high-falutin' advanced degree and then come back to Minneapolis and try taking over the print shop," said David, wiping the corners of his mouth with his napkin.

"Why do you say that?" asked Jon, looking at his younger brother.

"Because I plan to take it over when Dad retires."

Adam was caught off guard. It was the first time he'd heard his younger son say he wanted to follow in his footsteps. He'd watched his work in the shop all summer long and had realized he had the makings of a fine printer. If that was what David really wanted, then that was fine with him.

MICHAEL MORGAN-HOUSEMAN lay very still, listening for the clock. Nanny Annabelle always left his bedroom door open, just wide enough so the five-year-old could hear the deep-sounding grandfather clock chiming out the hours down in the front hallway. After eight o'clock each evening, Annabelle would turn the switch in the clock so that the chimes would go silent during the night. In the morning, at ten minutes before seven, she would move the lever in the other direction. That way, young Michael could hear the clock sound out seven o'clock. He was not allowed to come downstairs before then.

The clock began to chime. One, two, three, four, five, six, seven. Michael's heart began to pound with excitement. He jumped from his bed, darted into the hallway, and ran all the way to the other end. He skidded to a stop in front of the last door, upon which he pounded with tight little fists. "Daddy, Daddy!" he shouted. "Get up! It's my birthday!" Michael was not allowed to open his father's bedroom door, so he stood on the outside and hammered away. But there was no reply.

Annabelle came hurrying up the stairs. She knelt down beside the child and said, in a voice as comforting as she could manage, "Master Michael, your father had to go to work very early today. He'll be here for your birthday supper tonight."

Michael turned and looked defiantly at his nanny. His stuck out his lower lip and summoned two angry tears, one in the corner of each eye. "Daddy *promised* me! He said he would stay home today, and help me celebrate my birthday. He promised me a present today."

Annabelle tried to comfort the little boy, but he would not be comforted. He ran past her, back down the hall and into his room. He slammed the door so hard it made the hallway pictures rattle. Annabelle got up off her knees, breathed in deeply, and exhaled slowly. She walked to Michael's bedroom and hesitated before going in. Even before she opened the door, she heard him sobbing.

She walked across the soft carpet and sat down on the side of the bed. Michael had his face buried in his pillow. She smoothed her hand along the little boy's back, waiting for the shuddering to subside. At last, he turned over, looking at her with pathetic eyes. The tears had streaked his cheeks. Annabelle produced a handkerchief and tried to wipe the salty stains away.

Still blubbering, he wailed, "Why did Daddy lie? Doesn't he love me anymore?"

Annabelle hated times like these. Why did Mr. Morgan-Houseman constantly create these situations, making promises he didn't keep, and then leave it to her to try to put the broken pieces back together again? She said, "Michael, your daddy had a really important meeting today. He had to be there early."

"He always has some bad old meeting."

She took a deep breath and said, "It wasn't really a lie. Your daddy really wanted to stay home today. You were already asleep last night when he found out he had to go downtown so early."

Michael sniffed, then tried to blink away the tears still in his eyes.

Annabelle said, "And your daddy really does love you. Really and truly."

The child sat up. His beseeching brown eyes almost broke Annabelle's heart. He asked, "Will Daddy bring me my present tonight?"

"Master Michael, your present is waiting for you in the playroom right now."

The youngster's eyes became wide with anticipation. "What is it?"

"It's a surprise. It's in a big box, all wrapped up, just waiting for you."

"Can I open it?"

"*May* I open it?"

"May I?

"Not until you've dressed and had your breakfast."

In the kitchen he wolfed down his scrambled eggs and toast. Annabelle said, "Master Michael, slow down. You'll choke on your food." Her words were wasted on him.

When he had wiped his mouth with the cloth napkin, and folded it properly as he had been taught to do, he laid it beside his plate, then begged, "Please, Nanny Annabelle, let me down, let me down!" She pulled his chair back and helped him climb down.

Like a filly startled by a backfiring Model A, he was out the door and racing up the stairs. By the time Annabelle reached the playroom, Michael had found the box and was busy tearing off the wrapping paper. He lifted the lid from the Dayton's Department Store container and pulled out a large rubber ball. It had colorful stripes running around it — red, blue, yellow and green. When he bounced it, it shot up, halfway to the ceiling. He squealed with delight and chased after it.

Annabelle said, "Now don't make it bounce any higher than you are. We don't want to start breaking things in the house."

"But I want it to go high, Nanny Annabelle!"

"Not in the house."

"Can I have it with me when I take a bath?"

"*May* I."

"May I? Please?"

"Yes, if you don't make the water splash out of the bathtub."

"May I take it to bed with me when I go to sleep tonight?"

"I think we should leave it in your toy box."

"May I take it with us when we go on the streetcar?"

"When would we go on the streetcar?"

"Today! Today's my birthday. Today I get to ride the streetcar. Don't you remember?"

Annabelle vaguely remembered a conversation about the streetcar, many months ago, during the wintertime. She did not remember actually agreeing to take Michael for a ride on one. But, neither could she remember specifically saying no to the idea.

"Michael, I don't believe big rubber balls belong on streetcars."

"Oh please, please, *please*. It's my birthday. And my daddy went away and left me all alone. So can't I please, please take my birthday present with me when we ride the streetcar?"

He looked at her with eyes full of hope, at once both earnest and pathetic. *Such an irresistible little minx*, she thought. How could anyone, except the most heartless, possibly say no?

DANIEL JONAS spent the morning knocking on doors in the neighborhood around the church building. He found that he got energy from doing it. It was interesting to him to discover how many Lutherans, of all sorts, there were living near St. Michael and All Angels. There were members of the Norwegian Lutheran Church, Swedish Lutherans, several kinds of German Lutherans, and a scattering of Danish Lutherans. In addition, there were a number of families who weren't sure what kind of Lutheran they were, nor where the nearest church building was, much less what their pastor's name might be. These, Daniel was convinced, were simply Lutherans who had lost their way. He offered each of them a warm invitation to worship at St. Michael Church, and left behind an attractive flyer, copies of which had been printed for him, at no charge, by Adam Engelhardt.

Others whom Daniel met had no ties to any church. He offered them the same invitation.

The young clergyman was no less enthusiastic in his encounters with complete strangers whom he might encounter up and down Bloomington Avenue, or in the stores and shops that lined the busy thoroughfare. People came to expect, and to appreciate, a cheerful greeting from the pastor of the flock that gathered at the frame chapel on Anderson Avenue. Even those who had no particular interest in joining with his congregation came to regard him as their friend. And, as for those who suggested they might have an interest, the standard reply he offered was not "I hope you can come sometime," but rather, "On which Sunday should we look for you?"

At noon, as he always did, Daniel went home to the small apartment above the print shop, to eat his lunch with Rosetta. She knew he would be prompt and was always ready at precisely twelve o'clock.

From their kitchen table they could view the activity on the street below. As they sat eating, on this late August mid-day, Daniel said, "I love my work here. Things are going well. I think we're going to fill the church building before much longer."

"Just remember," said Rosetta, lifting a spoonful of soup to her mouth, "you married me and not St. Michael and All Angels."

"Are you feeling it already? Am I neglecting you?"

"No. But pastors sometimes do. It can happen too easily."

He looked into her eyes. She had such a pretty face, he wondered how he'd been so lucky to have won her. "You're good for me, you know," he said.

She nodded.

"Do you have any regrets? I mean, so far?"

"Why would I?"

"Well, when we were courting, you said it wasn't proper for a pastor to live above a print shop."

"We won't be here forever. The congregation will grow. They'll provide us a parsonage one of these days."

He mulled the comment. The congregation was growing already, largely through his efforts. But their lunchtime conversation had started with Rosetta cautioning him not to overdo it, at her expense. Yet all the energy he was pouring into his work would probably get her a house to live in, sooner than later. He wondered if she saw the irony.

They finished their meal in silence.

As she began to clear the table, Daniel said, "I noticed your old roommate, Molly, was at worship the other Sunday. I think that's the third or fourth time she's shown up. She always seems to get away without shaking my hand. Did you get to talk to her?"

"Yes," Rosetta replied. She felt her pulse quicken.

"How is she?"

What should she tell him? What was she at liberty to say? "She's ... I don't know. She's just about the same as ever."

In the distance Daniel heard the northbound streetcar clanging its bell. Within a minute or two it would be passing the print shop. That was his reminder that it was time for him to go back to work. He pushed back from the table, stood up, walked to the sink and kissed his wife goodbye. Then he headed for the stairs.

Chapter 7

Annabelle wondered how many children of local millionaires ever rode through the city of Minneapolis on a streetcar. She realized the chances were remote that anyone on the crowded trolley would recognize who Michael really was. But she also knew that, if anyone did, and if the word got back to his father, there was the potential for scandal. The possibility didn't trouble her much. She herself had ridden the trolleys a hundred times. Like herself, the people who rode the city's streetcars were far removed from the upper classes.

Annabelle could hardly believe how packed the Bloomington Avenue streetcar was. The walk from the mansion to Fourth Avenue, and the ride east along Franklin Avenue, had been pleasant enough. They'd climbed off at Bloomington Avenue, and she'd had every intention of catching the next one westbound. But the Bloomington southbound had been standing there, waiting for boarding. And Michael, irrepressible in his enthusiasm, had begged her impatiently. "That one, Nanny Annabelle! Now we have to go on that one!"

She'd agreed to a ride down Bloomington Avenue and Michael was ecstatic. But when they'd left the southbound and boarded one heading north, there had been only one seat available. So now they were wedged in, on a trolley overflowing with lower-class passengers. Michael was perched on her lap, his birthday ball held tightly in his hands.

Rolling along in the direction of Lake Street, the conductor rang his bell and, for the 65th time, Michael squealed with delight. Annabelle decided perhaps the joy which the excursion had given him was probably as fitting a birthday present as she could have found for her young charge.

The streetcar lurched to a halt. Passengers standing in the aisle moved forward quickly, heading for the exit. The last one to come past Michael, a portly woman with too many packages, bumped him accidentally, but kept moving, eager to get off. As she passed, the big rubber ball was jostled out of the five-year-old's hands and bounced down the aisle, toward the fare box.

In a flash, Michael was off Anabelle's lap, dashing down the aisle after it. The ball rolled down the stairs and out into the street. The youngster was close behind it, not looking left or right. With his eyes fixed only on the striped sphere, bouncing toward the intersection, he ran as fast as his small legs would carry him.

The driver of the motorized van, entering the intersection from the side street, saw the youngster race in front of his vehicle. He braked, but not soon enough. He felt the impact and felt a sick feeling in his stomach. Shoving into neutral, he yanked on the emergency brake and scrambled down.

The passengers on the streetcar, along with pedestrians from both sides of the street, had seen the accident. They were collecting around the perimeter of the space where the youngster now lay, not moving. Nobody was blaming the driver. It had clearly not been his fault.

DANIEL JONAS reached the bottom of the stairway and sensed immediately that something was amiss. The streetcar was not moving. A commercial van was standing halfway into the intersection. And a crowd of people were milling around in front of its bumper. He pushed his way through to the inside of the circle. Before him was a distraught young woman, on her knees, cradling an unconscious child in her arms. She was slowly rocking back and forth, weeping inconsolably.

Daniel knelt down next to her. He said, "I'm a pastor. Can I help?"

"He needs an ambulance," she said, through heavy sobs. "Please call an ambulance."

Daniel looked up. One of the bystanders explained an ambulance was on the way. He looked back at the young woman, and then at the youngster. There was no sign of blood. But neither was there any sign of life. He lay his hand on the boy's chest. He could feel him breathing, but just barely.

He said, "I'm so sorry about your little boy."

"This is all my fault," she said miserably, continuing to rock. "This is all my fault."

The ambulance came. Daniel said to her, "Would you like me to go with you to the hospital?"

She didn't respond, but just kept rocking.

Two attendants lifted the child onto a stretcher. Daniel helped the woman to stand, then assisted her into the ambulance. He sat down beside her, not sure what to say. The doors closed and the vehicle began to move. Daniel felt paralyzed. He could hardly believe he had found himself in this situation so suddenly and unexpectedly. He didn't know what to say to this troubled young woman. And he didn't know what he should say if she asked him anything — anything at all.

What he did know was that the woman and her little boy needed help. And he desperately wanted to offer some. He wished he could remember learning something at seminary that would help him just now. But he couldn't.

The ambulance pulled up in front of Fairview Hospital. Daniel climbed down, after the stretcher, then turned to help the woman. When she was out of the ambulance, she thrust a folded piece of paper into his hand. She said in a near whisper, "Please call Michael's father. This is his phone number."

He nodded, indicating he would do so. He followed the stretcher into the hospital. When he turned back to speak again to the woman, she was gone.

THE LOWLY FILE CLERK, temporarily seated at Molly Lundgren's desk, was fit to be tied. It was simple enough for Gladys Higby to field phone calls, and to promise that the company president would return them in due time. But what was she to do with the message jotted on the pad in front of her?

She studied her own handwriting. The man on the phone had told her in no uncertain terms that it was an emergency and that it should not wait. And yet, when Mr. Morgan-Houseman had gone into his inner office with Molly, he had instructed Gladys, in equally certain terms, that they would be in consultation for an hour, and that under no circumstances were they to be disturbed.

Gladys had specifically asked whether she might interrupt them for a serious emergency. The answer she had received still echoed in her ears: "Not if you value your job here."

She hated being caught in the middle this way. But caught she was, and there was nothing to be done about it.

And so she sat and studied the note in front of her, looking furtively from time to time at the locked door, beyond which the company president and his executive secretary were closeted. What sort of consultation, she wondered, could possibly justify the inflexible sort of instructions she'd been given? What indeed? She was well aware that Mr. Morgan-Houseman had a divan in his office. She had seen it. And everybody knew he had eyes for Molly. Rumors were, he sometimes visited her apartment on Park Avenue, at the end of the work day. Rumor had it, he even had his own key.

Gladys realized her imagination was running wild with such thoughts, but she couldn't put the idea out of her mind. It had now already been longer than the hour he'd said they would need, and they were still in there.

She looked at the note again. *Who was this Daniel Yonas person?* she wondered. *A client worried about his portfolio?* She knew that in the stock market, timing was everything. *What if waiting an hour and twenty minutes to execute a trade was costing him a lot of money? Who would get the blame?*

At long last, the door to the inner office opened. Mr. Morgan-Houseman came out. Alone. She handed the telephone message to the president of the firm and said, "Mr. Yonas said it was extremely important. But you said …"

"Yes, yes, I know," he replied, sounding distracted — and a little disoriented. He studied the message and said, "Go back to your filing."

Gladys lingered just outside the outer office door, waiting to see if Molly would re-emerge. When she didn't, the file clerk went back to her work station, half fearing she might get a scolding for having waited with the message. But there was no scolding. Instead, five minutes later, she looked up to see her employer, sprinting with the speed of a Minnesota University quarterback, through the office. Before he reached the lobby he collided with a typewriter table, sending the heavy Underwood upright crashing to the floor. He swore an obscenity, but kept right on going, until he disappeared, out into the hallway where the elevators were.

Never in her life had Gladys seen her employer move so fast.

DANIEL JONAS sat in a chair across from Michael Morgan-Houseman, in the small waiting room. They had been there together for two hours. Somewhere down the hall a medical team was doing what they could for the wealthy stockbroker's son. The youngster had not stirred since having been brought in. Only his shallow breathing gave assurance there was still life in him.

Morgan-Houseman had spent his first half hour at Fairview Hospital abusing the young pastor with angry outbursts. How could this have happened, he had demanded. What was his son doing on a streetcar? What had gotten into his nanny to permit such a thing? How could a whole streetcar full of people allow the boy to get off the trolley all by himself? And what was the matter with that delivery van driver? Failing to get satisfactory answers to those questions, he'd turned his rage on the doctors and the nurses. Why was it taking them so long to tell him anything? And, what in hell were they doing down there, at the other end of the hall, anyway?

Daniel had considered offering words of assurance, but nothing remotely comforting came to mind. He felt impotent. And that feeling made him angry. He was angry over the outpouring he'd been forced to endure for the past two hours. This man was not even his parishioner. And, so far, he'd not heard a single word of appreciation for his efforts on behalf of the man's injured son.

He realized that, were he in the place of this distraught parent, he would likely pour out some anger of his own. But he hoped, should he ever be put in that position, that he'd exercise a little more control. He realized he had no idea what he might really do in such a situation.

Morgan-Houseman had sat in sullen silence for the last quarter-hour. Daniel felt apprehensive, waiting for the next volcanic eruption. Instead, he heard something unexpected. The stockbroker, belligerent no more, began to sob. Quietly at first, then more audibly, he allowed his grief to flow with his tears.

Daniel was glad to see that the hard-driving businessman could show a more vulnerable side. But this display caught him off guard. He was unsure what to say, so he said nothing.

In broken syllables, Morgan-Houseman choked out the words. "This is my fault. This is my fault. I promised him I'd stay home today. It was his birthday, for god's sake." He was shuddering. He blubbered miserably, "All he wanted was a goddam birthday with his daddy. And I had to go to a breakfast meeting and leave him at home without his own father there to watch him open his birthday present."

Daniel really wanted to say something now, but he was tongue-tied. Morgan Houseman continued, "What kind of father leaves his only child alone on his birthday, after he promised he'd spend the day with him?" He looked Daniel in the eye, as if accusing the young pastor of something. He said, "Tell me, what kind of father does that?"

Daniel finally found his voice. "Mr. Morgan-Houseman, you mustn't blame yourself."

"Why the hell *not*!" he demanded, in a voice that almost knocked Daniel over. "Who the devil else *should* I blame? Don't you see what I've done? I've *killed* him. *I've killed my only son!*"

Surprising himself, Daniel got out of his chair. He crossed the small room and sat down on the short couch next to Morgan-Houseman. He lay his hand on the distraught man's wrist and said, "Your son is still alive. Don't give up on him. Don't give up on the doctors. And don't give up on God."

"God! You dare to mention *God* to me? Where *is* your God? What *good* is he? Where in hell was your goddam God when my son was being hit by a delivery van? What kind of God lets that happen to a little boy?"

Daniel cringed. But he understood the rage. Still, he wished there was something useful he could say or do.

Morgan-Houseman's mood shifted. "What kind of father lets that happen?" he slurred. "It should have been me. I'm a poor excuse for a human being. A stinking poor excuse." He turned toward Daniel and demanded, "Why wasn't it me?"

Daniel said quietly, "We're going to get through this, you and I together."

The businessman stared at him, trying to absorb what he'd just heard. Then he began to sob again, reaching out to grasp Daniel's forearms for support, shaking uncontrollably. His anger spent, there was nothing left in him but anguish. With great, pathetic wails, he wept without shame. Until there were no tears left.

LITTLE MICHAEL MORGAN-HOUSEMAN lingered between life and death for eight days, never regaining consciousness. Each day Daniel returned to the hospital. The young boy's father was always there when he arrived. Over the span of days, he came to tolerate the young clergyman's company, then to expect it, then to crave it. On the evening of the seventh day, quite unexpectedly, he asked Daniel to say a prayer for his son. Daniel was quick to oblige.

On the evening of the ninth day, during the supper hour, Daniel received a phone call. He was asked to come to the hospital immediately. When he arrived, he was ushered into the room where the youngster had lain motionless for so many days. He was informed that Michael had died within the hour.

Down the hall, in the same waiting room where he had so often sat with him, he found the boy's father, alone with his grief. Michael Morgan-Houseman looked up and said, tears staining his face, "You'll have his service, won't you?"

Daniel replied, "Yes. Of course."

THEY BURIED HIM next to his mother, at Lakewood Cemetery. After the graveside service, Daniel said to the stockbroker, "I want you to call on me at any time, for any reason. Do you understand?"

"Yes," he replied somberly. "I expect to be calling you. Before too long. There are things I need to say to you."

Daniel wasn't sure exactly how to interpret those words, but decided not to think too much about them. There were other things on his mind. He had a list of six new families who had asked about membership in St. Michael Church. All were waiting for a visit. And next Sunday's sermon was hanging over his head.

A week later, Morgan-Houseman phoned Daniel. He wanted to speak with him in person. He said he would send his car to pick him up. Daniel offered to come on his own, but the businessman insisted on sending his chauffeur with the Packard.

Seated in the parlor of the brown brick mansion, the two men faced one another across a richly woven Turkish carpet. Light streamed in through the leaded windows, the stained-glass insets creating colorful images on the shiny parquet floor.

"Brandy?" the host offered, pouring one for himself. Daniel smiled politely and declined. It was only ten o'clock in the morning, and he wasn't a brandy drinker anyway. To say nothing of the fact that Prohibition was the law of the land.

"I'm going to miss that little rascal," Morgan-Houseman said. He twisted his face into a thoughtful scowl. There were no tears today, but it was clear to Daniel that grief and remorse were burrowing into him.

"He must have been very special to you," Daniel said. The comment sounded lame to him as soon as it was out of his mouth.

The businessman did not reply, but instead changed the subject. "Do you have any idea what was so infernally important that took me downtown for breakfast on my son's birthday?"

Daniel had no clue.

"It was a meeting with one of the richest men in Minnesota. Wilbur B. Foshay. Here's a tycoon with way more money than he can ever spend. I've been after him for six years to let me manage his investments. It would be a major accomplishment for my career if I could snare him. The commissions would be phenomenal. I figured it out. I could almost run my entire operation with a single client — if he were the client."

Probably a risky strategy at best, Daniel thought. But he kept still.

"We didn't ink a deal that morning. But I received great encouragement. He told me he thought he might like to work with me." He paused and sipped his brandy. "Now, that's no binding commitment by any stretch. But it has the makings of a gentlemen's agreement. Anyway, it's more than I've ever gotten from him before."

Chapter 8

The stockbroker got up from his chair, the brandy snifter still in his hand. He began to pace. Daniel watched him with fascination and thought, *this man is in possession of more money than I've dreamed of having. And he's in the process of accumulating a good deal more. What am I doing, sitting in this lavish residence, listening to all of this?* And, he wondered, what did this talk of investment opportunities have to do with the death of this man's little boy?

The stockbroker was becoming animated, as if he had just figured out a way to corner the market in wheat futures. He stopped walking, turned toward Daniel, and said, "Think of it! Wilbur Foshay's stockbroker! I was so euphoric, I went straight back to my office and spent the morning plotting how I might reel him in. At mid-morning, I dictated a letter. It was a masterpiece of persuasion, if I may say so. My executive secretary had it ready for my signature by lunchtime."

He stopped and seemed to lose his focus. His mind raced back to the mid-day tryst with his employee. The realization, that it had been precisely then that his son had been struck down in traffic, gnawed at him.

But it was not what he had done with his secretary that troubled him. He felt no guilt about that. It was her job to give him what he wanted. That was what he paid her for. What was chewing at him was the neglect he had shown toward his son. As he considered the long string of broken promises he'd made, he felt weakness in his knees. He returned to his chair, dropped heavily into it, and set the empty glass aside. When he spoke again, the euphoria was gone. His voice was full of self-recrimination. "And so, while I was celebrating the greatness of me, the almighty, all-powerful Michael Morgan-Houseman, I was unavailable to my son." He looked off into space. "I'll never see him again."

The room fell silent. The ticking of the grandfather clock in the great front hallway suddenly seemed loud.

Daniel waited for what he decided to have been a decent interval before speaking. "How exactly can I help you, Mr. Morgan-Houseman?"

The host blinked, twice, and then seemed to come out of his trance. He said,

"Call me Mike. That hyphenated last name's a mouthful. And, anyway, I want to speak personally now, man to man."

Daniel nodded and tilted his head slightly, preparing himself.

"Mr. Foshay's building that amazing skyscraper down there on Ninth and Marquette. The damn thing's going to dwarf the City Hall clocktower. Just imagine that."

The young pastor had been past the Foshay construction site. To him, it looked like the Washington Monument with windows. But it was, truly, an amazing thing to see, rising above the mostly-squat city skyline.

"People like to build monuments, don't they," Morgan-Houseman said, sounding almost philosophical. "When my wife died, I put up a fancy marker for her, down at Lakewood. You saw it when we buried little Michael. Carved nymphs with their flower baskets, standing on top of the tombstone. One of the finest pieces in the cemetery."

Daniel nodded. It had been overdone, he'd thought.

"Well, that was for her. Now I need to think about my son. I want a monument to his memory, too. Something fitting."

"Were you thinking of an elaborate grave marker for him as well?"

"Oh, god, no!" Mogan-Houseman replied. Immediately he colored. "Pardon my French, Reverend. In the business world, we sometimes use … well … colorful language."

It was not the time or place for a sermonette on taking the Lord's name in vain, Daniel decided.

"I want to do something that will keep his memory alive, possibly forever." Daniel wondered how that would even be possible. "And I want it to be something that will touch a lot of people. Something that will … you know … help them. Make their lives better."

Now Daniel was tuned in. What did the millionaire really have in mind?

"You know," Morgan-Houseman said, crossing one leg over the other and leaning back, "I've been meaning to talk to you. Especially about that first day at the hospital."

Daniel cringed just thinking about that nightmarish experience. That day had, in his own mind, been the most anemic pastoral performance he had ever managed. He'd hoped to be able to forget about it. This conversation wasn't helping.

"I haven't had a lot of dealings with clergymen, but I know something about how a lot of them operate. They're so goddammed eager … Excuse my French again … They're so all-fired eager to tell you what they want you to know and hear and think and believe, they just don't know when to shut up and listen for a change."

Daniel was caught off guard. He felt a surge in his pulse.

"But you didn't do that. You didn't say anything. You just let me rant and rave and roar and say all the things I needed to say. You didn't walk away. You didn't scold me. God ... golly ... I don't know how you managed that. I thought sure there would be a sermon in there somewhere, at least a little hellfire and damnation about the way I neglected my son and all. Either that's one helluva seminary they sent you to, or you're a lot wiser than your years. Maybe some of both."

Now Daniel really was dumbstruck. He had no idea his feeling of ineptitude on that awful day at Fairview Hospital would be interpreted in such a way. He decided to allow the stockbroker to nurture his own perceptions of what had transpired.

"Which is a roundabout way of saying that I've come to have a lot of respect for you in the short time I've known you. I mean, you didn't know me from Adam. You didn't know my son. You didn't have to come to the hospital. You could have watched them load him into that ambulance and then have walked away, and nobody would have thought the less of you."

I would have thought less of me, Daniel thought.

"And yet you came back, again and again, all those tough and terrible days. I know you had other things to be thinking about. Nobody was paying you to show up at the hospital. You just came."

Seelsorge, Daniel remembered his pastoral care professor at the seminary having called it. Care and cure of souls. Why he'd learned the expression in German, he was not sure.

"So, here's the deal," said Morgan-Houseman, uncrossing his legs and looking intently at his guest. "I want to create a living monument for my son. And I want you to help me do it."

Daniel nodded carefully. "A living monument? What might that entail?"

"Last Sunday morning I drove past your church building. People at the hospital told me where it was. It was a warm day, perhaps you'll remember. The windows and the front door were open. I could see all the way down the aisle, to the front. That place was packed. If I'd wanted to go in, I would have had to stand. Of course, I had no intention of going in. I'm not religious, you see."

Daniel wanted to have a friendly argument with his host about that. He was confident everybody was somehow religious. But he held the thought.

"It's obvious to me," Morgan-Houseman went on, "that you need a bigger church building. Now, maybe not the size of that stone palace that Central Lutheran just put up, down there on Twelfth Street. My stars, that place is big as a cathedral. But you and your congregation need something bigger than you've got now. And, as it turns out, I need a way to honor the memory of my son. I'm thinking, why don't you let me build a new church building for you? Perhaps you'd consider naming it the 'Michael Morgan-Houseman Jr. Memorial Church.'"

Daniel should have seen this coming. He said, "In the first place, that would be quite a mouthful, don't you think?"

Morgan-Houseman offered a thoughtful scowl, then grinned.

"In the second place, the congregation already has a name, and there are some pretty stubborn Germans over there who are not going to sit still for you or me or anybody else fiddling with the name they gave it when they first started out. That name was there before I became their pastor. Besides, it's an excellent name for a congregation: 'The Lutheran Church of Saint Michael and All Angels.'"

"And you think *my* suggestion was a mouthful!" The stockbroker laughed heartily. And, in spite of himself, Daniel did too.

"But, in the third place — and I know you may not appreciate my saying this, but I have to say it anyway — in the third place, it would be really bad theology to name a church after a person."

"What do you mean?"

"The church honors God, not people."

"Nonsense! There's St. John's and St. Matthew's and Saint who-the-hell-else. There are churches like that all over town."

"Those are apostolic saints. They were faithful followers of our Lord. They're mentioned in the Bible. And all of them lived lives that pointed to Christ, not to themselves."

The host stroked his chin thoughtfully. He said, "Well, all right. The name is fine the way it is. In fact, I guess my son's name is already in it, isn't it?"

Daniel grinned. "Your son, and you, both have a fine biblical name. Do you know what 'Michael' means in Hebrew?"

Morgan-Houseman shook his head.

"It means, 'One who is like God.'"

The businessman roared with laughter. He said, "That doesn't exactly describe me." His face turned sober. "But little Michael? Yes. It may describe him. He wasn't like me. He loved everyone. He was ..." Tears began to form in the corners of the older man's eyes.

"He was a wonderful little boy," said Daniel. "I never knew him. But I know, from what you've told me, he was an absolutely wonderful son. And you can be thankful to God that you had him for five years."

"Five wasted years, as far as I can tell," Morgan-Houseman said ruefully. "*Damn!* How I wish I could go back and live those years over. What was I *thinking*? What was the *matter* with me? How could I have missed so much of his life?"

Daniel had no answers to offer.

Morgan-Houseman said, "All right, then. The church keeps its name. But would you be willing to put my son's name somewhere inside? You know, not too prominently. But somewhere so I could come sometime and look at it and remember him?"

The pastor was thinking fast. He amazed even himself by what he said next. "I can envision a fine new stone building, twice or three times as large as our present structure. Stained glass windows. Two chapels, one on either side, in transepts near the front. On the left could be a Chapel of the Victors. There could be a great colored window, picturing the scene from the Book of Revelation — the Archangel Michael, and all his angels, driving Satan out of heaven. And facing it, on the other side of the center aisle, there could be a Children's Chapel. There could be a wonderful stained glass window, showing Jesus and little children. And there could be an inscription, at the bottom, etched right into the glass itself. We could have it read, 'Sacred to the Memory of Michael Morgan-Houseman Jr.'"

Morgan-Houseman seemed enchanted. He said, "And, when the window is designed, could we have a little boy in it, one who looks just like my son?"

Daniel gestured to the framed painting above the fireplace. "We can send his portrait to the stained glass studio. They can replicate it. That would be a wonderful tribute to him."

The businessman gripped the arms of his chair, leaned forward and said in a hoarse, almost mysterious whisper, "Yes. By God, *yes!*"

MOLLY LUNDGREN stirred the cream into her coffee, watching the swirls the motion created in her cup. When she looked up, her friend, Rosetta sat looking at her expectantly. From their second-floor perch at the kitchen table window, overlooking Bloomington Avenue, they could see the mid-morning traffic moving busily up and down. But Molly wasn't thinking about the traffic.

"So, tell me," said Rosetta, "what was so urgent that it made you want to come all the way down here in the middle of a work day?"

Molly looked furtively at her, then pursed her lips.

"Oh, Molly," Rosetta said, "you finally confronted him. You've lost your job."

"No. I haven't lost my job. But ..."

"But what?"

"But I did confront him. Sort of. And, I don't work there any more."

"What happened?"

"He left town on business yesterday. He'll be gone a week. I waited until he was out of the office. And then I wrote my letter of resignation. I left it on his desk."

Rosetta nodded slowly. She said, "Well, it was for the best, Molly. That was a hellish situation to be in."

Molly looked at Rosetta with a face that seemed old. There were creases where the pastor's wife had never seen any before. Molly said, "I've missed my period for two months in a row."

Rosetta was speechless. Her mouth dropped open.

Molly's lower lip began to quiver. "I don't know where to go. I don't know what to do. I have no job. I have nowhere to live. I can't go home. I ... I can't have this baby." Her face was twisted into an angry scowl, and now the tears came cascading down. She continued, "And up until this minute, I haven't been able to talk to anybody about any of it." The river of tears became a flood. She sobbed so heartrendingly that Rosetta jumped out of her chair and hurried to Molly's side.

"Come with me," she said, pulling her up, and helping her into the small living room. When they were seated next to one another on the second-hand sofa, she circled her arm around the distraught young career woman's shoulders and held her tight. Molly cried nonstop for nearly a minute.

Afterwards, when her eyes were dried, she said, "I have to go away somewhere. Anywhere. Just far away. Until I can figure out what to do."

"Molly, don't go anywhere. Stay here."

"Here? In this tiny little apartment?"

"No, here in the neighborhood. We'll find you a place."

"I don't want him knowing where to find me."

"He doesn't *have* to know."

"I need a place soon. Like, right now."

"Molly, how much longer does your lease run on the apartment?"

"It doesn't matter. He was paying it. I've turned in my keys. I just wanted out of there. All I could think about when I went into that bedroom was that … that monster … and how he sullied my bed with his … Oh, God, I can't even talk about this!"

"Don't talk about it. Just put it out of your mind."

"What am I going to *do*, Rosetta?"

"Well, for tonight, you're going to sleep right here, on this couch."

"Will Daniel be all right with that?"

"He will if he values our marriage," she said sternly. Then she grinned. "Of *course* he'll be all right. Daniel has a pastor's heart for everyone. Sometimes I think just a little too much of a pastor's heart. But that's another story. Just plan on staying with us." She paused momentarily, and then asked, "Where are your things? You know … your clothes."

"I … I was too embarrassed to bring them into your home. At least, right away. I … well, I left them out on the landing, at the top of the stairs."

"Well, let's go and get them then!" said Rosetta, heading for the door.

Chapter 9

"You're not pulling our leg, are you, pastor?" asked Jake Bauer, leaning his forearms on the table. As other members of the parish council focused on Jake, he looked intently at Daniel.

"No," the clergyman replied. "It's all as I've described it. The account is set up, at our bank. It's in our name."

"And the only condition is, we have to build a new church building, with stained glass windows?" Fred Stumpf said.

"Well, one stained glass window in particular. And I don't exactly like donors telling us specifically how we have to spend the money. But it's one inscription, at the bottom of one window, in a side chapel, where it won't be too obvious."

"You're absolutely sure that's the only condition?" asked Willie Langholz. "This pandering to rich people always makes me a little nervous. We don't want him coming in here later on and adding more requirements to what he said at the beginning."

"I have a document from Mr. Morgan-Houseman's attorney. It's all spelled out. In fact, I want all of you to read it before we make any recommendation to the membership. They would really have to approve this."

"Even though it won't cost the congregation a red cent?" asked George Kleinhans.

"Yes. Of course. Absolutely. We're not the final governing body for the congregation. The members are. And besides, would you want to be responsible, as a group of six, for the disposition of five-million dollars?"

"All I can say," chimed in Andy Scheidt, "is this guy must have one extra-king-size guilty conscience, to want to give a church that much money in honor of his son."

"Oh, I don't know," said Jake. "If he's got the money, maybe it's not a big thing for him. I mean, look at the size of some of those houses over there on Groveland and LaSalle and Pillsbury and places like that. Carriage houses, servants' quarters, iron fences running around a half block of property. I say, since the guy has the money, let him share it with people who can put it to good use."

"He wanted to spend one-million dollars for each year of his son's short life," Daniel explained. The idea sounded preposterous to him as soon as the words came out. No wonder, he thought, his council members were having trouble believing it.

"Anybody think about what it might cost to take care of a big stone church building with fancy windows?" Fred asked.

Daniel said, "Twenty-percent of the bequest is to be a separate endowment, set aside for that. We'd only be allowed to spend the interest. It would be a perpetual fund."

"He's thought of everything, hasn't he," said Adam Engelhardt. "Don't get me wrong. I really like the idea that a benefactor has come forward like this. And we really need more space. It's a credit to our pastor that we have this situation facing us so quickly. But there is one thing that bothers me.

The other men waited for Adam to finish his thought.

"What kind of stewardship will this encourage in our members, if they think we have all this money in the bank and don't need to put anything in the offering plate? That's really not a healthy situation, when you think about it."

"Well, people are putting a lot of money in the offering plate right now," said Jacob. The young bank clerk was in charge of counting the offerings every Sunday after worship. "But it would be a shame if that started to dry up."

"I think we can find plenty of other ways to spend our offerings," said Andy. "We should be thinking about increasing our pastor's salary to full-time, so I don't have to keep paying him."

"You getting tired of that already?" asked George, grinning at the young carpenter.

"No. He's a great worker. And he's down to an hour and a half a day working for me. But he needs more time to do what he's doing in the congregation now. It's a wonder his young bride ever sees him at all." He looked at Daniel and said, "She *does* see you sometimes, doesn't she?"

Daniel grinned sheepishly and nodded.

"Well, I've got other guys ready and waiting to work for me. I think it's time we set our pastor loose to do parish work full time." He paused, but only briefly. "And, then, there's St. Paul Luther College and Seminary. They need every nickel people send to them. We could be helping them out. After all, everybody in this room, except Adam here, went to that school. We should be helping support the place."

Everyone was nodding. So was Adam, whose two sons had both enrolled there.

Andy continued, "And then, there's the matter of the pastor's living arrangements."

Daniel felt uncomfortable about how the conversation had turned. But he held his tongue.

Andy said, "I think it's time we consider buying — or building — a decent parsonage. It's great, Adam, that you're providing that upstairs apartment rent-free. But you can't have the pastor of a big stone church living above a print shop. And besides," he continued, looking at the pastor, "what does Rosetta think about living up there for who knows how long?"

Daniel colored. But he knew exactly how his wife felt. He said, "She'll be ready for a house of her own. Whenever it's practical."

"Well, then," said Andy, triumphantly, "so much for stewardship concerns. We have a bunch of good places to be spending our Sunday offerings. I'd say we'll be needing *more* in the collection plate, not less."

AS THE MEETING broke up, and the other council members began departing, Daniel lingered in Adam's living room. When they were alone, the pastor said, "Do you have a few minutes?"

"Certainly." The two men sat down again.

Daniel said, "Maybe you're aware that we have a sort of, well, situation. Up at the apartment, I mean."

"Molly Lundgren?"

"Somebody told you, then."

"Your wife."

"Well, how much has she told you?"

"Molly's a former roommate of hers. She's in the family way and she has no husband. And she's sleeping on your couch."

"Anything else? Did she say anything else?"

Adam said, "It's always hard for me to tell when Rosetta is hinting and when she's asking, so I'm not real sure about this. But I think she may be ready for some other living arrangement for Molly."

"It's been three weeks."

"Pretty crowded up there, right?"

"We both love Molly. But you know how much space we have. And it can't be good for Molly either. She's living out of her suitcases."

"What are your thoughts about what to do, then?"

"Well, since your two boys are both away at college, I have to assume you have a spare bedroom or two upstairs. So, naturally … "

Adam cut him short. He called toward the kitchen: "Elsa! Can you come in here for a minute, please?"

Daniel said in a low voice, "Adam, I didn't want to draw Elsa into this conversation yet ... "

"I think you already have. And that's fine. We need to talk about this together."

Elsa came into the living room and sat down. Adam said, "Pastor Daniel has been telling me about Molly Lundgren."

"What's to become of her?" asked Elsa, concern in her voice.

Daniel said, "Well, we need to find a place for her until her baby comes. After that, I guess I don't know."

"Why haven't you asked us to let her stay here?" asked Elsa. Adam looked at her in surprise. Elsa continued, "She can't keep sleeping on your couch."

"I ... well ... I wasn't sure what you might say."

"You weren't sure because you didn't ask."

The two men looked at each other. Daniel said, "It would be a seven-month commitment, Elsa."

"So?"

"So ... I wasn't sure you'd want to take on something like that. I mean, your boys come home on weekends sometimes."

"We have two empty bedrooms," she said. "And a couch. I'm willing to bet the couch is about as comfortable as a dormitory bed. So, what's the problem?"

"The problem is, I don't think she'll be able to pay you anything for room and board."

Elsa's eyes narrowed. "How much is she paying you?"

"Nothing."

"Then that's how much *we'll* take."

"IT LOOKS LIKE A CLOISTER!" said Sam Warner, nudging his wife with his elbow.

"Not so loud," Susan scolded. "It's just a proposal."

"The way Pastor Jonas is talking up there, it's what he really wants the new building to look like."

"Well, he knows something about these things. Don't they have to learn about church design in seminary?"

"But it looks *Catholic*!"

"He's a Lutheran pastor. We like him, don't we?"

"Yeah. So?"

"So, has he done anything yet that's disappointed us?"

"No. What's your point?"

"I think we should trust him on this."

The discussion period was over. Daniel took his seat in the tiny chancel. Adam Engelhardt took the floor. He looked over the crowded nave. Members were filling all the pews and standing around the edges. It looked to the print shop owner as though they were probably violating some sort of fire code. All the more reason to get this meeting over with.

"The vote today is to approve receiving the generous gift from our donor, for the specific purpose of building a new and larger church building, with the condition that the new structure will include one inscribed window in a side chapel. Please mark the paper ballot you've received. Vote yes or no."

The congregation bent to their task. When the folded slips of paper were sent to the center aisle, Fred Stumpf and Andy Scheidt came along with offering plates and collected them. While the tellers were tallying the results, Daniel asked Elsa Engelhardt to come to the upright piano. The congregation sang all the stanzas of "Built on a Rock the Church Doth Stand," followed by all the stanzas of "The Church's One Foundation." By the time they were finished, the counting was, too.

Andy handed a folded piece of paper to the president of the congregation. Adam opened it, studied it for a moment, and then announced, "There are no dissenting votes. The motion is adopted unanimously."

The congregation broke into applause. Adam declared the meeting over. He felt relief. It had been a long Sunday morning. The worshipers had remained after the second service for the special meeting, and other members had returned, after having come to the earlier one. During the meeting itself, Adam had wondered whether or when a contrary opinion — or several — might not extend the day even longer. But the discussion had been civilized, and not too protracted.

Adam marveled at how the vote had gone. In retrospect, he realized it was less difficult to achieve consensus when you're spending someone else's money.

As the congregation began to disperse, members of the parish council gathered at the front of the nave, in the vicinity of the ambitious architectural sketch displayed on the easel. Fred Stumpf said, "To build all of this, we'd need a whole block, not just two lots."

George Kleinhans replied, "I saw this coming."

"What's that?" asked Fred.

"When the chapel started overflowing and we went to a second service, I could see we'd need more space. You can't build a decent sized church and a parish house and offices on two lots. So, I got options on the next five adjoining."

"How did you do that?" asked Fred.

"Very quietly," the young real estate salesman said. "I knew two of them were coming up for sale before too long, so I talked to the owners separately. I told them I might or might not be interested. They were ready to sell. I've got first right of refusal. The family in the third house wants to move out to St. Louis Park. They didn't require very much persuading. The other two were owned by absentee landlords. Turns out both of them were open to selling."

"So now we have to buy the lots from your company, right, George?" said Fred, dryly.

"Well, we're not in business for our health. You don't expect us to give them away, do you?"

Fred colored. "Well, no, of course not."

"Don't worry. The church will get a good price."

"THANKS, ADAM," said Daniel, as the last two hangers-on moved toward the door of the church. "You ran the meeting well. No great controversy. I'm relieved."

Adam said, "Looks to me like you're going to get to serve in that Fremont-sized church building after all. Except in Minneapolis."

"Well, it's not going to be identical. But the same architect was available, and eager to do another building in a similar style. It makes things easier."

"It was clever of him to draw the plan so we don't have to tear down the chapel until the new building is completed."

"What else would we do? Worship in the street?" The two men stepped out onto the small front step.

"Well," said Adam, turning the key and locking the front door, "I seem to recall we once did this in people's living rooms."

"That was fine when there were fourteen of us. Now we have over 300. Can you believe it?"

"Well, some days, not really. I think we have to be careful not to let you work too hard at this. The congregation is growing like a weed. But I worry about your marriage some days. Are you spending enough time with your wife?"

"Believe me, things are better now that Molly is living in one of your spare bedrooms."

"We're delighted to have her living with us. She won't stop thanking us for our hospitality. She's no problem to have around. And, she's an incredible cook, by the way. Some days she almost pushes Elsa out of the kitchen."

"How does Elsa feel about that?"

"The first couple times she was sort of resentful about it. I mean, let's face it, Elsa is twice Molly's age. She thinks she knows a few things about running a kitchen. But then, she thought it over and decided it wasn't such a bad deal. After all, it gives Molly something to do, and she's really good at it. That mother of hers, out there in Litchfield, must have done a few things right."

"So, it sounds like things are okay with Molly."

"Well, most things."

"I'm sure the pregnancy has to be ..."

"It's not the pregnancy."

"What then?"

"Well, to be truthful, Pastor, she's really angry about this vote we just took."

"How could she be? We just took it."

"She's upset we're even *talking* about receiving a gift from Mr. Morgan-Houseman."

"I guess I can understand that."

"And she's really angry about the idea that his name will end up etched into stained glass."

"But it will be his *son's* name."

"It doesn't matter. It's the Morgan-Houseman name." He paused, sighed, and added, "She says if we build this new church, she may never set foot inside it."

Chapter 10

That night Daniel did not sleep well. He was wide awake at two o'clock in the morning. When Rosetta realized he was missing from their bed, she came out into the kitchen and found him standing at the window, staring down at the street.

"Daniel, what's wrong?" she asked, snuggling up behind him and flattening her palms across his sighing chest.

"I had this dream," he said.

"What sort of dream?"

"I was over at the church building. Except, it was the *new* church building. The three-story parish house and the enormous nave those Boston architects, Cram and Ferguson, designed for us."

"What was it like?"

"It was amazing. It looked just exactly the way I'd imagined it would look. It was a glorious building."

"And that was what you dreamed?"

"There was more." He turned to face his wife. "You know, we've never had any discussions yet about what the windows might look like, aside from the two in the side chapels." His expression was one she could not read. He continued, "But in my dream, there was a large stained glass window, high in the chancel, up behind the altar. It was a picture of God on his throne."

Rosetta asked, "You mean Christ?"

"No. God the Father." She returned a look of puzzlement. He continued, "Do you find that peculiar? Well, you should. I certainly do. Rosetta, nobody knows what God looks like! And yet, there he was, in our stained glass window."

"Well," she prodded, her curiosity getting the best of her, "what did he look like?"

"I don't know. I don't exactly remember. I mean, God was *there*, but he was ... well, whatever he looked like, he wasn't very friendly."

"What do you mean?"

"It was as if I was on trial. God said, 'Daniel Wilhelm Jonas, I am gravely disappointed in you.'"

"Those were his words?"

"I remember them clearly. They were cold and cruel and angry."

"Why was he disappointed?"

"He asked me a question. He said, 'Whose house is this?' I answered, 'I don't understand. This is *your* house. We built it for you.' And God said ... no, it was more like he shouted at me ... he said, 'You have *not* built this house for *me*. You have built it for *yourself*! You have committed the sin of pride! I am not pleased with you!' And then ... and then the whole building began to shake and I was certain it was going to collapse on top of me." He paused, feeling his pulse increasing. " And that was all. The dream ended there."

Rosetta cradled her husband's face in her hands. She said, "You're warm. And you're perspiring. And you're shaking."

He drew his arms around her and held her close. He said, "Are we making a mistake? Are we doing the wrong thing, building this church?"

She looked into his eyes and said, "You need to search your heart, Daniel. Do you think you're doing it out of pride? Or is it for the glory of God?"

He looked at her with the look of a lost child, not sure how to find his way back home. He said, "I wish to God I knew."

THE NEXT DAY, Daniel stayed at home. Rosetta sensed he needed time to himself, so she made arrangements to go to the Engelhardt residence to visit with Molly. She left him sitting at the kitchen table, staring absently out the window. After she had gone, he closed his eyes and sat perfectly still, for what seemed to him to have been a full half hour. He tried, as best he could, to calm his spirit and to listen for a word from God. When no message came, he began to speak to God instead. He said, "Lord, you called me to serve you. I want to be faithful. I don't want to make this ministry about me. You have given me wonderful gifts. You gave me a love for people ... an ability to remember their names ... a heart that wants to listen ... a caring spirit. I know people love these things in me. But I know I can use them to build up my success, and my own self-importance, and not remember you."

He sat listening to the silence. He continued, "Lord, we have come a long way very quickly. A year ago I was a seminary student and there was just a living-room church. Now there are three hundred members in this congregation, and more are coming every week. And we have the opportunity to build this amazing new building. Is it wrong to spend all this money on a church building? If it is, please make it clear. We can give the money back. We can build a smaller building. Help me ... help me know what you want me to do."

He felt exhausted. He sat perfectly still, listening to the faint sounds of the traffic outside his window.

When Rosetta returned at lunchtime, Daniel was sitting on the living room couch, turning the pages of his Old Testament. He said, as if he had made a new discovery, "God wouldn't allow David to build the temple because he was too warlike." Rosetta nodded but did not comment. "But Solomon built the temple, and he spared no expense. And afterwards, he dedicated everything to God."

His wife sat down next to him on the couch. She said, "Then that's what you must do." She placed her hand on his shoulder and smoothed it down to his elbow. "Do it for God's glory."

ONE EVENING in November, shortly after Herbert Hoover had been elected the new President of the United States, Molly surprised both Adam and Elsa Engelhardt by asking, "Do you suppose there is anything useful I could do over at the print shop?"

Adam's left eyebrow arched, but it was Elsa who spoke. "Molly, you don't have to work there. You're four months along."

"But I'm feeling like I'm a burden here."

"You're no burden! You prepare half our meals. I rather like that, if you want to know the truth of it."

"Yes, but … well, I never go out. Not even on Sundays."

"You're welcome to come to worship with us," Adam said, avoiding a judgmental tone.

"You know how I feel about that," Molly said. "I just don't feel comfortable being there."

"You know," Adam said, "it's really not fair to blame Pastor Jonas for receiving a gift from … well, you know."

Molly sighed. "I know. We've talked about this again and again. I don't know why, but I just can't deal with it. Can you understand that?"

Adam nodded. He said, "If you really want to get out more, I can surely find some things for you to do at the print shop. And, you're adult enough to know when enough is enough. If at any point you decide it's becoming too tiring, you could simply stop and come home."

Molly liked the sound of the word "home." She had really come to feel that way about the Engelhardt residence. "Thank you. I may just take you up on that."

DANIEL WAS LOOKING for a new winter coat. The shops and stores along Bloomington Avenue had yielded nothing, so he had decided to pay a visit to the business district along east Lake Street. As he stepped down from the streetcar, the display window of an automobile dealership caught his eye. He'd seen the place before, but the shiny new sedan now on display had not been there previously.

He paused and admired the vehicle, trying to imagine how many years' salary he'd have to surrender to own a car like that. As he nurtured the fantasy of motoring off to Robbinsdale or Columbia Heights, carefree in his "merry Oldsmobile," he began to hum the tune to the commercial jingle he'd heard, not long before, on WCCO radio. Had he paid more attention to those around him, he'd have noticed he had company.

"She's a beauty, isn't she?"

Daniel looked to his right. There stood a gentleman in his mid-thirties, wearing a three-piece suit. His shiny black hair had a wave, the sort Daniel imagined one might get in a salon. His thumbs were tucked into the pockets of his trousers.

"Yes, she's a beauty for sure."

"You want to take a ride in one?"

"Oh, no. Not really. I mean, sure, I'd enjoy that. But I'd absolutely be wasting your time. I'm not in the market."

"Maybe I could help you get there," the stranger said, in a voice so smooth it made Daniel uncomfortable. The man extended his right hand and grasped Daniel's with a firm but agreeable grip. "My name's Joe. Joe Pavelka. I own this dealership. And I can tell just by looking at you, you belong in an Oldsmobile."

"How can you tell that, exactly?"

"You have a discerning eye. You look for quality. You're pretty sure you know what you want. And, you wouldn't be caught dead driving a Ford!" He laughed at his own joke, with a merriment that made Daniel grin, in spite of himself.

"Well, I'll tell you what," said Daniel, "I may enjoy window shopping for Oldsmobiles, but I have to be careful not to covet them. My budget would never cover the payments."

"You might be surprised. People are buying everything on credit today. One of these may just be a lot more affordable than you think."

"You're very good at what you do, Mr. Pavelka. You're making a very persuasive argument."

"Call me Joe. Everybody calls me Joe. And what shall I call you?"

"Well, I'm a Lutheran clergyman. If you were one of my parishioners, I'd want you to call me Pastor Jonas. But, since you're not, I think you should call me Daniel."

"How about Dan? Would that be okay?"

This man, Daniel decided, was going for instant intimacy, with visions of selling an expensive automobile on the near horizon. Ignoring the last question, he said, "I don't know if you know much about clergy salaries, but some of us don't receive enough to buy automobiles, not even on the installment plan."

Joe's mouth was open, ready for the next part of his pitch. Before he could offer it, Daniel said, "And, besides, it's a matter of stewardship with me."

"I beg your pardon?"

"Minneapolis has a wonderful streetcar system. I like streetcars. They take me everywhere I need to go. It would actually be an irresponsible way to spend a lot of money, most of which I don't have, to buy a car I don't need, in order to get me where I can already go on our excellent urban transit system."

Pavelka broke into a broad grin. "I like you, Daniel."

Daniel noticed, with appreciation, that the salesman had not presumed to address him by using a name he himself did not ordinarily answer to, and which he had not given him permission to use. "But not as much as you'd like to sell me this Oldsmobile, I suspect."

"You're onto me. But the reason I like you is, you speak your mind. You think about things. You know what you believe — and why. But, I guess I should expect that from a man of the cloth."

Daniel's natural instincts kicked in. He asked, "So, Joe, do you have a place where you worship?"

"No disrespect, Reverend, but I'm beyond all that."

"I beg your pardon? How could anybody get 'beyond' the need to worship God?"

"You're good at what you do, too, you know that?"

"Thank you," Daniel said, smiling. "But I'm quite serious about that question."

"Listen, you have time to come inside? I'll give you a cup of coffee. On the house. And I can tell you more about why I left the church."

Daniel was torn. He had a winter coat to find. But here was a new acquaintance who was ready to talk about God. It didn't take much for him to accept the persuasive car salesman's invitation.

In Joe Pavelka's private office, they sat sipping coffee. The businessman said, "We're doing really well here. Sales are booming. Before long everybody in Minnesota will be driving a car. And, no disrespect to your views intended, the automobile is going to put the streetcars out of business. At least, I sure as hell hope that's the way it turns out!" He laughed again, with a joviality that seemed infectious.

Daniel wondered if the invitation to come inside had been a thinly-veiled ploy to get him to talk about automobiles, and possibly about purchasing one.

Pavelka said, "So, here's the thing about me and religion. I grew up in a good Catholic family. Over in St. Paul. Parochial school with the nuns. Confirmed in the cathedral. The whole bit. My parents were so loyal to the church, you wouldn't believe it. They trained the twelve of us ..."

"Twelve!" Daniel was used to hearing about large Roman Catholic families, but the ease with which the number rolled off this man's tongue caught him off guard.

"I said I was Catholic, remember?" Pavelka let roll another hearty laugh. "You know what? You Protestants could learn a thing or two. If you don't start having bigger families, the Catholics are going to take over the world. I *mean* it. It's just a matter of arithmetic."

Daniel nodded slightly, but kept his eyes focused on the businessman. Pavelka continued, "The rest of my family's still over there in St. Paul. They all still go to Mass, as far as I can tell. Wouldn't be caught dead not going to Mass. I mean that literally, you know. Gotta keep that slate as clean as possible."

There was a hint of sarcasm in his voice. Daniel wondered why Joe Pavelka had become his family's black sheep.

"Well, I met this nice Presbyterian girl. That was the first problem. Catholics aren't supposed to marry Protestants, in case you haven't heard."

Daniel nodded knowingly. His own pastor, back in Fremont, Ohio, had made it very clear that dating a Roman Catholic was the first step on the road to endangering your faith, and putting your salvation at risk.

"Well, she was a Presbyterian, but her name was Mary. So that made my folks, and the priest, feel a little better. They figured there was still hope for her. So, anyway, we dated, and everybody wondered why she wasn't making any move to convert."

He drained his coffee cup and set it down. He continued, "In parochial school I learned that Protestants aren't very firm in their faith. If you play your cards right, you can convert them every time. Well, they didn't know much about Mary. Talk about devout! She had a question for every answer I gave her. You know — about the Pope, and purgatory, and the rosary — all of it. And when I asked her questions, she had answers like I never heard from anybody. I was really impressed. So, anyway, she wasn't going to budge. She told me she wasn't going to become a Catholic, and I could take it or leave it."

Daniel thought he knew where this was leading, but he got a surprise.

"So I broke it off. Good Catholic boy. Did the right thing." He pursed his lips and narrowed his eyes, as if getting ready to close a deal. "It almost killed me. I couldn't live without her. I told the priest, and my parents, I was going to marry her no matter what. You know what they told me?"

The pastor could only guess.

"They said, 'Okay. Marry her. But it has to be a Catholic wedding. And you have to figure out how to convert her afterwards. And the kids all get raised Catholic.' See, the thing is, with Catholics, the church gets it all. You don't compromise. But the other thing is, Mary wouldn't buy all that garbage."

"You think it was garbage?"

"I didn't at the time. But later on, when I realized I was going to lose her if I pushed all this Catholic stuff on her, I began to see her point. I mean, think about it. Here's a person who has a perfectly good way to worship God. She takes it seriously. It's important to her. She's sincere. She's devout. And then I come along and tell her that's all crap. Well, what's crap is what my church was trying to make me do."

Daniel hadn't heard a Roman Catholic, even a lapsed one, put it quite that way before. But, obviously, this wasn't the end of the story.

Chapter 11

Daniel shifted in his chair. He finished his coffee and set down the cup.

"How about a refill?" Joe Pavelka asked, getting up. Without waiting for an answer, he took both cups and walked across the room to the coffee pot. As he filled them, he continued his monologue.

"So, anyway, we got married. In the Presbyterian Church, I might add. Needless to say, I'm not welcome in my family any more. Of course, that's crap, too. Who are these people to tell me I don't belong?"

The automobile salesman was really rolling now. "And, of course, Mary had her own ideas about how many kids she wanted. Which meant, of course, not so many. She'd be damned if she was going to have ten or twelve, she told me. Well, she didn't say it just like that."

Daniel grinned.

"And, of course, my mother was really steamed when she heard about that. It was the first time in my life I told my own mother, politely of course, to go to hell. I guess I broke one of the commandments when I did that. But dammit, they try to keep their hooks in you even after you've walked away from them."

"So, I guess that pretty well explains why you're no longer a Roman Catholic."

"You're damn right it does." Pavelka was seated again, finishing his second cup of coffee. He said, "Of course, you can take the boy out of the Catholic Church, but a little bit of Catholic always stays with the boy."

Daniel looked puzzled.

"I'm sure it's true with you Lutherans, too. If somebody messed with you and got you to become, say, a Baptist or something, you'd still have your Lutheran way of looking at things. Am I right?"

The pastor suspected he was.

"So, here I am, a sort of bastard Presbyterian … " He glanced surreptitiously about the room, as if looking for spies. "Man, don't ever tell Mary I said that. But, you know what I mean. I don't know much about Presbyterians. I haven't really joined Mary's church. She goes. I don't. But I still have this nagging feeling that, if I don't do things just right, I'm headed for hell. Isn't that the damnedest thing? I'm not even sure I *believe* in hell, and yet I'm still worried about *going* there."

"How do you mean, 'do things just right'?"

"You know. Toe the line. Stay out of trouble. Don't commit any mortal sins. And, if you do commit any, make sure you get them confessed as soon as you can. Don't get God mad at you, so he'll let you in when you die."

"So you do still believe in God, then?"

"Yeah. How could you not believe in God? I'd really like to believe in *Mary's* God."

"You think hers is different from yours?"

"Well, obviously not. There's only one God. But you know what I mean. The way she thinks about God is totally different from the way I do. She says God loves and forgives people. One time I told her that sounded too easy. What about paying for your sins? She says Christ did that. Catholics say that too. But you always get the feeling you have to help. You're never quite finished. There's always something else you should be doing."

"So, how do you deal with that?"

"The Catholic part? I say to hell with it. The Presbyterian part? I just can't get into it. So, I let Mary do the worshiping for the both of us."

Daniel remembered his confirmation pastor's argument for not marrying outside your faith. Religion was supposed to bring people together, not split them apart, he'd said. Here, before his eyes, was a living illustration of what he had meant.

"I will say this," Pavelka went on, "my Catholic training probably helped me succeed in business."

"How is that?"

"Well, it made me into an achiever. You know, when you believe you've never done quite enough, and then you transfer that to your career, it makes you a hard driver." His expression turned serious. "Mary says I'm a sales demon. She thinks I've made selling into my god. All I know is, I've really figured out how to sell Oldsmobiles."

Daniel thought he saw an opening. He asked, "Do you think she's right? Have you made selling your god?"

"Hell, I don't know. It's not the right question. I've made selling my *life*. I love this business. And, with the markets all going up so fast these days, the sky really may be the limit." He paused momentarily. "Business was great under Coolidge. It's going to be even better under Hoover, as far as I can see." He looked at the clergyman and asked, with a perfectly straight face, "Don't you think Herbert Hoover would look great, driving around in an Oldsmobile?"

He laughed so loud, Daniel wondered if people out in the showroom could hear. In spite of his coarse language, he found himself really liking this man's jovial manner. But he was determined to try once more.

"You know, Joe, things are going really well for you right now. And I applaud you for the way you're making this place thrive. But crowding God out of your life can't be a good idea."

Pavelka leaned forward in his chair. He said, "You've put up with everything I had to say to you, including my pitch for why you should buy one of my cars. And I thank you for that. Now you've told me what *you're* supposed to say to somebody like me. And that's fine. I expected that, as soon as I found out you were a man of the cloth. But let me tell you how it is with me. I've come to the conclusion that, if there *is* a god, and I suspect there might be, he hasn't done me any favors. Everything I have, I had to get for myself. And it's worked. I'm happy. I'm prospering. And, I've got my Sundays to myself. Life could hardly be better. So, I ask you, with no disrespect intended, why in hell do I need God?"

JON AND DAVID ENGELHARDT came home for the Thanksgiving break. With Molly in Jon's bedroom, the older boy slept on the living room couch for three nights. His mother had written him a letter, explaining things, so it was no problem. In fact, he seemed cheerful about the fact that he could be of some help to a young woman in distress. At the dinner table on Thanksgiving Day, after Molly offered her fourth apology for having displaced him, Jon said to her, "Listen, stop worrying about it, okay? This is my last year of college. After Christmas break I won't even be around here any more. I expect to be moving to Ohio when I graduate. So just consider the room yours."

Molly offered him a grateful look. She didn't bring it up again.

For his part, David found himself wondering what it might be like to go dancing with Molly. Or ice skating. Or a ride in the country. That was, of course, if she hadn't been pregnant and everything. She was his age, and he rather liked her unassuming, yet amusing demeanor. He liked her clever way with words, and there was a winsome sort of quality about her that pleased him a lot. He was tempted to tell her what a pretty young woman he thought she was. But, he never worked up the nerve to do so. Besides, every time he started a conversation with Molly, his older brother had the bad habit of cutting in with some irrelevant comment or another.

ONE DAY in early December, a middle-aged woman came to Daniel's tiny office at the chapel on Anderson Avenue. She removed one of her gloves, extended her hand to shake the pastor's, and introduced herself. "I'm Mary Pavelka. You've met my husband."

"Oh. Yes. The Oldsmobile dealer."

She nodded. "May I sit down?"

"Please." She slipped out of her winter coat. He found a place to hang it.

"I'm a Presbyterian. I think he told you that." Daniel nodded. "Well, I don't know much about Lutherans. I know there are a lot of them around here. I've always had the impression they're standoffish and aloof, and about as stubborn, where doctrine is concerned, as Catholics are. So, I've never gotten too close to any of them."

Daniel stifled a grin. He admired her courage for having walked into a Lutheran pastor's office, given what she had just said.

"Joe has been talking about you."

"I beg your pardon?"

"He said he and you had quite a conversation one day a couple months ago."

"Well, he tried to sell me an Oldsmobile."

"Oh, he tries that with everybody. That's what he does. But, you and he talked about religion. At least, that's what Joe told me."

"Yes. We did. I must confess, your husband did most of the talking."

"That's Joe for you. A natural-born conversationalist. I guess I shouldn't complain. He does so well selling those cars, we're more comfortable than I'd ever have expected we would be. But sometimes I think he talks too much for his own good. I wish he would do a little more listening."

"How can I help you, Mrs. Pavelka?"

"I'll come right to the point. I'm worried about Joe."

"In what way?"

"I … I don't know if he really believes in God any more. He says he does. Sort of. But it's not any God I know anything about. I just worry, you know, if something would happen to him … I worry about his soul."

"I'm sure you and he have had many conversations about this."

"Of course. But I'm afraid he's gotten himself stuck. He won't go back to the Catholic Church. Partly because he knows I wouldn't go with him, but partly because he's terribly angry about how he thinks his church has treated him. And, in spite of everything I've been able to say to him, he can't find his way into the Presbyterian Church either."

Where, Daniel wondered, was this leading?

"And, at this point at least, I'm not sure I could become a Lutheran. Or would want to become one. But ..."

"But?"

"But I wonder if you'd be willing to talk to the two of us together sometime. Not in a class or anything. But just to talk about how you understand God and things. And to let Joe ask questions. Believe me, he has a ton of them."

"Why are you coming to me?"

"Because Joe likes you."

Daniel arched an eyebrow. "We only talked once."

"I know. But Joe's a very good judge of people. He was really impressed with you. He said you know how to listen."

"I pretty much had to. As I said, he did most of the talking."

"Yes, I'm sure that was how it was. But he doesn't say that about very many people. He says you have a kind of sense for what people need to say. You don't make him feel like apologizing, or defending himself. You just seem like a good friend."

"Like I said, it was only that one conversation."

"He also said he likes the way you disagree, but that when you do, it's with good arguments — and common sense." She paused and looked down at her lap for a moment. She said, "I suppose you're going to get a really big head listening to me say all this. But it's just what Joe told me."

"Does Joe know you're here talking to me today?"

"No. I didn't tell him I was coming."

"What do you think he'd say if you told him?"

"I don't know. He may tell me to mind my own business. But I thought it was worth taking a chance." She paused for a deep breath. "The thing is, I'm just getting really weary of going to church without him. The children and I have been doing that for fourteen years. And now we have a teenager. I think Thomas may decide to imitate his father, including his ideas about God. I don't want to see that happen."

A WEEK LATER, Daniel went back to the Oldsmobile dealership. Joe Pavelka was in his office, visible at his desk behind a large plate glass window. When he saw the Lutheran pastor, he eagerly waved him inside. As Daniel closed the door, the salesman said, "Ready for that test ride?"

Daniel surprised himself by saying, "Yes. I think so. As long as you understand there probably won't be a sale for you."

"No problem. You know, some of my best customers are people

recommended to me by other people who never buy a car, but liked what they saw. So come on. Maybe a test ride will get me some new customers from over at your church."

Daniel had never looked at it in quite that way. Suddenly he felt less guilty taking up the car dealer's time. Besides, he really did want to find out what it would feel like, riding in a brand-new Oldsmobile.

"You ever drive one of these?" asked Joe, standing by the driver's door.

"My father has a delivery truck. He owns a lumber yard in Ohio. I used to drive the truck for him."

"This, my friend, will be nothing like a delivery truck, believe me. Here, you take the keys."

"No," Daniel said, shaking his head. "You drive, I'll ride. I haven't driven for a few years. I don't want to take a chance steering this nice new car into a lamp post."

"Probably not a possibility," said Joe. "But, as you wish." He climbed into the driver's seat and waited for Daniel to join him on the passenger side.

As they rode along Lake Street, heading west, the dealer said, "My wife came to talk to you. She told me."

Daniel didn't reply.

"That was okay. I don't mind that she did that. She probably got her hopes up. I told her I'd had a really good conversation with you. I hope you felt it was."

"I thought so," Daniel replied.

"But here's the way it is. Mary wants me to get back into church. I just don't want that. I know it's hard on her, having to go without me. I feel bad, doing that to her. But I have to be true to myself. And, at least for now, who I am is somebody who is perfectly happy the way he is."

They crossed Lyndale and continued west, along the broad avenue. "I mean, look at me. I'm a respected businessman. Every one of my brothers is doing manual labor over in St. Paul somewhere. None of them is going to amount to a hill of beans. They're stuck in their labor-class jobs, with way too many kids apiece, scraping and bowing to the padre on Sundays. That's one way to live. But that's not for me."

They crossed Hennepin Avenue and arrived at the perimeter road that ringed Lake Calhoun. As they circled the lake, Pavelka said, "Isn't this a beautiful city? Isn't this a beautiful country, where the son of European immigrants can become a wealthy man in only one generation?" He paused to admire the wintry landscape, and the frozen surface of the lake. He continued, "And isn't this a beautiful Oldsmobile?"

Daniel laughed out loud. "Joe, you are the best car salesman I can imagine there ever being. That was the smoothest lead-in I've ever heard. And I'm in the persuasion business myself."

"Thanks for the compliment, Pastor Daniel. But I meant everything I said."

Daniel took significance from the fact that, for the first time, his host had addressed him as "pastor."

Chapter 12

ON CHRISTMAS EVE, two worship services were held at the Church of St. Michael and All Angels, one at seven o'clock and another at eleven. The first was designed for families with young children. The six couples from the original living-room congregation had made plans, several weeks before, to attend the earlier Christmas Eve service together, and then to gather at the Engelhardt residence for coffee and conversation. Although they hadn't said it publicly, they had planned the gathering at the Engelhardt home because most of them had not yet received more than a casual introduction to the elusive Molly Lundgren. Her refusal to show her face at St. Michael Chapel had guaranteed that.

In deference to Molly, the pastor had not been invited.

While the others were at worship, Molly finished glazing her freshly-baked nut-and-fruit-filled pastry ring, checked on the tempting hot beverages simmering on Elsa's stove, and spent more time than necessary fussing over the already-perfect dining room table setting. It was a festive display of German and Swedish Christmas breads and cookies.

Elsa and the two boys arrived first. When Molly heard them stomping the snow off their overshoes, out on the porch, she retreated into the kitchen, as though she were not really invited to the party. She worried she might have to justify her having stayed away from worship once again, especially to Adam and Elsa's guests.

Jon came breezing into the kitchen. He'd become a conversation partner of Molly's during his three days home at Thanksgiving, and she felt especially comfortable around him.

"Hey, Molls, what's cookin'?" he asked, sticking his nose close to the simmering pan of mulled cider. "We missed you at church." She felt her pulse increase, but he didn't give her five seconds during which to answer. He said, "Big crowd coming. They're on the way. Get ready." She smiled shyly, wondering whether she was really prepared to deal with the approaching hordes.

Jon said, "Dining room table looks sensational." And then he was out the door.

know what I like most about you, Molly?" She looked up from the
was drying. "I like the way you laugh. It's musical."
re just sweet-talking me, David Engelhardt."
n it. I really enjoy your company. And another thing … "
"
ire your courage."
your pardon?"
re willing to go through with having this baby. A lot of young women,
stances like yours, would consider … well, you know … getting rid

d never do that. It would be murder."
w. But it still takes courage to go through with it."
id, "I think you're embarrassing me now."
led the plug and let the water drain from the sink, then found another
to help her finish. He said, "What are your plans for tomorrow
?"
ing special."
d you like to take a walk with me, in Powderhorn Park?"
ou asking me on a date?"
ust a walk in the park."

WALKED SLOWLY, enjoying the sound of crunching snow
eir feet. David felt as though it would be the gentlemanly thing to do
r his arm, but he wasn't sure she'd take it. So, they walked, side by
ot touching, their mittened hands thrust inside the pockets of their
ter coats.
said, "You're at the print shop quite a lot these days. Dad says you're
d help down there. But he's feeling a little guilty, letting you work in
tion."
s thoughtful enough to take me away from the counter and give me
. It's getting harder to stand for so long."
robably were on your feet too long yesterday, then."
the work needed to be done."
reful for yourself," he said solicitously. "You need to watch out for
uy."
k her that he had decided she was carrying a boy. "And you need
ut for yourself," he added.
as if you've appointed yourself my guardian or something."

Elsa came into the kitchen and found an apron to wear. "Thanks, Molly," she said, checking on the fruit soup. "You saved me a half day's work. You're so good with everything."

The front door opened again. The house began filling up with noisy, jovial houseguests. Elsa said, "Come on. We have to greet people, and get you introduced."

In the living room the hubbub soon became a roar. The guests went looking for places to lay their wraps, then, couple by couple, introduced themselves to Molly. She promptly forgot all their names and everything else they told her. It was all too overwhelming. Suddenly, Adam was standing next to her, circling her with his arm and giving her shoulders a gentle squeeze. He said, "Quiet, everyone. Settle down now. You're as bad as a bunch of unruly Sunday school children."

There was laughter. Adam said, "Most of you have already been introduced to Molly Lundgren. She's our houseguest, and for the next few months she's also a part of our family. And, she's helping out a bit, down at the print shop."

Even though she was beginning to show, Molly was thankful Adam had made no reference to her pregnancy.

Elsa said, "Come to the table, fill your plates, and then find a place to sit. If anything looks German, I made it. If it's Swedish, Molly did."

Molly retreated to a corner of the dining room, where she stood sentry while the guests filled their plates and cups. She made frequent short trips to and from the kitchen, with the result that nobody invited her to sit with them. Anyway, she didn't feel included in the conversations that were going on.

Nor did she feel particularly comfortable with the whole scene. David Engelhardt sensed it, and came into the dining room. Pulling out a chair for her, and another for himself, he said, "Sit down. You don't have to spend the whole night on your feet."

Molly followed his lead. As they sat sipping their cider, she tried to avoid staring at the handsome college boy sitting next to her. His light brown hair tumbled agreeably down over his forehead, accenting his bright blue eyes. His square Germanic features gave his face a finely-chiseled look. She wondered how many girls he might be stringing along just now.

"It's really not fair to put you up against this bunch," he said, smiling at her. "They're pretty close-knit. You're an outsider, so they have all the advantages and you have none."

She nodded with appreciation.

"But you're being a really good sport about this."

She wondered why the two of them hadn't spent more time talking with one another at Thanksgiving time. Then she remembered. Every time David had tried to start a conversation with her, Jon had finished it. She'd enjoyed the give and take with Jon, but David had seemed content to stay on the sidelines. Tonight, however, Jon was in the living room, mixing it up with the guests. And, while David could have stayed there too, he'd decided to show her some consideration. Or was it pity?

"Jon's really steamed you've laid claim to his bedroom," David said, mischievously. Molly's mouth dropped open. Jon had said exactly the opposite to her. "Just kidding," David said, grinning broadly.

"Don't joke around like that," she scolded.

"Sorry. Actually, we're all glad you're living here."

"Well … thank you. This feels like home to me. For now."

"How are you doing? I mean, you know, with everything?"

"With the pregnancy?"

"Yeah. Especially that."

She sighed. "Okay."

"Not really, huh?"

She grimaced. "I really don't want to have this child."

He exhaled. "Yeah. I've heard you say that."

"But it's not the baby's fault. I'm … I'm going to give him for adoption." She said it with a hint of apology.

David nodded and offered a thoughtful frown. "Has to be hard, carrying a baby you don't expect to raise."

"Can we change the subject now?"

"Sorry." He took a bite of glazed sweet roll. "I guess it has to be tough, not being with your family at Christmas."

"I'm *with* my family."

"I mean, your family in Litchfield."

She scowled. "You certainly know how to pick uncomfortable topics, David."

"Okay. You pick one."

"Tell me how your studies are going."

"They're okay. I wish I was done with them."

"You don't like college life?"

"I want to get it over with. I want to work in the print shop."

"You really like working there, don't you?"

Elsa came into the kitchen and found an apron to wear. "Thanks, Molly," she said, checking on the fruit soup. "You saved me a half day's work. You're so good with everything."

The front door opened again. The house began filling up with noisy, jovial houseguests. Elsa said, "Come on. We have to greet people, and get you introduced."

In the living room the hubbub soon became a roar. The guests went looking for places to lay their wraps, then, couple by couple, introduced themselves to Molly. She promptly forgot all their names and everything else they told her. It was all too overwhelming. Suddenly, Adam was standing next to her, circling her with his arm and giving her shoulders a gentle squeeze. He said, "Quiet, everyone. Settle down now. You're as bad as a bunch of unruly Sunday school children."

There was laughter. Adam said, "Most of you have already been introduced to Molly Lundgren. She's our houseguest, and for the next few months she's also a part of our family. And, she's helping out a bit, down at the print shop."

Even though she was beginning to show, Molly was thankful Adam had made no reference to her pregnancy.

Elsa said, "Come to the table, fill your plates, and then find a place to sit. If anything looks German, I made it. If it's Swedish, Molly did."

Molly retreated to a corner of the dining room, where she stood sentry while the guests filled their plates and cups. She made frequent short trips to and from the kitchen, with the result that nobody invited her to sit with them. Anyway, she didn't feel included in the conversations that were going on.

Nor did she feel particularly comfortable with the whole scene. David Engelhardt sensed it, and came into the dining room. Pulling out a chair for her, and another for himself, he said, "Sit down. You don't have to spend the whole night on your feet."

Molly followed his lead. As they sat sipping their cider, she tried to avoid staring at the handsome college boy sitting next to her. His light brown hair tumbled agreeably down over his forehead, accenting his bright blue eyes. His square Germanic features gave his face a finely-chiseled look. She wondered how many girls he might be stringing along just now.

"It's really not fair to put you up against this bunch," he said, smiling at her. "They're pretty close-knit. You're an outsider, so they have all the advantages and you have none."

She nodded with appreciation.

"But you're being a really good sport about this."

She wondered why the two of them hadn't spent more time talking with one another at Thanksgiving time. Then she remembered. Every time David had tried to start a conversation with her, Jon had finished it. She'd enjoyed the give and take with Jon, but David had seemed content to stay on the sidelines. Tonight, however, Jon was in the living room, mixing it up with the guests. And, while David could have stayed there too, he'd decided to show her some consideration. Or was it pity?

"Jon's really steamed you've laid claim to his bedroom," David said, mischievously. Molly's mouth dropped open. Jon had said exactly the opposite to her. "Just kidding," David said, grinning broadly.

"Don't joke around like that," she scolded.

"Sorry. Actually, we're all glad you're living here."

"Well … thank you. This feels like home to me. For now."

"How are you doing? I mean, you know, with everything?"

"With the pregnancy?"

"Yeah. Especially that."

She sighed. "Okay."

"Not really, huh?"

She grimaced. "I really don't want to have this child."

He exhaled. "Yeah. I've heard you say that."

"But it's not the baby's fault. I'm … I'm going to give him for adoption." She said it with a hint of apology.

David nodded and offered a thoughtful frown. "Has to be hard, carrying a baby you don't expect to raise."

"Can we change the subject now?"

"Sorry." He took a bite of glazed sweet roll. "I guess it has to be tough, not being with your family at Christmas."

"I'm *with* my family."

"I mean, your family in Litchfield."

She scowled. "You certainly know how to pick uncomfortable topics, David."

"Okay. You pick one."

"Tell me how your studies are going."

"They're okay. I wish I was done with them."

"You don't like college life?"

"I want to get it over with. I want to work in the print shop."

"You really like working there, don't you?"

"I love it. It's what I'm meant to do."

"How does a person know what he's meant to do?"

"I don't know. You just do. It feels right. It's what you're good at, the thing that gives you satisfaction." He wiped the crumbs from his mouth and laid his napkin down. "What about you, Molly? What feels right for you?"

She sighed and slowly traced her finger around the rim of her cider cup. "I don't know. I thought I had the career I wanted. Then that turned into a nightmare. I thought I wanted to be a mother some day. That's become a disaster." She looked at David, and discovered his eyes were locked on hers. There was empathy in his eyes. She said, "I wish I knew what I was meant to do. But for now, I feel like I'm running out of dreams."

David laid his hand on hers and said, "Something good is waiting for you, Molly."

"Do you think so?"

"I'm sure of it."

BY ELEVEN the guests had all gone. Elsa began clearing the dishes and putting food away. After two trips to the kitchen, she said, "Oh, it's late. Let's just leave the dishes for tomorrow."

She was surprised to hear her younger son say, "You and Dad go on up. Molly and I will take care of this. You don't want to come down on Christmas morning and find all this stuff not put away."

Elsa said, "You're sure? It's not like you, David."

"I know. But it will give Molly and me a chance to talk."

She said, "Molly, are you sure? You must be tired."

"It's okay. I'm fine."

"Well, close the kitchen door then. Jon will be sleeping on the living room couch, and I think he's about ready to turn in."

When they were alone in the kitchen, Molly said, "Are you sure you want to help with all of this?"

"Sure. Come on. I'll start the dishwater."

As they washed and dried the plates and cups and silver, David said, "I just wanted a little more time to talk. I was enjoying our conversation earlier."

"What more do we have to say to each other?"

"Well, for one thing, I need to apologize to you. I said some insensitive stuff to you. I'm sorry. I don't want you getting the wrong idea about me. I can really be quite charming when I work at it."

She laughed softly. "You college boys are the limit."

"You know what I like most about you, Molly?" She looked up from the plate she was drying. "I like the way you laugh. It's musical."

"You're just sweet-talking me, David Engelhardt."

"I mean it. I really enjoy your company. And another thing … "

"Yes?"

"I admire your courage."

"I beg your pardon?"

"You're willing to go through with having this baby. A lot of young women, in circumstances like yours, would consider … well, you know … getting rid of it."

"I could never do that. It would be murder."

"I know. But it still takes courage to go through with it."

She said, "I think you're embarrassing me now."

He pulled the plug and let the water drain from the sink, then found another dish cloth to help her finish. He said, "What are your plans for tomorrow afternoon?"

"Nothing special."

"Would you like to take a walk with me, in Powderhorn Park?"

"Are you asking me on a date?"

"No. Just a walk in the park."

THEY WALKED SLOWLY, enjoying the sound of crunching snow beneath their feet. David felt as though it would be the gentlemanly thing to do to offer her his arm, but he wasn't sure she'd take it. So, they walked, side by side but not touching, their mittened hands thrust inside the pockets of their warm winter coats.

David said, "You're at the print shop quite a lot these days. Dad says you're really good help down there. But he's feeling a little guilty, letting you work in your condition."

"He was thoughtful enough to take me away from the counter and give me a desk job. It's getting harder to stand for so long."

"You probably were on your feet too long yesterday, then."

"Well, the work needed to be done."

"Be careful for yourself," he said solicitously. "You need to watch out for that little guy."

It struck her that he had decided she was carrying a boy. "And you need to watch out for yourself," he added.

"I feel as if you've appointed yourself my guardian or something."

86

"Sorry. Was I out of line?"

"No. Not really. I rather like the feeling, being fussed over once in a while."

He hadn't realized that was what he was doing.

They reached a bench near the frozen lake. She said, "I really need to sit down for a little while." He used his mittened hand to sweep the snow off the seat, after which they sat down together.

He said, "Do you like to ice skate?"

She sighed. "We went skating all the time when I was younger."

"Who's 'we'?"

"My brothers and sisters and I. There's a pond on our farm. We always had a grand old time on it in the wintertime."

"How many of you are there?"

"Eight, counting my parents. Three sisters. Two brothers."

"Which one are you?

"What do you mean?"

"In the pecking order."

"I'm in the middle."

"Where are they — your brothers and sisters?"

"They're all still around home. My oldest brother wants to stay on the farm with Dad. My brother Martin may go to Gustavus Adolphus College. If my folks can afford to send him. My sisters will probably all end up marrying fellows from the neighborhood. Nobody goes much of anywhere in Litchfield."

"Except people like you."

She nodded, but said nothing. She studied the perimeter of the lake.

David said, "I know you probably wish you hadn't come to the city. But you did it in good faith. None of what's happened is really your fault."

She turned suddenly and looked ferociously at him. "But it *is* my fault. You don't know that it isn't."

"How could it be?"

"I was foolish. And naive. I should have known a young business school graduate wasn't likely to start out as an executive secretary to the owner of an investment firm. I deceived myself into thinking it was my professional skills that got me the job. How *could* they have been? I didn't even have a track record yet."

"But what he did was inexcusable."

"I should have realized that was why he hired me."

"Molly, stop blaming yourself. You should be blaming *him*!"

Chapter 13

When Daniel arrived at the Gaytee Art Glass studio, Michael Morgan-Houseman was already there. The artist had spread two large sheets of paper on a drawing table, each displaying a sketch depicting a scene that would appear in stained glass in the new church building. Morgan-Houseman looked up when he saw the pastor come in. He said, "Come here, Reverend! Come look at this!" There was exuberance in his voice.

Daniel looked at the enormous drawings. One showed a titanic battle in progress. Michael the Archangel, wearing armor and equipped with powerful wings, was seated on a rearing horse. He was pointing a sharp sword at the heart of a demon like figure, crouching near the horse's front hoofs. All around the two central characters, in a swirl of motion, were ranks of angelic warriors, closing in on the devil, who looked defiant and was fitted with stubby horns and bat-like wings.

It made Daniel's heart race to think this panoply would grace the chapel wall of St. Michael Church. He looked up from the penciled sketch and said to the artist, "It's a masterpiece."

But the businessman was not interested in the colossal depiction of war in heaven. He grasped Daniel's coat sleeve and tugged, like an impatient schoolboy. "This one!" he said. "Look at this one!"

The second drawing pictured Jesus, seated on a huge granite boulder, with a flock of young children surrounding him. He had a kind expression. Daniel thought his face looked a little too sentimental, but realized every window portrait of Jesus that he had ever seen looked very much this way.

Morgan-Houseman jabbed his finger at the drawing of a young boy, seated on the ground near the center of the picture. Daniel studied it, then noticed the portrait of young Michael, on an easel next to the table. It was a near-perfect likeness. The stockbroker said, gesturing toward the artist, "This man is a genius. An absolute genius."

Daniel found his patron's enthusiasm infectious. He said, "It's a fine rendering. Very, very nice."

The businessman said, "When will the building be finished?"

"Well, it's a big project. We've shown you the architect's plans. We break ground after Easter. They're telling us it may take two years."

"That's a long time to wait," Morgan-Houseman said, returning his gaze to the drawing of Jesus and the children.

"It will be worth waiting for," Daniel said. He realized there was still a long way to go. For one thing, none of the designs for any of the other windows had even been decided on.

TWO DAYS before Ash Wednesday, four hours before dawn, Molly had a frightening dream. Michael Morgan-Houseman had somehow discovered where she was staying. He had come into her bedroom and stood waiting, at the foot of her bed. Next to him stood Pastor Daniel Jonas. They were speaking to one another. As she stared at them, they seemed not to notice her.

It made no sense. How could they not see that she was now awake? She tried to cry out, to learn how and why they had come into her room, and to demand they leave at once. But her voice was mute.

And then she heard their conversation. Morgan-Houseman was saying, insistently, "She has to give him to me. He's my only heir." And Pastor Jonas replied, in a soothing, pastoral voice that, for some reason, made her skin crawl, "Just tell her you're the father. Once the child is born, I'm sure she'll hand him over, if you ask her nicely."

She felt panic, anger and revulsion, all at once. She tried to scream, but no sound came. She climbed from the bed, hurried from the room, and headed for the stairs. At the landing she stumbled. Unable to reach the railing, in order to break her fall, she tumbled down the entire flight of stairs.

Elsa heard the commotion. Thinking a burglar was in the house, and convinced her husband would probably sleep through the Second Coming of Christ, she shook Adam, waking him out of a deep slumber.

They found Molly, lying unconscious, on the lower landing. Adam tried in vain to waken her, then rushed to the phone and called for an ambulance. Elsa knelt beside her, urgently speaking her name, over and over again. By the time the medics had arrived, Adam was dressed, and insisted on going with them to the hospital.

Molly had been only two weeks short of going full term with the infant baby girl who was delivered stillborn. When she regained consciousness, and learned the news, she showed no emotion.

Daniel conducted the funeral for the child, whom Molly refused to name, at a service from which she would have stayed away, had she had the strength to leave her hospital bed.

The day she was released, Adam came to Fairview Hospital to take her home. She sat quietly on the passenger side of the print shop owner's new Ford, staring blankly out through the windshield, toward the traffic moving along Riverside Avenue.

As they set off, past Augsburg College, toward Cedar Avenue, then south toward Lake Street, Adam struggled with what to say. Nothing appropriate came to mind. Molly saved him from having to start the conversation. "I suppose I'll need to be thinking about moving out soon," she said. There was no feeling in her voice.

"Is our house too full of bad memories for you now?" he asked, turning onto Lake Street and watching for the Bloomington Avenue intersection.

"No. It's not that. It's just that, there's really no good reason for me to stay with you any longer."

"I think there's every reason. We consider you a member of our family."

"I couldn't impose on you. You've done too much already."

Adam turned onto Caldwell Street, then Anderson Avenue. He pulled up to the curb, where he cut the engine. Then he turned and looked at Molly. She continued to stare out through the windshield, looking miserable. He said, "Where would you go? What would you do?"

"I don't know," she said, quietly but firmly. "But I have to go."

"Would you consider staying for my sake?" She didn't reply. "For Elsa's?" He thought he saw tears begin to form in her eyes. He said, "Let's go inside and talk to Elsa. If you and she agree it's time for you to leave, then I won't stand in your way."

Molly nodded. Adam climbed down, came around to open the door for her and, taking her arm, led her up the sidewalk. The rapidly-melting snow was almost gone, exposing large green patches of lawn on either side.

Elsa saw them coming and opened the front door. She led them into the dining room where, on the table, a steaming pot of tea was waiting. She said, "Adam, sit down. Molly, will you pour the tea, please?" Without waiting for an answer, she disappeared into the kitchen and returned with a plate of sliced nutbread. Setting it on the table, she said, "It hasn't been the same without you here, Molly. I've had to do all the serving by myself."

Molly returned a faint smile. She finished pouring the tea and set down the pot. When they were all seated, Elsa said, "Molly, I don't know what your future plans are. But I want you to promise me one thing."

"What would that be?" Molly asked.

"Before you make any decisions about anything, I want you to talk with David."

"Your son?"

"Yes. He's coming on Friday. For the weekend. He cares for you, Molly. A good deal, in fact. And, if you left us without saying goodbye to him, I think it might just break his heart."

AFTER HE'D STOKED THE COALS, David waited near the fireplace until the flames began to dance. Finally satisfied with his handiwork, he returned to the couch and took a seat next to Molly. She sat with her hands folded in front of her, watching as the fire illuminated the otherwise dark living room.

"It was a wonderful supper," he said, moving as close to her as he dared without actually touching her. "Sure glad I didn't stay on campus this weekend. The food at college is … well, let's just say it leaves a lot to be desired."

Molly exhaled heavily. She appreciated David's attempts at small talk, but she was absolutely not in the mood.

He turned on the couch, looking at her. "When Dad told me what happened, it almost killed me," he said. There was no response. "It must have been … " He saw her pained expression. "You don't really want to talk about this, do you?"

She shook her head, ever so slightly.

"What can we talk about, Molly? You only said six words at supper. You haven't said anything since my folks went up to bed. Are you … are you mad at me, by any chance?"

She looked at him with pooling eyes. "David, this is not about *you*. It's never been about you. My life is a mess. I have to find a way to get it fixed."

"Are you thinking of going back to Litchfield?"

"I could never go back there. I could never explain things to my parents. And I won't lie to them. I won't make something up."

"Then stay with us. Stay here with my folks. This is where you belong, Molly."

"I can't stay here. It just doesn't feel right any more."

"Listen to me. You have no prospects. It makes no sense at all for you to go off somewhere. You know what happens to girls who have no prospects and then end up desperate, don't you? Especially a girl as pretty as you."

She returned a shocked look. "Is *that* what you think I'll do?"

"That's what I think could happen. Believe me, this city is full of unfortunate young women who ended up with ruined lives."

"Just how else would you describe my life right now, David Engelhardt?"

He hated it when she used his full name. She only did it when she disapproved, or was really angry. "Well, it sure isn't like *that*," he replied. His voice was edgy.

"I want to ask you something," she said.

"All right."

"Your mother told me that you care for me. Is that true?"

"She told you that?"

"Yes. Why did she say that?"

"Well ... because it's true. I just didn't remember giving her permission to tell you."

"Were you planning to keep it a secret?"

He wondered whether, in the gloom, she could tell that he was blushing. He said, "I would have told you. Eventually."

"She also said that, if I left here, it might just break your heart."

"I never told her *that*."

"But is it true? Would it?"

"Oh, Molly ... "

"Is it true?"

"Of course it is."

"What do you really think of me, David?"

He felt his face growing warm, and it wasn't because of the fireplace. He said, "Boy, if I'd known you were going to ask me *that*, I would have done some rehearsing."

"I don't want a rehearsed answer. I want to know the truth. What do you think of me?"

He took a deep breath and let it out slowly. Then he said, "I think you're the most wonderful young woman I've ever met. My mother's right. I really do care for you. A lot. I told her that because ... well ... I think she was starting to figure it out anyway."

"I think it's really sweet that a young man would tell his own mother that he cares for a girl."

A large log fell with a loud crunching sound. A spray of sparks went up. Then the embers began to settle again.

David said, "The truth is, ever since Christmas, I haven't been able to stop thinking about you. I dream about you. I have trouble doing my homework." He moved closer, until his leg was touching hers. He lay his hand, tentatively, on her arm. She let him keep it there. He said, "Molly, I think I'm falling in love with you."

She backed away. "No. You don't want to do that."

He looked confused. "Why don't I?"

"Because. Just because."

"Because *why*?"

"David, you know as well as I do. I'm used merchandise. I'm not fit for any man now."

His expression turned from confusion to shock, and then to anger. "Molly, is *that* what's bothering you? That some man ... excuse me, I should say, some *poor excuse* for a man ... has had his way with you? And now you think you're worth less than you were? Don't you *ever* think that, not for one minute."

She was taken aback. The ferocity with which he said it caught her short.

"Now you listen to me, Molly Lundgren. There's nothing the matter with you. If anything, you're a better person now than you were before any of this happened."

She was extremely dubious about what she'd just heard, and her face showed it.

"You remember that stuff in the Bible? About the refiner's fire? Well, that's where you've been. You went through the fire. And fire can do one of two things. It can either destroy you, or it can make you strong. And the fire hasn't destroyed you, Molly."

She pursed her lips and swallowed hard. This, she decided, was the strangest sort of affirmation she'd ever heard. But it was affirmation, nevertheless, and David's sincerity was real. She was sure of it.

"If I had my choice, between a woman who knows nothing about life, on the one hand, and a woman who's been through the fire, on the other, I'd take the one who's been through the fire. Any day."

Molly began to cry, silently at first, then with soft whimpers, then with deep, heartrending sobs that put her at full flood. David moved close to her, circled her shoulders with his arm, and pulled her close against him. "Go ahead, sweetheart, just cry out all the tears."

Had he called her "sweetheart"? He hadn't planned on that.

He found a handkerchief in his pocket and thanked his stars it hadn't been used yet. He helped her to dry her face and her eyes. She took time to compose herself, then handed back the soggy cloth. She said, "David Engelhardt, you're too good for me. I don't deserve somebody like you."

"You deserve a helluva lot better than you've gotten so far," he said, quickly adding, "and excuse me for the rude language. I don't ordinarily talk to women, or anybody, like that."

For the first time since he'd been home, she laughed, a soft, rhythmic shudder. In spite of himself, he laughed along with her. Then he said, "I've been wanting to ask you something since last Thanksgiving."

"I admire your restraint. What is it?"

"I've planned this for four months. Now I'm not sure I have the nerve."

"Well you'd better not leave me hanging. Ask."

"May I kiss you? Please? Just once?"

She couldn't hold back the grin that crept across her face. "Yes. You may."

He leaned close and kissed her tenderly on the lips. He backed away and said, "Do I have to ask permission for a second?"

It was so very dark, so far from the fireplace, that he couldn't tell for sure, but he thought he saw her eyes begin to sparkle.

Chapter 14

It seemed surreal to Daniel, walking up the sidewalk toward the front door of the modest frame chapel, seeing the great excavations crowding up against the building. At mid-May, construction on the ambitious new worship center was well underway. Before long the walls would begin to rise and, he suspected, Mr. Morgan-Houseman would take up his post as sidewalk superintendent.

The custodian had already unlocked the door to the little frame chapel, and had turned on the lights. The bright sunlight of an early Sunday morning streamed in through the rectangular clear-glass windows. Daniel realized that turning on the lights in this already-bright room was probably redundant. But, it was part of Karl Rausch's Sunday morning ritual, and Daniel was not about to override the routine of his faithful elderly volunteer.

He walked down the center aisle of the quiet sanctuary, toward the modest chancel. Karl was standing at the altar table, checking to see that the candle wicks were of sufficient height so that they could easily be lighted without the youthful acolytes having to struggle with them. The refugee from World War I Germany offered his familiar, heavily-accented greeting.

"Guten Morgen, Herr Pastor! Another Sonntag, another Gottesdienst." Karl had still not mastered the English language, and seemed perfectly comfortable slipping back into German when it suited him.

"Yah. Another Gottesdienst," Daniel replied. "Another chance to worship God together."

"Drei! Gott in himmel! Drei!" the old man exulted. Karl had been delighted to see the fledgling congregation expand its Sunday morning worship schedule from two services to three. But, with services now being held at eight o'clock, nine-thirty and eleven, Daniel was finding that his Sunday mornings were becoming something of an energy drain. Still, he had nobody but himself to blame for swelling attendances.

Himself and the Holy Spirit, he realized, giving himself a quick humility check.

"You know, Herr Pastor," Karl said, stepping down into the aisle, "es ist wunderbar we now have the Gottesdienst drei … three … times every Sonntag. Aber …"

"But," Daniel said, translating aloud.

"Yah, yah. 'But.' But the candles, they burn down schnell."

Daniel smiled. "Yes, they go down fast. Just like our lives, Karl. Before long, we come to the end of our days."

The old man nodded, patted the clergyman on the shoulder, and shuffled off, down the center aisle, to check, for the third or fourth time, that the worship folders, printed the day before at Engelhardt Printing, were still in order, stacked on the little stand out in the compact vestibule.

Daniel stepped into the chancel, paused before the altar table, and made the sign of the cross, tracing his middle finger and thumb from his forehead to his sternum, and then from one shoulder to the other. Since Easter morning, he had become intentional about encouraging — even urging — his flock to begin to trace the same sign on themselves, as a way of remembering that they were baptized. He'd taken to printing little crosses at places in the order of service where signing one's self was appropriate, and then had preached a sermon about it. Nearly one-third of the congregation was now following his lead.

He opened the door to the sacristy, just off the altar area. The crowded little room, that doubled as his office, had space for his desk, a small bookcase, and one visitor's chair. If more than one person came to speak with him at the same time, the three of them needed to retreat to the nave, where they would sit, not very comfortably, in a church pew. It would be good, he realized, to be able to move into a roomier office. He wondered if he had the patience to wait another year, until it would be ready.

He pulled his sermon notes from his coat pocket and lay them on the desk, then sat down, flattened the folded sheets, and began to make final pencil revisions. He was only vaguely aware that someone had come into the room. Looking up, he expected to see Karl, or perhaps Elsa Engelhardt, with last-minute questions about the hymns or the liturgy. Instead, there stood before him a striking young woman, perhaps twenty-five. Her soft blonde hair fell down around her shoulders. She wore a bit more makeup than most of the women Daniel was accustomed to greeting at the church door after a Sunday morning service. But it was not overdone, he thought. Her dark blue dress was set off with a white lacy ruffle that formed its collar and came to a V in front. That, he thought, was a bit daring for Sunday morning attire. But, still, she had come to worship, and he didn't want to discourage that.

He wondered if he hadn't seen her somewhere before. And, he wondered whether, in spite of himself, he wasn't staring at her.

Without his suggesting it, she sat down on the folding wooden visitor's chair.

"The service begins in fifteen minutes," he said. "This may not be the best time for a conversation."

"This won't take long," she said. Her voice was soft, with a curiously lilting quality to it. He was positive he'd never spoken to her before. "I need your guidance."

"Concerning?"

"It's complicated. Could I make an appointment to speak with you again?"

"Well … yes … I think so." He pulled his calendar book out of his suit jacket and turned the pages. "Wednesday? In the morning?"

"Ten o'clock would be fine. May I come then?"

"Yes. Now, if you'll excuse me …"

"Of course. Your sermon. You're still not ready."

After she had gone out, he scanned the manuscript before him. It wasn't that the message wasn't ready. He was simply not completely sure he was really ready to deliver it. Because of what he intended to say. But, he decided, laying it aside, and getting up from his chair, he could trust his flock. He knew them all by name, even though there were now several hundred of them. And he was confident he had earned their trust.

Today, he realized, would be a test of that.

Through the wall he heard Elsa begin a prelude on the old upright piano. He knew the second-hand instrument, that was hard to keep in tune, was a frustration to her. But she never complained about it. Still, playing an acceptable church prelude on an old piano had to be a challenge to any musician. If only …

As he fastened the long row of buttons on his black cassock, he reminded himself of the virtue of patience. The bequest the congregation had received would include the price of a brand-new pipe organ for the balcony. He knew that would bring challenges not yet confronted. Elsa was a piano player, but she had never tackled the organ. She had already announced to the pastor that her service as a worship accompanist would end on the day the pipe organ was dedicated.

He pulled his white surplice over his head, turned to the framed prayer on the sacristy wall, crossed himself once more, and said, just loud enough for him to hear it himself, Frieda Stellhorn's familiar invocation:

Oeffne, Gott, meine augen und mein herz fur dein erscheinen. Ich sehe wie du mich liebst. Du bist da.

Then, in English, he revised the sentiment slightly: "Also open, O Lord God, the eyes and hearts of all who gather here for worship. And make them receptive to what your Spirit leads me to say to them today."

His softbound copy of the *Evangelical Lutheran Hymnal* had seen so much use, the corners were becoming dog-eared. His parents had given him this book on his confirmation day. It had gone with him to worship ever since, first in Fremont, Ohio, then at Capital University in Columbus, and then at the seminary in St. Paul. And now, here it was, guiding his worship in this modest chapel in south Minneapolis.

The entry hymn ended. He walked to the altar table and, taking advantage of the fact that it was free-standing, stood behind it, addressing the congregation. He realized that probably made him seem too "Protestant" for a few, just as his invitation to them to cross themselves frequently made him seem too "Catholic" to some of the others.

The liturgy and Scripture readings seemed to him to fly by quickly on this day. Suddenly he found himself standing in the pulpit, inviting the congregation to be seated. He looked at his manuscript and quickly decided, as he often did, that he would probably not need to look at it. He scanned the congregation, which filled about two-thirds of the seats. This was the early service. The second one would be fuller. The third would be overflowing.

The congregation was looking expectantly at him. He had waited longer than normal before beginning to speak. He said, "Has anyone here ever been to Jerusalem?" No hands went up. "Have you ever wanted to go?" Some heads were nodding. "Well, get ready. Today we're going to Jerusalem."

There were appreciative grins from a few, and some of the children leaned forward, caught with curiosity. He said, "We celebrated Easter not many weeks ago. What do you suppose it was like to be in the brand-new Christian congregation in Jerusalem, right after the very first Easter?"

He paused, then looked down at the page to which he had already opened the pulpit Bible. "Let's go to Jerusalem and find out. Here's what the Book of Acts says was going on." He scanned the words, paraphrasing and updating so that the language on the printed page didn't come across sounding stilted: "Day after day all the people went regularly to the Temple. In their homes, they broke bread together. Their hearts were full of thanksgiving. They were praising God, every chance they got. And, day after day, God made the church keep growing and growing."

He paused, sent a quick prayer heavenward, asking forgiveness for having taken so much liberty with the English translation, and then looked earnestly at the congregation.

He said, "What does that sound like to you?" There were puzzled looks. He said, "To me, that sounds a lot like us!" Now there were some nods of comprehension. "This is a picture of a great big family of believers who are so excited about God and the resurrection that they can't stop celebrating." He paused for effect, then continued, "Wouldn't you think they would have gotten a little tired of doing that, day after day?" He detected grins on some faces.

He said, "The resurrection of Jesus was so exciting, the people who found out about it simply couldn't help themselves. And so, they did what we do. They came to worship, in large numbers. And their numbers grew and grew. Now, I know it's the Holy Spirit who calls and gathers people into the church. But I also know that about half the people I see sitting here this morning are here because the other half listened to the Holy Spirit and invited them to come. So, you see, the way things are happening at St. Michael and All Angels right now, we're practically back in Jerusalem."

Then he stopped and took a deep breath, which he let out very slowly. He had reached the point where he needed to change direction. He said, "Did you notice anything in what I just read to you that does not sound so much like what we're doing in this congregation?"

There were no looks of recognition on any of the faces. He said, "Here's a little review. The people went to worship in the temple. They gathered day by day in their homes. They brought in more and more new friends and made the community grow. And ... " It was an artful pause. He had turned the entire congregation into a catechism class, and this was the teachable moment. Everybody knew the question, but nobody seemed to know the answer.

"They broke bread together," he said quietly. "Remember that part? Now, what was really going on? People who study the Scriptures have different ideas about this. Some people think this means they got together for lunch or supper. With all those people, it would have had to be like a Lutheran potluck dinner, don't you think?" There was audible laughter. "But I don't think that was it. Oh, they probably got together for meals, and had a great time when they did. But most of the people who have carefully researched what happened in the first Christian congregations are pretty sure this means something quite different."

He seemed to change focus when he said, "Do you remember how the

Apostle Paul scolded people in Corinth, Greece, for eating their meals in the wrong way? Was he talking about bad table manners?" He waited. Heads were shaking. Old-line Lutherans knew what he was getting at. "No. Paul was talking about the Sacrament. These people were celebrating Holy Communion in their homes, and they were turning a holy meal into something extremely unholy. Now, we all believe we should receive the Sacrament in a worthy manner, and what happened in Corinth is the reason we are so concerned about that. But the point I really want to make is that, when the first Christians broke bread together, what they were really doing was almost certainly celebrating the Eucharist, the Sacrament of the Altar."

Now, he thought, *I have to be careful what I say.* "So, just how often do you think those first Christians broke bread together? How many of you think once a year? Raise your hands." Nobody did. "How many think it was more often than that?" All the hands went up.

"How many of you think they broke bread together four times a year?" No hands went up. "How many of you think it was more often than that?" All the hands went up.

"How many of you grew up in a congregation where Communion was only celebrated four times a year?" Over half the hands went up. He said, "So did I. But that doesn't sound like what they did in Jerusalem, does it?

"How many think they broke bread together only once a month?" A few hands went up. "How many think more often?" A forest of hands appeared.

"How many think it might have been every day?" No hands went up. "How many don't think so?" Not a single hand. "How many aren't sure?" All the hands went up, and almost immediately laughter broke out. "I'm glad we can have a sense of humor about this," Daniel said. But then he said, in a serious tone, "If you read the story in the Book of Acts very carefully, you will be hard pressed not to conclude that these people celebrated the Sacrament every time they came together for prayers in their homes. And it's pretty certain that was at least once a week."

He felt his pulse increase and his face growing warm. But there was no turning back. "Now, I know there are some Protestants, and a lot of Lutherans, who think that if you celebrate Holy Communion every week, you're catholic." He had their attention now. "Well, you are. But not Roman Catholic. The Roman Church does that, of course, in the Mass. But we're not Roman Catholics here. Still, we are catholic. You spell that word with a small 'c.' It's a Greek word. It means 'according to the whole thing.' That's a pretty stilted way to say it. It means, 'the church community all together, everywhere.' In the first century, the Christian church, everywhere, all together, seemed to agree that when you come together to worship, that should include celebrating the Sacrament."

He paused and studied the faces looking back at him. He said, "How many of you would worry that celebrating Holy Communion too often would make it seem cheap and ordinary?" It was as if the congregation was trying to read his mind and figure out what answer he really wanted. Some hands went up, were held there uncertainly for a moment, and then went down again. About a third of the congregation raised their hands and kept them up.

Daniel said, "How many of you think it would cheapen your love for your children if you hugged them every single day?" Nobody responded, except with laughter. "What about your wife or husband? Would it make your love too ordinary if you kissed the person you're married to every single day?"

He'd made his point. Almost everyone was grinning. "So, if God wants to put his arms around us and give us an enormous hug, by feeding us with this wonderful heavenly meal, does it make sense not to let God do that for us every chance he gets?"

Heads were shaking.

It was time to finish. Daniel said, "Now, we celebrate Holy Communion here at St. Michael and All Angels on special days — only about eight times a year. As your pastor, I want to say to you that I believe that's not often enough. We're starving ourselves by limiting the Sacrament to so few celebrations. But, I also realize that some of us have traditions that taught us it should be very infrequent. We might want to remember that Martin Luther thought Holy Communion should be celebrated as often as the first Christians did it. Of course, Martin Luther grew up in the Roman Catholic Church. But Martin Luther was also the first Lutheran." There were some chuckles. "He didn't change his mind after he started the Reformation. And I don't think we should disagree with our spiritual Father in the faith."

He was becoming fatigued. And this was only the first service of three. He would have to do this two more times today. He said, "We have a brand-new worship and music committee here at St. Michael Church." He nodded toward the front pew, the end nearest the piano. "Elsa Engelhardt is the chair. She's an excellent choice to lead this group." Elsa smiled with appreciation.

"And the committee has agreed that, for the time being, we should continue our pattern of when to offer the Sacrament of the Altar. But, once our new church building is finished, we will begin to offer it every Sunday, at every worship service." He waited for an audible gasp, but none came. Maybe, he decided, it was because they would have an entire year and a half to get ready for the change.

He said, "And when that happens, we can read that Scripture portion from the Book of Acts again, and everything they were doing will then be true for us as well. We will have gone all the way back to Jerusalem. Won't that be exciting?"

Chapter 15

On Wednesday morning, Daniel sat at his office desk, waiting. It was already ten minutes past ten, and the woman who had come to speak with him on Sunday had not appeared. He wondered if perhaps he'd been stood up.

Then the door opened and she walked through.

"I'm sorry," she said, "I misguessed how long it would take to get here."

"You've been here before," he said, trying not to sound judgmental.

"On Sundays. The weekday traffic is always worse."

That was it. He finally realized why she looked familiar. He'd seen her at the early worship service, always sitting in the back. But, when the services ended, she was never there. He wondered about that.

She sat down on the folding chair and brushed her lustrous blonde hair back from her eyes. She said, "My name is Maureen Rawlins. I'm not one of your members."

"I know you're not. I know all of the members here."

"You do? All however many?"

"By now, nearly 400, actually."

"That's amazing. How do you do it?"

"It's not that difficult in a congregation this size. But, I don't think that's what you are here to discuss this morning."

She returned a coy smile. "Well, no. Actually not. I've … well … I've been listening to your sermons for the past several weeks. Since Easter Sunday, in fact. And I really like the way you talk. To the congregation, I mean."

Was she here to compliment his preaching?

"I think you sound like the kind of person who likes to listen to people's problems. And to help them." She blinked twice. Her long eyelashes seemed to flutter.

"Just what is it you need help with?"

"Well, it's about my husband. He's such a wonderful man. We haven't been married so very long, and it's been incredible. So far, I mean. But … " She opened her pocketbook, which Daniel noticed was perfectly coordinated with her smart light green outfit. Taking out a tissue, she began dabbing the corners of her eyes. "I don't have any really good evidence for this," she continued, now beginning to sniff softly and dab at the corners of her nose. "But I think he may be stepping out on me." She appeared about ready to burst out into tears.

Daniel was feeling uncomfortable. He wanted to show some empathy, but he was nervous about getting too close to this extremely attractive young woman. He wondered what sort of husband would step out on such a gorgeous partner. For that matter, how could another woman hope to compete with her?

She seemed to regain some of her composure. "I just don't know what I'm doing wrong. I try to satisfy him. I cook everything he likes. And, our lovemaking has been, if I may say so, incredibly good … "

Daniel was not liking the direction this seemed to be taking. He said, "What evidence do you have to suggest your husband is being unfaithful?"

"Well, he doesn't respond to me the way he used to. He comes home later and later from work. He never used to do that. And, last week, I found a letter in his dresser drawer, from someone named Gloria." No sooner were the words out of her mouth, than she broke into tears.

Daniel was tempted to move to the other side of the desk, but he resisted doing so. For once, he was glad there was only one chair there. He said, "Maureen, have you considered the possibility that there are perfectly logical explanations for everything you're telling me?"

"Oh, yes. Of course. I've tried to give Eddie the benefit of the doubt. For all of it. But it's getting harder and harder."

"Just where does Eddie work?"

"It's not important. What's important is that he used to love me and he doesn't any more." She reached in her pocketbook for more tissues.

"Maureen, I think you and I, and Eddie, should all sit down together and talk about this. Is that possible?"

She brightened. "Oh, that would be just excellent. Would you do that for us?"

"Of course. When could we meet with him?"

"Well, it would have to be some evening. He works six days a week. Business is so good, he has to work Saturdays. And, I surely wouldn't expect you to use the Lord's Day to make a home visit."

"You talk to Eddie. Find a day and a time. And then let me know."

She stood up, a look of relief on her face. She reached into her pocketbook once more and withdrew a folded piece of paper. Handing it to Daniel, she said, "This is our address. We live in an apartment. On LaSalle. And the phone number is there at the bottom. Just in case you need it."

After she had gone, Daniel sat studying the piece of paper. Should he find it odd, he wondered, that she hadn't been willing to divulge where it was that her husband worked? He thought about it. Perhaps it was one of those sensitive jobs that required discretion. He mulled it further. For the life of him, unless it was the FBI or work as a private investigator, he couldn't think what such an occupation might be.

ON THE DAY that Jon Engelhardt graduated from the University of Minnesota, his parents held a reception for him in their home. As Andy Scheidt stood chatting with him, sipping a cup of Elsa's gourmet coffee, he asked the new graduate why it was that his younger brother had a girlfriend and he had none. Jon made sure David was within hearing distance when he replied, "Well, I could have had Molly Lundgren if I'd wanted her. But, then, what would my baby brother, David, have done?"

David stepped up and said to Andy, with thinly-veiled sarcasm, "Or, it could simply be that my older brother is actually allergic to girls."

"Or maybe not," said Jon. There was something in his eyes that told David there was more to the story.

"Is there someone else?" Andy prodded playfully.

"Let's just say I'm holding out for an Ohio girl."

"Have you found the *right* Ohio girl?"

"I'm not sure yet. While I was working for my Uncle Adolph, I had plenty of time to meet the young ladies. There are just so many to choose from. But, if and when I finally do settle on one, there's a fair chance her name might turn out to be Susan."

Now his brother's curiosity was fully aroused. "You have a lady friend named Susan?" Why hadn't he mentioned it before?

"That's for me to know, little brother. And for you to find out."

Three days later, Jon was on his way to Columbus, Ohio, eager to go back to work for his Uncle Adolph.

ONE WEEK after she had come to his office, Maureen Rawlins called Daniel. She asked him to come to her apartment that evening. She promised that her husband would also be there.

At seven-thirty, Daniel knocked on her apartment door. When it opened, she was standing there, wearing a dark red dress which was a bit too revealing for his comfort. She welcomed him inside and gestured toward the couch. He looked around and admired the well-appointed living room, with comfortable furniture and two matching floor lamps with poles of polished brass. There was an exquisite oil painting, a verdant landscape in an expensive frame, decorating the wall above the couch. He asked the obvious question. "Where's Eddie?"

She returned a look of frustration. "When it came right down to it, he told me he couldn't go through with it. He hasn't talked to a minister for years. He told me he couldn't bring himself to do it now. Then he told me he was …" She paused dramatically, reached for a handkerchief, and dabbed her eyes. " … he was going to spend the night downtown."

Daniel couldn't tell whether the tears were genuine, but they were flowing. She said, "Pastor, I've lost him. What am I going to do?"

It was clear she wanted some physical contact. He was determined not to offer any. He felt a little cold-hearted about it, but knew how vulnerable both of them were just now. He said, "You're going to need to try again, Maureen. If he's not here, I can't stay."

She began to weep. "Don't tell me you're going to abandon me too!"

His heart went out to her. What could it hurt to share one innocent hug? She came to him and wrapped her arms around him. He was at a loss to know what to do with his hands. He grasped her shoulders and gave them a gentle squeeze, saying, "You'll get through this. I'm sure you will." He felt her shuddering.

She looked at him through tear-stained eyes and said, "Will you come back again? In a few days? And make sure I'm okay?"

"I'll be in touch," he said huskily. He had rarely felt so uncomfortable. Somehow, he disengaged and found his way to the door. He let himself out. In the hallway he felt his heart racing. What had just happened? And, what was he going to tell Rosetta?

WITH THE SPRING TERM at an end, David came home for the summer. Back in his old room, he was happy as a squirrel on a nut pile, knowing that Molly Lundgren was still occupying the room adjoining his. Elsa had taken her son aside the day he'd moved back, warning him, politely but firmly, not to invade Molly's privacy. His father had put it more directly. Fully aware that his son's hormones were likely in full flow, he instructed him, simply, "No funny business."

David was heartened to see how Molly's spirits had improved since her miscarriage. It appeared to him that the delightful young woman he'd encountered last Christmas had returned. What he wasn't so sure about was what she was hoping for. He asked her about it one evening in early June. They were relaxing on the front porch of his parents' home, seated side by side in a couple of rocking chairs. It was nearly nine o'clock, but the sun had still not quite disappeared.

"Molly," he said, looking out toward the street, "what do you want to do with the rest of your life?"

"I still don't know. Your parents keep saying I can stay as long as I need to. But I can't tell if they're only saying that to be polite."

"Boy, things have really changed since that Friday last March, when you and I sat in our living room, with the fire going."

"That was really a hard time for me."

"You know, I worried all spring that I'd come home from college and find you'd gone away."

"Where would I go? You told me yourself I didn't have any prospects."

"Things will get better for you."

"You're such an everlasting optimist," she said. "But, I guess I prefer that to the alternative."

"Thank my parents for that," he replied. "I learned it from them." They rocked in silence. He said, "Are you still mad at Pastor Jonas?"

She didn't answer.

"I wish you'd come to church with me."

She sighed. "I may be mellowing on that. A little."

He looked at her hopefully, but said nothing.

"Since I lost the baby, I've been thinking about things in a different way. I guess I shouldn't blame the pastor for accepting all that money for the congregation. I probably would have done it." She paused, then said, "One night, not so long ago, while I was lying in bed, not able to sleep, it occurred to me that, when he was offered the bequest, he didn't even know there was a connection between that evil man and me."

"Really? Are you sure?"

"Well, yes, actually, I am. When I moved in with them, Rosetta didn't tell him who'd gotten me pregnant. That didn't come until later. So, I suppose I have to accept the fact that he probably accepted the money in good faith."

They rocked some more in silence, except for the creaking of their chairs on the wooden porch floor.

David said, "I'll bet you miss your family."

She didn't answer.

"How long has it been since you last wrote to them, anyway?"

"The day I moved out of my Park Avenue apartment."

"What did you tell them?"

"That my situation was changing. That I'd explain everything to them when I had a chance."

"Holy Toledo! That was last fall. For all you know, your folks are downtown right now, knocking on doors, trying to find you."

"I suppose it's possible," she admitted.

"I think it must be hard for them. I know, if I went off somewhere and never told my folks where I was or anything, they'd probably have the sheriff out looking."

It was nearly dark, but he could still see her face. He found her expression impossible to read.

A WEEK AFTER he had been to Maureen's apartment, Daniel received another call from her. She asked if he would come by once again. He asked if her husband would be there. She explained he hadn't returned, and that she was feeling terribly abandoned. He told her he would come to see her later that evening.

When Maureen opened her door at seven-thirty, she was wearing a silky black negligee and high heels. The lights were turned low. She offered him a seductive smile, and beckoned him to come inside.

Daniel said, "I brought a friend."

A look of puzzlement crept into her face. She said, "I thought you were coming alone."

He said, "I don't like to leave Rosetta alone when I go out at night."

"Rosetta?"

"Maureen, I'd like you to meet my wife." Rosetta stepped out of the shadows, smiled at the scantily clad woman, and walked into the apartment with her husband.

Maureen cleared her throat uncomfortably and said, "You know, Pastor, I'm really doing much better than I was. But thanks to both of you for stopping by."

"Any time I can be of help," he said.

When they were back in the hallway, and the door had been shut, his wife said to him, "It sounds as if someone in there just smashed a vase or something."

Daniel circled his wife's waist with his arm and said, dryly, "Do you suppose?"

AS THE WALLS on the new church building began to rise, people from the neighborhood began to linger on the sidewalk, watching the workers manipulate the large blocks of white stone. All through the month of July, the great project continued to take shape. It was clear that, before long, the frame chapel on the corner would be dwarfed by its magnificent replacement.

One Sunday at mid-month, as Daniel was hanging up his vestments in the sacristy, Elsa came to the door and said, "Do you have a minute?"

He turned to look at her. "Certainly. What is it?"

"I hate to do this to you, but I'm feeling the need to give up the Sunday morning piano playing. Sooner than later. I haven't minded doing it, but three services on a Sunday morning are beginning to take a toll. Do you suppose there's another volunteer who could take over for a while?"

He nodded thoughtfully, and then said, "Instead of another piano player, I think we need to start looking for a musician who can play the new pipe organ we're going to have in about a year."

"Well," Elsa said firmly, "that's definitely not me. I play piano. I'm not an organist. I never have been. And, I don't want to learn."

He asked, "Can you hang on until the first of September?"

Chapter 16

The building committee meeting was breaking up. As the men began to leave, Sam Warner, one of the participants, stayed behind to fold up and stack the wooden chairs and then collapse and store the long folding table. Daniel decided to help him. As they did so, the pastor asked Sam, "When's Susan's baby due?"

"November. We're really excited."

"I'll bet you are," he said, adding, "as if you haven't done your part to help this congregation grow already."

The comment appeared to amuse the young Minneapolis policeman, who added, "We try to do our part." He said, offhandedly, "I haven't seen Dolly Winters in church for a while."

"Pardon me? Who's Dolly Winters?"

"She used to come to early worship and sit in the back. I thought you knew her. You don't seem ever to forget a name."

"I've never heard that one."

"Well, maybe she never told it to you. But I know she was there. I saw her several Sundays in a row. Long, flowing blonde hair. A good dresser. Made up fit to kill. I remember that Sunday you preached about having Communion more frequently. She came out of your office, just before church. Susan and I had just walked in, and I remembered thinking, 'Hey. What do you know? Pastor's having a chat with the unforgettable Dolly Winters.'"

Daniel stopped folding chairs. "She told me her name was Maureen Rawlins."

Sam grinned. "Wouldn't surprise me. Dolly's not exactly what you'd call transparent. I thought maybe she'd decided to come to you to get herself straightened out."

"Of all the pastors in the city, why would she have chosen me?"

"Well, to be blunt about it, you're a fairly good-looking young man. That always seems to figure into the equation for her."

"How do you know her?"

"For a while, my beat was Hennepin Avenue, down where the clubs and joints are. Dolly works as a stripper. At least, she did then. I saw her in action a few times. Not that I was patronizing her act or anything. A couple of us were down there in plain clothes. We had a tip the club was bending the rules on Prohibition. Didn't see any evidence of that. But, get this. After her act, she came down in the audience and propositioned me! We took her in for soliciting. Of course, she argued it had all been a misunderstanding. Said I looked like somebody she recognized. Turned on the tears to the chief. Darned if he didn't let her off."

Daniel felt his skin begin to crawl.

Sam said, "We also had a situation involving her one other time. Some young bank officer, a handsome fellow as I recall, came into the station and said Dolly had tried to entrap him."

"How do you mean?"

"Well, turns out he'd stopped by her club and, before he knew it, he found her sitting at his table. She gave him some sob story about how her husband had deserted her. That was why she had to work in that lousy club. Anyway, that was the bank officer's story. He said she gave him a pretty good line, all about how she was afraid to go home alone, and would he please escort her? Well, he took pity on her, and gave her a ride back her to her apartment. Over on LaSalle someplace."

Daniel's stomach was getting queasy.

"According to him, she invited him in for a drink. They hit it off pretty good. She told him how lonely she was and how good it made her feel that he'd shown her such kindness. That sort of garbage. Anyway, according to *his* story, he started going back there. They got involved. She actually got him into bed at one point. After they'd done their business, he went to sleep and she went through his clothes. Took pictures of his kids out of his billfold, to use to prove to his wife he'd been doing it with her. Then she said she'd ruin him if he didn't start making payments to her."

Daniel's knees were feeling weak. He unfolded one of the chairs and sat down on it.

"Of course, it backfired," Sam continued. "She didn't think he'd go to the police, but he did. They brought her in. She denied everything. But then they found the pictures in her apartment."

"What did his wife say?"

"I don't think she ever found out. And, after that, Dolly dropped out of sight for a while. Not sure what she's doing now."

"What about her husband? What does he have to say about any of this?"

"Are you kidding? Dolly's not married. Never has been."

DANIEL WAS READY for a break. It was August and he was beginning to feel drained. Besides, he'd finally received an answer to the letter he'd sent to the head of the conservatory of music at Capital University, and that was going to require a visit to Ohio. In addition to everything else, he and Rosetta were feeling overdue for a trip back to Fremont. It had been more than a year since their marriage, and their families were dropping not-so-subtle hints that it was time for them to come back home for a visit.

So, he made arrangements with St. Paul Luther Seminary to provide students to fill the pulpit for two Sundays, and, on a warm Monday morning, the young clergyman and his wife boarded a train for Chicago, and then Toledo.

Somewhere in Wisconsin, as the hills and barns were flying by their window, Rosetta said to him, "Do you think there's room for a baby crib in our bedroom?"

He looked at her in surprise. "Are you pretty sure we're going to need one?"

She nodded. "I'm pretty sure."

ROSETTA'S BROTHER, George Siegel, met them at the Fremont station and took them to her parents' home. That afternoon, Daniel walked along State Street, to Grace Lutheran Church's new building. With admiration he studied the construction work on the three-story parish house and the wonderful new nave. The congregation had raised sufficient funds to start the new building they'd planned for so long, and the walls were now rising. He marveled how different it was in the case of St. Michael and All Angels congregation, where the funds were already in hand and plans to construct a new worship complex had come together very quickly.

He wondered which building would be completed first.

WHILE ROSETTA STAYED in Fremont, Daniel took the train south, to Bucyrus. As he settled into his seat, he pulled out the letter he'd received from the conservatory of music, and the one from Bucyrus, folded in with it. He had almost memorized the messages by now. But still, he found himself reading both letters again.

He had written to the school of music in late May, explaining the opportunity that was soon to open at St. Michael Church. He'd told the director he wanted an accomplished musician, but one willing to start at the bottom of the pay scale. That, it had seemed to him, most logically pointed to a recent graduate of the Capital University conservatory. The ace up his sleeve, he figured, was the fact that his church council had approved the idea of a fully-salaried position, something most Lutheran congregations he knew about were not willing to consider.

As he'd hoped, the conservatory director had jumped at the opportunity to see one of his graduates launched into a full-time music career.

When he stepped down onto the platform in the small county seat town, he asked directions to south Sandusky Street, then set off on foot. It was only eight blocks to the address he'd been given. The young woman he was coming to visit had assured him she would be waiting for his arrival. She was a public school teacher, but it was August, so she would be home all day.

On the front porch of the two-story frame house, he knocked and waited. There was no response. He realized this would have been a long trip to make, only to discover there was no one here. At last, the door opened. On the other side of the screen stood a tastefully dressed young woman in her early twenties. Her wavy hair was attractively styled, almost as though she had done it up for a social occasion.

He occurred to him that, from her perspective, that was probably what this was.

"Lillian Gardner?"

"Yes?"

"I'm Pastor Daniel Jonas."

"A good Reformation name if ever I've heard one," she said, catching him off guard.

"You know your church history," he said, impressed.

"Justus Jonas. One of Martin Luther's associates. Every good Lutheran should recognize that name."

Perhaps so, he thought. *But not very likely.*

"Please come in," she said. "How was your trip from Fremont?"

"Very pleasant, thank you."

She led the way into a modestly appointed parlor and gestured toward a worn but comfortable-looking sofa. As he sat down, he noticed an upright piano against the far wall. On its rack several pieces of sheet music were spread.

Gardner sat in an upholstered chair near the couch, lay her hands confidently on the arms, and said, "How is your ministry progressing in Minneapolis?"

Daniel wondered for a moment who was going to be interviewing whom.

But, he decided, it was a reasonable question. "Quite well. Thank you for asking. I mentioned something of that in my letter to you."

"Yes. A very good letter. Thank you."

Now she was critiquing his writing style? He admired her self-assurance. In terms of what he was looking for, that might be a good sign.

"I understand you're a school teacher."

"Yes. At Kilbourne Elementary. It's just two blocks from here."

"And you play the organ on Sundays."

"At Good Hope Lutheran. I also direct the choirs."

"And Good Hope has a pipe organ."

"My dear Pastor Jonas, we're the largest church in the county. What else would we have?"

He felt as though a schoolmarm had just dressed him down. He wondered if she was as confident at the console as she seemed to be in conversation. He suspected she probably was. He took a deep breath and chose his words carefully. "What's your philosophy of church music ministry?"

"What, exactly, are you getting at?"

"Are there styles of music you shy away from when planning for worship?"

"Of course. The worship service ought to be in praise of Almighty God. Nothing less. And that means our texts and harmonies can be nothing less than worthy musical offerings."

He thought, *I'm talking to a conservatory graduate, no doubt about it.*

"Which means," she continued, "that there's no place for sentimentality in church music. It ought to be objective and God-centered."

"Does that mean," he responded, feeling playful, "that you would refuse to allow, let us say, 'Beyond the Sunset' at a church funeral?"

She looked at him askance. "You're toying with me, aren't you?"

He grinned.

"I enjoy a clergyman with a sense of humor." Getting up, she said, "I have tea and cakes. Would you like to come into the dining room?" It was spoken as a question, but she had already decided what the answer should be.

He followed her into the next room. As she filled their cups, he asked, "Are you alone here?"

"I beg your pardon?"

"I'm wondering whether you share this residence, perhaps with other school teachers."

"Oh, heavens, no. This is my parents' home. They did me the favor of going up to Chatfield for the day. That's our ancestral home. So we have the house to ourselves, as long as we need."

"How was it at the conservatory?"

"How should it have been?"

Obviously his questions were going to require more precision. "What I'm asking you is, did you feel as though you got a good musical education there?"

"Well, if I hadn't, I'd expect the bursar to refund my tuition." She said it with a straight face, but the sharpness of her wit was unmistakable.

"I really appreciate a musician with a sense of humor," he said, lifting his teacup.

She returned a smile that seemed to say, *now we're even.*

He asked, "Is there a possibility you would consider coming to Minneapolis to play our new pipe organ?"

"It's an intriguing thought," she said, breaking the dainty cake on her plate into two pieces.

He said, "The candidate we select would need to be somewhat flexible. We need a person to begin next month. But the organ won't be ready for another year. That means that, during the interim, it would require accompanying three Sunday morning services on the piano."

"What impresses me is that you're offering a full position. Your letter said the candidate would be responsible for playing your new pipe organ, directing the choirs, and developing a music program. What it doesn't say is how she — or he — would be helped to survive your brutal Minnesota winters. Does this position include provision of a parka and galoshes?"

He smiled and said, "I was raised just up the road, at Fremont. This is my fourth year in Minnesota. Believe me, you get used to the cold. The good side is, Minneapolis is a very beautiful city. We have lakes and parkways, and a famous waterfall, all inside the city limits."

She nodded. He wondered what she was thinking. She might be intrigued, but was she actually considering it?

She said, "I think you would be remiss, considering me for this position, without having first heard an audition." She stood up and said, "Good Hope Church is only four blocks. Shall we go over? I have a key. I think you should hear me play something."

He was delighted at the suggestion. They left the house and walked together, toward the church building with the tall, slim spire that could be seen from everywhere in town. Along the way he asked, "How would the principal at Kilbourne Elementary School deal with the possibility that you might not return for your second year of teaching, and that you might leave on such short notice?"

"Well, you be might be interested to know that I was offered the teaching position last year only after the school term had already begun. I waited all summer for that appointment, and nobody thought to apologize for stringing me along. I wouldn't feel too guilty about giving them short notice."

Inside the cavernous nave of Good Hope Church, he took a seat near the front and turned to watch the keyboard artist behind and above him, in the balcony.

It was silent for perhaps a half minute. She took her time, selecting the music, setting the organ stops and mentally preparing herself. Then, without warning, the great instrument exploded into glorious sound. The music of the great north German composer, Dietrich Buxtehude, filled the worship space.

And Daniel was convinced he had found his minister of music.

Chapter 17

For David Engelhardt, it had become an idyllic summer. He'd known since Easter that Molly was growing more attracted to him. Coming home from his brother's college graduation, she'd snuggled close to him in the back seat of his father's Ford and allowed him to hold her hand all the way back to Anderson Avenue.

Things had only gotten better. While she'd resisted coming back to work in the print shop, even for an hour or two a day, she'd begun to find excuses to spend time with David, and to ask him to take her places. At first he'd thought it was just a sign she was finally ready to put an end to her morbid obsession with the sad tragedy that had afflicted her for so long. But, soon, it became clear to him that she was genuinely interested in him — as much as he was in her.

He'd originally thought he'd want to spend all his time during the summer helping with his father's business. But his days there soon began to seem long. He found himself counting the hours until mid-day, when Molly would come by with a lunch to share with him — and until closing time, when he could spend more time with her.

One Sunday afternoon in the middle of June, his mother took him into her bedroom, closed the door, and said, "David, I know you care a lot for Molly. But I want you to be careful. You've got two more years of college. Your father and I really want you to graduate. And Molly ... none of us wants to see her get hurt again. So please, be very careful. All right?"

"Mom, we aren't going to do anything we shouldn't. I promise."

"I'm sure you don't plan to, David. But you're a young man and you're full of energy and strong feelings. And they can get away from you. Trust me."

That little talk turned out to have been the best thing he could have heard just then. He'd been thinking seriously about dropping out of school, going full time in the print shop, and asking Molly to marry him. But, as he began to think about it, he realized how unwise that would be. For one thing, in spite of their spending more time together, he still didn't know her all that well. Not really. And for another, he'd never even met her parents.

The problem was, she wasn't ready to deal with her parents either. How would she explain the fact that she had stopped writing to them? Or, why she hadn't been home since before Thanksgiving? Or, what had happened to her?

So, David and Molly spent all their free time in each other's company, neither sure where it all might lead. They walked through Powderhorn Park so frequently, it began to feel as if it was theirs. They went to Minneapolis Millers baseball games at Nicollet Park, and she pretended to enjoy them as much as he did. They went to Minnehaha Falls and watched the water spill over the outcropping, while he recited Longfellow to her. They took the streetcar up Central Avenue, to the popular new Heights Theater in Columbia Heights. And, when he'd saved enough money, he took her to a performance of the Minneapolis Symphony, where he pretended to enjoy the concert as much as she did.

It was with conflicted feelings that they made plans to attend the Minnesota State Fair at summer's end. They were eager to spend an entire August day together at the great annual statewide exposition. But the coming of the state fair meant that school would resume almost immediately thereafter. They tried not to think about the fact that he would soon be heading off to the University of Minnesota for his last two years of study.

They took the streetcar to the fairgrounds, arriving just after opening time on a Saturday morning. They wandered, hand in hand, along the midway, where he tried without success to win a stuffed animal for her. A fortune teller assured them they were destined to be soul mates. They walked through the food court, where they filled themselves with wieners and sauerkraut, lemonade, and ice cream.

They rode the Ferris wheel and, when it stopped with them suspended at the very top, imagined they could see the print shop, on the green southwest horizon, far beyond the curve of the Mississippi River.

Finally, when they'd done everything David could think of to do, Molly said, "Come on, we have to see the farm displays."

"But I'm not a farmer. Do we have to?"

"Yes. We do. I used to bring my 4-H projects here when I was still home on the farm. Let's go see the prize-winning animals."

He really wasn't all that keen on it, but Molly wanted to make the rounds, so he agreed to go along with it. He figured, as long as he had her hand in his, nothing else mattered much.

They went to see the sheep and swine and cattle, and he found himself beginning to enjoy the tour. Then they were off to the home economics building, to survey the winning entries in the cooking and baking contests, and to see which sewing projects had earned blue ribbons.

It was while she was admiring a finely stitched tablecloth that Molly heard a familiar voice call her name. Three times she heard it. Looking up, she stared in disbelief, and whispered urgently to David, "It's my family!"

He looked in the direction from which the voice had come. A man perhaps his own father's age, but heavier, and balding, was dressed in farmer's work clothes. Beside him stood a well-endowed woman, short, with blonde hair, and wearing a peasant dress with festive designs stitched around the neck and hem. Four children, three girls and a boy, were with them.

There was a milling crowd of fair visitors separating them from Molly and David, which prompted him to whisper, just as urgently, "Are you sure?"

"As sure as I'm standing here with you," she said.

She seemed unable to move. Firmly grasping her hand, he said confidently, "Come on, then, you have to introduce me."

"Oh, God in heaven," she said, sounding panicked.

As they approached, the two youngest girls came running, pushing their way through the ocean of people. "Molly, Molly!" the younger one squealed in delight. She leaped into her older sister's arms. Molly lifted her up and said, "Oh, Joanna! It's been such a long time since I saw you last."

"Where *were* you?" the youngster demanded, half scolding. "We thought you were lost."

"Well, I wasn't, really." She looked at the other girl and said, "Hello, Betsy. How's Murdo?"

"Still the best steer in the county. He'll be ready for the fair next year. I think he just may win blue."

"I'm sure he will," she said, smiling.

By now the rest of her family was standing nearby. David, sensing the awkwardness of the moment, said, as casually as he could manage, "Hello, My name is David. Molly allowed me to bring her to the fair."

The pleasingly plump farm woman had a look of consternation. But she smiled as best she could and said, "I'm Edna Lundgren. This is my husband, George. And these are our children, Anna, Martin, Betsy and Joanna. Our oldest, Forrest, is home running the farm today." She added significantly, "Molly is also our daughter."

"Why haven't you written to your mother?" asked George Lundgren, looking stern. "We haven't heard from you for months. And you don't come home any more. We started thinking the worst."

Molly said, "I'm sorry. Truly, I am. It's been a difficult time for me." She paused, not knowing what to say next.

David seemed to know. He said, as if he'd rehearsed it, "Molly had some bad luck. Her job at the investment company came to an end. It wasn't through any fault of hers." He looked at Molly's father, who seemed confused. "She was given expectations that were impossible to meet. If I were her, I would have gotten out of there even sooner."

Please be careful what you tell them, Molly wanted to say. But she only thought it.

David continued, "So, my father offered her a job in his print shop. She's really good at what she does."

Molly thought, *I haven't worked there since I lost the baby.*

He continued, "She was really upset about how her previous job ended. It was hard for her to talk about it, even to us."

Her younger brother said, "But, how come you didn't talk to *us* about it, Molly? How come you never came home?"

She had a trapped look about her. David saw it, as well as the continuing look of consternation on her father's face. He said, "You know, there's a pavilion next door with tables and chairs. Why don't we all go over there and sit down for a little bit? That way, we can talk more privately."

That appeared to everyone to be a good idea. He led the way, steering Molly along with a hand placed on her shoulder, while the others followed, like ducks looking for a pond.

When they were seated, there was an awkward moment of silence, broken by Molly's mother. She said, "Are you all right, dear?"

"Mom, I'm fine. I'm doing well."

"And, what is your relationship to this young man?"

"Well, he's my employer's son," she said, aware that she was perpetuating a half truth. "He's been an excellent friend. He was especially so when I was grieving."

"Grieving?" her older sister, Anna, said.

David took charge again. "You know, when you prepare yourself professionally for something, and then you get it, only to discover they won't let you keep it, that can be a terrible disappointment. It's almost like there's been a death."

Anna nodded with understanding. Molly looked sideways at David. She marveled at his diplomacy, and his quickness. She felt like giving him a kiss, but realized this was not the time or the place.

George Lundgren asked, "Is your present job enough to cover your room and board, then?"

"Daddy, it's all taken care of. Everything's just fine."

"So, where are you living?" Edna asked.

David said, "That was one of the benefits my father was able to offer her. There was a spare room in our home. Molly's been using it. She helps with the cooking. It's a fair trade."

"Well," said Edna, relaxing, "that sounds creative." She looked at Molly and asked, "So, are you happy, then?"

"Yes. Yes, Mother, I really am."

"And, just what do you do?" her father asked David.

This time it was Molly to the rescue. "He just finished two years at St. Paul Luther College, right here in our capital city."

"Oh," said Edna. "So, that's a Lutheran school, then? Sort of like Gustavus Adolphus?"

"Very much like that," said David, smiling.

Molly's parents both seemed impressed, learning this extra bit of information.

"And he starts at the university in just a few weeks," she added.

"But are you ever coming home again?" asked fourteen-year-old Martin.

"Why don't you come for Thanksgiving?" Edna interjected. "Perhaps this fine young man could bring you. We'd be happy to have you see the farm, David. And you could be our guest."

"I don't know much about farming," David admitted. "But I'd love to see your farm. And I think Molly must be eager to come home again, at least for a visit."

He looked at Molly. Her eyes were pooling. He found a handkerchief and handed it to her. The gesture was not lost on Edna Lundgren, who smiled with appreciation.

DANIEL RETURNED to the Gaytee Art Glass studio in late September. The craftsman assigned to begin preparations on the ten stained-glass windows still to be designed was ready for some guidance.

Daniel had invited Michael Morgan-Houseman to come by as well, but the businessman had begged off, arguing he had some urgent business to attend to. Seated across from the designer, the clergyman handed over a set of carefully typed pages, a summary of what each window should look like. He'd worked with the property and building committee, as well as with members of the worship and music committee, and, finally, the church council. The designs had come at his initiative, and no one had offered serious disagreement.

Daniel explained to the glass merchant what was already on the ten sheets. He said, "We're asking for a series of eight large windows, four on each side, running from the back of the nave up to where the walls open into the two side chapels. There's a sequence, starting on the north side, at the back, and ending on the south side, also at the back."

The designer nodded, reading avidly. Daniel continued, "All the designs incorporate angel themes. We want worshipers to feel that they're in the presence of angels when they come into the nave. The first will picture Adam and Eve, expelled from the Garden by an angel with a flaming sword. The second will show angels speaking to Abraham, as he learns what God has planned for him. The third will be of warrior angels driving the Assyrians back from the besieged city of Jerusalem. The fourth is an angel in the Jerusalem Temple, touching a burning coal to the mouth of the Prophet, Isaiah."

He paused, considering what the array of leaded glass might finally look like. It made his heart beat faster. "The first window on the south side will picture the angel Gabriel, announcing to Mary and Joseph that they will become Jesus' parents."

The designer interrupted. "I thought the angel only came to Mary."

"Well, there's another story in which God speaks to Joseph in a dream, with essentially the same message. There will only be so many windows available, so we're combining those two stories into one."

The artist nodded. "Very creative. And a good solution, too."

Daniel appreciated the fact that the glass worker was so well versed in Scripture. He realized, with all the church buildings for which his firm created glass, it was the better part of wisdom that they hire someone with a grasp of the Church's tradition.

"Window six will show the angels at the empty tomb. And the last two are … well … non-biblical. Number seven is to depict Martin Luther, seated at the Wartburg Castle, translating the New Testament into German, while angels hover over him. And, finally, we want a contemporary window."

The artist studied the last page of description. He said, "This will be a fun window to work on. I see you have the new church building pictured in the center, surrounded by scenes of the Twin Cities." He mulled it as he muttered softly, "Upper left: Minneapolis City Hall clock tower and Foshay Tower — but without Foshay's name on it — good idea; I always thought he was a scoundrel. Upper right: the academic building at St. Paul Luther College — you're going to have to give us a drawing of that one. I don't know what it looks like. Bottom right, the state capitol building. And, bottom left, a two-story print shop on Bloomington Avenue, with a streetcar out in front."

He looked up at Daniel and said, "And angels, with their trumpets, in the sky above. It sounds ambitious .... maybe even a little cluttered for one window ... but entirely manageable. We'll enjoy putting that one together." He paused, as if to rethink the comment. "Of course, we'll enjoy doing *all* of them."

Daniel said, "The window above the balcony at the west end is to be a rose window. You select the pattern and the colors. The organ pipes will surround it without obscuring the design. Make the color tones rich." The artist nodded, his eyes bright with anticipation.

"And, the great chancel window, above the altar, will picture Jesus, flanked by the archangels Michael and Gabriel. All three are to be robed, surrounded by a swirl of stars and planets."

The glass designer set the sheaf of papers aside, stood up and grasped Daniel's hand. He said, "We're eager to do this project. We assure you, you will not be disappointed."

"I've seen your work in other churches," Daniel said. "Your designs for Mount Olive Lutheran, on Chicago Avenue, are quite nice, although the symbols in the window above the altar are much smaller than I would have wanted. But that's just a matter of taste. I'm confident you'll do excellent work for us."

As he turned to leave, Daniel came face to face with Michael Morgan-Houseman. The stockbroker said, "My meeting ended sooner than I'd expected. Have I missed anything?"

Chapter 18

As the two men stepped out onto the sidewalk, Daniel said, "You missed the whole discussion about what the stained glass windows will look like. But, I suspect there's only one in the set that you really care about."

"And don't you go changing a single detail of it without consulting me."

"There are no plans to change it."

"Excellent. By the way, there's no point in you waiting for a streetcar. Come on. Wesley's here with the Packard. We'll give you a lift."

Daniel gladly accepted. He'd enjoyed a brief chat with the chauffeur on a previous ride, and had found him to be an interesting conversationalist. But this time there was no opportunity for give and take with Wesley. Michael Morgan-Houseman was eager to discuss a topic of his own.

"I've just done something that I'm almost too embarrassed to mention."

Daniel's ears perked up. Was the back seat of this automobile about to become a confessional?

"Of course, remember," the stockbroker continued, "you're talking to a person with adventure in his blood. I'm a man who likes taking risks. Big ones, sometimes. And, you probably have noticed, these are times when the aggressive investor can multiply his worth — two and three and four times over."

Daniel took a deep breath. He'd been reading stories in the *Minneapolis Tribune* about the theories of some high-profile economists. They warned the money boom could easily become a bust. He wondered if it was his place to say anything to the self-confident entrepreneur.

Morgan-Houseman said, "It's a good thing for your congregation that I've already transferred all your funds into the separate account. You've got the money for your building, all tucked away, safe and sound."

"And, why do you say that's a good thing?"

"Because, as of ten o'clock this morning, I've leveraged all my available assets."

Daniel had only a vague idea what that might mean.

"It means I've gone out on a limb. It means I'm now heavily invested in a dozen high-flying equities — all purchased with money I don't actually have. At least, not just yet. Of course, when the stocks appreciate, I'll have the money I need to pay for them, along with an incredible profit. I've gambled the market will keep going up. When it does, and when I cash out, I'll be one of the richest men in Minnesota."

"I thought you already *were* one of those."

"Well, I just gave away five million dollars. I have to find a way to get that back." He looked at Daniel, who was clearly taken aback. Then he erupted in a tidal wave of laughter, slapping the pastor on the knee so vigorously Daniel's flesh was stinging. "That five million I gave your church," Morgan-Houseman asserted, "was the best goddam investment I ever made. And, once again, you'll have to pardon my French."

The direction the conversation was taking was making Daniel increasingly uncomfortable. He could not shake from his consciousness a parable in the Gospel of Luke, about a farmer who kept building bigger barns. He said, "And, just in case the market goes the other way, what then?"

"Well, I'd be ruined, of course. But that's what the gloom peddlers warned would happen last year, when I gambled that share values would go up. They told me I was taking far too many risks. Of course, since then, I'm eight million dollars richer than I was before."

Daniel wondered if there was such a thing as investors' addiction. If so, he was pretty sure he was looking at an addict's addict.

The automobile pulled up in front of St. Michael Church. Morgan-Houseman surveyed the construction in progress and said, "Looking good. Looking *very* good." The rising new stone structure's walls were now nearly up to window level. The two men climbed out, and Daniel led the way to the place in the floor plan where the Children's Chapel was beginning to take shape.

Morgan-Houseman said, "When you get this finished, I'll come back, and sit in this chapel, and say a prayer for Michael." He looked wistfully at the structure which was yet to be. He turned toward the pastor and said, "And then you can try to convert me!" He slapped Daniel on the back, almost as hard as he had before.

Then he was gone, and Daniel was left staring at the walls of the rising complex, listening to the chipping and scraping sounds of the masons' trowels.

LILLIAN GARDNER walked through the rooms on the second level of the large house on Caldwell Street. Matronly Wilma Shaughnessy, a 70-year-old widow and a devout Roman Catholic, conducted the tour with enthusiasm. "My bedroom is downstairs, so you would have the run of the entire floor. You've got the bathroom back here … This room was a bedroom, but I've turned it into a sitting room. It has a day bed, so you could have an overnight guest sometime … This next one is a bedroom too. Except, this one actually has a bed." She laughed softly, as if she'd told a joke on herself.

"And this room in the front has a nice bay window, with a view to the street. It would make a nice upstairs parlor. You know, in case you wanted to entertain."

Lillian studied the room with eager eyes. The furniture looked antique, but serviceable enough. But she had something else in mind for this room, assuming she signed the lease.

"And," Wilma continued, "you'll have access to the kitchen. You could fix your own meals, or you could eat with me. Either way."

They'd returned to the top of the stairs, ready to go down. The homeowner said, "I like nice, quiet renters. The last one had one of those Victrola machines. He played jazz records on it. Really loud! I thought I was in a honky tonk! I said a prayer of thanksgiving to Saint Patrick the day he moved out, let me tell you."

Lillian said, "Just how quiet do you expect your next tenant to be?"

Wilma flashed a look of uncertainty. "Oh, saints in heaven, do you have a Victrola too, my dear?"

The young musician grinned. "No. But I couldn't help notice you have a piano in the downstairs parlor."

"I used to play it for Barney in the evenings. God rest his soul."

"I know this may sound presumptuous," Lillian said, choosing her words carefully, "because you and I haven't even come to an agreement about whether I should be your next renter. However, I need to have you understand something. My salary at the church is going to be, well, let's just say, on the lean side. So, if I'm to be able to afford a place like this, with all the wonderful space you're offering here, I would need to supplement my income. By teaching piano."

"And you want to use *my* piano?"

"Well, I was hoping we could discuss that."

"Nothing to discuss. That piano hasn't played a note since the day Barney died. We need a little civilized music in this house again."

"Maybe I could pay you an extra something each month for using the piano."

"Oh, heavens, child, absolutely not. I wouldn't hear of it."

126

"Are you certain you wouldn't mind having music pupils going in and out of your downstairs parlor, afternoons and Saturdays?"

Wilma screwed up her pudgy face in a pleasant, thoughtful scowl. She said, "I'll tell you what. I'll have the piano moved to the upstairs parlor. That could be your music room."

"Are you certain you want to go to that trouble?"

"Well, only on two conditions, of course."

"Which are … ?"

"First, that you sign the lease. Today. And second, that if you ever do get a Victrola, all I'm going to hear on it is concert hall music."

ADAM ENGELHARDT finished his meal and lay down his fork. He said, "Molly, it's really been good having you working full-time in the print shop. Thanks for agreeing to come back to work."

"It's been good for me," she said, folding her napkin. "Thank you for letting me take charge of the bookkeeping. Now I'm back to using some of the skills I learned in business college."

"Is it just my imagination, or is business picking up?" Elsa asked. She poured herself a cup of coffee and added cream. "Every time I come over, there seem to be more customers waiting than there were the last time."

"It's not your imagination," Adam replied. "Two pressmen and one counter clerk can hardly keep up now. Some days I wish David was home working full-time, like he was last summer. But I won't pull him out of college just for that." He looked at Molly and winked. "Besides, he'd probably be such a distraction, Molly would end up making a mess of the books."

Elsa flashed a look of mock reproach to her husband. Molly blushed.

"I'm seriously thinking of a larger building," Adam said.

"You're *what*?" asked Elsa. It was the first she'd heard of such an idea.

"We could double our business. We've got customers bumping into each other in that crowded customer area. And I think we're close to the point where we could afford something bigger."

"Where would you find another building?"

"We wouldn't. We'd build one."

Elsa registered a look of surprise.

"There's a vacant lot further down Bloomington. A nice corner site. It's zoned commercial, and George Kleinhans says he knows who owns it. He could get it for me at a good price."

"But then you'd have to pay builders!"

"Yes, we would. But I've been doing the arithmetic. I think we could do it. As early as next year. It would stretch us a little. But, wouldn't it be great to welcome David into full partnership in a brand-new building?"

"Well, yes, I suppose so." She sipped her coffee. Then a look of concern crept into her face. "Where would Pastor Daniel and Rosetta go if you sold the building?"

"Well, maybe it's time the congregation faced up to its responsibility and found a decent residence for the pastor. Especially now that there's a little one on the way."

"*What*!" both women responded together.

"Oops," he said sheepishly. "I wasn't supposed to say that yet."

"Yet!" said Elsa, sounding betrayed. "How does it happen you know that Pastor and Rosetta are having a baby, and nobody else does?"

"Well, Pastor Jonas made mention of it. In confidence. He said they wanted to announce it when they were ready. I don't think they're ready yet. So, that means you two have to keep your lips sealed."

"Well, what did the pastor tell you, exactly," Elsa demanded.

Adam sighed. "I hate getting caught in things like this."

"What did he *say*?"

"I was in the pastor's study, at the chapel. We were discussing the church council agenda for next month. He said he didn't want to make an issue of it, since we're in the middle of a huge building project right now, and even though offerings are good, we just recently started paying him a full salary. And, on top of everything, we've hired a full-time music director. But, in spite of all that, he thought I should know that the two of them were expecting. And, that sometime next spring, things might start getting pretty crowded up there over the print shop. The point he was making was, he wondered if we could approach the council, and then the congregation, about possible alternative housing for them."

"Well, then, I guess it doesn't make much difference whether you keep the old shop or not. They have to get out of there. That's only sensible."

Molly was beaming. She said, "I'm really happy for Rosetta!" She considered what she'd just said, then added, "Well ... and for Pastor too, of course."

Elsa smiled. She said, as gently as she could, "You're still just a tiny bit unhappy with him, aren't you?"

"I'm actually getting over it. I've been thinking about that a lot. It's not the pastor's fault that Mister you-know-who did what he did. And, if Pastor Jonas had known everything right at the beginning, maybe he wouldn't have accepted the money in the first place. But he did, and he did it in good faith, and what's done is done."

Adam said, "Molly, I'm really pleased to see how you seem to have gotten this settled in your mind."

"Well," she said darkly, "just because I've made my peace with Pastor Jonas doesn't mean I have with that monster. And I know it isn't Christian, but I still have days when I find myself wishing — and hoping — that he would end up frying in hell." She paused, looked down, and traced her finger slowly across the tablecloth and then back again. She looked up again, and said, "That's a sin, isn't it? I know I shouldn't think that way. But it's how I feel." She was looking repentant. "So, I've decided, I really need to start going to church again."

Elsa's jaw dropped. She'd always avoided pressuring their long-term house guest on that subject. She said, "Molly, whenever you want to come with us …"

"Next Sunday. I think next Sunday."

WITH GREAT DIFFICULTY, the four athletic-looking young Irishmen tugged and coaxed and maneuvered and finessed the upright piano up the stairs, one excruciating step at a time. Wilma Shaughnessy stood at the bottom of the stairs, wringing her hands, fearing at any moment all four of them, and the piano, might come tumbling down. Lillian Gardner stood in the doorway of the upstairs parlor, watching and waiting. When one end of the piano came to a temporary rest on the upper landing, she breathed an audible sigh of relief.

Ten minutes later, the instrument was safely in place, against one wall of the upstairs parlor. In spite of the fact that all four of the muscular young laborers were emitting a rich aroma of perspiration, she shook each one's hand, congratulating them for exceptional effort, and thanking them profusely for their service.

Wilma came into the room and said, cheerfully, "Oh, you don't have to thank any of them, dear. They're all family." She pinched the cheek of the youngest-looking one, embarrassing him, and said, "But I'll thank them anyway."

Lillian asked if she could offer them something for their services. Wilma said, "Don't be silly. I've been doing favors for these rascals since they were in diapers. They owe me."

The four young men all grinned. One of them said, "See you later, Auntie." Down the stairs they went, the steps reverberating beneath their work shoes.

She shouted after them, "Tell your mother I'll have some preserves ready for her on the weekend."

Lillian said, "Are they all from the same family? They look like they're practically the same age."

"Those four? They're all nine months apart," Wilma replied with a twinkle in her eye.

Chapter 19

The morning began uneventfully enough. Michael Morgan-Houseman arrived early, as usual. As he consumed his first cup of coffee, he turned the pages of the financial section of the morning paper. He took satisfaction that the equities in which he was heavily invested were still going up. He went to the stock ticker and read the tape for three or four minutes. There was nothing exceptional to note.

But an hour later, the phones began to ring. And they continued to ring, all morning long. His clients were calling to ask whether their stocks were still good to hold, or whether they should be thinking of selling. Neither he nor his sales staff had heard questions like that from clients in a good long while. For weeks — months — customers had wanted to buy, not sell. They had feared being left behind, getting caught paying too much for equities whose values appeared to be heading for the moon.

At first, he thought it was only natural there should be some skittishness, given the fact that some of these investors had not experienced a down market for very long time. In addition, there were no doubt clients out there who had ridden the market up. They were ready to take some profits, regardless how high their stocks might continue to rise once they got out. So, he instructed his brokers to execute the trades as the requests came in.

But the requests, when they started coming, were all to sell. And the calls became increasingly urgent. He went back to the ticker and read the tape again. Something had changed. The markets were trending down. For the first time in recent memory, prices were falling. And, they were falling fast. It was obvious to him that people were selling out, and buyers were scarce.

He returned to his office and closed the door. Sitting at his large mahogany desk, he tried to calm himself. He was tempted to pull a bottle from his bottom right desk drawer. But it was still early in the day. And, besides, he wanted to be sharp. He needed a clear, unimpaired mind.

He waited, not exactly sure for what. Beyond his office door, out in the bull pen, where transactions were executed, he heard a rising clamor. His brokers appeared to be shouting. That, he thought, was extremely unprofessional. He decided to calm things down. He went back out. The phones would not stop. And his clerks, impatient — almost panicky — were actually yelling into their phones. "Calm down! Just relax! Everything is under control! We'll get you into a sell position! Try to be rational about this!"

But the brokers weren't sounding rational themselves.

He went back to the ticker tape, watching the numbers cascade downward. His twelve hot-as-a-rocket companies were faltering. How could that happen? They had shot up for weeks and weeks. Furthermore, how could he deal with their going down? He was heavily leveraged, and had far too little in liquid assets to buy himself clear.

He began talking to the ticker tape machine, as if it could hear him: "This is temporary. This happens in the market. The trend is undergoing a correction. People are taking profits. That's their privilege. We always told them they could sell whenever it was in their best interests. By the end of the session, things will have turned around."

But the market did not turn. It went down, like a gangster in a cement suit, trying to tread water.

One of his brokers came running across the floor, toward him. The frantic young man said, "What shall we do? Can we stop taking sell orders? Can we tell them trading is temporarily suspended?"

Michael Morgan-Houseman said, in a voice so calm he wondered if it were his own, "No. Give them what they want. And, as you do, assure them that the market is about to turn upward again. Ask them if they really want to miss the next big climb."

The broker looked dubiously at his employer, but then nodded and raced back to his desk, where the phone had been ringing nonstop ever since he'd left his post.

All day the news was bad. At eleven-thirty, Morgan-Houseman closeted himself in his inner office and locked the door. He turned on the radio and listened, as his legs turned to jelly and his brain to mush, to the unending reports of panic selling on Wall Street. The bear market had created a psychology and a momentum of its own, and was not being slowed. It appeared there was no stopping it.

Instead of going out for lunch, he stayed at his desk, where he finally did pull out the bottle of brandy. Still, he wanted to be certain he could think with reasonable clarity. So, he set it on the desktop, unopened, where he studied it while thinking about what he might do, just in the rare, unlikely, unthinkable, surely-never-to happen circumstance that he would have to make good on his unsecured financial commitments.

He knew his bank accounts were considerable, but if this run continued, they would be wiped out. He wondered what his mansion might be worth. He wondered whether, in the event he actually had to consider selling it, a buyer could be found quickly enough to give him what he'd need from the sale.

He was fully aware that he could not sell the elegant house for enough to make up the difference.

Anyway, what was the point of speculating about it? The market was going to turn. There was nothing different about the companies whose stocks had been so valuable the day before, that should be making them less appealing today. All of this was purely irrational, stupid behavior. Why couldn't people see that? It was their hard earned money, for god's sake. Why wouldn't they want to keep their stocks from becoming worthless?

At last, an eternity of chaos later, the market closed in New York and the ticker tape machine fell silent. But the phones did not. He made a bold decision. He walked out into the bull pen and instructed each of his brokers to begin answering phone calls with this message: "The market in New York is closed. So are we. We'll take your calls tomorrow."

His brokers seemed relieved with this directive.

IN THE FRONT PARLOR of his mansion on Franklin Avenue, Michael Morgan-Houseman sat in the dark, watching the flames leap up in the fireplace. He took no comfort from them. He was on the edge of panic. But he refused to let himself quite go there. He poured himself a brandy, then downed it quickly. He slumped lower into his chair and, for the tenth time since noon, did the arithmetic in his head. The numbers always came out the same.

For one fleeting moment, he thought, *I wonder if that church over on Anderson Avenue would consider giving my money back. Just temporarily*. But he dismissed the idea as quickly as it came into his head. Come hell or high water, he was not going to disturb the legacy he was creating for his son. And, besides, there was no way he could legally do so. The funds had been transferred, fully and finally. They were now beyond his reach. He had seen to that himself.

An hour later, with three empty brandy bottles littering the carpet before him, he fell into a stupor. When, much later, the embers in the fireplace burned themselves out, he was not aware of it.

WHEN DANIEL STEPPED into the pulpit at St. Michael Church, he faced a congregation full of uncertainty. He knew most of his congregation had no money in the stock market, although a few surely did. But, he also knew there was growing unease in the city about what the bear market in New York might do to their way of life. He, himself, had had great misgivings about some of the aspects of what many had taken to calling the "Roaring Twenties." As far as he was concerned, there had come to be entirely too much roar in them.

He had adopted the astute practice of beginning his sermon preparation on the previous Monday, selecting and studying the Scripture text early in the week, and then letting it "incubate," inside his heart and brain, all week long. On Monday he had decided he would use as his preaching text Psalm 46, the one appointed for Reformation Sunday. It had seemed astonishing to him, as the events of the week had unfolded, just how appropriate those words became.

"God is our refuge and strength," he read solemnly. "A very present help in trouble. Therefore, we will not fear, though the earth be moved, and though the mountains be toppled into the depths of the sea."

Was it his imagination, or was the chapel even fuller than normal today? He could not tell.

"Friends, these words inspired our father in the faith, blessed Martin Luther, in his time of darkest need. They became the basis for his great Reformation hymn, 'A Mighty Fortress Is Our God.' Read Psalm 46 for yourself, and think about the words in this hymn."

He looked to the end of the front pew on the piano side. He was still getting used to the fact that Elsa Engelhardt was no longer sitting there, but rather Lillian Gardner. She looked back at him, with an expression that seemed to say, *Yes, the hymn is ready to go. So, what else do you have to say?*

He glanced at his manuscript, but decided not to use it. "Nobody knows what will happen on Wall Street. A few are predicting that, when the markets reopen tomorrow, it will go right back up to where it was last Wednesday. And many in our community hope that's what happens. But, for people of faith, the stock market is never the place to put one's confidence."

He glanced at the open Bible lying on the reading stand. "*God,*" he said, giving the divine name extra emphasis, "*God* is our refuge and strength. It is God who surrounds us with his holy angels, the heavenly messengers who remind us constantly of his unfailing promises."

Suddenly an image crept into his mind. The multi-millionaire, Michael Morgan-Houseman, was surely a troubled man today. What sort of refuge was he finding? He wondered whether he ought to phone him. Perhaps tomorrow he would.

He said, "Martin Luther grew up in a church that encouraged people to put their faith and hope in a corrupt empire. I hate to sound too harsh toward another branch of the Christian church family, but it's the truth. Luther was angry about what was going on in his own church and, if I may beg your indulgence for what I'm about to say, he raised holy hell about it."

There were some nodding heads.

"It's the promises of God, always good, and always dependable, that provide the refuge and strength we need in stormy times. Not false promises, about how you can buy a guarantee of God's love. Not success in business. And not a rising stock market."

MICHAEL MORGAN-HOUSEMAN sat in his office, staring out the window at the contours of the sleek, obelisk-like Foshay Tower. It occurred to him that Wilbur Foshay had never responded to his proposal that the Morgan-Houseman firm take on his portfolio. On this grim Monday morning, the financier couldn't decide whether that had been a bad thing or a lucky circumstance. He wondered what Foshay's portfolio was worth now, in the midst of an unrelenting five-day-long bear market.

He studied the stair-step pyramid atop the new monument, just blocks away, and remembered the festive launch that Foshay had given to his new building just over two months ago. Morgan-Houseman himself had stood in the courtyard with the dignitaries and listened to the optimistic speeches. He'd taken the elevator to the observation balcony, from which he'd seen his city as few ever had before.

He wondered if he should have accepted the opportunity to move his offices over there. When the invitation had come, along with the proposed rent schedule, he'd dismissed the idea out of hand. It would have tripled the cost of his floor space to gain such an exalted overlook.

Still, Foshay had told him the invitation was open-ended. He should feel free to come to the observation balcony any time it suited his fancy. He'd only done it once.

His office door was open. He'd left it that way deliberately. He wanted to hear the ticker tape machine, the moment it started its noisy clacking. When it finally started up, he found himself frozen to his chair, dread and trepidation chewing at him. He thought to himself, *Michael, get a grip. It's Monday. It's a new week. The market has had time to cool down. Investors will see that, with prices artificially depressed, today will be a great time to buy bargains.*

But when he went to the stock ticker, and began studying the results from New York, he realized his optimism had been misplaced. It was the beginning of still another disastrous day for the stock market.

AT MID-DAY, Daniel phoned Michael Morgan-Houseman's office. The businessman had gone out. Nobody was sure when he would be back.

LILLIAN GARDNER and Wilma Shaughnessy sat facing one another, across the widow's kitchen table. They had taken to eating their meals together. Lillian had resisted at first, feeling she ought to pay her landlady something for the food, and take her turn at preparing meals. But Wilma had refused to hear of it. "Dearie," she'd said, in a voice Lillian found both charming and disarming, "you don't know how happy this old lady is to have a renter as congenial — and as trouble-free — as you are. Just let me do the cooking. Besides, I love to listen to you talk."

Wilma hadn't explained herself, but Lillian knew intuitively what she meant. The young music teacher had a witty, sometimes sardonic, always respectful way of nurturing a conversation. She refused to let things lie on the surface, but always took the conversation deeper. This noon-day was no exception.

"I suspect some of the wealthy businessmen of our city aren't breathing so easily about now," Wilma said.

"Well," Lillian replied, "given the appearance of some of the houses they've built themselves to live in, I'd say it might be good for a few of them to rethink their spending priorities."

"I always wondered what it would be like to live in one of them fancy mansions," Wilma confided. "But, when you're married to the owner of a coal delivery business, God rest his soul, that's never much of an option."

"What I want to know," Lillian said sardonically, "is exactly how many bedrooms and bathrooms and fireplaces does one family need? Who gets it when you die?"

"Well, your relatives, I guess. Or the government."

"So, why not spread some of it around while you're still here? Make a few people happy who really need it."

Wilma nodded. She buttered a piece of her own homemade bread and added a dollop of the strawberry preserves she'd cooked on her stove the previous summer. "Sort of like that rich fellow who gave all the money for your new church, then."

Lillian thought about it. "I have mixed feelings about that too, I must confess. How much money do we really need to spend on a church building?" She finished the last of her soup and lay down the spoon. "But, then, there's the selfish side of me that says, if it wasn't for that big building, there wouldn't be a wonderful new pipe organ coming. Which I can hardly wait to get my hands on."

NO ONE HAD STOPPED HIM when he entered the elevator carrying his brown paper bag. As he rode the car to the observation floor, those around him guessed, from what was on his breath, what was also in the bag. But it was not their job to enforce the increasingly-ignored Prohibition law, so nobody paid much attention.

Standing on the balcony, he admired the panoply before him. The clock on the sun-washed city hall tower read three seventeen. Beyond it were the mills that had made the Washburn, Crosby and Pillsbury families wealthy, along with the city itself. He studied the span of the Hennepin Avenue bridge, and the Mississippi River, slicing through the middle of the expanding city. He traced its progress south, past the university campus. He thought he made out the roofline of Fairview Hospital, where his son had died.

He felt a wave of melancholy. A swig from the bottle inside the brown bag failed to dispel it. He took another. In his mind he saw five-year-old Michael's face. He saw him running toward him. Or was he running toward his nanny instead? Where in hell was that goddam nanny, anyway? Where had she run off to after the accident? He'd never paid her for her last half month's wages. How could he? She'd disappeared. And why should he pay her, anyway? She'd caused the death of his only child. Goddam nanny! Why hadn't she come back and faced him like a man?

His mind went back to the day the news had come of Michael's accident. He would have learned it sooner, except that he'd been pleasuring himself, behind a locked office door, with that Molly Somebody-or-other. What the devil was her name? He'd completely forgotten it. And what had ever happened to her? She'd just sort of disappeared. He'd never paid her for her last month, either.

What was wrong with these women, running away like that?

Far below, he saw the roofline of the building where his offices were located. He knew the markets were still open, and that the ticker tape was still clacking away. *Bad news, bad news, bad news, bad news, bad new*s. That was all that seemed to come from that impudent little machine. Yesterday had been Bad News Monday. And today was Bad News Tuesday. The idiots! Why were they selling? They were complete idiots, all of them!

He tipped the bottle to his lips, emptying it. He dropped it over the side. It seemed to float, carefree, down into the garden twenty-five floors below. That was what he needed now. To be carefree. To float.

He climbed up onto the railing and spread his arms, as far apart as he was able. He felt like an eagle. He leaned forward. And, suddenly, he was flying.

Chapter 20

It was a somber gathering. Members of the church council seemed to have little to talk about. When Adam Engelhardt called the meeting to order, he said, "I'd ordinarily ask the pastor to begin with prayer. But, if it's acceptable to everyone, I'd like to offer one of my own."

There was no dissent. Daniel, who had been consulted in advance, nodded his own approval.

Adam began, "Almighty God, we are your humble servants. Our times are in your hands. Keep us mindful of that truth, those of us who are gathered in this place to do the work of this congregation. Protect us with your holy angels, and give us the mind and spirit of Christ our Lord. Amen"

There was a pause, before Adam, in his role as council chairman, began to speak. He said, "As you know, this is a special meeting. There are three items on the agenda, and three only. For the first, I defer to Pastor Jonas."

Daniel looked around the table. These were all his friends, and he was not feeling particularly insecure. Nevertheless, he was mindful of the fact that there had seldom, if ever, been a meeting of this group when such weighty matters were lying on the table.

He cleared his throat and said, "There have been some questions raised — quite a few questions, in fact — by some members of our congregation about my decision, ten days ago, to officiate at the funeral for this congregation's major benefactor." None of this was news to anyone. But Daniel wasn't sure what the members of his council really thought about what he had done.

"Since the service was held at a funeral chapel, and not in our church building, you might think what I did might not be of any special interest to any of our members. Of course, the difficulty arises from the fact that Mr. Morgan-Houseman ended his own life. And some of our members have taken offense from the fact that I consented to conduct the funeral, and the graveside service, for a person who died while deliberately breaking one of the Ten Commandments."

He could not read their faces. He continued, "I have even been accused of compromising my Christian convictions, by doing one last favor for a wealthy man, supposedly only because had previously given this congregation several million dollars."

He took a deep breath. He realized that, if any of the membership had any inkling that it had been Michael Morgan-Houseman who had gotten Molly Lundgren pregnant, the grumblings might instead have become an uproar. But, evidently there had only been two families in the congregation who had learned of it.

He said, "I want to assure the members of our council — and, in the next news bulletin we send to our members, I will also want to assure all of them — that I had one motivation, and one motivation only, when I agreed to officiate. It was compassion. It was the same compassion I felt when I sat with this gentleman for nine days, over at Fairview Hospital, while his son was dying. And, gentlemen, if the situation should arise again in similar circumstances, I would do the same thing a second time."

His council members were hanging on his words.

"I do not believe," Daniel continued, "that it is our business to consign people either to heaven or to hell. I have no idea what was going through Mr. Morgan-Houseman's mind when he jumped from the top of the tallest building in our city." Well, he realized, he had a pretty good idea what it might have been. "Whatever it was," he said, "his destiny is in God's hands, not mine. And I have no interest in presuming to read God's mind."

He said, "If we'd buried him in sacred ground, some might have argued we had committed sacrilege. Of course, he was buried at Lakewood Cemetery, not in a parish churchyard. Had it been attempted in the latter, the cemetery board would probably have forbidden it." His mind went back to the tiny Lutheran cemetery in rural Ohio, where his grandparents were buried, a graveyard that completely surrounded the tidy red brick building. He knew that no member whose life ended in suicide had ever been permitted to be interred there.

There were other items on the agenda. He sensed he'd spoken long enough. He concluded, "Some of you may or may not be aware that there are four families who have decided to leave St. Michael and All Angels Church because of this. I'm sorry to have to report that. But I'm not sorry for what I did."

Members of the council were nodding in silent affirmation.

Adam asked, "Are there any questions for the pastor about this?" There were none. The chairman said, "We turn, then, to the question of our current building program. I'm going to ask the chairman of our building and property committee to speak to us about this." He looked across the table, where Andy Scheidt was shifting uncomfortably in his chair.

The young carpenter said, "I'm hearing some questions being raised in the congregation about our new building." He cleared his throat. "The argument seems to be that, we're spending a lot of money on a very expensive project, while some of us are in danger of losing our jobs, what with the economic mess we're all in right now. To say nothing of the increasing number of unemployed people out there in the city who aren't even our members."

"What are these people proposing we do?" asked Jake Bauer. "Stop construction and shut it down? The walls are nearly up now."

Andy replied, "Some of them think it doesn't look good for us to be spending all this money on a church that's going to be too big for our members anyway, once it's finished."

Fred Stumpf jumped in. "The way this congregation is growing, I'd say that new building might be just about the right size by the time we get it dedicated." He looked at Daniel and said, "How many do we have coming to the three services now, Pastor?"

"Almost two-hundred-twenty-five. There simply aren't seats for more than that."

"And how many did we have last spring?"

"Well, before we went to three services, there were around one-hundred-fifty."

Fred said, "Let's do the arithmetic. By next spring, we may have three-hundred. Assuming we want to add a fourth service. "

"Of course, that assumes the pastor would want to do worship four times on a Sunday," Will Langholz interjected.

"I've been considering adding a Sunday evening service, at least until the new building is ready," Daniel said. "That is, if I can talk Lillian Gardner into it — and my wife."

There was laughter.

"So, back to my point then," Fred said. "Our congregation needs this building. Size isn't the issue. And, if you're going to build big, you have to pay for it."

Adam said, "Andy, are people uncomfortable that we have all this money in the bank right now?"

"Well, I guess that's some of it. People don't seem to understand that those are designated funds. We have to spend them for their intended purpose. And, since they were a bequest, it isn't really costing the congregation anything."

"Besides," said George Kleinhans, "look at all the people we're keeping employed by keeping the project going. If we stopped now, we'd just be adding to the number of people without jobs."

Daniel asked to be recognized. He said, "I think we should be sensitive, however, to the concerns of those who worry about so many people being thrown out of work. And the problem is likely to get a lot worse before it gets better. I think there are ways this congregation could respond to that."

"Such as … ?" George prompted.

"Such as a meal program for hungry people. And a food shelf for those who can't buy groceries. And even providing a temporary place for people to sleep, in our new parish hall. When we get it finished."

"Sounds like a lot of new projects," said Andy. He hastened to add, "Not that any of them aren't excellent ideas. But we'd really have to get some help to do all that."

"Well," said Daniel, looking at the carpenter who had once been his employer, "we now have six-hundred members. I'd imagine we could find some ready helpers. Maybe we could begin with the ones who are raising the concerns we've been discussing."

The members of the council looked at one another. It seemed like a reasonable idea.

Adam said, "I sense there isn't a need to take a vote on any of this. We're all in pretty solid agreement that the building project should proceed." He turned to the pastor and said, "Maybe when you write to the congregation about the funeral service, you could explain some of this also."

Daniel nodded.

Adam continued, "That brings us to the third and final item on the agenda. And, for this one, I've asked Pastor Jonas to leave the room. I think he, and we, would be more comfortable if we handle it that way."

As Daniel pushed back his chair and got up, the other council members looked on in puzzlement. What could be so sensitive that the pastor couldn't stay to hear about it?

When he was gone, Adam said, "We've just had two tough topics to chew on. This last one may seem the toughest one of all to some of you. Because it could require us to spend some of our own money."

Immediately he had everyone's attention.

"It wasn't long ago that we began to salary our pastor full-time. As we should have done. And, we've been paying full salary for the past two months for our new music director … "

"If you can call what we give her a full salary," said Andy, sardonically.

"That will get better in time, if I have anything to say about it," Adam cut back in. "The point is, we've added two new financial obligations recently. Of course, with a growing membership, our contributions are going up. Or, at least, they have been. We have to be hopeful about the markets and all. And, believe me, I'm as concerned about that, with my own business, as anybody else. But, to get to the point, things are changing for our pastor and his family."

"There's just the two of them," said Fred.

"Well, so far," said Adam. "But sometime next spring, as it happens, they're going to be outgrowing that little apartment up above my print shop. So, I think it's time we began discussing plans for a parsonage for the three of them ... "

DAVID ENGELHARDT turned off the gravel county road, and steered his father's Ford along the lane toward the farm buildings in the distance. As he did so, he reached over to where Molly was seated and affectionately squeezed the back of her neck. "Good navigating," he said. "We didn't make any wrong turns, and it looks like we're right on time."

She patted his knee and said, "I know it's been a while since I've been home, but didn't you think I could remember how to find my own farm?"

"I'm just giving you the business," he said. Then he exhaled heavily and said, "Hope your folks like me."

"Couldn't you tell at the state fair?"

"I think maybe your mother liked me, a little anyway. Your dad? Boy, I'm really not so sure about him."

"He's just a gruff old Swede. It takes a little time to get him warmed up. Don't worry. We've got the whole day to work on him."

He pulled up in front of the white frame farmhouse with its long front porch. Smoke was coming from the kitchen chimney, rising into the chill, gray November sky. As he climbed down and headed around to Molly's side, chickens scattered around his feet. A black and white dog came racing toward him, from the nearby barn, barking welcome or warning, David wasn't sure which.

As he opened Molly's door, she said, "Don't worry about Roscoe. He's harmless. But he may try jumping up on you. Be careful."

The dog came bounding toward them, then slowed, wagged his tail energetically, and studied the scene. He seemed confused about which of the two to assault. He chose Molly. She grasped his paws, trying to keep him from depositing straw and chicken droppings on the top half of her best coat. As she did so, David stroked the animal's head and ears.

Roscoe led the way up the porch steps, his "yarf, yarf, yarf" signaling to the family waiting inside that their guests had finally arrived.

Betsy and Joanna Lundgren were both waiting to greet them when the door opened. "They're here! They're here!" Joanna shrieked joyfully, running away into the kitchen.

Betsy said, "How was your trip? Aren't we lucky it didn't snow? Are you hungry?"

David wasn't sure to which question he ought to respond. It didn't matter, because Molly spoke for both of them. "We had a very nice trip. Did you see the new car we came in?"

Betsy pushed past them, to poke her head out the door and take an admiring look at the shiny new Ford with which David's father had entrusted him for the day.

Molly's mother came into the entryway. She wore a patterned apron over a dark blue dress and smelled of roast goose. "Welcome, welcome," she said, looking at David. Turning to her daughter, she said, "We're so happy you've come home."

"Only for Thanksgiving day, Mama."

"Oh, I don't care. I'm just so happy you've come."

Molly showed David where to put their coats. Then she took him into the parlor, where they sat down and tried to catch their breath. Joanna came in as well, but Betsy came after her, saying, "We have to set the table. If we don't, we have to wash the dishes. So come on. *Come on!*"

Without getting the first word out of her mouth, Joanna retreated with her sister.

As they sat on the upholstered love seat, David said, "I'll bet you left a lot of memories here."

"All good memories," she said with contentment.

"Do you ever wish you hadn't left?"

As soon as the words were out of his mouth, he worried they might stir ugly memories in her. But she said, without hesitating, "No. Because if I hadn't, I would never have met my two best friends."

"Namely?"

"Well, Rosetta, obviously."

"Obviously. And … ?"

"Oh, I don't know," she said with a coy smirk. "Let's see. Your brother Jonathan, I think."

"Jonathan, in your *dreams!*" he whispered in mock anger. He wrapped his arms around her in a playful bear hug.

At precisely that instant, Martin Lundgren appeared at the parlor door. When David realized they had company, he straightened up, sending a glance toward Molly's younger brother that suggested this was ordinary behavior for guests in someone else's parlor on Thanksgiving day.

"We're ready to sit down," Martin said, as seriously as he could. He flashed a grin at David, and then disappeared.

"Well, I'd say things are off to a pretty good start," said David, getting up and offering her his hand. "Do you suppose he'll blab that all over the house?"

"Martin? Oh, probably not. Not if you slip him a quarter, or maybe a half-dollar."

He found himself fishing in his pocket for coins, before he noticed she was dissolving in silent mirth.

Chapter 21

"Your mother is an excellent cook," said David, walking toward the barn with Forrest Lundgren.

The oldest of the six children, Forrest was also the quietest. Stocky and well-muscled, he had an almost sullen demeanor about him, armor that Molly had told David would fall away once you got him into conversation. So, David was working at it. But so far it had been a monologue.

They reached the barn. Forrest pushed the heavy sliding door open. Inside, the rich smells of hay and animal manure filled their nostrils. "We milk thirty cows," he said. "Plus, there's the hogs, the sheep, some chickens. And the field crops. Keeps us busy."

David said, "So, what time do you get going in the morning?"

"Dad and I get up around four."

"Ouch," David said.

"City boy," Forrest said, chuckling. He led the way, out the other end of the barn, toward the hog shed, then past the chicken coop and into the machinery shed. For David it was a perilous journey. Unlike the farmer's son, who'd strapped on his work boots, he was wearing the same pair of shoes he ordinarily wore to Sunday worship. And there were nasty looking piles of barnyard refuse everywhere they went. As he navigated the obstacle course, he caught sight of the smirk on Forrest's face. Clearly, his predicament had become a source of great amusement.

As they were heading back to the farmhouse, the young farmer said, "Let me ask you something."

"What's that?"

"What are your intentions toward my sister?"

David was caught off guard. "What do you mean?"

"How good a friend of hers are you?"

"Well, quite good, actually."

"You planning to marry her?"

"I …" Nobody had ever asked him that before.

"Because, if you aren't, I don't want to have you messin' around with her. Okay?"

"I have nothing but the highest respect for Molly."

"Because, if you get messin' with her, and get her pregnant, I might just come after you and mess *you* up a little bit."

ALL THE WAY BACK to Minneapolis, David debated whether he should tell Molly what Forrest had said to him. He decided not to mention it. But her burly older brother's warning kept chewing at him. Enough so, that, when he came home for Christmas vacation, during one of their walks around frozen-solid Powderhorn Lake, he asked her if she would marry him. She said she would, after he finished college, if her father gave his consent.

David was relieved she hadn't stipulated that he get Forrest's permission as well.

LILLIAN GARDNER opened the cardboard container and pulled out the book she had ordered. She'd read in the *Lutheran Standard* that, with the coming merger of the Ohio Synod with three other Lutheran groups, there would be a new hymnal to help cement the union. She was holding a copy in her hands. Turning the pages of the *American Lutheran Hymnal*, she savored the new-book smell and looked for favorite hymns, as well as new ones she could begin to learn.

Her worn, leather-bound copy of *Evangelical Lutheran Hymnal*, a confirmation gift from her parents, had borne the imprint "Lutheran Book Concern, Columbus, Ohio." This new volume was also published in Columbus, but the Ohio Synod publisher had faded into history. Although still housed in the same building, the new firm carried the name formerly used by the Iowa Synod — "The Wartburg Press."

She'd heard some rumblings, in correspondence from Ohio, in letters to the editor of the *Lutheran Standard*, and through conversations with Pastor Jonas, to the effect that church leaders in both of the two largest combining synods felt they were getting shortchanged. Iowa had to give up their publishing house and headquarters, along with the name of their church magazine. But the new church was keeping the name of their publishing house, and Iowans had the assurance their seminary in Dubuque, Iowa, would be allowed to continue. At least, for now.

The Ohio Synod people were grousing about the fact that there would be two seminaries in the new church, not just one — theirs. How, they wondered aloud, could you have a common theological position when you had two seminaries? To make things worse, in Dubuque, classes were still being taught in German. When were these people planning to join the twentieth century? And, topping everything, the president of the Iowa Synod had insisted on language in the statement of doctrinal affirmations for the new American Lutheran Church that was not what Ohio Synod people would have asked for. So, did that mean Iowa was really getting the last word?

Lillian didn't have the answers. She only knew that, if a merger was like a marriage, as people kept saying, then there were bound to be fights and disappointments. Her own parents' experience convinced her of that. And that made her wonder whether staying single might not just keep things a whole lot simpler.

She opened the new hymn book, set it on the music rack, and began playing through the Advent hymns. The harmonies floated out the door and down the stairs, to where Wilma Shaughnessy was finishing supper preparations. When she called from the foot of the stairs, the piano fell silent.

It was Lillian's turn to offer the table blessing. In words that took her back to her childhood on the farm in Crawford County, Ohio, she prayed, "Heavenly Father, bless this food, to your glory and our good." Then she added a sentence she'd heard Pastor Jonas use, especially since the stock market crash: "And keep us mindful of the needs of those who are less fortunate than are we. Through Jesus Christ, our Lord. Amen."

Wilma crossed herself and said, "I like your Lutheran prayers. They're not so terribly different from our Catholic ones."

Lillian sighed. "I rather thought these prayers might all have come from the same place, once upon a time."

"Oh, you think so? Well, then that would certainly make it easier for God not to have to sort them out, one from the other."

In spite of herself, Lillian laughed out loud.

Wilma ladled out two servings of the main course, and set one before Lillian. She said, "Things are getting pretty serious, with the workers, you know."

Lillian lifted a forkful of Irish stew to her mouth, considering the truth of what she'd just heard. Her family in Ohio had been writing to her about unemployment and unrest in Toledo and Cleveland. Every time she received a letter, more people had lost their jobs. Factories were closing, and businesses were having a harder time selling their goods and paying their employees.

Wilma continued, "My sister's boys — you remember them four strappin' lads who came and moved the piano that time —"

"I remember them perfectly well," Lillian replied. "What about them?"

"Well, they were working over on the east side of St. Paul, in the factory, don't you know. And every one of them, one after another, has lost his job. Now they're all four looking for something to do."

"Do they have families to support?"

"Oh, merciful St. Patrick, no! And, under the circumstances, that's the lucky part, I guess. They all live at home with their mother and dad. Eddie's with the railroad. Still has his job, saints be praised. But that's four extra mouths to feed, and you saw the size of them lads. They don't just nibble, come mealtime. They all four used to help with the expenses. No more. It makes it hard."

Lillian nodded. Her eyes indicated she was sympathetic.

"The worst of it is," Wilma said, "young fellows like that are going to get restless. They have nothing to do but wander the streets, and maybe start mixing it up. Of course, they're all good, God-fearing boys. But, you know what they say about idle hands."

Lillian knew what they said.

"What I want to know," Wilma continued, "is how some of them families will manage when nobody at all is bringing home a week's wage. That's when it's going to start getting dangerous."

"How dangerous?"

"Well, there's even talk here in Minneapolis about the laboring folk going out on strike. They want the government to do something. And you know, we might even get a socialist governor in the next election. That Floyd Olson fella is their favorite, you know, and they even say he might turn out to be a Communist or something."

"Well, do we really know that about Mr. Olson?"

"Of course, I don't know that personally. But you hear a lot of people say it."

"You hear people say a lot of things, Wilma. We shouldn't believe everything we hear."

"No, I suppose not."

"For example, I read in the morning *Tribune* that they might have to auction off that new skyscraper."

"The Foshay Tower? It's not six months old!" Wilma wiped the crumbs from her mouth. "But, they say Mr. Foshay has lost all his money now." She thought about what she'd just said. "Of course, I can't prove that."

"Just think about how foolish a rumor like that really is," Lillian said. "Nobody has any money, and they're supposedly going to auction off a skyscraper? Why would they waste their time with an auction? Who would buy it?"

DAVID ENGELHARDT CAME HOME for spring break. Even though he'd taken to returning every weekend since Christmas, to help out at the print shop, this time he had nearly a week at home. During one of the rare moments when he was able to pry him away from Molly, Adam sat down in the front parlor with his younger son and said, "Are you going to survive one more year?"

"At the university? Sure."

"I meant, until you'll be free to marry Molly. It's turning out to be a long wait for the two of you."

David sighed, with a combination of resignation and contentment. "Yes. It's getting to be a pretty long time. But it's worth the wait, Dad." He looked at his father, thinking. Then he said, "You know, Molly says I have to ask her father for permission to marry her."

"That sounds appropriate."

"But it occurs to me, I've never really asked *you*."

"For *my* permission?"

"Well, yeah."

"Believe me, David, if I had any objection, you'd have heard about it long before now." He stroked his chin, thinking. "What does your mother say?"

"I haven't really asked her, in so many words."

"What do you *think* she'd say?"

"She'd say, 'Ask your father.'"

They both laughed.

Adam said, "I'm glad St. Paul Luther is only a two-year program and you're already finished there."

"Why is that?"

"Well, for one thing, the school is almost out of money."

"That place has always been run on a shoestring."

"It's a lot worse now," Adam said. "Pastor Jonas tells me both the college and seminary are in pretty bad shape. People are losing their jobs, and it's getting really hard for some of the students to pay the tuition and the fees. Plus — and you might find this hard to believe, David — some of the professors are even talking about moving into the same dorm rooms the students live in. Maybe as soon as next term."

"Why would they do that?"

"Because the college can't pay their salaries. So they can't pay their rent. I guess the school thinks they should just teach out of the goodness of their hearts."

David said, "Well, it's too bad what's happening over there. This depression is getting to be a little scary. Some of my classmates at the university are talking about dropping out, too."

"I suppose you've thought about that, especially since Molly has agreed to marry you."

"Well, I'm determined to finish." He looked uncertainly at his father. "That is, if you can still afford to send me back next fall."

"We'll find a way to do it, David. If we have to move heaven and earth, we'll find a way."

ON THE TWENTY-SIXTH DAY OF MAY, in the lobby of Minneapolis City Hall, an auction was held, for the announced purpose of selling the Foshay Tower. The great public space was packed with reporters and curious citizens. But there were no bids offered.

One week later, Daniel and Rosetta, along with their first-born, Hannah Ruth, moved from the apartment above the print shop, into the congregation's newly-purchased parsonage. The substantial two-story home, a block north of St. Michael Church on the other side of Anderson Avenue, was encased in white wooden siding, with red brick facing up to the first-level windows. It had come on the market at Christmastime, when a local merchant, whose business was beginning to fail, saw the handwriting on the wall and sold the house before he was faced with a mortgage in default.

Even though the dwelling had been offered at a distressed price, there had been no funds in the congregation's budget with which to purchase the home. But the whirlwind campaign to secure the needed funds had been an easy sell for members of the church council. The fact that the pastor's wife was due to give birth sometime during March had convinced members of the congregation that it was past time to find a house for them. The entire amount needed was in hand by the time Rosetta Jonas gave birth to Hannah Ruth.

THE DAY THE ROOF WAS FINISHED on St. Michael Church's new building, Daniel received a letter from his parents. They explained that the members of Grace Lutheran Church in Fremont, Ohio, had decided to stop construction on their ambitious new worship center. They had put a roof on their new nave, but then decided to leave it an empty shell — until the economy improved. Their three-story parish house had been completed, and it included a large assembly room, where they would worship. At least for now.

Chapter 22

In the middle of July, Daniel took a streetcar to Lake Street, then changed to another. He was heading toward an apartment complex, where an elderly member was waiting to receive home communion. As the trolley rolled along, he absently watched the storefronts passing him by. Here and there he saw a shuttered shop. That would not have been part of the scene just one year ago.

Suddenly his eye caught sight of a familiar building. His heart leaped into his throat. The sign was still painted on the glass: Pavelka Motors. But the showroom was empty. There was not an Oldsmobile to be seen. Nor a customer.

The streetcar stopped in front of the building, but Daniel had an appointment he needed to keep. As he continued his ride along Lake Street, he found his heart racing. What, he wondered, had become of Joe Pavelka?

On the return trip, he climbed off in front of the now-defunct dealership. Walking to the window, he peered inside. The place looked like a tomb. He tried the door, which was locked. He went into a nearby clothing store and asked the clerk, "What's become of the dealership on the corner?"

"Closed up. Went four months in a row without selling a car. They had to fire all their salesmen. Then they auctioned off the cars. Not sure about the building. Don't think they were able to sell it. You know somebody who wants to buy it?"

Daniel shook his head. "Mr. Pavelka — do you know where I can locate him?"

"Not sure. After the auction, he used to come around once in a while. But then I'm not sure what happened. He just disappeared one day and never came back. "

Daniel felt a wave of profound sadness washing over him. Not only for Joe Pavelka, but for the man's wife and children.

WILMA SHAUGHNESSY waited until the piano lesson was over and the sixth grader had come down the stairs, before ascending to the music room. The door was open. She found Lillian seated in the chair she kept next to the

152

piano bench, writing notes on the session just ended.

The landlady hesitated, then tapped softly on the door. "Was that your last pupil, dearie, or are there more to come?"

"No, that's the last one. What do you need?"

"There's a gentleman caller in the downstairs parlor. He's here to see you."

"Did he tell you his name?"

"He said 'Chrysostom.' Did I pronounce that correctly?"

"Yes. Perfectly. Is that his first or his last name?"

"I asked him that. He said Chrysostom was the whole name."

Lillian pondered it. She remembered someone having had that nickname once. But who? And where?

"Do you want him to come up, or do you want to come down?"

Just in case this was someone she didn't really know, there was no way she was going to have him come up to her private quarters. "I'll come down," she said, getting up and following Wilma into the hall.

At the foot of the stairs, she looked with puzzlement at the young man sitting on the couch. He was slim, with dark brown hair combed straight back. His dark blue suit was set off with a striped red tie. His felt hat was resting on the seat beside him.

When he saw her, he stood up and broke into a broad smile. "Hi, Lily Pad. Remember me? Chrysostom. From Capital. Remember?"

She hated it when people played with her mind. Desperately she tried to make sense of his lingo. Then it started coming together. *Chrysostom. The Bishop of Constantinople. Fourth Century. Church history class. The name means "golden voice."* But at Capital University, when she'd been at the conservatory of music, that was the nickname everyone had given to the captain of the tenor section in the Chapel Choir. Even though he was a history major, and not even a music student, everybody raved about the golden tenor voice of ...

"Luther Fischer," she said, half in a trance.

"Long time, no see. Remember those choir concerts when you'd sit in the front row and swoon over my solo parts?"

"Oh, piffle," she said, using an expression she hadn't summoned since college. "You always did have an ego three times too large," she said. But she couldn't suppress a grin.

Wilma decided it was probably safe to leave the two of them alone together. She retreated to the back of the house.

Luther stepped toward her and grasped her hands in his. "You're looking swell."

"How did you … how did you figure out where I was? And what are you doing in Minnesota? In the middle of August?"

"Sit down," he said cheerfully. "I'll tell you everything."

She took a chair across from the couch. He sat and crossed one leg over the other. "After I graduated from Capital, I decided to teach high school history. I went back to Crestline and got a job at the high school. One year was enough. The kids weren't all that interested. In the meantime, my major advisor back at college kept on me to consider a PhD in history. He said I really belonged on a college faculty somewhere. That sounded good to me. He had me all set up to do the graduate work at Ohio State. But then … "

"But then *what?*"

"But then I found out you were moving to Minneapolis. I told myself, 'Chrysostom, you can get this degree at the University of Minnesota just as well as at Ohio State.'"

"You came up here to do graduate study just because I'm living here now?"

"That's about it."

"Well, that sounds rather presumptuous, if I may say so."

"Lily Pad, that's what I like about you — you're a woman who knows her own mind, and speaks it."

"Stop trying to flatter me. Tell my why you're here."

"I already told you."

"I mean, here in my landlady's front parlor."

"Oh. Well, I just wanted you to know I've arrived. Classes start in a few weeks. I'm in an apartment over near the university."

"So, how did you get from there to here?"

"You have a wonderful streetcar system in this town. Or haven't you noticed?"

"Luther, if you think I have any … you know … romantic interest in you … in us … you're taking an enormous gamble."

"Whoever said I had such an interest."

She remembered his unsuccessful efforts at dating her during college. She'd put him off, remembering her parents' warning that romantic entanglements can ruin a young woman's career before it gets started. And, then, after graduation, she'd gone back home to teach school and play the church organ, and not heard from him again.

"Luther," she said, "is there, by any chance, a young woman in your life right now?"

"Nope. I'm footloose and fancy free."

It was just as she'd suspected. She wondered whether she could ever have a satisfying relationship with someone as jovial and half-serious as Luther "Chrysostom" Fischer. She seriously doubted it.

"I'm curious," she said. "How did you find me?"

"Nothing to it. I figured the head of the conservatory keeps track of former students. That's how I found out you'd come here, to be the music director at this brand-new congregation. And, when I got here, it was fairly easy to track you down."

"Well," she said, "I guess I should be flattered that you cared enough to look for me. And then to show up as you have."

"You always seemed special to me, Lily Pad."

She was trying to remember when he'd started using that name for her. At a reception, following one of her piano recitals at college, she thought. It was her own fault. She'd never told him not to call her that. Maybe she should have.

"I thought I'd come by on Sunday and listen to you tickle the ivories."

"I don't think you'd find that very satisfying."

"Why in the world not?"

"Well, mainly because the congregation uses an old, beat-up second-hand upright piano, that's constantly going in and out of tune. In spite of my best efforts, it's not all that musically satisfying."

"Well, then maybe I should wait until the new church building's finished. I understand you're getting a crackerjack instrument."

"It will be a Reuter. I helped to make the selection."

"You're going to be in heaven playing that."

"Yes," she said, smiling, "you might just be right about that."

"I suspect that's the real reason you moved up here to this icebox."

"It's August, Luther. Not an igloo anywhere."

"I've heard about winter around here. Blizzards to stop the traffic in its tracks. I'm curious. Do the streetcars keep running in the wintertime?"

"I lived here through last winter. They ran then."

"Great. Because I don't have a car. Yet. And I don't want to miss any of your preludes and postludes and choir anthems. Oh, and that reminds me. Could you use another tenor in your adult choir?"

How was she going to say no to an offer like that?

Wilma came to the doorway. "Lillian, would you like to have your gentleman friend stay for supper? We've plenty."

Lillian hadn't considered the possibility. But who was she to tell her landlady whom she might invite to dinner? She said, "For all we know, Mr. Fischer has other plans."

Luther stood up and said, "Thank you for the kind invitation, Mrs. Shaughnessy. I'd be delighted to join you."

AS THE CASSEROLE went around, Wilma said, "I just love having an excuse to eat in the dining room." She looked apologetically at Lillian and said, "No offense intended. You and I could eat in here anytime we wanted to, of course."

"Nonsense," said Lillian. "Why would just the two of us want to rattle around in this big room? There should be at least three."

Wilma said, "So, Mr. Fischer, you know Lillian from your college days, then?"

"That's right," he replied. "She was a music major. I wasn't. But I was in the choir, and she came to the concerts. And I love piano music, so I went to her recitals."

"So that's how you met then."

Lillian interjected, "Actually, we both grew up in the same county in Ohio. Our homes were only twelve miles apart. But we never met until college."

"Well, doesn't that beat all," Wilma exclaimed, sending around the vegetables.

"How did you meet your husband, Mrs. Shaughnessy?" Luther asked. He looked sideways at Lillian, and realized from the scowl on her face he might just have committed a faux pas.

Clearly Wilma didn't think so. "Oh, Barney, God rest his soul. Thank you for asking. Nobody's inquired about him for twenty years."

Luther stole another quick glance at Lillian, who was now rolling her eyes, as if to say, *okay. I was wrong.*

Wilma said, "I was a young lady growing up in Chicago. Some of my girlfriends were being courted by young men in the church league. It was a baseball competition between some of the Catholic parishes. They dragged me along to the games, so we could all cheer for their young men. That's where I met Barney. Later when we were engaged, his mother said to me, 'We named him Barnabas. Why won't anybody call him that?' Well, he didn't look like a Barnabas to me. He was a Barney, sure as God made Ireland green. And there he was, one day, pitching for one of the teams in the church league."

"Pretty good, was he?" Luther prodded.

"Oh, the best. He could strike 'em out like the best of them. I went to all the games after I first spotted him. But of course, I wasn't really there to see the games, just this one handsome young pitcher. And, of course, they didn't always let him pitch either."

"So, how did you meet him then?"

"Well, after each game, the young men on the team would take their girlfriends to the tavern for drinks and bragging time. Barney was there right along with the rest of them. My girlfriends went too, so I came along. He bought me a glass of beer. I hate beer, but I never told him that. I just drank it. And that was how it all started."

"Chicago's a long way from Minneapolis," Lillian interjected.

"Yes. Indeed it is. So how did we get up here? Well, Barney and his brother were working in the coal yard. And then, their cousin Nick came up to St. Paul, and got started in the coal delivery business. He did so well, he told Barney and his brother they should come up here and try doing the same. There was room for another operator on the Minneapolis side, he said. Well, his brother didn't want to leave Chicago, but Barney was ready. So the two of us came to Minneapolis. We've been here ever since."

"What about your children?" Luther asked.

Lillian shot him another disapproving glance. She knew the answer to this one.

"No children. I guess the Lord didn't want us having any." Her expression suggested she had somehow disgraced herself.

"I'll bet you turned out to be the mother every boy and girl on the block always wished they could have had," Luther said, smiling.

Wilma blushed. "Well, I guess I did have a little bit of that sort of reputation."

When Luther looked back at Lillian, she was wearing an expression that said, *okay, so I was wrong again.*

AFTER THEY HAD CLEARED and washed the dishes, put away the food, and tidied up the counters, Wilma turned to Luther and said, "So, you have a lovely tenor voice then."

"I beg your pardon?" he replied.

"In that choir you sang in. I overheard you say you were a tenor. When I was standing in the hallway."

What else did she overhear, he wondered.

"So, now that we've fed you, you have to sing for us," said Wilma, mischievously. "And, Lillian, I really think you should accompany him. In the upstairs parlor."

Lillian said, "Well, I'm not sure I've got anything appropriate in the piano bench."

"Doesn't matter," said Wilma, pulling out a drawer built into the dining room cabinetry. "Barney was a tenor, too. He sang with a men's group a long time ago. Here. See if any of these look good to you." She produced a dog-eared stack of sheet music.

"Well," said Lillian, apprehensive about what might be in the collection, but not about to get into an argument with her landlady, "let's see what we've got here. Come on." The three of them went up the stairs together.

And, for the next hour, she played and Luther sang. And Wilma swooned.

Chapter 23

The huge congregation filled the small frame chapel and spilled out onto the front lawn. There were more waiting outside than seated in the pews. Many stood peering in at the windows, whose sashes had been thrown high to give the overflow congregation access to the proceedings inside. Elsa Engelhardt, Lillian Gardner's recruit for this lone task, was seated on the piano bench, waiting to accompany the single hymn they would sing before processing into the grand new edifice next door.

Daniel stood before the congregation, made the sign of the cross and declared the invocation. He noted with satisfaction that nearly everyone present traced the same sign upon themselves. He said, "Two hymn numbers are posted. We sing the first as we leave this building, and the second as we enter the new one. Bring your hymnals along. The service will continue inside the new sanctuary."

With that, Elsa played the introduction, fully cognizant of the fact that this would be the last time the tired old piano would be used for worship. Then the congregation began to sing, in a tidal wave of song, "Now thank we all our God … !"

Kevin Krambeer, a member of the newly-formed youth group, lifted the processional cross from its stand and began moving, in front of the pastor, down the aisle. The cross had been crafted by the accomplished wood carver, John Diekhoff, a local carpenter who had recently joined the congregation. For the chancel of the new building, Diekhoff had also fashioned an elaborate wooden lectern, carved in fine detail and having the appearance of a warrior angel, whose outspread wings formed the table on which the Bible was placed.

When the cross passed each row, the worshipers turned, as they had been instructed, to face it, then followed the pastor, all of them singing the stanzas of Martin Rinkart's hymn of thanks. Out the front door of the chapel they moved, onto the sidewalk. Turning north, they heard the sound of the chapel piano, growing faint. But they persisted, now singing a capella, until they had exhausted all the stanzas.

Before the great front doors of the new stone edifice, Daniel turned to face the waiting worshipers, now crowded around the front steps, with more behind them on the sidewalk, all the way back to the curb. The police department had temporarily closed off Anderson Avenue immediately in front of the building, allowing more of the crowd to overflow out into the street.

Daniel read from Psalm 100.

Make a joyful noise to the Lord, all the earth.
Worship the Lord with gladness;
Come into his presence with singing.

Following in their printed programs, the great crowd responded:

Enter his gates with thanksgiving, and his courts with praise.
Give thanks to him, bless his name.

Then the doors were opened and, suddenly, the sound of the enormous Reuter pipe organ could be heard, introducing the great hymn in celebration of the Trinity and drawing them inside. Following the crucifer and the pastor, the gathered throng began to move, singing, "Holy, holy, holy, Lord God almighty, early in the morning our song shall rise to thee!"

As Daniel moved down the center aisle, toward the distant altar, he felt a chill race down his spine. He wondered whether the Emperor Justinian must have felt this way on the day they dedicated the great domed Church of Holy Wisdom in Constantinople, 1,500 years before.

The new nave had been designed to seat eight-hundred worshipers, more than seven times that of the chapel on the corner. As Daniel stood at his chair, on one side of the chancel, watching the congregation fill the pews, he realized there might not be an empty seat today. He also realized that, with six-hundred-fifty members, and a current Sunday attendance of around four-hundred, that was not likely to happen again soon.

Lillian Gardner had instructed the custodian to turn all the chairs in the Children's Chapel around, so that they faced away from the side altar and toward the nave. As soon as the hymn was ended and the congregation was seated, she signaled from the organ bench in the balcony to the twenty children in her cherub choir to stand. From their places in the side chapel they watched for her direction, then broke into a harmonious rendition of an Anglican anthem based on a psalm text.

I was glad, glad when they said unto me:
Let us go into the house of the Lord!

It was as if youthful angels had inhabited the nave.

Daniel went to the marble free-standing altar, faced the congregation, motioned for them to stand, and began the service. "Our help is in the name of the Lord," he said.

"Who made heaven and earth," came the unison response.

Lillian gave the tone for the congregation and the sung liturgy began. The congregation, bathed in a rich rainbow of light from the multi-colored angel windows, sang the texts of Holy Scripture which had been intoned by saints before them, throughout the Christian world for the past nineteen-hundred years.

In his sermon, Daniel reminded the congregation that the new building was God's house, not theirs, and that nothing should happen within its walls that did not glorify God. He said, "It may seem like a difficult thing to practice humility in such a grand space, but a congregation that gives itself over to pride is one that will decline and die."

He thanked the members of his steadily growing flock for bringing their friends and family to the service. He said, "Running out of seats, as we nearly have today, is a wonderful problem to have. Perhaps you could convince those whom you brought with you today to keep coming back."

There was some laughter. He added, "I'm really quite serious about that. This congregation has grown surprisingly fast. Some of you think it's because of the way the pastor preaches. Some of you think it's because the pastor is friendly, and isn't afraid to talk to strangers. Some of you think people have started coming here because of this wonderful new building, and our excellent new pipe organ, and our exceptional organist."

In the balcony, Lillian Gardner felt a surge of well-being, but made sure nobody in the senior choir, sitting behind her, noticed. The pastor said, "Well, all of those things may be true, but they're not the real reason we've grown so rapidly."

He gave the congregation a moment to try to guess what he would say. A few did, because they'd heard him say it before. "It's the Spirit of God, and nothing else, that builds a community. Those of you who learned the words from Martin Luther's *Small Catechism* know what I'm talking about. 'The Holy Spirit calls, gathers, enlightens and sanctifies the whole Christian Church on Earth.'"

After an artful pause, he said, "What's amazing about the people in this congregation is how you've opened yourselves to letting the Spirit push you — into talking about this place with friends and neighbors, inviting them here, taking them by the hand and bringing them." He said, "Most Lutherans I know are too shy to do anything like that. So, all I can conclude is, we must have a church full of imposters here today, masquerading as Lutherans." There was hearty laughter.

But, from where he sat, in the fourth pew, Adam Engelhardt thought to himself, *the Holy Spirit may very well be moving us to make all this happen, but without this pastor's skillful leadership, none of this would ever have come about.*

As the offering baskets were distributed, Lillian motioned to the adult choir to stand. With the bright light of a late September morning streaming in through the deep hued blues and reds of the great rose window behind them, they began to sing an anthem she had written and composed for the service:

Lord, your people gathered here
Lowly bend with holy fear,
Seek your Spirit's surging power
For your guidance in this hour.

The text, rendered in simple harmony, quickly expanded into a complex choral fugue.

As the Eucharistic liturgy began, one visitor was heard to whisper urgently to her neighbor, a member, "This has been a wonderful service. But now they're going to serve communion to all these people? This could take all day!" Her friend replied, "It's part of the liturgy. We do it every Sunday."

In fact, it was only the beginning of every-Sunday Eucharist, but members had been well prepared for the fact that the pattern was now changing. And, they had been coached not to get into the practice of walking out when the liturgy of the sacred meal began. The pastor had said, in a sermon not a month ago, "To do that would be to come for the salad and the vegetables, and then to go home, leaving the meat and potatoes and dessert uneaten on the table."

During the distribution, the children sang again:

Lord, I want to be a Christian, in my heart, in my heart ...
Lord, I want to be more holy ...
Lord, I want to be like Jesus ...

After they had received the sacrament, members of the adult choir began to sing the text of a hymn for the Festival day of St. Michael and All Angels. It had not made the transfer from the Ohio Synod hymnal into the American Lutheran Church's hymn book. That hadn't stopped Lillian Gardner, who liked the text, and had thought it especially fitting for this day and place.

In exquisite harmony, using a new melody Lillian had composed, they sang the words Rabanus Maurus had penned 1,100 years before:

Jesus, brightness of the Father,
Life and strength of all who live:
In the presence of the angels,
Glory to thy name we give,
And thy wondrous praise rehearse,
Singing in harmonious verse!

Daniel offered the closing prayers and then declared the benediction. Kevin Krambeer lifted the richly carved cross, on its wooden pole, high into the air and moved into the center of the chancel, ready to step down into the aisle. The great organ intoned the last eight notes of the Doxology. As the crucifer and the pastor began to move toward the door of the church, the congregation joined in singing the familiar Trinitarian text:

Praise God from whom all blessings flow!
Praise him all creatures here below!
Praise him above, ye heavenly host!
Praise Father, Son and Holy Ghost!

With less than ten seconds of silence, Lillian Gardner launched into a thunderous rendition of a glorious fugue by J.S. Bach. The music filled the nave and seemed to shake the newly-installed stained-glass windows. The dedicatory service for the amazing new building was ending. And there was a palpable sense of anticipation among the departing worshipers, whose excited conversation was now rising to the level of a roar. They were convinced they had just helped begin something extraordinary, the ending of which they could not imagine.

THE NEWLY-FORMED Women's Missionary Federation gathered in the spacious community room at St. Michael Church the following Tuesday morning. There were thirty-five who showed up. Martha Pellner and her sisters, Gretchen and Gertrude, had appointed themselves a committee of three, responsible for coordinating the serving following the meetings and seeing that refreshments were provided. They busied themselves in the adjoining kitchen, making sure that the coffee would be ready at precisely the moment the discussion was ended.

Pastor Jonas was ready with a brief Bible study and prayer. When he was finished with his presentation, he thanked the women for inviting him to launch their organization, and began to move toward the door. But the group's new president, Marjo Hummel, asked Daniel to stay for a few moments. "I think you can help us with a question that's been going around," she said.

Daniel found a chair near the front of the room and sat down. Mrs. Hummel said, "First of all, Pastor, we want you to know how impressive the service was on Sunday. It was just amazing, all of it."

He nodded, appreciating the comment. He'd felt the same way.

"I'm hearing people say ... some of the visitors, I mean .... that they might come back to worship, simply on the strength of the music and the choirs."

"Lillian Gardner really has a gift," he replied, stating what he thought was obvious.

"Oh, but that's not to say anybody wouldn't come to hear you preach!" said Margie Cornelius, hastily. A dozen voices quickly affirmed her sentiment.

"As I said in Sunday's sermon," Daniel replied, "it's not the preaching or the music that's the reason to come to worship. It's a hunger for God's promises, and openness to the Spirit's tugging at us."

"Well, of course that's all true," said Margie, "but great preaching and excellent music can't hurt." There was polite laughter.

Daniel looked at Marjo once again. He said, "I'm curious about the question you mentioned was 'going around.' Did you want to share that with me?"

"Well," the group president said, "I think Alma Feuerbringer would like to do that."

Matronly, fifty-year-old Alma, hints of gray accenting her otherwise wavy brown hair, was seated in the third row. She stood up, smiled deferentially at Daniel, cleared her throat, and said, "Pastor, there was a stranger at worship on Sunday ... "

"I dare say there may have been as many as three-hundred visitors," said Daniel.

"Well, this one was a woman, about thirty I would think, with red hair and just a few freckles. She had sort of a coarse voice, as if she might have spent a lot of her time shouting at children on a playground." Or, smoking cigarettes, she really wanted to say, but didn't. "You couldn't have missed her."

Daniel said, "She does sound unforgettable, but I'm still not sure … "

"The point is," Alma interrupted, "she came into church without a hat on her head. She was the only woman in church who did."

It was deadly silent. Daniel wracked his brain. In the great crowd he'd greeted at the front door after worship, he'd missed noticing such a person. He wondered how he could have. And, he wondered, but only for a moment, whether Alma Feuerbringer had actually taken the trouble to scan the heads of all the women in the congregation.

A polite, almost too-soft voice was heard, coming from the back row. "Excuse me. I think I know who Alma's talking about." It was Linda Dietz, an immaculately dressed 30-year-old single woman who had just recently become a member. She said, "Her name is Margaret Washington. She sat in my pew on Sunday."

Now everyone was looking at Linda. She seemed temporarily uncomfortable with all the attention focused on her, but continued, "We talked briefly in the aisle going out. Then she asked me where the ladies' room was, and disappeared. She must not have come out the front door. I think Alma's right. If you'd met her, you'd have remembered her, Pastor."

"You're pretty confident of that?"

"Oh, I'm pretty sure. She's really … well, she's not shy. And when she talks, it's … well, let's just say she doesn't hold back. She speaks her mind. I actually enjoyed talking with her, but I can see how she might offend some people."

"Well, she offended *me*," said Alma. "You don't go to worship without a hat on your head. Not if you're a woman. It just isn't done."

Daniel had not thought much about it, but now he realized that it was true. Every woman who came to worship always wore a hat. It had been true in his home congregation, and in every one where he had ever visited.

Alma said, "I'm curious, Pastor. If this Washington woman …"

"Let's call her 'Mrs. Washington,'" Daniel broke in.

"All right. If this Mrs. Washington had come through the line and shook your hand after the service, would you have said anything to her about the fact that she wasn't properly attired?"

Daniel realized he probably would not have. He tried running a detour. "Alma, this is a matter of real importance for you, isn't it?"

"Well," Alma said, almost hyperventilating, "I would think it would be for any right-thinking Christian woman."

"And why is that?"

"It's very clear. The Bible directs women to cover their heads in church. I thought we all learned that in catechism."

Daniel knew the Apostle Paul had written something about women covering their heads at worship. But he'd never spent much time meditating on it. And, as for what Lutherans learned in catechism class, he also knew that the content was usually determined by the pastor who taught the class. He had no memory of having had such a discussion with his own confirmation pastor.

"And what do you recall being taught about that in confirmation, Alma?"

"It's not the sort of thing you like to mention in polite company," Alma said.

Mildred Heins spoke up. "My confirmation pastor told me that a woman who goes to worship without covering her head is advertising to everyone that she's a woman of the evening."

There was a buzz in the room now, as the women began sharing their own views on the topic with those seated next to them.

Daniel looked at the president, who returned a perplexed look. He said, "I have a suggestion. How would it be if, at the beginning of your October meeting, I lead you in a Bible study about what the Apostle Paul says about women covering their heads at worship?"

There was immediate unanimous agreement.

"In the meantime," he said, "if anyone knows how to find Margaret Washington, please let me know. I'd be eager to have a conversation with her."

"Well, I would think you would," said Alma Feuerbringer.

Chapter 24

On the following Sunday, worship attendance was down by one-third. Daniel had steeled himself for the possibility that it might even go down by half. It seemed good to him that, not since the early months of worship in the frame chapel, had it been possible for all in attendance to worship together in the same room. And, even though there were 300 fewer in the pews today, given the exceptional acoustics in the new nave, the sound created when they sang together was quite extraordinary.

As the worshipers filed out afterwards, greeting him at the church door, he caught sight of her. Margaret Washington was standing at the back of the line, waiting to come through.

She wore a plain dress, carried no purse, and her bright red hair fell comfortably down to her shoulders. Linda Dietz had been right about the freckles. She had what Daniel thought was an attractive sprinkling of them. And, true to reports, she wore no hat.

"I'm Maggie Washington," she said, in a slightly raspy voice. She thrust her hand forward and grasped the pastor's vigorously. "Sorry I didn't say hello last Sunday. I had to see a man about a horse."

He laughed to himself. Here, he decided, was a woman who did what she wanted and said what she thought. "I'm pleased to meet you, and pleased to see you here at worship."

"Yeah. Well, I like this place. It has some dignity. People need that, you know?"

He nodded. That was certainly his philosophy.

She said, "You grow up in the Pentecostal church, you get to missing the mystery, the quiet, the elegance."

He nodded again. "Listen, Margaret ..."

"Maggie. I prefer Maggie." There was mischief in her eyes and intensity in her voice.

"Well ... Maggie ... do you have five or ten minutes to visit with me, or do you need to be on your way quickly?"

"What? No. Yes. I mean, I have time. You want to chat, let's chat."

Why did he have the feeling he'd just made a dinner date with a hungry tiger?

As they walked through the courtyard, flanked by column-borne arches on the street side, on the way toward the offices, she said, "This is one fancy layout. I can hardly believe the spread you've got here. I know, I know, they gave you the money and you had to use it this way. But, my stars, a place like this could really turn your head, if you're not careful."

They reached Daniel's office. He opened the door and let her go in first. He said, "Well, the architecture does speak of the dignity you said you like."

"I *do* like it. I like it a *lot*, I also like the Taj Mahal. But, you have to be careful, you know, so you don't give people the wrong impression." She sat down in one of the chairs on the visitors' side of Daniel's desk. He took one of the others. "I mean, there could be a lot of people out there who'd take one look at this place and decide it was just too uptown for them. You get my point? They wouldn't feel welcome."

Daniel nodded. That risk had occurred to him the day Michael Morgan-Houseman had offered to give the congregation the bequest. But he hadn't ever really confronted the problem. Until now.

"How did you find your way to St. Michael and All Angels?" Daniel asked.

"I was looking for a big church."

Daniel thought, *People look for big churches so they can get lost in them, without having to take responsibility for anything. Or, they pick big churches because it makes them feel important.* He said, "And why did you want a big church?"

"Because big churches have more resources. I want to get involved with a service project for the community, for people who are being left out. Since the stock market went smash, there are more of them out there than ever. And, I figure, a large church could support something like that."

Daniel said, "Well, Central Lutheran Church, downtown, is a lot bigger than we are."

"Too far away. I live in *this* neighborhood. I don't want to go halfway across town to church."

"If I may ask, are you married?"

"Oh, yeah. Henry brings home the bread. He's a plumber's assistant." She paused, then said dryly, "Henry's also a socialist."

"I beg your pardon?"

"Class struggle. Power to the workers. That sort of thing. Henry's a great fan of our new governor."

"Floyd B. Olson."

"Great man. Henry worships him."

"You don't actually mean 'worship.'"

"Actually, I do. Henry doesn't subscribe to the tenets of any church. He's made his passion for the labor movement his religion. I'm convinced he's prepared to die for it."

"But you're here at worship."

"Henry and I don't see eye to eye on everything. But we do agree on some things. Like, for example, the fact that people in need deserve to be helped. That's why I want to start some kind of program for them."

"How did you meet Henry?"

"At a labor rally, actually. Hit it off right away."

"So, Henry is not religious, and you grew up a Pentecostal."

"The jumpin' up and down, clappin' your hands, rollin' on the floor and talkin' weird languages variety. We just hung everything right out there on the washline. It was my diet several times a week when I was growing up. But, it gets old. You get hungry for something different, something better. I got to the point where I didn't just want to get all stirred up every time I had an encounter with God. I mean, how many times can you authentically get yourself converted, or give your heart to Jesus, for God's sake?" She watched to see if he would flinch, but he did not. "I stumbled into an Episcopal church service once in my late teens. That was really amazing. I liked it a lot."

"Why aren't you an Episcopalian then?"

"You'll laugh."

"No, I won't. Tell me."

"Because I didn't have a hat. And all of them did."

Daniel could not believe the direction the conversation had suddenly taken. "Women wear hats in this congregation, too. Perhaps you've noticed."

"Yeah, well, I'm putting St. Michael Church to the test on that score. I want to see how many weeks I can come here before somebody tells me I'm not welcome because I don't dress the right way."

"Did they do that at the Episcopal congregation?"

"Not in so many words. But I was just outclassed. In every way. It was very uncomfortable. Here, for the last two Sundays anyway, I've noticed the people are sort of on my level. Ordinary folks. Oh, they dress up for church and all that. But no pretensions. Several people talked to me both last week and today. Treated me like part of the family, almost. That was pretty impressive."

Daniel was gratified to learn that his members were doing what he'd encouraged them to do. "So, what sort of ministry did you think you might like to help get started?"

"You have a wonderful parish hall and a fabulous church kitchen. I took the tour after the dedication last Sunday. You won't be using those much on week days, I'd guess."

"Not right away," Daniel admitted.

"So, I'm thinking, this would be a great place for a soup kitchen and a shelter for homeless people. Short term, of course. They couldn't camp out here permanently."

"That would take some serious planning, and some good help from a lot of people."

"I'll bet you've got a women's group here that would be just the ticket. What would you think if I showed up at their next meeting and shared my idea?"

Daniel wondered if that wouldn't be like pouring gasoline on a fire. He found himself saying, "As it turns out, I'm supposed to lead a Bible study at the next meeting of the Women's Missionary Federation. About why women wear hats at worship."

"You're joking, right?"

"No. I'm serious."

"Of all the important stuff in the Bible, and you're talking about why women wear hats in church?"

He nodded. Suddenly it did seem a little ridiculous to him.

"Well, you can count me in!" she said. Her eyes were blazing. "I wouldn't miss that meeting for anything!"

ON THE FIRST THURSDAY of November, the women's group assembled in the parish hall at St. Michael Church. At the pastor's request, all of them had done some advance reading, of the first half of the eleventh chapter of First Corinthians. And, all of them had brought their Bibles with them.

There was no hiding the fact that Maggie Washington had also shown up. She was seated in the front row where, as it turned out, she ended up sitting by herself. Until Linda Dietz, who was feeling increasingly uncomfortable about how that looked, went to the front of the room and sat down next to her.

Daniel said, "As you will have discovered, the Apostle Paul does have some specific things to say about women covering their heads at worship."

"It doesn't actually say 'at worship,'" Maggie interjected.

Daniel's gaze went immediately to the fourth row, where the expression on Alma Feuerbringer's face seemed to say, *How rude! Interrupting a clergyman in the middle of his remarks.* For his part, Daniel decided it didn't hurt to have the monologue livened up a bit. He said to Maggie, "You're right. It doesn't say that precisely. But from the context, what would you imagine Paul might otherwise have meant?"

"They could have been praying in their homes," Maggie said.

"They probably were," Daniel replied.

"I beg your pardon?"

"That's almost certainly where they worshiped in the Corinthian congregation. In people's homes."

"So, you're saying," Maggie replied, "he's most likely talking about worship, then."

"Well, I can't imagine Paul was arguing women should cover their heads for family devotions when only their husbands were present."

Everyone, including Maggie, laughed.

Daniel said, "The question is, why did Paul want women to cover their heads at prayer, and men not to?"

"Well, a man could hardly be mistaken for a lady of the evening," said Lois Brockmeier. There was more laughter, this time more scattered.

"Is there anything in this chapter that suggests a woman who doesn't cover her head may be mistaken for a woman of the street?"

All eyes were on their Bibles. Linda Dietz said, "It sounds like women are supposed to cover their heads because they're subordinate to their husbands. And men aren't supposed to, because they are superior to their wives."

"Then why do we have this other verse, that says men and women are really subordinate to each other, and neither is greater?" Mildred Heins asked.

Daniel said, "Very good, Mildred. You spotted that." Mildred was happy for the affirmation, but her face showed she was still bewildered. The pastor continued, "Some who teach the Scriptures for their profession believe Paul wanted to keep good order in the church, so he asked women to let their husbands lead."

"That isn't it," Maggie said, cutting in. "He's arguing that it's an order of creation. God set it up that way on purpose."

Mildred wasn't finished. "But then he seems to change his mind. First he says that man should lead because he was created before woman. But later, he argues that woman gives birth to man, so neither is superior. It sounds like he can't make up his mind."

"A little bit like thinking out loud, deciding what he wants to argue as he goes along?" Daniel suggested.

"Yes, almost," said Mildred, uncertainly. "But it's in the Bible. So that can't be what's really going on."

Daniel said, "Well, it's in the Bible, but how many of you think Paul expected his letters to be part of inspired Scripture when he wrote them?" Nobody raised their hand. "Is it possible he was simply trying to help his congregation discover how to live like Christians, and he was searching for the best argument?"

"I thought God told the Apostles what they were supposed to say and do," protested Margie Cornelius.

"Well, some of them didn't always get it right, did they?" Daniel said.

"What do you mean?"

"Think about the natural leader among the original twelve, Simon Peter. He got scolded by Jesus more than once. And then he got scolded by Paul, who describes it in one of his letters. What does that tell us?"

There was confusion in the room. Maggie piped up, "I think it tells us these apostles understood the main thing — that Jesus is Lord and that he took care of our salvation. But on day-to-day issues, like how to make sense of it when applying it to situations, they had to do what we have to do — try to figure it out as you go along. And, they might not always have gotten it just right."

"So, you think Paul may not have gotten it right when he told women to cover their heads at worship?"

Maggie said, "Well, the way he changes his argument, I'd say he isn't too convincing."

"So, then, should we require women to wear hats in church or not?"

Alma Feuerbringer's mouth was already open, but she wasn't quick enough for Maggie Washington. The newcomer said, "I want to get something straight here. Paul says it's a shame for women to have short hair and men to have long hair. That's in this chapter too. But that picture of Jesus, right over there on the wall, shows Jesus with hair longer than mine." There was a confused murmur behind her. "And, Paul says women should submit to the authority of their husbands, but also to the authority of Christ."

She took a breath. "Now, here's a question for you: I believe in Christ, but my husband just may be an atheist, for all I can tell. So, should I submit to my husband or to Christ? And, if my husband isn't the final authority over me, then do I have to wear a hat to church, even though he's never in a million years likely to show up there with me?"

Alma's mouth went shut.

Daniel seemed to change the subject. He said, "How many of you think we should take that picture of Jesus down from the wall?"

No hands went up.

"How many think Paul was right about how long or short women's and men's hair should be?"

A few hands tentatively went up.

"So, maybe it's possible that what Paul asked Christians to do in his community was shaped by his culture, and not necessarily a rule that should apply at all times in every generation?"

Every head was nodding.

Then he asked, "How many believe a woman who comes to worship today, without a covering on her head, is advertising her services as a streetwalker?"

No hands went up. Daniel said, "Neither do I."

Chapter 25

The day before Thanksgiving, Rosetta told Daniel another child would be coming. The clergyman was delighted. There was plenty of room in their recently acquired parsonage for a houseful of children, he was convinced. He realized he'd never really spoken with Rosetta about how many they should think of having, altogether.

After the Thanksgiving day meal, Daniel walked the long block, along Anderson Avenue, to the church parish house. He'd promised to help serve the community meal that had been hastily planned at the last women's meeting. How that had come together so quickly was still a blur in his mind.

When Marjo Hummel had opened the business meeting, Maggie Washington had immediately asked for the floor. Instead of proposing a soup kitchen and a shelter, items sure to generate complex debate, she'd cleverly asked whether the women wouldn't consider serving a Thanksgiving day meal to hungry people. Linda Dietz had immediately — and enthusiastically — supported the idea, and had then nominated Alma Feuerbringer to run the kitchen. To Daniel's astonishment, Alma had taken that as a high compliment, and had signed on without resistance.

As he entered the large assembly room, the pastor was met with a crowd of hungry people — men, women and children — all of whom were strangers to him. His first thought was, *what are we going to do with all these people?* His second was, *this is a great thing our women are doing!*

In the kitchen, Maggie and Alma were joking together about disastrous Thanksgiving dinners they could remember. Daniel could hardly believe what he was seeing and hearing. Maggie greeted Daniel with a wry comment: "I didn't realize they allowed men in the kitchen."

Daniel joked, "I was hoping you'd say that."

"Not so fast," the redhead replied. "There are tables to be served. You can help my husband."

Daniel's eyes grew wide. "Your husband is here?"

"Wouldn't have missed it," she said. "This is about as close as Henry is likely to get to a church. Serving hungry people is something he can get excited about."

"Where is he?"

"Out in the fellowship hall, helping people find places to sit. Come on, I'll introduce you."

As he was being whisked away, Daniel looked sideways at Alma, who had a twinkle in her eye. Clearly the chemistry between Maggie and her had turned out to be good — perhaps even exceptional.

Henry Washington was a weathered-looking man of perhaps thirty. He wore a plaid shirt and work trousers. His sleeves had been rolled up almost to the elbows. His wiry, sandy hair looked as if it had been rearranged a time or two by a recent gust of wind.

"Henry, this is Pastor Jonas. Pastor, this is Henry."

The plumber's assistant was in the process of pulling back a chair and lifting a small child onto it. He looked toward Daniel and said, "Glad to meetcha, Reverent." It wasn't the first time the pastor had heard the mispronunciation. He was certain it wouldn't be the last.

Daniel said, "What a great crowd for dinner!"

"Yeah, well, there has to be fifty times more people out there that need a meal like this. And, the other problem is, where will these people eat tomorrow or next week?"

One step at a time, Daniel thought.

The two men worked the room for an hour, bringing meals to the tables and seeing that everyone was fed. Daniel thought a serving line at the kitchen window might have made things go faster, and have saved work for Henry and himself, but Alma had insisted that this was a special meal and should be a sit-down dinner. So they did things the way Alma preferred.

Afterwards, as they were clearing the tables, Daniel said to Henry, "It was great to have your help."

"Yours too," Henry said. "'Course, you probably showed up to get leads for a buncha new church members." He laughed a deep, throaty laugh. "In my case, it was a matter of survival."

"How's that?"

"Well, simple. If I didn't show up to help, Maggie wouldn't have fed me for a week or so afterwards." He laughed again, even more heartily than the first time.

THE PARISH SECRETARY, Rebecca Olson, surprised Daniel by turning in her resignation on the Thursday after Thanksgiving. Even though she explained, reasonably enough, that her husband had been laid off at the bank

— an increasingly familiar story during the deepening depression — and that they were heading to Colorado to accept a work opportunity for him, it threw Daniel into a panic.

Seated in her office, whose inner door provided access to his own, he said, "Rebecca, can't you wait until after Christmas? We're coming up on a really busy time. December is a terribly complicated liturgical season, as you know, and we have all the music and worship events to think about."

"I'm sorry," she said, "but James has been out of a job for six months now. My work here has kept groceries on the table, but he really needs work. You see, we want to start a family. And, when he found this new job in Colorado, well, it just didn't make sense not to take advantage."

"So, when will you be leaving?"

"In two weeks, I'm afraid."

He sagged in his chair and looked dejected. He said, "Rebecca, where are we going to find someone on such short notice? I could run a classified advertisement in the *Minneapolis Tribune*. But we may not even get a response, much less a candidate half as dependable as you."

"I knew this was going to create a problem," she said, "so I have a suggestion." She had his attention. "Why don't you interview my sister, Luise?"

"Do I know her?"

"I don't think so. She's been attending University Lutheran Church of Hope."

"Tell me about her."

"Well, she graduated from Fairview Hospital School of Nursing last spring. She moved in with us for the summer and started looking for work. She hasn't found anything."

"There are no nursing positions available? Not even at Fairview?"

"Well, that's the thing. She figured out, sometime during her training, that she didn't really want to be a nurse after all. She worked in the nursing school library when she had the time. Turns out, she'd rather have become a librarian. Of course, there aren't any jobs out there for librarians right now. Nobody's hiring anybody for anything."

"Could she do your job?"

"I'd think so. She's good with language. You'd never have a misspelled word in a worship folder or a newsletter. And, she probably could tell you the difference between 'affect' and 'effect.'" It had become a standing joke in the church office that, whenever one of those two words showed up in a sentence,

Rebecca would go looking for the dictionary.

Daniel grinned. He said, "Why don't you speak to Luise? Ask her if she'd like to come by for an interview."

The following Monday morning, Luise Mensing was seated in Daniel's office. She looked professional in her trim outfit and white dress gloves. The pastor saw some physical resemblance between the two women. He chatted briefly with her, asked whether she was aware of the tasks her sister had been completing for the congregation for the past two years, and whether she would feel intimidated about stepping into the role on such short notice. Confident she would be a good match for the job, he asked, "When would you be available to start?"

"Oh, sometime last week," she dead panned.

He hired her on the spot.

ON CHRISTMAS MORNING, as the service was ending, Adam Engelhardt stepped up to the lectern, just as Lillian Gardner was positioning her music for the postlude. She, the pastor, and the crucifer had all been alerted that there would be a brief interruption in the liturgy at precisely this moment.

Adam looked out over the congregation, then across the chancel to where the pastor was seated. He cleared his throat and said, "This has been a remarkable year for St. Michael and All Angels Church. We have dedicated this astonishing new building. We have purchased a parsonage. We have seen our membership continue to grow. And, in the midst of a great financial crisis in our country, we have seen our congregational stewardship expand at a healthy pace. We have no debts. We have been blessed."

He paused, then looked back toward Daniel. "We have also been blessed with the inspired leadership of our pastor. In fact," he said, looking back at the congregation, "his success — under the guidance of the Holy Spirit, of course — has created a new problem for him, and for us. We have an increasing number of members who do not live within walking distance of the church building. And a streetcar ride is no longer an easy way to reach some of our homes. So, with the approval of the church council, and with the support of you, the members of St. Michael, we have completed, since Thanksgiving day, a secret collection."

He pulled an envelope from his inside suit pocket. "Pastor, please step over here. On behalf of the congregation I want to give you this cashier's check, funds sufficient to purchase the automobile of your choice — well, your choice of a modestly-priced car, at least." The congregation laughed. Daniel was now standing next to Adam, who handed the envelope to him. "Please receive this as a token of our affection and esteem."

The entire congregation rose and began to applaud. Daniel was surprised and overwhelmed. Tears were flooding his eyes. For once he was speechless. As the applause went on and on, he spread his arms wide, in a gesture of appreciation, and bowed before the gathered throng.

And then the great Reuter pipe organ sprang to life, full volume, with a festive postlude based on Isaac Watts' hymn tune, "Antioch," a melody which evoked the carol "Joy to the World!"

DAVID AND MOLLY missed the Christmas morning worship service at St. Michael Church. They had gone to Litchfield, to celebrate with the Lundgrens. A Christmas Eve worship service in Molly's home congregation had been followed by a gift ceremony at the farmhouse. The shoebox-sized container David presented to Molly created great curiosity among the other members of her family. When the wrapping was removed, the opened carton yielded a smaller one inside. Increasingly smaller boxes had been nested, one inside another, until the smallest one appeared. It had a hinged lid and was covered with blue velvet. It was clear to Molly, and to everyone else, what was inside even before she lifted the lid.

As she removed the diamond ring from its slot, and allowed David to slide it onto her finger, there was wild excitement in the room. Nobody was really surprised, and yet everyone appeared to be.

The couple had already set their wedding date for the following June, after David had graduated from the University of Minnesota. Now they made it official, announcing their plans to her family.

On the afternoon of Christmas Day, when the meal was over and the dishes had been washed and put away, Martin Lundgren challenged David to a game of Categories. Seated at the dining room table, they matched wits, one naming a category while the other listed every item that might fit, before the one-minute time limit ran out. Then the other took his turn. Martin's younger sister, Betsy, sat nearby, keeping score, enjoying the way the lead moved back and forth. And Joanna, to whom David had given his watch, studied the sweep second hand, announcing when the minute intervals had run out.

Meanwhile, in the kitchen, Molly, her mother, and her older sister, Anna, discussed wedding plans. The service would, of course, be held in Litchfield. Guest lists were discussed, and food for the reception considered.

Then the matter of Molly's wedding dress came up. Her mother said, "I have a seamstress friend who will make the finest white wedding dress you have ever seen."

Molly surprised her mother and sister by saying, quietly, "Not white. I want a pale green wedding dress."

There were looks of shock and disbelief. Anna said, "What are you talking about? Nobody wears green for her wedding. Maybe the bridesmaids could wear green, but not the bride."

"Why not?"

"Because it's not done."

"White is traditional, dear," her mother said, finally finding her voice.

"But how do traditions get started? And how do they get changed?"

"Don't you like white?"

"Mother, I've been worshiping in David's church for more than a year now. They are very liturgical. I've learned to appreciate the seasons of the church year in ways I never did before. In June the season will be Trinity. That's green. I want a pale green dress."

Her mother drew a deep breath and exhaled heavily. She said, "Well, I suppose the seamstress could do a green dress … "

"Of course she could," Molly replied. "If she can do bridesmaids' dresses in green, she can certainly make a bride's dress from the same cloth."

"But," her mother said, "what will I tell her? How will I explain it?"

Molly said, "Why do you have to tell her anything? It's not her wedding."

"Maybe not," said Anna, frowning, "but we have to live here and you don't."

"What's that supposed to mean?" Molly shot back.

"It means that you're off in the big city, living your own life. The rest of us are still here, in little old Litchfield, where people don't understand newfangled ideas that come out of places like Minneapolis. And when I go into the market or the post office or the bank, and people know you're not having a white dress for your wedding, they're going to wonder exactly what sort of weird sister I've got. And that's going to make me look weird too." The words came tumbling out of her.

Molly said,"You know what, Anna? Nobody can make you look any way you don't choose to look. Nobody can define your life for you — except you. I'm really tired of people telling me who I have to be, or what I have to think or feel. What I like most about David is that he lets me be the person I am. And, while I'm really sorry that I'm ruining your life by making you look weird because I want a pale green wedding dress, I'm not going to do something just to please everybody else. I've already done that in my life, too many times. This time I won't."

Edna Lundgren was uncomfortable with the fact that her daughter's face was turning so crimson. She said, "All right, darling, it's not worth a fight. And it's not worth ruining Christmas over. If you want a pale green dress, then a pale green dress it will be."

"Thank you, Mama," Molly said. She looked at Anna and said, "I'm sorry. Will you still be my maid of honor?"

Anna returned a pouty look, but then she mellowed. A faint smile crept into the corners of her mouth. She said, "Of course, you silly goose." And then she smiled broadly.

Suddenly, from the dining room, there arose a shriek. Betsy Lundgren could be heard to shout, "Martin, you won! You won!"

They hurried to the door and looked in on the scene. Young Martin Lundgren was waving the score page in the air, announcing proudly: "248 to 241! I'm the Categories champion of the world!"

David looked at Molly and offered a shrug, and a mock look of dejection.

Chapter 26

One day in early January Daniel boarded the Bloomington Avenue northbound streetcar, then changed for the Lake Street westbound. He'd heard advertisements on WCCO announcing the opening of a new Chevrolet dealership somewhere along the street, and inviting customers to "come on in and test drive the most affordable, dependable automobile in America."

He wasn't so sure about the claims, but decided it was time to start doing some research. As he approached the address he'd jotted down when listening to the radio ad, he got a strange feeling. Then he realized why. The new "Lake Street Chevrolet" dealership was now occupying the building once home to the now-defunct Pavelka Motors.

He left the streetcar and stepped up to the window of the showroom. There were three new vehicles on display on the other side of the glass. Suspecting a Chevrolet might be in his price range, he went inside. An eager young salesman was on him like a fly on honey. That made him uncomfortable. But, he realized, with such tough economic times, the commission from the sale of a new automobile would mean a considerable boost to a salesman's take-home pay.

"Isn't she a beauty?" the young man asked rhetorically. Daniel nodded, studying the exterior and peering in at the dashboard.

"What are you driving now?"

"What? Oh. Nothing. I don't own a car."

"So, nothing to trade then. That's to your advantage. No haggling."

"I'm not sure I'm going to buy a Chevrolet. I remember there used to be an Oldsmobile dealership here, up until last year."

"Too bad about that," the salesman said. "Actually, I worked for them, almost until they closed."

"So you know what happened to the owner then?"

There was a pause. The salesman seemed to be weighing his words. "That's a really sad story."

Daniel felt his heart skip a beat. *What had become of Joe?* he wondered, fearing the worst.

"It had to be hard — maybe even a little humiliating — for him, losing the business, and then having to come back as a salesman. Poor guy, he's working right alongside me. And he used to be my boss. Doesn't seem right, does it?"

Daniel's heart leaped into his throat. "Joe Pavelka is working here selling cars?"

"One of our best salesmen. Shouldn't be surprising, should it?"

"I should say not. May I speak with him, please?"

"You know him?"

"Actually, I do."

The salesman hesitated, as though he could feel a commission slipping away. He said, "He's off today. He'll be back tomorrow."

"No disrespect," said Daniel, "but if I buy one of your cars, I'm going to have to buy it from Joe."

"Why is that? Do you owe him?"

"No. Let's just say, I wouldn't feel right if I didn't."

DANIEL RETURNED the next morning. When he walked in, Joe was showing a car to a young couple. It became quickly apparent to him, unintentionally overhearing their questions, that they were probably not going to be able to afford a new automobile. At least not yet. Joe's final suggestion to them was, "Why don't you take a look at our used cars? The lot's just across the street."

As they turned to leave, Joe's eyes met Daniel's. The salesman appeared, momentarily, to be disoriented. Then there was a look of recognition, followed by a split second during which he seemed to hesitate. But then he broke into a broad smile. Daniel couldn't decide whether it was genuine or forced.

"Good morning," he exclaimed. "We meet again!" Daniel approached and extended his hand. Joe grasped it solidly. "Glad to see you again. Mother of God, a lot of things have changed since I saw you last."

You can't take the Catholic out of the boy, Daniel remembered Joe once having said. He replied, "I'd sort of lost track of you, after the dealership closed."

"Yeah. Rotten business. In more ways than one." He studied the pastor's face for a second, then switched easily into selling mode. "Listen, you want to take one of these for a spin?"

Daniel didn't need persuading. "Sure. But keep in mind. I travel by streetcar. I may need some coaching."

"I'm a great coach! Just watch and see. Come on." He led the way, out the door and down the block, toward a lot where a row of new Chevrolets were parked. Fishing a key from his pocket, he handed it to Daniel and opened the driver's door on one of the vehicles. He said, "Climb in. You're gonna love this car."

As they drove along Lake Street, and then south on Chicago Avenue, Joe extolled the car's features. Daniel listened carefully, realizing it could be information he might soon need. Joe had already told him the asking price, and it was within his range. And, he admitted to himself, he really did like this car.

He turned left onto Forty-Second Street and headed east. He said, "How are you doing, Joe?"

"In what way?"

"Well, you're working again. That has to be good." Joe nodded, but didn't comment. "It has to be difficult, going to work for somebody else — in a building you used to own."

Joe sighed. "It was really tough, swallowing my pride and going back in there, asking for a job. I don't know if they hired me out of pity or what, but they didn't hesitate for five seconds." He paused, studying the passing scenery. "Lucky for them they didn't."

"So you're doing well for them."

"Damn right!" There was an awkward silence. "Darn right. I'm the best salesman they've got."

So much for swallowed pride, Daniel thought. He said, "How long did you go without work?"

"About six months. We had some savings. We managed to pretty much spend all of it. Then this new dealership opened up. I decided there wasn't any point moping around, living in the past. So I went in and hired on with them."

Daniel turned north on Anderson Avenue. He said, "This isn't an Oldsmobile, but I'm not Herbert Hoover, either."

It took Joe a second to catch the significance of the remark. When he did, he broke into hearty laughter and slapped his knee with the palm of his hand. "No, it's not an Oldsmobile. But, you know what? I've come to really respect the quality of these cars. You know what they say on the radio about Chevrolets — they're affordable and they're dependable. And, honest to God, they really are."

Daniel drove through the intersection at Caldwell Street and pulled up in front of St. Michael and All Angels Church. He said, "Joe, this is where I lead worship on Sundays. Have you ever been here?"

Joe looked with admiration at the white stone complex. "Never. Nice place you have here, Padre."

"Tell you what," said Daniel."You come to worship here with your wife and kids. Just once. And then I'll buy this car."

Joe looked at Daniel and his jaw dropped down. "Are you having fun with me?"

"I'm serious. You do what I ask, and I'll do what I said I would."

Joe looked incredulous. He said, "You don't really have to do that, you know."

Daniel said, "Joe, just think about it."

The salesman grinned. "Okay. I will."

The pastor said, "I live another block north of here. What do you say we drive on up there and see what my wife and daughter think of this fine new Chevrolet?"

THAT EVENING, the sad news came that Karl Rausch, the gentle old one-time custodian, had died. Karl had given up his duties when the congregation moved out of the chapel on the corner. He'd been wise enough to know he wouldn't have the stamina to care for a sprawling complex. Daniel had offered him a symbolic role, supervising the ushers or changing the hymn numbers on the boards, but the elderly German refugee had seen through it. "Nein, Herr Pastor," he had said, laying his hand on Daniel's forearm. "It's time for younger folks to take over now. We'll let them have a turn. Es ist gut. Sehr gut."

Karl had eaten his supper — a bowl of soup, a piece of bread and a slice of cheese — and then had gone into his tiny living room. His landlady had taken to checking on him every morning and evening. When there was no response at eight o'clock that night, she'd let herself in and found him, seated in his old padded rocking chair, a copy of *Kirchenblatt*, the German language Lutheran newspaper, spread across his knees. He had fallen asleep and never awakened.

Daniel conducted Karl's service on Saturday afternoon. It was the first funeral ever conducted in St. Michael Church's new building. That, the pastor thought, seemed entirely fitting.

THE NEXT MORNING, the Pavelka family was at worship. At the church door, Mary came through first. Her expression was radiant. Daniel said in a near whisper, so as not to let Joe hear, "I apologize if I coaxed you away from your Presbyterian congregation for a day."

"Listen," she said in a conspiratorial tone, "don't apologize. You've accomplished something I haven't managed since my children were toddlers. I haven't sat in a church pew next to Joe for more than a decade. This is almost a miracle."

"Well, at least we got you all into a worship service for one Sunday."

"If I have anything to say about it, this won't be the last time you'll see all of us here."

"We'd be delighted to see you here anytime," he said.

Next came the Pavelka children. Mary introduced them to the pastor. "This is Margaret. She's eight. This is John. He's eleven. And this is Thomas, our teenager."

Thomas shook Daniel's hand. The pastor asked, "How was it this morning? Were you glad you came?"

"Yeah … well … Dad made us come."

Daniel grinned. "Are you sorry he did?"

"No. Not really. I really like your organ. And the choir is really good. And the stained-glass windows are really nifty."

"How about the sermon? Was that okay?"

"Huh? Oh, sorry. Yeah. That was first-rate, too."

Daniel almost broke out laughing. "Well, I'm glad you didn't sleep through it, then."

Thomas grinned, then headed out the door with his mother and siblings.

Finally, Joe stepped up. He said, "This should reaffirm your belief in miracles, Pastor. We're all here. At the same time. And your roof didn't fall in."

"It's a brand-new roof," Daniel said. "What are the odds?"

Joe said, "You have to come back and talk with me some more."

"I know. I have to order a new car. Right?"

"No. You really don't. That's not what I want to talk to you about."

"Joe, I'll talk to you any time you want. About anything. Just name the day."

ON THE SUNDAY AFTER EASTER, Lillian Gardner offered a recital featuring a dozen of her piano students. She had realized, early on, that there was no way to fit all the children and their parents into Wilma Shaughnessy's upstairs parlor, so she secured permission to hold it on a Sunday afternoon in the fellowship room at St. Michael Church.

By the time all the parents, grandparents and family members had taken their chairs, there were nearly sixty people in the room. The youngsters, beginning with a shy second-grade boy and concluding with an extremely confident sixth grade girl, played their pieces with very few stumbles. Lillian had coached them in the social graces. It was with considerable pride, then, that members of the audience watched their sons bow smartly before climbing onto the piano bench, their daughters curtsy, and then to see them do the same when their performances were finished.

At the conclusion, filling out the program, Lillian performed a piece of her own, a Beethoven sonata. It was as though she was communicating to the parents, *You see, you keep your young people coming for piano lessons, and one day they'll be playing pieces just like this one.*

She had recruited the Pellner sisters, always ready to spread a festive table, to manage the reception which followed. Coffee, tea, punch, dainty sandwiches with the crusts cut off, and cookies of three kinds, were consumed in an atmosphere of high-decibel joviality. At one point, Lillian quieted the crowd, many of whom had already thanked her personally for having taught their little prodigies to play with such skill. She said to the group, "Your children have musical gifts which should not be limited to the keyboard. I want to encourage you to help them develop their vocal skills as well."

She continued, "A few of you are members of this congregation. Others of you have churches of your own. For those of you with nowhere to go on a Sunday morning, I have a little proposition to make." They were listening keenly now. "One of the things I do at St. Michael Church is direct the children's choir. We have room for more singers. If your son or daughter is not a part of this group, and becomes a member when we organize again in the fall, and if they continue faithfully with the group, not missing any rehearsals or Sunday mornings when we sing, I will award them, at our piano recital one year from now, a certificate good for … " She paused dramatically before completing her sentence: " … six free piano lessons."

The crowd was abuzz with the news. During the next twenty minutes, there were a half-dozen inquiries from parents wanting to know more about the children's choir. And, she discovered that the law of unintended consequences was also now at work. Members of all four families whose young people were already in the choir came forward to ask whether their youngsters were also eligible for the free piano lessons. Chagrined, she quickly decided they were.

As the crowd began to thin, Lillian caught sight of Luther Fischer, chatting with Gretchen Pellner. Why, she wondered, hadn't she noticed him before? He came her direction.

"Wonderful concert," he said. "Especially that last piece."

"Oh, piffle," she protested. But inside, she was glowing.

"Listen," he said, "Gretchen told me that you and Wilma made all the sandwiches and cookies, and they want you to take the rest of them back for her and you to enjoy later on."

"What? There are still some left?"

"I realize you had a good crowd here, but it looks like you prepared enough to feed a small army. Yes, there are still some left."

"Maybe the Pellner sisters would like to have them."

"They think *you* should have them. So, here's the deal. Your hands are going to be full, carrying all that music and everything. So, I'll carry the food."

"Well, that's a nice offer. But why would you do that?"

"Because then I'd have an excuse to walk you home."

"Do you *need* an excuse?"

"I don't know. Do I?

She rolled her eyes. "Just get the sandwiches and the cookies."

Chapter 27

Daniel sat in the front parlor of the Pavelka residence. It was a large, comfortable house on Park Avenue, an impressive dwelling Joe Pavelka had managed to save from foreclosure during his bankruptcy. As Daniel finished his coffee, Mary came offering a refill. He declined, so she took the cups away. When they were alone in the room, Joe said, "I really appreciate how you got me off dead center."

"What do you mean?"

"I wasn't planning to go back to church again. Ever. You sort of called my bluff."

"Just doing my job, Joe."

"Don't be modest. You did exactly the right thing. I don't mean that goofy offer to buy a car if I brought my family to church. I mean, what you said the other time we talked. About how a person needs God in his life. In a really substantial way, I mean."

Daniel couldn't remember exactly to which part of their previous conversations Joe was referring. But, he realized, it didn't really matter.

Joe said, "Your sermon last Sunday wasn't all that different-sounding from the kind of stuff I heard in the Presbyterian Church. Of course, I'm a little vague about that. It's been a long time since I ever went there. But what you said last Sunday was ... I don't know ... I guess I'd say hopeful. Sensible. You didn't hit me over the head. That was good. But you didn't make it sound too easy, either. I don't like it when people make it sound too easy. Because I know living with God isn't always easy. And it shouldn't be."

"It's an interesting paradox," Daniel said.

"Don't use those preacher-type words. What are you saying?"

The pastor grinned. He liked how the car salesman cut to the chase. "A paradox is a combination of two ideas. They sound like opposites, or contradictions, when you say them together. Lutheran theology has a lot of them. What you were just talking about reminded me of one of those paradoxes."

"Okay. I'm listening."

"Here's the thing. You grew up believing your salvation depends on living a good life. It doesn't. Being right with God depends on God. It's a gift. You and I don't deserve it. We just get it because we need it. We call that grace. Of course, when Martin Luther started to teach that — it wasn't his idea, by the way: the Apostle Paul said it first — but, when Luther talked that way, his enemies in the church all accused him of making it too easy. They said that, following his argument, people would stop doing the right things and take advantage of God and try to sail right into heaven with a free pass, no matter how rotten their lives had been."

Joe said, "I hate to tell you this, but that's what I learned about Protestants, growing up in St. Paul."

"I'm not surprised," said Daniel. "But that's only half of the paradox. We believe salvation doesn't cost you *anything*. But we also believe it costs you *everything*."

"Excuse me?"

"Jesus said, 'Come to me and I will give you rest.' But he also said, 'Take up your cross and follow me.' Do you know what happens to people who take up crosses? Sooner or later, they get nailed to them."

"Holy crap!" Joe exclaimed. Immediately, he blushed. "Sorry." He tried to get past the embarrassment he was feeling. He said, "What you just said sort of takes all the appeal out of being a Christian."

"I'm not saying a disciple will literally end up getting physically crucified. Although, that's been known to happen to some of the faithful. What it *does* mean is that, once you get serious about living with this free gift from God, it's going to cost you something. If it doesn't, it may not be the real thing."

"So, which is it, then? Is salvation free? Or is it expensive?"

"Both. That's the paradox."

"Sounds like a pretty slippery argument. I'd hate to have to use that kind of double-talk to try to sell Chevrolets."

"Let me use an illustration. You and Mary have three wonderful children. Did you make them promise you they'd do something for you, before you agreed to love them, and give them food and clothing and a roof over their head, and hug them when they need it? Or do you give them all of that without condition?"

The answer was too obvious. Joe didn't bother to reply.

"But, as your children have grown older, and figured out how to think for themselves, and make choices — including some really risky ones — do you just stand back and let them do whatever they want? Or, do you lay some conditions on them, and expect certain kinds of behavior of them, and discipline them when they need it?"

Joe was nodding.

"Well, those are the two sides of the paradox. You love your children without condition. That's what parents do. That's a gift you give them. But then you show them what they have to do in order not to get themselves killed, and in order not to break your heart. You wouldn't let them play out in the middle of Park Avenue where the traffic could come along and cut them down. Sometimes love says *yes* and sometimes it says *no*."

"So, being a Christian means getting something for free, but then paying for it later."

"You could say that. Except, we can't really pay God for anything. All we can do is thank him for what he gives us. It's like, if you found your son, Thomas, cornered in an alley by bullies ready to beat the daylights out of him. You rescue him and bring him home safe. Thomas feels really guilty about having gotten himself into the fix in the first place. And, he's so thankful you came along at just the right time, that he wants to do something to pay you back. Of course, you're wise enough as a parent to know he can't ever possibly do that. So you tell him, 'Thomas …'"

"You can call him Tom. We do," said Joe. "Sorry for interrupting."

"Okay. So you tell Tom, 'Look, I love you. You're my son. You can't pay me back for saving your life. All I want from you is to show me, in everything you do, that you're glad to be my son. And, of course, stay out of dark alleys.'"

Joe had a broad grin on his face. "It's like that story about the son that ran away and then his dad let him come back. That's in the Bible, isn't it?"

"Jesus' parable. The Prodigal Son. Yes, that's the same idea."

"So, you Lutherans don't really believe God gives you a free ride after all. That's a relief. But now I'm irritated."

"Why?"

"Because I've been fed a bill of goods about you people all these years."

"Well, I'm sure you can find a few Lutherans out there who think they don't have to behave like disciples, since God already gave them their salvation. But they don't properly understand Lutheran theology. And they also don't know the meaning of the word *disciple*. We're all disciples, you know, not just the original twelve followers of Jesus."

"One of the only sermons I ever remember hearing in the Presbyterian Church was about being a disciple," Joe said. "The minister said it was from the same word that means 'discipline.'"

"He was right. And, I'm impressed."

"About what?"

"That you still remember that sermon after all these years."

Joe stared out the window for a moment, then turned his attention to Daniel once more. "I think I'm ready to spend some more time with you, talking about this."

"Lutheran theology?"

"Yes. And what we need to know in order to become Lutherans."

"We?"

"I wouldn't do it without Mary."

"She'd consider giving up her Presbyterian church membership?"

"If I told her I was considering joining a church with her, yes. She'd do it in a heartbeat."

"Well, we have membership classes from time to time."

"Do we have to wait for one of those?"

Daniel thought about it. "No. I guess not. You want to have me come and meet with just the two of you?"

"Well, there's one more thing."

"What's that?"

"Tom's fifteen now. He's too old for your confirmation program. At least, I'm pretty sure he wouldn't sit still for classes with kids younger than himself. So, I'm thinking … "

"It wouldn't be a problem. Tom could take the classes with the two of you."

"Great. We'll talk about it and get back to you."

"Have you spoken to Tom about this yet?"

"No. But I know he'll want to."

"Really."

"Of course. He's my son. He listens to me. He does what I tell him." He smirked. "Well, most of the time." Turning serious, he said, "Tom was pretty enthusiastic about our experience at St. Mike's."

"Actually, we call it St. Michael."

"No nicknames for you Lutherans?"

"It's a matter of theology."

"How's that?"

"We don't believe the church belongs to the saint. It belongs to God. So I don't even encourage our members calling us 'Saint Michael's.'"

"Hmmm," Joe said, mulling it. "Sounds a little fussy. But I get your point." He paused, then said, "I guess there's a lot this dyed-in-the-wool Catholic boy is going to have to get used to. The sooner we get those classes going, the better."

LUTHER FISCHER sat in Wilma Shaughnessy's parlor, waiting for Lillian to come down to Sunday supper. The week before, when he'd walked her home, Wilma had decided it was time to invite him to share another meal with them. He'd accepted with alacrity.

Wilma came to the parlor door and asked, "Would you like a glass of wine, Mr. Fischer?"

"Thank you, Mrs. Shaughnessy. I'd be delighted to have a glass."

"You can call me Wilma."

"Then you should call me Luther."

"You know," she said, lowering the tray for him, "I've never known a 'Luther' before."

"I beg your pardon?"

"Somebody named Luther. I've never known anyone like that. It's not such a Catholic name, you know."

Luther chuckled. "We drink wine just like Catholics do."

She said, "I have to tell you. That young Lutheran lady living upstairs is the best renter I've ever had. A lot better than some of the rowdy Catholic boys I've put up here over the years."

He said, "I think the issue is, what's inside a person, not what kind of label they wear."

"Truer words were never spoken. You know, my late husband, Barney, used to say some of the best customers he ever had — you know, the ones who actually paid their bills on time — were people you'd never expect. Like that Mr. Simmons, who used to live over on Anderson Avenue. Barney said he didn't think that man had any kind of religion at all. But he always paid for his coal, right on time."

"Whatever happened to him?" Luther asked, looking at the stairs and seeing no sign of Lillian.

"Well, his house burned down. With him in it. I just hope it wasn't the coal in his furnace that caused it."

Luther wanted to change the subject. He said, "Wilma, if you don't mind my asking, does Lillian ever talk about me?"

"Talk about you? How do you mean?"

"You know. Does she ... well ... Do you think she likes me much?"

"Why, Mr. Fischer. It would be presumptuous of me to speak for Lillian.

Why don't you ask her yourself?"

Luther sighed. "She has a funny way with words. You ask her a direct question and she gives you a sideways answer. You're never sure exactly what she's saying, or what she's thinking." He paused. "Actually, I rather enjoy that about her. Except, I really wish I knew what she thinks about *me*."

"Well, I can't prove it," Wilma said with a twinkle in her eye, "but as far as I can tell, she's really glad I invited you to supper tonight."

"Really? Did she say that?"

"Not in so many words."

"What did she say, exactly?"

"She said, 'Wilma Shaughnessy, how *dare* you invite someone to supper when I'm expected to be present and not consult privately with me first!'"

Luther gulped. "That doesn't sound too encouraging."

"Oh, you have to learn to read between the lines. If she'd really meant it, she would have told me the two of us would be eating without her. Instead, she asked me which dress I thought she should wear to supper."

Chapter 28

As the pot roast went around, Lillian said to Luther, "How is your doctoral program progressing?"

"Just fine," he replied. "Before long I get into the research for my thesis."

"And what will the topic be?"

He looked sideways at Wilma, then said, "Well, it wouldn't be polite to discuss it in present company."

"Why on earth not?" Lillian demanded, laying down her fork. She was staring hard at their dinner guest.

Luther shifted uncomfortably in his chair. Finally he said, "Root causes of the Thirty Years' War."

Lillian knew from her own church history course at Capital University that the conflict had been between Lutherans and Roman Catholics in Germany, and that her own ancestors had come to North America fleeing its aftermath. But, with the conversation now dead in the water, she pushed ahead. "And what argument are you planning to defend?"

Luther looked at Wilma again. He said, "Well … ahhh … I haven't really settled it in my mind … completely, that is."

"Well, you must have an idea," Lillian said impatiently.

In spite of the awkwardness it was causing just now, Luther liked it when she started sounding cross. It always made for a good head-to-head intellectual contest, and his experience sparring with Lillian was that both of them gave as good as they got. He took a deep breath and said, "I'm thinking of defending the thesis that the war was fought because Roman Catholics wanted to obliterate Lutheranism and recapture Europe for the pope."

Suddenly both of them were looking at Wilma, wondering what would come out of her mouth. Wilma cut a piece of meat and popped part of it into her mouth. She said, almost cheerfully, "Well, that should be an easy one to defend. That's what Father Hamilton taught us in Catholic school."

"It is?" said Lillian, wide-eyed.

"Certainly. He said if the Catholic generals had been a little smarter, they'd have done the job. But instead, everything ended up where it started, and all those innocent people got killed."

Luther said, "My heavens, Wilma. You actually discussed this in parochial school?"

"Certainly. It's part of the history of the Church, isn't it?"

"Well ... yes ... "

"But you know what Father Hamilton never told us, but should have?"

"No. What was that?"

"He should have said that the war should never have been started in the first place. Wars never settle anything. All they do is make people mad. And then the other side tries to get revenge. Just look at Germany and France. Whose turn is it to invade who? I mean, how ridiculous can you get?"

The room fell silent. Then Luther said, "Wilma, you should consider becoming my thesis advisor!"

She looked at him and beamed. "You really think so, dearie?"

DAVID ENGELHARDT borrowed his father's car to take Molly Lundgren to Litchfield for Mother's Day. It was her last planned visit home before the wedding. When they arrived, Martin was sitting on the top porch step in his stocking feet, carefully scraping chicken manure off his work shoes. David pulled up in front of the house and cut the engine. When he climbed down, the teenager shouted, cheerfully, "Back for more punishment?"

It took David a split second to realize the challenge was coming from the self proclaimed Categories Champion of the World. He shouted back, "I'll take care of you in due time, young man! This time I won't be half so easy on you."

"Hah!" retorted Martin in jolly defiance. His happy-go-lucky demeanor was what made David like him so much. Why, he wondered, couldn't some of it rub off onto his sullen older brother, Forrest?

On Saturday afternoon, after they had been at the farm for almost four hours and Forrest hadn't shown himself, David decided to go hunt him down. Martin said he thought his brother was cleaning the hog pens. Remembering his previous experience with Forrest, David had come prepared. He tugged off his dress shoes and pulled on an old, scuffed pair.

In the yard he saw Molly's father, guiding a horse and wagon full of corn cobs toward the far edge of the yard. He shouted a hello and waved. George Lundgren waved back, but kept on going.

David walked through the cow barn and then the machine shed. Finally, he saw Forrest at work, just where Martin had guessed he would be. The stocky twenty-year-old seemed preoccupied, hefting pig refuse with a scoop shovel. David approached and shouted, in as friendly a voice as he could manage, "Forrest! Hello!"

Forrest straightened up, turned and studied David for a moment. Then he returned to what he'd been doing, as if ignoring his guest would make him disappear. David leaned on the top of the fence enclosure and watched in silence as the young farmer continued to shovel and pitch, shovel and pitch, shovel and pitch.

Finally, without looking up, Forrest said, "You want a shovel? If you're gonna stand there, you might as well help."

David hadn't expected the invitation. On the other hand, he was dressed casually enough that, if some of the slop got onto his trousers, it wouldn't be a disaster. He said, "Sure. Show me where one is."

"Over there," he said, pausing and pointing. "Tool shed. Just inside the door."

As he walked toward the shed, David wondered whether he might have scored a breakthrough with Forrest. On the other hand, it might just be that he was about to be shown what a poor farmer he would likely make. He decided it didn't matter that much, either way.

With scoop shovel in hand, he headed back to the pig pen. Trying to sound casual, he said, "Okay, boss, what do I do now?"

Forrest stared at him with a look of incredulity. He said, "Listen, city boy, if you don't know what to do with a scoop shovel in a pig yard, you've got even less upstairs than I thought."

David felt his temperature rising. He leaned the shovel against the fence and grasped the top rail with both hands. Looking over the barrier, he said, "What exactly is your main problem with me, Forrest? I'm trying to be a friend to you. So far, all I've gotten is angry talk and sarcasm. Is it me in particular you don't like, or people in general?"

Immediately he wished he hadn't added the last phrase. But it was too late. He'd said it. And part of him took curious satisfaction in the feeling it gave him.

Forrest set down his shovel and stepped up to the fence, his face so close to David's it made him uncomfortable. He also didn't exactly appreciate the scent of stale breath he was being made to endure. But he wasn't about to back away, even though the farmer's son was a third larger than he was.

"Here's the deal," said Forrest. "I like people who know what the score is. I like people who keep their noses clean. I like people who don't meddle in other people's business." There was a snarl in his voice.

"You think I'm meddling, Forrest?"

"Damn right, city boy."

"You know what would help things a whole lot right now?"

"What's that?"

"If you'd just lay off calling me 'city boy.'"

"Yeah, well, that may just be too bad for you. Because that's pretty much the way I see you, okay?" With a sneer he added, "Ya' don't even know what in hell to do with a scoop shovel."

"You ever go to the city, Forrest?"

There was no answer.

"You should try it sometime."

"There you go again. Meddlin'. That's one of the things you do real good, ain't it?"

"I don't get it."

"Naw. You wouldn't. See, it's none of your damn business if I go to the city or not. That's *my* business, not yours. That's what I mean by meddlin'."

David was considering retreating to the house. But he couldn't think of a way to do so without looking, and feeling, humiliated.

Forrest kept right on going. "'Course, there's a difference between meddlin' and messin'. You remember that little conversation we had at Thanksgiving, when I warned you not to go messin' with my sister? Well, seems like you didn't get the message."

David was puzzled.

"And now she ends up wearin' a green dress to her own wedding, not a white one." He reached across the fence and grabbed David by both sides of his shirt collar, yanking him so close he thought Forrest was going to jump right down his throat. "A green dress, because you went and messed with her before the wedding. You just couldn't wait, could you?"

Forrest dragged David off his feet, up against the fence. There was hostility in his eyes. Just as suddenly, he released David, half dropping, half shoving him away from the fence. He landed on his rump, in the pig slime. He sat there, stunned, feeling the slop oozing through the seat of his trousers.

MOLLY SAT on the bed, next to David, rubbing some of her mother's homemade skin soothing remedy across his red, irritated chest. It was the first time she had seen him with his shirt off, much less touched him there. She said, "This is going to be all right. There's no broken skin. But it doesn't look very pretty."

"It doesn't feel so great either." He winced as she spread more salve onto the tender spots. "I guess Forrest and I aren't going to make it as best friends." He put his hand on Molly's, stopping her momentarily from her work. He said,

"Promise me you won't let him sit next to me in church tomorrow."

She said, "This is all so wrong. So pathetically wrong! You're the man I'm going to marry, and my own brother is roughing you up. Just what, exactly, did you say to him out there?"

"Why are you assuming it was *me*?"

"Well, you must have said *something*. If you don't say anything to Forrest, he pretty much leaves you alone."

"You could say that about a grizzly bear, Molly."

"Well, I've never heard of him attacking anyone before."

He lifted her hands away from him and looked at her, incredulous. "Are we having our first fight?"

There was a look of surprise on her face. "Oh. I hope not." She began to rub his chest once more. "It's just that, I feel as though I'm caught between loyalties. I want to defend my brother, and I'm hopelessly in love with you."

"Well, I'm not sure what Forrest did was defensible, if you want to know my opinion."

She turned toward him and took his hands in hers. "What actually happened? Just tell me."

"Well, I thought I was being friendly. I tried making conversation. I even offered to help clean the hog pen."

She smirked.

"Yeah. That was pretty much his reaction. You know, I guess I can overlook him calling me 'city boy' all the time. I think he may just resent an outsider coming in and taking his little sister away. As if that was really the way it was."

"He's always been a little protective of the rest of us kids. But that's no excuse for him threatening you."

"The thing is, he seems to be all worked up about the fact that you're planning to wear a green dress at your wedding."

"Oh, no. He mentioned that?"

"*Mentioned* it! He as much as implied that I'd violated your womanhood. And, as a result, now you can't wear white."

She had tears in the corners of her eyes. "This is my fault. I should have explained it to them. Nobody understands why I want to wear green."

"Do you really want to?"

"Yes. Of course. Anyway, I have to."

"No, you don't."

"Yes, I do."

"It's because of ... of *him*, isn't it? You think he's soiled your reputation."

"Well?"

"Molly, Michael Morgan-Houseman is *dead*!" It was the first time he'd ever said the name in her presence.

"It still happened. And I still remember it."

"Molly, I know. I understand. But don't you see what's happening? He's controlling you from beyond the grave. That's not right. You can't let him do that to you. He's done enough to you already."

Tears were streaming down her face. "It would be a lie for me to wear white."

"No. It wouldn't. Because none of that was your fault. You have to get beyond all of it, and treat it for what it was — an ugly business not of your choosing, over which you had no control."

She was fumbling around for a handkerchief. The nearest thing at hand was his shirt, which she'd pulled off him ten minutes earlier. He offered a corner of it to her. She dried her eyes.

David said, "I think I said this to you one other time, back in Minneapolis, but I guess I didn't say it very well. So, here goes again. Molly, in my eyes — and, I'd think in God's, too — you're still pure and unspoiled. You have a right, a responsibility — to yourself and your family and me — to wear white at your wedding."

She looked miserably at him, as if his words were soaking in, but it appeared to him she could still use more convincing.

He said, "And I won't have some uppity bastard from the other side of Park Avenue stealing that right, and that privilege, from the woman I love."

His fierce language seemed to work in her the cleansing she had needed for so long. She exhaled so heavily, he feared it might be her last breath. He was beginning to regret his strident language. But Molly set his heart and mind at ease when she said, "The seamstress has already started the dresses. Mine's half done. I can't tell her not to finish it."

He grinned. "Tell her to simplify it. Tell her you'll take it with you on our wedding trip. Tell her I'm going to take you dancing in it. And, tell your mother I'm buying that one. It will be my wedding present to you."

Her eyes glistened. He climbed off the bed and pulled her up with him. Drawing her close, he kissed her tenderly, his hands circling her face. Then he took her hand in his and placed the other along the slim line of her waist. He whispered seductively, "Dance with me."

"There's no music."

"I hear music. Don't you?"

"Someone may come in."

"Let them."

A half-audible laugh escaped her throat. It sounded a little bit like a whimper. She drew her hand around him, smoothing her fingers against the bare skin of his back. And, in the silence, with the old plank flooring of Molly's childhood bedroom groaning and creaking beneath their feet, they danced together in the silence.

Chapter 29

Luise Mensing stood at the pastor's office door and tapped softly. When he looked up, she said, "Do you have a minute?"

"Certainly. Come in."

She sat down across the desk from him and said, "I have a question."

"All right."

"The Reformation Room. How are we planning to use it?"

He considered her question, visualizing the large space just down the hall from the church offices. It had been his special project to get a panoply of stained-glass installed there, picturing five significant locations in the life of Martin Luther. But the room itself, originally intended for a comfortable lounge, had instead become a storage room, while a friendly but intense disagreement had stopped further development of the space.

The men of the church had wanted to claim the room for their meetings, but so had the youth group. Both had decided it would be a very good thing to hold their gatherings where richly detailed scenes of Worms, Augsburg, Eisenach, Erfurt and Wittenberg adorned one entire wall. But several members had campaigned to have the room put off limits for meetings of any kind, suggesting it would not do justice to the dignity of the space.

It had even come up at a church council meeting, where representatives of both the men's group and the Luther League had made their case. In one memorable showdown, a father and his son had squared off, offering opposing arguments. That had led the council to decide not to open the room to any group, including the women. Since then, the youth had taken to meeting in the church basement, the men in the community room.

"I think the Reformation Room would make a wonderful library," Luise declared. "A church this size needs one. It would be the perfect location. Right in the middle of the window you've got the Wartburg Castle, the place where Martin Luther translated the New Testament."

Daniel thought about it. "The council would have to approve it. It's not a bad idea, really. I could put it on the agenda." He thought some more. "We'd need a librarian."

Luise said, "I'd like to volunteer for that."

"Wait a minute. You already have a full-time job running the church office."

"I'd find the time. I really like library work. I think I'd be good at it."

"I have no doubt that you would be. But, there are no shelves in there."

"We have the endowment. I've been reading the file documents. Mr. Morgan-Houseman's bequest allows us to spend the interest for improvements and maintenance. Library shelves would certainly fit that description."

"Yes. I'm sure they would. But we have no library books. How would you propose to build a collection?"

"Well, there are lots of possibilities. We could ask people to donate them," she suggested.

"You mean, from their home libraries?"

"I wouldn't recommend that. We'd get all sorts of things we wouldn't want. No, I was thinking more about having people give money to buy books. We could put the names of people they want to honor on bookplates, inside the front covers."

He nodded. "That might work."

"But there's another possibility."

"What's that?"

"A few thousand dollars from the endowment fund would buy a lot of books."

He frowned. "I don't know whether library books would qualify under the terms of the bequest."

"How could we find out?"

"Well, I could speak with the trust officer at the bank. But don't get your hopes up. These bankers tend to be pretty conservative."

"It would be a shame if he said no. There's a lot of interest accumulating in that account now. We should be spending some of it."

DANIEL WALKED INTO THE LOBBY of the Minneapolis Bank and Trust Company and looked around. He'd not been here before. He approached a uniformed guard. "I need to speak with Mr. Jorgensen," he explained.

"Do you have an appointment?"

"Yes."

"Right over there." He pointed toward a desk where a secretary was busily typing forms. She looked up and said, "Reverend Jonas? Mr. Jorgensen is expecting you. Go right on in."

Daniel stepped into a richly-paneled office. Jens Jorgensen, a dignified forty-year-old gentleman in a three-piece suit, had thinning dark brown hair that he combed straight back, perhaps to cover any hints of baldness. He looked up from the document he was studying, then got out of his chair and came around the desk. Grasping Daniel's hand, he shook it warmly and said, "We meet at last."

"I beg your pardon?"

"I've been managing this bequest for your congregation for the past year and a half. I've always wanted to meet the clergyman whose congregation got all that money."

He gestured toward two leather upholstered chairs. When they were seated, the bank officer asked, "How can I help you?"

"I wondered if you could answer a question for us. We're planning to establish a library at St. Michael Church. We're pretty sure we can use interest earnings for bookshelves, since they'll become permanent fixtures."

"That's correct."

"What about library books?"

"Probably not. I was reading the terms of the bequest just before you arrived. They make it clear that you can use the funds to paint the walls, or repair the roof, or even add onto the building. But nothing may be spent for consumable materials. So, for example, you can't use the funds to purchase office supplies — and certainly not office salaries."

"We hadn't considered doing that."

"But, neither can you spend the funds for things like Sunday school books, or Bibles, or hymn books. Those things get worn out and discarded. So they wouldn't qualify."

"But what about books in a permanent library?"

"How do you mean?"

"Well, I agree with you that a Bible or a hymnal would get a lot of regular use, and eventually would wear out. But a permanent collection, such as books that will be on the shelves for years and years, and possibly never wear out, might be more like equipment and less like supplies. We understand, for example, that we're allowed to buy furnishings, like a new piano or a new table. But I can imagine a chair or a piano could wear out before a well-bound library book."

The banker smoothed back his thinning hair. His dark eyebrows furrowed. He rubbed his trim moustache with his thumb, as though formulating an argument. Then he said, "You've obviously thought about this. And it's an interesting argument. But I know what happens to library books. If they're in much demand at all, they wear out. Like Bibles and hymnals do."

Daniel suspected he'd lost the argument. But then Jorgensen said, "On the other hand, if you wanted to buy reference books, I'd think those would qualify. For example, if you wanted to buy a complete set of *Luther's Works*, those aren't likely to get worn out quickly — if ever."

The pastor said, "You've heard of *Luther's Works*? Are you Lutheran?"

"Well, culturally. I'm Danish. I guess that makes me an automatic Lutheran."

"So, are you from Denmark, then?"

"Not quite. Des Moines. My wife and I were active in a congregation there. You can't find a lot of Danish Lutheran congregations around here. In Minneapolis we have Norwegians and Swedes coming out of our ears, of course."

Daniel smiled. "And quite a few Germans."

"Yes. Of course."

"You know, we have a growing number of Scandinavians at St. Michael Church. Some German families started the congregation, but we've grown large enough that others are now joining us. We don't wear our German heritage on our sleeve. I'm not aware we have any Danes there yet. But it would be wonderful to add one or two of them."

Jorgensen smiled. "Did you really come here to talk about your endowment fund, or to get me back to church?"

"I had no idea what I'd encounter when I walked in here today, but with a name like Jorgensen, I suppose I might have guessed."

"In my family we have a saying: 'With a name like Jorgensen, you're either Lutheran or you've been tampered with.'"

Daniel laughed. He enjoyed the banker's quiet sense of humor. He said, "Here's a suggestion. You owe it to yourself, professionally, to see the place where all the money in your trust fund is getting spent ... "

"It's actually *your* trust fund."

"Of course. But you're the fund's custodian. So, why don't you come by some Sunday morning and look our building over? And you could stay for worship."

"I may just consider that. I'm sure Ingrid would be happy to have me show a little more interest in a church. She's the religious one. She doesn't nag, but I know she misses it."

"Well, visit us any time. You'd be more than welcome."

"Thank you for coming by. I realize we could have handled this on the phone."

"I like to put a face with a voice," said Daniel. "Besides, you never know when you'll run into someone who might need a church home."

"I'll mention you to Ingrid," Jorgensen said. He got up from his chair and ushered the pastor out.

ON THE DAY OF PENTECOST, the entire Pavelka family became members of St. Michael and All Angels Church. There were six other families who joined along with them.

One week later, as he was coming out of worship, Joe's teenage son paused at the church door and said to Daniel, "I'm curious about something."

"What's that, Tom?"

"The boys who carry the cross into church at the beginning of the service, and out again afterwards. How do they get to do that?"

"Do you mean, what kind of training do we give them?"

"No. I mean, is there some way I could take a turn at it?"

"You're interested in becoming a crucifer?"

"Yeah. I guess that's what I mean."

"There's always room for one more. Come by the church office some day next week. We'll show you what you need to know. And then we'll put you into the rotation."

From the broad smile on his face, Daniel would have thought the lad had just scored the winning touchdown for the Minnesota Gophers.

Chapter 30

The day after David Engelhardt graduated from the University of Minnesota, his father made him a junior partner in the printing business. Three weeks before, Adam had asked Luise Mensing at the church office to run a notice in the *St. Michael Messenger*, requesting used furniture. As a result, by the time David was out of college, the long-vacant apartment above the print shop was fully furnished. He and Molly would be able to move right in, following their honeymoon.

Molly went home to Litchfield after David's graduation. He would not see her again until the wedding. He spent the last two weeks as a single man working in the print shop, discussing with his father possible ways to move the business forward, thinking about Molly, and waiting for the arrival of his brother from Columbus, Ohio.

Jonathan returned to Minneapolis two days before the wedding. He regaled his parents and his younger brother with stories of life in the clothing store business. He explained that sales were down dramatically, that Uncle Adolph had been forced to let over half his workers go, and to close one of the stores he owned. Still, the company was holding on, and Jonathan was feeling hopeful they'd get through the downturn in one way or another.

He also announced he'd become serious about a young woman, whom he'd been seeing. Her name was Susan Schmidt, he explained, and she was "the most wonderful person he'd ever met" — present company excepted, of course. He'd come to know her at Trinity Lutheran Church in German Village. That was all he was willing to disclose. David wondered whether a second wedding might be on the horizon.

ON THE LAST FRIDAY MORNING in June, the Engelhardt family loaded into Adam's Ford and headed west, toward Litchfield. Along the way, Elsa kept turning around to talk to the groom-to-be, riding in the back seat. She peppered him with questions about his future in-laws. It was obvious to David that his mother was nervous about meeting the Lundgrens for the first time. He assured her everything would be fine. He took pains to speak glowingly of

Molly's mother, because he was confident the two women would get along famously.

What he said about Forrest was only what he felt compelled to share, which was very little.

The Lundgrens had arranged for the Engelhardts to stay in two nearby farm homes, Adam and Elsa with one family, David and Jonathan with the other. It was not until a half hour before the rehearsal that the parents of the bride and the groom met, in the church nave. David and Molly introduced everyone to everyone else. Forrest was conspicuously absent. When David asked Molly about it, she said he didn't have a part in the service and didn't need to be present.

Afterwards, the group went to the church basement, for a meal served by the women of the congregation. Jonathan, the best man, offered a toast to the bride and groom, as did Molly's older sister, Anna, the maid of honor. Again, David asked Molly what had become of Forrest. She told him he'd chosen to stay at home.

The next day, at two o'clock in the afternoon, David and Molly were married. The church was full. Molly's family and friends far outnumbered those who had made the journey from Minneapolis, in support of the Engelhardts.

Molly was radiant in white as she came down the aisle, on her father's arm. For David, the service was a blur. It seemed to him to have been only about six minutes before the pastor declared the benediction and they were headed back to the church basement, for the reception.

What Molly knew, but David didn't, was that her father had instructed his older son to make a public apology to the groom, before the couple left town. George Lundgren had learned the full story of Molly's ordeal from her own lips, and had passed the essence of it along to Forrest. He had also told his son that his behavior toward David had been inexcusable and that he had better find some way to make things right, or he could forget about inheriting the farm one day.

But Forrest was nowhere to be seen.

The wedding cake was cut and the bride and groom took turns feeding each other. Twenty minutes later, after the last of the crowd had been served, Molly stood up and asked for the group's attention. She thanked everyone for coming, and for the gifts which, she explained, would be opened after the honeymoon. Then David joined her, and added his own words of appreciation.

Forty minutes later, the couple began to move toward the door. Suddenly a loud, booming voice sounded through the room.

"Wait!"

It was Forrest, standing at the bottom of the basement stairs. Although not in what David would have called Sunday best, the young farmer was better dressed than he'd ever seen him.

Forrest walked to the head table and motioned for the crowd to be seated. He said, in a voice that was at first halting, "I ... have to apologize ... for missing the wedding and the reception and everything. I had work at the farm."

There was not a single person in the room who believed him. He said, "I want to congratulate the bride and the groom. I hope they'll be very happy together." David thought his words lacked conviction.

Then he said, "I also want to say something to my new brother-in-law." He looked at David directly. "I want to apologize for the way I've treated you the past few months. It was ... " He stopped in mid-sentence. It was as if he'd learned a script and then forgotten it. "It was wrong. I behaved like a jackass. I shouldn't have done it. And I'm sorry. Very sorry."

The crowd listened in stunned silence. Except for David, Molly and her parents, nobody had the first idea what he was talking about.

And then, as quickly as he had come, Forrest disappeared.

THE MAID BROUGHT the last of the evening meal to the table, and then dismissed herself. Jens looked toward his wife. For some reason — he could not remember exactly why — he had always deferred to her to ask the blessing for the food. Sometimes Ingrid Jorgensen spoke the prayer in Danish, as had been her custom as a child. This evening she chose English.

Lord God, who gives us every good,
We ask your blessing on this food.
Nourish our bodies with this meal,
And for our lives your will reveal. Amen.

"Amen," Jens muttered. He opened his eyes and looked toward his daughter. He wasn't sure whether Sonja had said Amen or not. He decided that was between her and God.

As he dished vegetables onto his plate, Ingrid asked, "How was your day, dear?"

"We're still letting employees go," he replied. "The markets are in the tank. Nothing's getting better. If this keeps up, I'll have to give up my job in the trust department and go to work as a teller."

Ingrid looked out through the dining room window, across the intersection, to the stately homes in her line of vision. She wondered, now that the Depression was throwing so many people out of work, whether she ought to feel guilty, living so comfortably in the upscale Kenwood neighborhood. But, as Jens kept reminding her, he was a bank officer and it was almost expected that they live in such a house.

Jens said, "I still think President Hoover is the right man for the job. But he just doesn't seem to know what to do about stopping the downward business spiral. He says things are bound to get better. But it's getting harder and harder to believe him."

Fifteen-year-old Sonja was growing impatient with the conversation. "Daddy, you always talk about business at the supper table. Why can't we discuss a happier topic for a change?"

Jens looked at his only child. He thought, *Ingrid can't have any more children, and the one I have has absolutely no interest in banking. I'm never going to have a male heir, unless I adopt one. What's to become of this family?* But his daughter's complaint had some legitimacy, he decided.

"All right, Sonja. What do you suggest we talk about?"

"Good news of some sort, if you don't mind."

"Well, do you know of any at the moment?"

She'd turned the conversation in exactly the direction she wanted it to go. "As a matter of fact, yes!" There was elation in her voice.

"Well, don't keep us in suspense. What good news do you know?"

"You remember I told you the kids at Luther League are going to put on a play for the congregation?"

The Jorgensens had started worshiping at St. Michael Church in late summer. Even before Jens had applied for formal membership for his family, Sonja had joined the church youth group. It was clear to him that one particularly handsome young crucifer, with black curly hair, had provided a lot of the incentive. She'd discovered he was an active Luther Leaguer, and shortly thereafter she'd begun attending meetings of the youth group.

"Well," Sonja continued, "we had tryouts at our meeting last night, and I got one of the main parts!"

"Sonja!" her mother said, beaming. "That's wonderful. What part will you have?"

"This should please Daddy," she said, looking at her father. "I'm a rich man's wife."

Jens was impressed, but also puzzled. "What sort of church play has a rich man's wife in it?"

"It's called 'Holy Joe's Uptown Adventure.'"

"That's a sassy sounding title for a church play," Ingrid interjected.

"Oh, Mom, it's written for young people. You have to jazz up the title a little, so kids will be interested."

Her father said, "Well, okay. What's the play about, exactly?"

Sonja said, "It's a morality play. This farmer boy's older brothers all are going to inherit part of the farm, except for Joe. He gets crowded out. So, he leaves home and takes up with this traveling salesman. The salesman shows him how to sell stuff out of the back of his wagon. But then one night, while they're sleeping, a thief gets away with all the merchandise. And the next morning the salesman thinks the farmer boy is in on the robbery. He's so mad, he sells him to a traveler for enough money to pay for what was stolen."

"Sounds a little unbelievable," Jens said.

Sonja seemed not to hear the comment. "And so then he gets sold again. To a really rich businessman, who wants a servant to run his property. And while the businessman goes off to the office, the rich man's wife tries to get Holy Joe to make love to her. But he won't do it. That's why they call him 'Holy Joe.' So, when her husband comes home, she lies to him and says Joe did it to her even when he didn't."

"This sounds like a fairly rude story," Ingrid objected.

"It's based on a Bible story, Mother. Anyway, Holy Joe ends up getting blamed for something he didn't do — for a second time! So, he goes to jail. And the governor accidentally discovers him there when he's giving pardons to prisoners. Holy Joe tells him how he was falsely accused, and the governor finds out he's really good with numbers and everything, so he puts Joe to work in the state banking commission. And he rises right up to the top, until he's the governor's advisor."

"So, in other words, it's about not losing your integrity," Jens said. "That sounds like a good theme for a church play."

"But the businessman's wife sounds like a hussy," Ingrid remarked. "Does that part have to be in there?"

"Sure, Mother. It's what makes the story interesting. Besides, I'll bet things like that actually happen in the real world. Don't you think so?"

"Well, maybe," Ingrid said. "But that sounds like a play for a theatre on Hennepin Avenue, not on a church basement stage."

"Mu-thurrr!" Sonya said, sounding irritated.

"Don't use that tone with your mother, young lady."

"Well, criminy, Daddy ..."

"And don't bring that slang into this house either."

Sonja sighed heavily. "Here I am, telling you really good news, and you're just making it sound like something terrible."

"You said the play was based on a Bible story," Ingrid said. "Which one?"

"Joseph in Egypt," said Sonya, sounding sullen. "It's in the Book of Genesis."

Her father said, "Really! Well, that's very creative." He looked at his wife and said, "I think that's a wonderful way to give that story a modern meaning."

The stressful look on Ingrid Jorgensen's face seemed to fade. She said, "All right, dear. We won't say anything more about the play. As long as the Luther League sponsors think it's okay."

"They *suggested* it, Mother!"

"Fine. And you said your part is the rich man's wife?"

"Yes. I get to try to seduce Holy Joe."

Ingrid gasped. "Did you have to take that part?"

"Well, no, I could have been one of the boring dancing women, who show up at the rich man's party and never get to say anything."

Jens said, "Just out of curiosity. Who will play the part of Holy Joe?"

"Tom Pavelka," Sonja said. "He's such a dreamboat. I get to kiss him, right on stage."

Her parents looked at her wide-eyed.

"Don't get all excited about it. It's only a pretend kiss." She paused, then said, "Unfortunately."

Chapter 31

Frieda Stellhorn rocked slowly back and forth, reminiscing. Daniel always enjoyed visiting in her cluttered apartment, with antiques and memorabilia all about. There were members of St. Michael Church who were pretty sure Frieda was an antique herself. Daniel was not one of them.

"It's changing, Pastor," she said philosophically. "St. Michael Church isn't what it was back in the beginning."

Daniel chuckled silently. 'Back in the beginning' was scarcely four years ago, when the congregation had been organized as a living room congregation. But he knew what she meant.

"Who would have thought our little flock would have grown so fast?" she said, seeming to marvel at it all. "Who would have thought we'd get such a fine young pastor, with the ability to draw so many people together?"

"Who would have thought a philanthropist would have given us five million dollars?" Daniel interjected.

"But that's all part of it, don't you see? If you hadn't paid attention to a stranger, and behaved like a true shepherd, just when you did, that bequest would never have come to us."

Daniel had been working on humility lately. He wanted to steer the conversation in a different direction. "Frieda, how are you doing?"

"What do you mean?"

"Well, you'll be eighty-two next month. And you're still taking the streetcar over to St. Paul Luther College to help out. Aren't you getting a little tired, doing that?"

She looked sternly at the pastor. "Now you listen to me, young man. That college is my life. I've poured a decade of love into that school. They always tell me they appreciate it when I come."

"Oh, I don't doubt that's all true," Daniel said. "But it's a long trip from here, all the way to the east side of St. Paul. And you do it all by yourself."

She smiled. "It's nice you worry so much about a frail old lady. That's what I mean about you. You're a good pastor. You pay attention to people. But, Pastor …"

"Yes?"

"Don't worry about Frieda Stellhorn. She can take perfectly good care of herself, thank you very much."

She got out of the rocking chair and walked to the door leading to her tiny kitchen. Turning back toward Daniel, she said, "I've got tea ready. You'll drink some, of course."

She said it as if it was a declaration of fact.

Daniel heard the kettle whistling on Frieda's stove. He got out of his chair and prowled about the living room, looking at the collector's items the congregation's matriarch had accumulated over the decades. His eyes came to rest on an engraving inside an old molded frame, the wood almost black beneath layers of lacquer. It was a picture of an old brick building on a city street, with a horse and carriage passing its front door. The caption beneath read:

> *First home of the Lutheran Seminary*
> *Joint Synod of Ohio and Other States*
> *Canton, Ohio*

He remembered from his course in American Lutheran church history that the German pioneers had started the school there in 1830, only to move it to Columbus a short time later. He was not surprised that Frieda kept this relic from her hometown on her living-room wall.

Suddenly he heard a noisy clatter coming from the kitchen. He dashed across the room, to the doorway, and peered inside. Frieda was lying on the floor, not moving. Around her lay the debris from the spilled serving tray — cups, saucers, spoons, a broken sugar bowl, and a plate, its cookies scattered. Fortunately, she hadn't yet poured the tea.

Daniel knelt beside her and said, "Frieda? Are you all right?"

The elderly woman moaned softly, then said, "I'm fine. Just let me be for a moment or two." Her eyes remained closed, but her breathing seemed steady.

He began picking up the items littering the floor and piling them onto the table. Frieda moaned a second time. He knelt beside her again.

"You can help me up now," she said, opening her eyes. There was a drawn, distant look on her face.

He lifted her from the floor and guided her to the nearest chair. She sat quietly, calming herself, breathing deeply. He sat next to her, watching with concern. Finally, she said, "I'm better now."

"Frieda, has this happened to you before?"

"Sometimes my heart beats a little faster than I think it should. It makes me dizzy, just for a moment or so. But I've never fallen down before." She looked at the broken sugar bowl. "I'm so sorry. I wanted to give you a nice cup of tea."

"Listen, Frieda, I want to take you over to Fairview Hospital."

"No."

"Just to have them check you over."

"No. I've never been inside a hospital in my life. And I'm not starting now."

"You know, with you living here alone and everything, something could happen to you when nobody's around. There wouldn't be anyone to help you."

"I'm not a helpless old woman," she snapped crossly.

"Well, you are eighty-one. And there's no shame in having a few health problems when a person reaches your age."

She glowered at him. "All right. You can take me to the hospital. But I'm not staying there. Do you understand? I'm *not staying*!"

"I understand," he said. He went to the stove and turned off the flame beneath the whistling teapot. Then he went to find Frieda's coat.

INGRID JORGENSEN picked up the meat platter and passed it to the fifteen-year-old seated at the end of the table. "Have some more, Tom. You look like you're a hungry young man."

"Thank you, Mrs. Jorgensen," Tom Pavelka replied. He forked another slice of roast beef and moved it to his plate.

"That was a fine play," Jens Jorgensen said, looking down the length of the table. "You young people did an excellent job putting it all together."

Sonja Jorgensen looked proudly at Tom. She could hardly believe her parents had agreed to invite him to Sunday dinner.

"After we saw what a fine young actor you are," said Ingrid, "we decided we really needed to get to know you better. Especially if you're going to be kissing our daughter right out in public."

Tom blushed. Sonya scowled at her mother. But Ingrid was having a little joke, and Tom quickly realized it. "My own mother wondered about that scene, when I first told her about it," he confessed.

"I've met your mother," said Ingrid. "She's a delightful woman. We spoke during the coffee time at church not long ago."

"Sonja tells us you've become quite active in the Luther League at St. Michael Church," Jens said.

"It's a great group," Tom replied. "Our family hasn't been in the congregation so very long. The kids in Luther League have made me feel welcome in a hurry." He looked at Ingrid and said, "Besides, that's where I met your daughter."

Her parents looked from Tom to their daughter and back again to Tom. Tom said, "I was wondering. Would you permit me to take Sonja to a motion picture show sometime?"

Jens looked at Ingrid. Her eyebrow arched ever so slightly, but then he thought he saw her nod. He said, "Not on a school night."

"I was thinking of a matinee."

"I don't think going to the motion pictures on a Sunday afternoon would be a good idea," said her mother. "It's the Sabbath, you know."

"I was thinking of Saturday," said Tom.

"You'd bring her home right afterwards?"

Tom nodded. He glanced at Sonja. She seemed embarrassed by the grilling she thought he was receiving. Tom winked at her.

"Of course, you'd treat her the way a gentleman should," Jens said quietly.

"Oh, yes, sir. A *perfect* gentleman. I wouldn't kiss her in public or anything like that."

He wished he hadn't said it, but it was too late. He looked at Sonja's mother, afraid he'd just ruined his chances. He needn't have worried. Ingrid Jorgensen was pursing her lips, poorly concealing her amusement.

"We like you quite a lot, Tom," she said. "We're sure the two of you will behave yourselves."

Tom said, " Did Sonja tell you we're already thinking about another play for the Luther League to perform? Next year, right after Easter."

"No," Jens said. "But I think that's nice. Will you be in it, Tom?"

"I hope so. Especially if Sonja gets a part."

IT HAD BEEN A MONTH since Frieda Stellhorn collapsed on her kitchen floor. The physician at the hospital had told her she'd had a mild heart spell, and that she should not continue to live alone.

Daniel had discovered that his office manager was at the end of her lease and, since the rent was going up, had decided not to renew it When Luise Mensing learned that Frieda was a retired librarian, she offered to move into the spare room in the older woman's apartment and help whatever way she could.

At first Frieda had refused, but when she realized she might otherwise not be able to stay in her apartment, and that Luise would pay half the rent, she reluctantly agreed.

Luise's apartment had been furnished, so she had only her clothes and a few other things to bring along. During the first three days of the new arrangement, Frieda laid down the law. She was constantly reminding her new housemate how she did things and how she was not about to change to accommodate to someone else. She was constantly snapping at Luise, after which she would apologize. But, a short time later, she would be back at her snappishness.

Luise finally went to Pastor Jonas with her concern. She said, "I'm not sure this is going to work out. I'm really frustrated. I can't do anything right. Frieda is always complaining about something. I almost wish I had just paid the higher rent and stayed in my old place."

Daniel listened, nodding with understanding.

Luise said, "She seems so … I don't know … angry, I think."

"Well, you would be too if someone told you to share your space, after sixty years of living alone, and suddenly having to give up the freedom and independence you'd always had."

Luise nodded.

"And there's the fact that she's been a librarian for forty years, and a very good one. For the last ten years, she's volunteered over at St. Paul Luther College. That's been a source of real fulfillment for her. Now, suddenly, she's not allowed to do that any more. I might be a little angry, too."

Luise looked disappointed. She had hoped for a solution, and wasn't getting one. She sighed heavily. "Is this what it means, having a cross to bear?"

Daniel smiled. "No. Cross-bearing is usually life-threatening. Or, do you think this is in that category?"

Luise grinned. "No. I guess not. It's probably in the category of me feeling sorry for myself." She sighed again. "But I wish there was something we could find for Frieda to do."

"Well," Daniel said, "have you considered asking her to become your assistant in the church library? You've got all those new reference books and they're still in the cartons. When were you planning to catalog them?"

Luise became defensive. "I haven't exactly been sitting around, twiddling my thumbs. This is getting to be a big congregation. Being an office manager is a full-time job."

"That's what I suggested to you when you volunteered to start the library."

She looked sheepish.

He said,"I'm not saying that to criticize you. I brought it up because it occurs to me that Frieda would make a great assistant church librarian. If you want to have her do it. And if she wants to volunteer her services."

Chapter 32

David Engelhardt crawled into bed and, turning on his side, snuggled up against the back of his sleeping wife. Molly had been in bed for an hour. He smoothed his hand along her side and felt her breathing. He moved his fingers down across her smooth belly, searching with his finger for her navel, through the fabric of her nightgown. He moved his hand higher, to discover the round contour of her breast.

He sighed contentedly. They'd become one flesh for the first time on a warm June night, six months before, in a little shoreline summer cabin on the edge of Lake Superior. Since then, their lovemaking had been a delight to both of them.

Until now. With the arrival of winter, Molly had begged off becoming intimate with him. She began complaining of not feeling well. There had been times of crankiness, followed by apologies, and then more crankiness.

At first he'd wondered whether she had relapsed into the nightmares that used to plague her. Maybe, he thought, she was remembering how she'd been violated by that vile stockbroker. And, maybe going to worship each Sunday in a building her former employer had paid for was finally beginning to take its toll on her.

He cupped her breast with his hand and, drawing closer, kissed her softly on the back of her neck. She stirred, murmured, and then turned onto her back. She opened her eyes, looked at him in the semi-darkness, and said, "I'm sorry, David."

"It's okay. I'm just going to go to sleep now."

"No. That's not what I mean."

"Excuse me?"

"I'm sorry for being so hard to live with for the last two weeks."

"It's okay."

"I didn't understand why I was feeling so grouchy all the time."

"Hope it wasn't anything I said or did."

"Well, actually it was."

"I beg your pardon?"

"You've gotten me pregnant, you silly goose."

LUTHER FISCHER STEPPED away from the piano. He cleared his throat. Singing the difficult tenor solo had given his vocal chords a workout.

Lillian Gardner turned around on the piano bench and said, "So, what do you think?"

"It's wonderful. I love that piece. I love the entire score of *Elijah*. But do you really think the senior choir would be up to performing it?"

"I don't know why not. Church choirs sing *The Messiah* — until people get sick of hearing it, if you want my opinion. But how often do they get to hear *Elijah*?"

"Well, not very often, I have to admit."

"Of course you do. Because I'm right."

He grinned at her. The feistier she became, the more he liked her.

"Come on," she said, getting up. "Wilma has tea ready."

As they descended the stairs, he said, "If your landlady keeps inviting me over here, I'm going to have to start paying rent."

"You take that up with her," Lillian said, leading the way into the dining room.

As the tea was being poured, Wilma Shaughnessy said, "You two certainly do make beautiful music together."

"Why, thank you," said Lillian.

"I wasn't talking about what I just heard upstairs, although that was awfully nice, too."

"Wilma, you're talking in riddles," said Lillian.

"I'm talkin' about the two of you. You're such a pair. Half the jokes you tell go right over the top of my head, but the two of you know exactly what you're talkin' about."

Luther sipped his tea, then set down the cup. "It's just banter, Wilma. We're having a contest to see who can make the wittiest comment, or the cleverest comeback."

"Well, whatever it is, you're awfully good at it. So ..."

"So?" Lillian responded.

"So, are you an item yet? The both of you together?"

Luther had an amused look on his face. But Lillian was looking stern. She said, "Listen, any relationship I have with Luther is strictly platonic."

"It *is*?" Luther said, half surprised, half irritated.

"Absolutely."

"Well," said Wilma, spooning sugar into her cup, "you can be as platonic as you like. But I've seen plenty of mis-matches in my day. And, as far as I can tell, this is definitely not one of them."

ON HIS SON'S SIXTEENTH BIRTHDAY, Joe Pavelka gave Tom a used Chevrolet. There were conditions attached. Tom had to submit to driving lessons, provided by his father. He had to inform his father before he drove the car anywhere, explaining where he intended to go and why, and when he expected to return. That requirement, Joe explained to his son, would continue until he was eighteen. Then he'd be on his own.

In exchange, Joe agreed to pay for maintaining the car, buying the gas and oil, and providing the insurance. Tom was delighted with the gift, especially since he hadn't expected it. His unhappiness about the rules his father laid down was balanced with the fact that he could now drive to Luther League, and to Sonja's home in Kenwood. And they could have more privacy on their dates.

The first Saturday out with Sonja in his very own automobile, Tom took her on a ride along the south Minneapolis parkway, beginning at Lake of the Isles, then down to Lake Calhoun, Lake Harriet, and along Minnehaha Parkway, to the famous falls near the Mississippi River. They spent a long time watching the water cascade into the pool below the overhang, before Tom said, "You want to be my special girl, Sonja?"

She looked at him with puzzlement. "What do you mean, Tom?"

"Just promise to go on dates with me and nobody else."

She grinned. "That's what I'm doing now, I think."

"I know. But promise me it will keep on being like that."

"Well, it will. Until one of us decides it's time we should stop going together."

"That won't ever happen, will it?"

"Tom, how could I be so sure? We're still in high school. Maybe we'll both go off to college and meet other people."

"Golly, I hope not."

"Well, right now, I hope not either. My folks really like you."

He beamed with appreciation. "I think my folks like you, too."

"But you're not quite sure?"

"Well, my dad doesn't always say exactly what he means. My mother likes your parents, and especially your mother. And she's said she thinks you're a lovely young woman."

"What does your father say?"

"So far, the only thing he's really said about us is, 'Tom, don't do anything foolish.'"

"Well, so far we haven't, have we?"

"No. But you know what? There are days when I'd really like to."

"Tom, what are you saying?"

"Sonja, I think about you all the time when we're not together. I don't know if I'm in love with you, because I don't know what that's supposed to feel like. But if it means being sick in your stomach, and being short of breath, and having your heart beat faster than normal, and not being able to sleep at night, then I'm head over heels."

"I really like you a lot, Tom. I haven't felt sick in my stomach yet. But once in a while I do get a little dizzy, thinking about us. And all my friends say you and I make a really keen couple."

He pulled her close to him and kissed her.

She sighed with contentment. But then she said, "I think we'd better keep in mind what your father told you."

LUISE MENSING peered in at the door of the Reformation Room from the doorway. Frieda Stellhorn was seated at one of the library tables, eating the lunch she'd brought with her. Luise said, "You certainly do know library work, Frieda. This place looks wonderful."

Frieda said, "I've only been helping out here for six weeks. Maybe a year from now you'll change your mind."

"I can't imagine I would," Luise said, stepping inside. She studied with admiration the stained-glass window panel picturing the Wartburg Castle. At mid-day, the sunlight came streaming through, giving the mountaintop fortress an ethereal look.

"Come here. Sit down a minute," said Frieda. "I want to show you something."

Luise took the chair next to Frieda. The older woman lifted a small volume with blue binding. She said, "I took this little book out of my personal collection. I'm donating it to the church library."

She handed it to Luise, who held it with both hands and read the gold lettering on the front cover: *History of the Joint Synod of Ohio*. The author was C.V. Sheatsley. She opened the cover and read, "From the personal library of Frieda Stellhorn."

Frieda said, "We can cover that up with a bookplate."

"Are you sure you want to give up this book?" Luise asked.

"Well, I suppose we could order a new copy from the Wartburg Press. But why do that? I'm giving you this one for free."

"Yes, but, this is your personal copy."

"Listen," Frieda retorted, "I'm eighty-two years old. I'm not going to live forever. When I die, who's going to get my things? I'd rather decide that for myself."

"Well, nobody's planning on having you die, Frieda."

"Nobody ever *does* plan things like that. Today I feel fine. Next month I might not. Let's be realistic about this."

Luise was getting uncomfortable with the discussion. She said, "Thank you for giving this book to the church library. I assume you've read it."

"Every page. It's not perfect. But it has some good information."

"What's not perfect about it?"

"Well, it talks a lot about Capital University. But it's pretty thin on St. Paul Luther College. *Extremely* thin."

Chapter 33

The batter sizzled as it hit the griddle. Joe Pavelka watched the four pancakes he had just poured spread out on the hot surface, then began teasing at them, around their edges, with his spatula. When he'd waited just the right length of time, he slid the flat utensil under each of them, flipping them over.

As he did so, he looked to his left, where Jens Jorgensen was trying to keep up with him. "Thanks for helping out in the kitchen," Joe said. "You're making those hotcakes like a professional."

"I'll bet you never thought you'd see a banker in an apron," Jens replied.

"All for a good cause," said Joe, shoveling the finished pancakes from his griddle and piling them onto a plate. "If it wasn't for the likes of you and me, there wouldn't be any Shrove Tuesday supper at all."

Jens looked out through the serving window, into the fellowship room. He said, "Where are all these people coming from? Do you suppose we'll run out of food?"

"Are you kidding? We've got enough pancake mix here to feed everybody in south Minneapolis."

"I certainly hope we don't have to do that," said Jens cheerfully, clearing his griddle. He poured four more cakes onto the hot surface.

"Jens, there's something I've been wanting to ask you," Joe said.

"What's that?"

"From your perspective, as a bank officer, just where exactly do you think the country is headed? I'm talking about the economy."

The banker sighed. "It's not a pretty picture. We're still seeing company foreclosures. The number of people out of work is still going up. I don't see our president offering any good ideas. At this rate, we're likely to end up with a Democrat in the White House."

"Would that be bad?"

"Well, I don't know, exactly. Part of me says, stay with the party that's always been a friend to business. Another part of me says, nothing's working. We may have to try something else."

Joe said, "What about your bank? Are you doing all right?"

"We'll do fine. We've been careful, especially since the crash. Although, I feel sorry for a lot of people who used to be our customers. Some of them have lost everything."

The two men worked in silence. Then Jens said, "What about you, Joe? I know you had to give up your business, but that son of yours tells me you're the best Chevrolet salesman in town."

Joe smiled with pretended modesty. "Tom has a high opinion of his father."

"Well, Pastor Jonas tells me he's absolutely delighted with that new car you sold *him*."

"I got him a deal," said Joe. "Clergy discount." He grinned. Then he said, "Jens, what's your advice to someone who wants to think about taking out a business loan right now? Is this a bad time to do something like that?"

Jens laughed. "You expect a banker to tell you not to take out a loan?" He paused, as if pondering why the question had arisen. He said, "If the borrower has thought it through carefully, and has sufficient collateral, this could be a very good time for a loan. While I regret the unfortunate circumstances of so many people who have suffered reversals, it could be a time of great opportunity, for the person prepared to take advantage of the current situation."

He looked at Joe and said, "Sorry if that just sounded like I was reading from an investment prospectus. That's the way bankers like to talk."

"Don't apologize. I understood what you said perfectly well." He took a deep breath and exhaled. "Here's the thing, Jens. I really am doing well at the dealership. I'm now the top salesman for the firm. Maybe not the best in all of Minneapolis, but I haven't taken a survey to find out."

Jens laughed.

"But the owner of the dealership is experiencing some liquidity problems right now."

"He's looking for some ready cash."

"Exactly. And he's suggested to me I might want to consider buying into ownership. You know, become a partner."

Jens nodded.

"I've actually managed to save some money during the last couple of years."

"It's in my bank, I hope."

"I could move it there."

The two men laughed in spite of themselves.

Joe continued, "And, I have some equity in my house. I'd need to take a business loan for the rest. Which means, if I'd do this, I'd be pretty heavily leveraged."

"There's always a risk," said Jens. "But you're the sort of fellow who doesn't shy away from taking a reasonable one, I'm guessing."

"Well. Yes. That's true. But the thing is, I've been burned once already. I don't think I could survive losing a business a second time. So, I'm really hesitant to take a step like this. Unless I can feel confident — really confident — that it's a wise move."

"Well, people are making business investments every day. The clever ones will do just fine. You have to be careful. Don't take foolish chances. Our bank continues to make business loans. Of course, I'm not a loan officer. I'm in the trust department. But, if you think you're really serious about this, and want to explore it with us, come downtown and I'll introduce you to the right person. And I'll put in a good word for you."

Joe returned a thoughtful look. "Thanks, Jens. I'll think some more about this. And you may be hearing from me."

They continued making pancakes. Suddenly Joe said, "Oh, and there's one other thing I need to ask you."

"Yes?"

"Have you by any chance been considering taking out adoption papers on my son?"

"I don't understand."

"Well, Tom's spending almost all of his free time at your house these days. I thought maybe you were planning on adopting him."

Jens laughed. He said, "Well, if I thought he was available, I'd do it in a New York minute."

ON THE THIRD SUNDAY IN LENT, during the morning Eucharist, Rosetta Jonas brought her newborn son to the baptismal font. For the second time, Daniel experienced the high privilege of baptizing one his own children.

"Joshua Daniel Jonas," he intoned, while a riveted congregation looked on, "I baptize you in the name of the Father, and of the Son, and of the Holy Spirit. Amen." Then he traced the sign of the cross on the child's forehead.

At the conclusion of the Sacrament, Rosetta turned with the infant in her arms, back toward her pew. Her eye caught sight of the great stained-glass window in the side chapel. It wasn't the figure of Jesus that commanded her attention, but the image of a five-year-old boy, sitting at Jesus' feet. In that instant she found herself whispering what she later decided was a highly irrational prayer: "Lord, keep this child safe from on-rushing delivery vans."

AS THE REHEARSAL ROOM began to empty, Lillian Gardner remained behind to stack and store the music. It took her a few moments to realize there was a stranger standing at the door. At first she assumed it was Luther Fischer, waiting to walk her home. But then she remembered. Luther had stayed at home, in bed with a cold.

The man at the door was perhaps forty, dressed in the clothing of a day laborer. His dark brown hair was already showing hints of gray. He had an intense look about him. Without an invitation, he stepped into the room, which except for the two of them, was now deserted.

"May I help you?" Lillian asked, feeling vaguely uncomfortable. It was eight-thirty at night and she had no escort.

Without bothering to introduce himself, the stranger said, "Sounds like you're going to go through with it."

"I beg your pardon?"

"*Elijah.* You're actually going to perform it. I was standing in the hall, listening to your singers practice."

"Yes. That's right. The afternoon of Palm Sunday. Four o'clock. Come early and get a good seat."

"Oh, you won't be seeing *me* there."

She detected a hint of disdain in his voice.

"Why couldn't you have chosen *The Messiah,* like most churches around here do?"

"For precisely that reason. If everybody else does the same thing, what's the point of one more rendition?"

"You could have picked John Stainer's *The Seven Last Words.*"

"Rather sentimental, wouldn't you say?"

"Oh, I don't know. It was good enough for the church I used to belong to."

"And where do you go now?"

"Lots of places. I travel around."

"And why is that?"

"To hear what preachers are saying. To make sure they're giving it to their people straight. So far, yours passes muster."

"I wasn't aware ours required a board of review," she said, barely hiding her sarcasm.

"Maybe he doesn't. But I think maybe *you* might."

She viewed him through slanted eyes. If he'd been her son, she would seriously have considered slapping him. "Just exactly what is your point?"

"My point is, you have no business performing *Elijah* in a Christian church."

"And how did you come to that discovery?"

"Mendelssohn wrote it, right?"

"Yes?"

"And you don't think that's a problem?"

"For your information, Felix Mendelssohn was a member of the Lutheran Church. Can I say the same for you?"

He ignored her question. "Mendelssohn was a Jew."

Suddenly it began to register. The man was an anti-Semite.

"I used to own a nice little store over on Chicago Avenue," he went on. "When the crash came, I had to sell out. Then some Jew family bought it. They're making money hand over fist. *In my store!*" His face was beginning to turn red. "People in this country had better wake up. The Jew class is taking over. Their slimy tentacles are going everywhere. They already have the banks. Now they're going after the businesses and the factories. When they get the churches, we're done for."

Lillian thought, *this man is making no sense whatsoever.* She said, "Did it ever occur to you that Jesus was a Jew? So were all of his disciples. If it wasn't for the Jewish people, Christianity wouldn't exist."

"That's just Jew propaganda. I've heard it all before." He moved closer to her, pointed his finger menacingly and said, "They've got the right idea in Germany. If the National Socialists get into power, they're going to round them all up and get rid of them. That's what we should be doing here!"

He shook his finger, his face boiling. But he'd spoken his last word. He turned and marched out of the music room.

And Lillian Gardner, weak in the knees, found it necessary to sit down. After she had done so, she realized her heart was racing.

Chapter 34

After the sunrise breakfast, the Children's Choir concert, and the festive Liturgy for the Resurrection of Our Lord, Daniel went home to dinner with his family. With Hannah Ruth in her highchair and baby Joshua cooing in his cradle nearby, they shared a quiet Easter dinner together.

While eating dessert, the pastor dropped a bombshell on his wife. He said, "I've been thinking about the future. I'll have been here five years next winter. I wonder if I should give my name to the President of the Minnesota District."

"What for?"

"To have it circulated. For possible call. To another congregation."

"Why on earth would you do that?"

"Because I think five years may be long enough to serve in one congregation. I don't want to become a fixture here."

She said, "Daniel, back in Ohio there were pastors who spent their entire ministry in one congregation."

"I'll never do that. Can you imagine how stale their preaching must have become?"

"Yours is giving no sign of doing that."

"That's why it might be the right time to consider a move."

"Daniel, have people been saying things to make you think it's time for you to go?"

"No. Well, maybe. Twice in the past week I've had people tell me that, in the neighborhood they're starting to describe St. Michael Church as 'Pastor Jonas' church.' That's not what I want to see happen. The church isn't *me*. It's the people God draws into this place for worship and service. If they start confusing it with *me*, we're in real trouble."

"You know, back when they started putting up the new building, you were worried about doing it out of pride. Remember how we talked about that?"

"How could I not remember that?"

"Well, I know pastors of large congregations can fall into the trap of thinking it's all about them."

"Pastors of small congregations can fall into the same trap," he admitted.

"But I don't think that's been the case with you. And, if you're worried about people identifying the congregation with you, why don't you preach a sermon about that?"

"Haven't I ever done that?"

"Not specifically."

"Well. Perhaps I should then."

"All I know is, if you offer to relocate now, there will be a lot of terribly disappointed people. And, to be honest, I'd be one of them."

"You really like it here, don't you?"

"How could I leave all our friends? And Molly hasn't even had her baby yet."

"She'll have it before summer's end."

"But I want to see him — or her — grow up a little bit. And, she's already told me, she hopes Hannah and Joshua can become playmates for her child."

"Well, we can't make decisions for the Kingdom of God based on things like that."

"Maybe not. But just keep yourself open to the possibility that God wants you staying in this part of the Kingdom, and not going looking for greener pastures somewhere else."

"I'm not looking for greener pastures. The pasture is pretty green right here. That's why I don't want to get too comfortable in it."

"Pray about it, Daniel."

"I will."

"And don't make it a one-way conversation when you do."

JENS JORGENSEN steered the Lincoln along the last half mile of the gravel road. The granulated surface crunched beneath the touring car's tires. He studied the road ahead, looking for the first signs of his destination.

"Thank you for taking a few hours out of your day to make this trip with me, Pastor Jonas," he said, glancing at his guest in the passenger seat.

"Always a pleasure to spend some time with you, Jens. Since we left Minneapolis, you've given me a very thorough update on our trust account, and a good reminder of how we can — and cannot — spend the earnings."

"Well, it never hurts to stay current," the banker said. Then a hint of excitement entered his voice. "All right, look up ahead now. You can start to see it."

Daniel studied the opening the road created through the thick stand of trees. He thought he saw a building of some kind. Suddenly the road became rough

229

and bumpy. But the pastor wasn't focused on that. "Jens," he said, "I expect this to be something really amazing. You've kept me in suspense for the past hour."

"Well," he replied, pulling into a clearing, "I was pretty amazed the first time I saw it." He pulled up next to a large wooden building and cut the engine. "Come on, let me show you."

They climbed out and Jens began conducting a walking tour. "This used to be an old youth camp," he said. "Some private group ran it for a few years. This big building here was a dining hall. Still has tables and chairs inside. The kitchen's pretty rudimentary." They walked to the front of the large structure.

"Jens, there's a *lake* out here!"

"With four little islands, out there in the middle. Each has its own small forest."

"And, look over there. Is that a dormitory?"

"More like a barracks," Jens replied. "That's where the young campers slept. There are still cots inside. Pretty musty and dusty, though." He pointed beyond the building to another like it. "There were two of them. One for the young men, one for the boys."

They walked along, through high weeds, across what clearly had once been a manicured campus. Jens said, "This place has been neglected for so long, it's all going to go back to forest in a few more years. Then these buildings will be hard to find."

"And what was this?" asked Daniel, peering in through a dirty pane of glass.

"An activity house. They did crafts in there. Stored some of their supplies. Mostly just trash in there now."

They kept walking. "Here's what used to be a canoe shed. You see, they had racks in here for twelve of them. Of course, they're all gone now. Out behind there's an old rowboat. I wouldn't be surprised if it was still seaworthy. Not sure I'd want to be the one to find out." He laughed. "And farther down the lake there are six cabins the counselors used."

Daniel said, "So, whatever happened to the camp? And how long has it been abandoned?"

"Well, the group that ran it had some wealthy patrons. They gave them a bigger campus, with buildings ready to go, on another lake, up by Crosby. That was almost ten years ago. So they moved the whole operation up there and let this place run down."

"Was it a religious group?" Daniel prodded.

"No. A private outfit. Some fraternal organization. A men's club that wanted to do work with boys and young men. They're still doing it, of course. Just not here."

They walked together, through the tall grass, down to the lakeshore. "The camp association actually owned all the land surrounding the lake. So that means they owned the lake itself, and those four cute little islands out there."

They approached the foot of a decaying dock. Jens said, "I wouldn't recommend walking on this. I might have to pull you out from between the planks."

Daniel said, "So, Jens, how did you become aware of this place?"

"Well, the fraternal started running short of money after the stock market went down. They'd always kept ownership of this place. I think they had the idea they might reopen it, as a second camp, if their program grew. Instead, their program got smaller. They're having trouble paying operating expenses on their campus up at Crosby. So they put this place up for sale."

"So it's available?" Daniel said. Beyond the rotting dock and sagging buildings, he saw all kinds of possibilities.

"Well, it *was*."

The pastor's heart sank. "Somebody's purchased it." He sighed. "Too bad we didn't know about it sooner. Maybe we could have found some funds to make an offer."

"You'd have had to bid against me," Jens said dryly.

Daniel looked at the banker, uncomprehending. Then he said, "*You* bought this old camp, Jens?"

"I bought the entire parcel. I'm now the owner of my own lake — and four little islands," he said proudly. "But I have to find a way to unload this camp property, so I don't have to worry about taking care of it. Or tearing it down." He looked impishly at Daniel. "You don't know any church that might be interested in having it, just in case I decide to give it to them, do you?"

"Heavens, I can't imagine," Daniel responded playfully.

"Well, in that case, I may just have to give it to some Quaker group, or maybe the Unitarians or the Christian Scientists."

"It's good to discover that you Danes have a sense of humor," Daniel quipped. He quickly added, "This would make a marvelous church camp. As if that wasn't already in your mind."

"It would take a lot of work. But we have a men's group that could make this a project. Lots of our members are in the building trades. And some who aren't are still pretty good with a hammer."

"To say nothing of the Luther League," said Daniel. "This could be a wonderful project for them."

"It would be nice to have a church camp just for St. Michael Church," said Jens. "Of course, I wouldn't give you the whole lake. Just the camp. Over on the other side of one of those islands, I want to build myself a summer home." He added, with a twinkle in his eye, "It's something I could never have done when I lived down in Iowa. There aren't too many lakes around Des Moines, you know."

Daniel said, "Just out of curiosity, does this lake have a name?"

"What would you think if I named it Lake Saint Michael?"

"Camp Saint Michael on Lake Saint Michael. That has a nice sound, doesn't it?"

Jens nodded, gesturing toward the parked touring car. As they walked toward it, Daniel said, "You still haven't answered my question, Jens. What do they call the lake now?"

"Well, it may have been from the terrible condition of that last section of road we drove in on, I'm not sure. But the plat book calls it Washboard Lake."

"That's not such a terrible name for a lake, I suppose."

"It gets worse. The papers they gave me when I bought the place indicate the campers gave it a nickname. Obviously it stuck, because that's the name on the documents."

"So what did they call it?"

"Nothing you'd want to use for the location of a church camp."

"You're not going to tell me, are you?"

Jens hesitated before replying, "They called it Dirty Woman Lake."

Chapter 35

"My dad's really changed in the last couple months," said Tom, stee second-hand Chevrolet along the gravel road. "Six months ago, if I'd I was going to take my girlfriend out to a deserted lake for the Fourth without any adults around, he'd have taken away my car keys. Instead gave me his regular little speech and told me to have a good time."

"What's the speech?" asked Sonja, moving closer to him on the fro

"What he always says when I take the car out. 'Just be careful.'

"Well, that's pretty good advice, don't you think?"

"Yeah. I guess it is." The sedan rumbled jerkily across the last str roadway and into the grassy clearing. He said, "You wouldn't believe he the weeds were in here before we cut them down on our work day last

"You've been chattering about this place ever since you were up he your dad, and the other boys and men from the church. I thought maybe discovered paradise, the way you talked about it. So far the place loo of shabby."

"Hey, watch your tongue!" he chided, turning off the engine. "We' gotten started. The buildings are old, but they can all be fixed up. And going to save us having to start from nothing. Mr. Scheidt says if we ; or seven more work days in before school starts, we can probably hav place ready for summer camp next year. Won't that be super?"

He walked her through each of the tired-looking old buildings, expl how filthy each had been inside before the crew had cleaned them out. I time they got to the canoe shed, she said, "Well, it's pretty rough lookin I'll bet it was really a lot worse when you started out."

"You can say that again. And look at this." He led the way to the ba the shed. "This old rowboat still floats. My dad and I took it out into the m of the lake."

She'd never heard him sound so animated.

"Come on." He took her hand and led the way to the lake shore. "See t four islands? We've already named them." He hesitated. "Well, actu David Engelhardt did. Kind of as a joke."

He pointed, starting with the one at the far left. "Matthew, Mark, Luke and John."

"Oh, honestly," she said, laughing softly. Then she said, "Actually, that's sort of clever." She studied the perimeter of the lake, captivated by the beauty all around them. "So, should we swim first or have our picnic first?"

"We should take the rowboat out first. And then have our picnic. Over there, on the Isle of Mark."

"What? You want to have lunch on some island?"

"Sure. Why not? It'll be an adventure. It can be our private island for today."

She looked dubious. "Are you sure about going out there, Tom?"

"Look, I've done it before. Dad rowed the boat out that other time. I rowed it back. He said I was a natural."

She looked around. "There's no really good place to have a picnic here, I guess."

"So, come on. Let's get our swimming gear and the food basket. Then you can help me pull the boat down to the shore."

ADAM ENGELHARDT stopped by the apartment above the print shop. He asked David if he and Molly were ready to go with him and Elsa, to the patriotic concert at the Lake Harriet pavilion. David told his father they'd decided to stay at home. Molly was tired and wanted to rest. In fact, he explained, she was still in bed.

So, Adam and Elsa went on their way, ready for a relaxing day away from ordinary chores. And David sat at the kitchen table, watching the traffic on Bloomington Avenue, thinking about the concert he and Molly would be missing.

THE ROWBOAT met the shore on the far side of the Isle of Mark. Tom had circled the small island, looking for a good beachhead. The only one he found was a tiny stretch, the length of two rowboats, the one place where trees did not come right up against the water.

He secured the oars, scrambled out, and towed the boat, with Sonja still in it, up onto the little patch of beach. Then he helped her step ashore and returned to retrieve the cargo they'd brought along.

Sonja had remembered to bring a blanket, and went looking for a place to spread it. There was a small clearing, just large enough, near the center of the island, where leaves and pine needles crowded out the undergrowth. She

spread the blanket and sat down on it.

Tom arrived with the lunch basket and the hamper with their beach towels. He sat down next to Sonja and studied the woods, surrounding them on every side. The sunlight of mid-day managed to send a few spears of light down through the stand of trees, interrupting the darkness.

"Isn't this amazing?" he said in a half-whisper. "We can't see the lake in any direction, yet we're only about twenty steps away from it, no matter which way we walk. It's like being in our own little kingdom. Nobody here but us, and the birds." There was a rustling nearby. "And the squirrels."

"But no snakes, I hope," she added, warily.

"If there are any, I'll cut their heads off."

"With what, exactly?"

He reached into his pocket. "Look what I found." He handed her an arrowhead. "We're not the first people to have been here."

"I wonder how old it is," she said, turning it over in her hand. "Where did you find this?"

"Right next to where we landed the rowboat."

She handed it back to him. He rubbed his finger carefully along the still sharp edge of the ancient blade. Then he scrambled up and, pulling away a sheath of loose bark from a nearby tree, began to gouge out a heart shape. He made it large, so there was room inside for the inscription he was formulating. As she watched, he cut the words into the tree, within the heart's border:

Tom + Sonja
July 4, 1932

Then he returned to the blanket and sat down beside her. "That's our tree now," he said. He placed his hand on her cheek, leaned close, and kissed her.

"It may be our tree, but my father owns the island. Don't forget that."

"We won't tell him. We won't tell anyone." Then he scrambled to his feet and said, "I say we swim now and eat later. That way, we won't get stomach cramps."

She nodded. But then her face took on a troubled look. "How are we going to do this? There aren't any changing rooms."

"I'm wearing my swimming trunks underneath," he said, opening his belt and pulling off his shirt and shoes and trousers. "You change here. I'll wait down by the boat. When you're ready, come on out."

She looked dubiously at him, but then smiled and said, "All right. But no peeking."

"No peeking," he said cheerfully. He took his towel and headed toward the rowboat.

DAVID HAD GONE downstairs, to find a book he'd left on his desk in the print shop. He'd decided that, if Molly wanted to stay at home on a holiday, he might as well find something to keep himself busy until she was up and about. It wasn't until he reached the landing at the top of the stairs and began to open the door to the apartment that he heard her cries.

"Molly! What's wrong?" He raced toward the bedroom, where his wife lay, the sheet kicked back, her face covered with perspiration. She lay on her back, her knees tented, holding her stomach. She was half moaning, half weeping.

"Is the baby coming, Molly? It's not supposed to for another three weeks!"

"Babies can come early," she said, clenching her teeth. "I think this one's coming now."

TOM AND SONJA FROLICKED in the cool lake water, just beyond the rowboat. Both were excellent swimmers, and used their aquatic skills to the full, as they took turns dunking each other and then trying to escape the payback which inevitably came. After twenty minutes they were exhausted and ready to get out.

"See you at lunch," he shouted after her, as she headed through the trees, walking carefully on the leaf-covered forest floor.

When she was out of sight, he stripped off his trunks and twisted them, squeezing out the water. He spread them on the side of the boat, so they could dry. He reached for his towel and began drying himself. Suddenly it occurred to him. He'd left his clothing lying next to the tree he had carved not forty minutes earlier.

He waited for what he thought was a decent length of time, long enough he convinced himself, for her to have dried and dressed herself a couple times over. Then he cinched the beach towel around his middle and walked, carefully in his bare feet, across the forest floor, into the woods. His eyes were on the ground, watching for sharp stones and roots.

When he looked up, he caught sight of her. She was standing, naked, her back to him, vigorously toweling her long blonde hair. Obviously it was taking a her long time to get it dry, longer than he'd counted on. His first instinct was to turn away, perhaps to return to the boat.

But his gaze was riveted on her. She had the appearance of a pale white

Greek goddess, a reminder to him of a picture he'd seen as a child, in a book of mythology which his mother kept on a shelf at home. He could not move. His heart began pounding so loudly in his ears, he was certain she could hear it.

Two voices sounded in his brain. One said, "Leave her." The other said, "Go to her." He obeyed the second voice.

He stepped quietly across the blanket and gently placed his hands on her sides, then moved them down to her waist. She let out a shriek, and turning toward him, tried to cover herself. He smothered her mouth with his, kissing her with more passion than he had ever shown her before.

FOR THE TENTH TIME David asked his gasping wife if he should go for help. And for the tenth time she pleaded, "Don't leave me. It's too late. The baby's coming." And then she cried, more desperately than before, "Oh, David, help me! *Help me!*"

And he realized the baby's head was presenting itself.

THE BRANCHES OVERHEAD sighed softly. A hundred thousand leaves danced in the gentle breeze of early afternoon. Beneath the thick canopy of trees, Tom and Sonja lay together on the blanket, their picnic lunch still waiting in the basket nearby. What little light penetrated the thick canopy overhead created a pale dappled pattern on their naked bodies.

"Oh, Tom. What are we going to do?" she asked, sighing heavily.

He enjoyed the feel of her breasts, moving against his chest. He smoothed his hand along her back, from her neck down to her waist, then back again. He groaned with contentment. "I hadn't really planned that we would do this," he said, nibbling the end of her nose with his hungry lips.

"Tom, what if you've gotten me pregnant?"

"We've only done it once. What are the chances? Really."

"It only takes one time, you know."

"You're so beautiful. I'm really glad it happened."

"Tom?"

"Yes?"

"What if we have to get married?"

"I'd love to marry you."

"We both have another year of high school. What would you do?"

"Live here with you on this island. And let the world go by."

"Boys don't worry about these things, do they? It's always the girls who have to."

He snuggled closer to her and smoothed his hand across her still-damp hair. "We'll think about it together. But not today. Today I just want to think about us. And about how hopelessly in love I am with you."

Chapter 36

Daniel had asked for extra time on the church council agenda. He'd explained he had a special concern to share, something of urgency.

Council president Norman Gerdes turned the meeting over to the pastor. Daniel said, "Many of you know Andreas Scheidt. Andy. He's one of our founding members. Andy's a carpenter. He builds houses, does some plumbing and electrical work. That sort of thing. He was also on church council, back before most of you were elected.

"Well, the Depression has thrown a lot people out of work in Minneapolis. And it's finally caught up with Andy, I'm sorry to say. People just aren't building houses right now. There's not much new construction of any kind. Andy got along for awhile doing repair and maintenance work for people. Then he resorted to odd jobs. Lately, there aren't even any of those. Not any that will earn him a living wage, anyway."

The pastor cleared his throat. "Andy and Lorene now have two young children, and a third one on the way. They really need some help."

"Do you have a suggestion, Pastor?" asked Roger Hanson, a skilled handyman himself.

"Well, I have an idea. This is not a solution for the long term. But it could help Andy for two or three months."

He paused and organized his thoughts. "The congregation is actually doing pretty well, financially. The Morgan-Houseman bequest has taken the pressure off building and grounds maintenance. We're out of debt. The parsonage is paid for. Attendance is strong and offerings are increasing."

"That's a tribute to your hard work, Pastor," said Rodney Oleson.

Daniel appreciated the comment, but didn't respond to it. He said, "As you all know, we now own a defunct lakeside camp. Many of you spent some of your weekends up there last month, helping to clean things up, and I understand you're ready to help some more, before summer's end. And, of course, Andy has been right in the thick of that work."

Where was the pastor going with this, Norm wondered.

"All of that is background to what I want to propose now. For one reason or another, we've never done anything about our little frame chapel down on the corner. I'm not sure why. Maybe it was nostalgia. It was, after all, our first building. But the fact of the matter is, it's being neglected now. Nobody ever goes in there. We're using it to store old hymnals, things like that. If the building wasn't there any longer, we could pave that space and gain some parking."

The council members were nodding. Clifford Rask, a young physician, the council secretary, said, "I recall reading in some old minutes that we voted to tear that building down. But nothing was ever done about it."

Daniel said, "One of the things I'd really like to see us do up at Camp Saint Michael is to construct a chapel. At first I thought we could use the dining hall. I'm more and more convinced that's not a very good idea. It just doesn't lend itself to worship. So, now I'm thinking that it would be an excellent project for us to support, if we hired Andy Scheidt to take down the chapel on the corner, truck all the lumber up to Camp Saint Michael, and put it back together."

There was a buzz in the room. Jake Bickford said, "Excellent idea. Creative plan. I'm for it." He paused to think about what he'd just said. "Could Andy actually do that — all by himself? And how long would it take?"

"He'd need an assistant," Daniel replied. "I've already floated the idea with him, just to see if it would be practical. And if he might be interested. Andy says he and a partner could take the building down in about a week and a half. Others would have to fill in the basement. We can find someone to do that. Then, after all the material is moved up to the camp, he thinks six weeks to two months might be about right. Possibly by early September, he could have it finished."

Rodney said, "I don't want to put a wet blanket on this, but do we have enough money to pay two people to do this work for us? It would have to be outside the budget we've already approved."

Harold Wilms, the treasurer, replied, "We're in very good shape. I think we can do this without too much difficulty. We're only talking about two months. Three at the outside."

Norm said, "Any discussion?" He waited, looked at the pastor, then ordered, "All in favor say aye."

There was no dissent.

THE TWO MEN carried the last plank to the platform and laid it into position. With Andy Scheidt starting at one end and Tom Pavelka at the other, they hammered it down. Andy stood up, slid his hammer into his carpenter's holster, and rubbed his hands back and forth a couple times.

"Good work, partner," he said, a hint of admiration in his voice. "Now we have a floor."

Tom enjoyed the feel of the warm August sun on his bare chest and back. He climbed up from his knees and wiped perspiration from his forehead with the back of his hand. "Now comes the fun part," he said. "Putting all the pieces back together again." He looked at the piles of carefully stacked lumber, and the salvaged doors and windows, lying nearby. "You sure we can figure out where everything goes?"

"Simple as pie," said Andy, confidently. "You numbered all the pieces. I made the chart. If this doesn't work, we're not as smart as we look."

Tom grinned. In the past three weeks he and Andy had become fast friends. The skilled carpenter had proven to be an effective tutor as well. The high school junior felt as though he could drive nails with the best of them. Of course, there was plenty Andy hadn't taught him yet.

"You know," Tom said, "with all the people looking for work these days, I can't understand why you picked me to work on this project with you."

"Several reasons," said Andy, pulling a dark blue bandana from his pocket and mopping his neck and chest. "First of all, you're family. Church family, that is. I believe in asking fellow members first. Second, you came up here on every single one of the work days the men's group had last month. You're the only fellow in the entire Luther League that did that."

Tom said, "I'm president this year. I had to set an example."

"But I could tell you really liked being here. And you worked like a trooper. I've never seen a high schooler take to physical labor the way you did. Farm boys, maybe, but not a city kid."

"Well, I was enjoying the work."

"And you did the job. Very well. I was impressed. Watching you doing repairs on those barracks, I thought, 'Now, here's a young man who'd make an excellent carpenter's apprentice.' 'Course, I knew you were only a high school boy. And your father probably has other plans for you after you graduate."

"My dad hasn't said anything about what I should be thinking about for the future. I'm not sure I want to sell cars. Not exactly sure what I want to do."

"The other reason I wanted you to help me out," said Andy, sitting down on the edge of the floor they'd just completed, "was that I think we need to pay special attention to our young people. Get to know them. They're the future. Including the future of the congregation."

Tom looked out, across the lake, to the four islands in the distance. He said, "I really love this place. It's so amazing. Water. And trees. And birds overhead. Loons on the lake. And no traffic. It's peaceful — and so beautiful."

Andy looked at his young co-worker. He said, "You'd just like to move up here and never go back to the city, right?"

Tom grinned. "I could do that. With the right person."

"And who might that person be?" Andy enjoyed how Tom looked at the floor, as if he had an embarrassing secret to hide. He prodded, "Could she, by any chance, be the daughter of the man who gave all this to the church in the first place?" Tom looked at him and nodded. "The fellow who's having me build him a summer home over there on the other side of the Gospel Islands?"

Tom looked surprised. "Really? Mr. Jorgensen is having you build him a place up here?"

"Soon as you and I get the chapel done. About the time you're going back to school. It's a great opportunity for me. I'll be able to keep working, and keep bread on the table. And do what I like doing best — building houses."

"Holy mackerel! That's great, Andy. How long will that take you?"

"Maybe I can finish by next spring or summer. I figure, if I can get it framed up and closed in, I can work inside, right through the wintertime."

"Man, I wish I could help."

"Well, maybe if you're free on weekends, and your parents don't object, you could come up once in a while and drive a few nails." He got up and admired the floor he'd been sitting on. "In the meantime, I think we'd better keep going on this project, or we're not going to get it finished before the end of August."

Tom got up and said, "Okay, chief. I'm ready. Let's do it."

Andy led the way to the stack of two-by-fours. "Let's see if we can figure out how to put some wall sections together," he said. "I'll read the numbers off my nifty little chart here, and you see if you can match them with what you wrote on these boards and two-by-fours."

Within a half hour, they had assembled a wall section and were beginning a second. As the sounds of their hammers echoed merrily, Tom found himself thinking about Sonja. The worst thing about investing so much time at the lake with Andy was, he had less time to spend with her. It was making his weekends in Minneapolis seem precious to him.

"Andy, can I ask you something?"

Andy didn't look up from his work. He said, "Ask away."

"How did you meet Lorene?"

"We grew up in neighboring towns, back in Ohio. We met at a Luther League rally. It was at St. Paul Lutheran Church in Toledo, as I recall."

"So, when did you know you were really interested in each other?"

"I'd say, about as soon as we met. It got a lot more serious one summer at church camp. Things just started sparking between us."

"Where was that?"

"We had to rent the Methodist camp, up on Lake Erie. A place called Lakeside. It was nice enough. Not private and unspoiled like Lake Saint Michael, though."

"So, what happened? When the 'sparking' started, I mean."

"Well, we started getting real serious, real fast. We were from different congregations, so it wasn't so easy. But we found ways to get together. We wrote a lot of letters. Then my folks moved up to St. Paul. I enrolled at St. Paul Luther College. But I never forgot Lorene. The week I finished my two-year course, I went back to Ohio and asked her to marry me. I was already doing carpentry in Minneapolis by then, but her dad wanted proof I was good enough at it to earn a decent living and take care of her. So I offered to build him a corn crib, to replace one that was falling down."

"How did that work out?"

"Perfect. He was really impressed with my work. Especially since I didn't charge him anything. Of course, he provided the materials." Suddenly there was a twinkle in his eye. "I never told him, but I also did a little mischief while I was at it."

"What do you mean?"

"Well, I left my calling card on that corn crib. Just before I painted it for him, I carved 'Andy loves Lorene' into a board on the backside. After the paint was dry, you could still sort of see it, if you knew where to look."

Tom's thoughts were suddenly on a tree on an island in the middle of the lake. And just as suddenly, an unexpected wave of shame washed over him.

Andy seemed not to notice. He said, "One thing I promised Lorene's father was, I would never do anything to hurt her, if I could help it. I've always tried to follow that." He paused, and his voice quavered momentarily. "Strangely, I guess I hurt her in spite of my best intentions. I ran out of work. It's really been tough on her, I know." He took a deep breath. "But, things are a lot better now. In fact, I can hardly believe it. I have work for another whole year!"

Tom was still thinking about the Isle of Mark and the fourth of July. He said, "Andy, were you ever tempted with Lorene? I mean, before you got married?"

Andy laughed out loud. "Is the Pope Catholic? Of *course* I was tempted. Man, was it hard sometimes, waiting until we got to the altar. Well, we made it. But just barely."

"Really?"

"Gosh, I shouldn't be telling this to a high school kid. It will give you all kinds of ideas."

"Too late," Tom said. "I've had the ideas. Plenty of times."

Andy grinned. "Just remember what the *Small Catechism* says."

"The *Small Catechism*?"

"Martin Luther's explanation to the Sixth Commandment. Treat that young lady in a way that's pure and honorable. You'll never regret it."

But regret was exactly what Tom was feeling.

Chapter 37

Frieda Stellhorn had just completed cataloging the new shipment of reference books and had lifted them into place on the appropriate shelves. As soon as she hefted the last of the heavy volumes, she realized that she had overdone it. Her heart began racing, unnaturally fast. And, for some reason, she could not make it stop.

She walked slowly to the door and considered shouting for Luise. But she was certain she would never be able to make herself heard that far away. So, leaning against the wall as she went, she eased her way down the hall, toward the church office. By the time she arrived, her face was ashen. She staggered into the room and slumped into the nearest chair.

Luise looked up from her typing and studied her housemate with alarm. Before she could speak, however, Frieda said, almost inaudibly, "I need to go to the hospital."

TOM PAVELKA had planned to eat his lunch in the high school cafeteria. But what he'd just learned had so upset him that he decided to go home instead. As he drove along Park Avenue, he tried desperately to rehearse what he would tell his father. But when he arrived, his mother informed him that he was downtown, at a business lunch of some sort.

Tom went searching in the icebox for a snack. His mother asked him if she could fix him something. He thanked her, but said he didn't want that much. He found an apple, and a wedge of cheese, from which he cut a generous slice, and a piece of his mother's homemade bread, upon which he spread a layer of butter. He ate in silence.

Twenty minutes later, he went back to school.

IN THE WAITING ROOM at Fairview Hospital, Luise Mensing paced the floor. It had been a half hour and she'd heard nothing. She was about to go looking for a nurse when a young physician came into the room. He had a look of compassion on his face. She wondered what to make of it.

"Miss Mensing?"

"Yes?"

"Sit down," he said cordially. "Let's talk a bit."

When they were seated, he said, "Your friend, Frieda, has had a heart spell. We're going to keep her here for a few days. If that's all right with you."

Immediately she liked his manner. She suspected his patients did too. "It's fine with me. I'd be surprised Frieda would agree to it, though. She hates hospitals."

"Well, she isn't protesting. She told me this had given her a real scare. She wants to stay as long as it takes to get her back on her feet."

"That's good news," Luise said. "I'm sure she'll be in good hands."

"Do you have time for a cup of coffee, by any chance?"

"Excuse me?"

"Frieda told me you attended our nursing school here. I thought it might be interesting to hear you tell a little bit about what that was like. My rounds are over now. I have a few minutes. If you do."

She shrugged. "Sure. Why not. Nobody's asked me about nursing school since I graduated." She studied the doctor's features. To her he appeared rather dashing, with his dark brown hair, carefully combed, trim eyebrows, and dancing brown eyes. She wondered why he wasn't wearing a wedding band.

He led the way out of the waiting room, and down the hallway, toward the smell of coffee.

AT SUPPER THAT EVENING, Tom poked at his food, scarcely eating. At first his father didn't notice. He was too excited about the approval of his loan request, and the fact that he was almost back to owning at least a part of the dealership he'd once had to give up. Mary and the two younger Pavelka children listened with interest to his hopes and visions for the business, and how Jens Jorgensen had smoothed the way for all of it to happen. Tom's mind was elsewhere.

When the dishes were being cleared, Tom followed his father into the parlor. He said, "Dad, I have to talk to you. Alone."

Joe looked at his son. "Something important?"

"Yes."

"Can it wait until I read the paper?"

"I'd rather not wait."

His father looked puzzled, but then said, "All right, slide the door shut. Then come, sit down. And we'll talk."

When they were seated, Tom leaned forward, propped his forearms on his knees, and began folding and unfolding his hands nervously. He looked at his shoes.

Joe said, "Well, I'm listening."

Tom reached into his trousers pocket and pulled out his car keys. He handed them to his father. "Here," he said. "I need to give these back to you."

"What for? How will you get to school?"

"I can take the streetcar."

"Tom, what's going on?"

"I can't keep the car anymore, Dad. I don't deserve it." He sniffed, then went reaching for a handkerchief. He blew his nose, then straightened up and looked at his father. "I've done something I'm not very proud of. In fact, I'm pretty ashamed."

For once, Joe was speechless. The silence seemed deafening, but he restrained himself and waited for the next sentence.

"I didn't listen to you. You warned me to be careful. I wasn't. And now ..."

"Tom, so far I'm not making much sense out of any of this. Did you have an accident with the car?"

"I've made a mess of everything."

"What have you done?"

"It's Sonja. She's pretty sure she's pregnant. And I'm pretty sure I'm the father."

IT WAS HER FOURTH VISIT to the hospital in as many days. Luise had so enjoyed her conversation with young Dr. Mason, when she'd brought Frieda in, that she made a point of going back just before she knew the physician was due to finish his rounds. He'd always taken time to sit with her, briefing her on Frieda's progress, but also chatting with her about the challenges of his profession. Since she was trained in nursing, he found her a ready listener with good questions and interesting observations about the practice of medicine.

As it turned out, John Mason, still single, was intending to work in Minneapolis for another year or so, and then join his father's practice. She decided, finally, to ask exactly where that was.

"Cedar Rapids, Iowa."

"Iowa! *I'm* from Iowa."

"Really? Where?"

"Waverly."

"I know where that is. There's a Lutheran college there."

"Yes. Wartburg. How do you know about Wartburg College?"

"I grew up in the Iowa Synod. I know about all three Wartburgs. Wartburg Seminary in Dubuque. Wartburg Teacher's College in Waverly. And what my pastor uncle jokingly calls 'The Preacher Factory' — Wartburg College in Clinton. Where all the seminary students come from." He paused, offered a thoughtful look, and continued, "I hate to say it, but Clinton has a nicer campus than Waverly. It's up on a hill and all."

"Well, the Waverly campus has more buildings," she said dismissively. She'd never been to Clinton, but she'd heard her home pastor talk about the other school.

The young doctor wondered if she wasn't just a tiny bit defensive about her hometown. He decided to change the subject. "We Iowans have to stick together, you know. These Minnesotans tell some pretty nasty jokes about our state."

"I've heard them all, believe me."

"Listen, are you seeing anyone right now?"

"I beg your pardon?"

"That was forward of me. I apologize."

"The answer is no. I'm not seeing anyone. Why?"

"Well, I have Saturday free. Would you be interested in going to a motion picture with me?"

She was flustered. She'd only known the physician for four days. But she was also flattered. She found him fun to talk to. He was intelligent, polite and good-looking. And, he was from Iowa. "Yes. I think that might be fun."

"Good. I'll come by for you around seven." A smirk crept onto his face. He said, "And, if the show's not much good, you can tell me more about why Waverly is such a great place to be from."

THE TENSION in Jens Jorgensen's front parlor was palpable. The bank officer looked at his wife, then at Joe and Mary Pavelka, and then at Tom and Sonja, sitting next to each other, but in separate chairs. He said, "We've all had a lot of time to talk about this situation. And I think we parents know what our children have to say for themselves."

Sonja was looking miserable. Tom had a contrite expression on his face. Both were looking at the carpet.

Jens said, "Sonja's mother and I want her to leave school after Thanksgiving. We want her to stay home until the baby comes. Then we can think about what to do next."

Joe said, "We've told Tom he has to finish his last year of high school. I know they want to get married. And I know Pastor Jonas would probably do it. But they're only sixteen."

"Dad, you're talking like we're not even here," Tom said.

Joe looked sternly at his son, but said nothing.

Jens said, "Ingrid and I agree. Sixteen is too young. We want Sonja to have the baby first. Maybe after that, the two of you can think about getting married," he said, looking first at his daughter, and then at Tom.

Joe looked at his son and said, "I'd really hoped you'd think about going to work at the dealership with me. After high school."

Jens, a college graduate, realized that Joe had only completed high school himself. He wasn't surprised to learn his friend wasn't setting his sights any higher for his son.

Ingrid said to her daughter, "Is there anything you want to say to us, Sonja?"

Her daughter shook her head, but then said, "Only that I love Tom." Her face was awash with tears.

Mary said, "Tom? What about you?

"I'm just sorry for everything. I wouldn't blame you if you kicked me out."

"Nobody's going to kick you out, Tom," Joe said. "You're still our son and we still love you. That doesn't change just because you make a mess of things once in a while."

"Well, I've really made a mess of *this*," he said.

Joe reached into his pocket and pulled out the keys to Tom's used Chevy. He walked across the ornamented carpet, to where his son was seated. He handed them back to him. "A month's long enough for you to go without your car. Especially since it's so clear to me how sorry you really are about this."

Tom felt like crying aloud, but he figured that wouldn't be manly. So, instead, he pursed his lips, vainly trying to hold back the tears, which flowed anyway.

"You're not the first young man to make a mistake like this," Joe said. He looked at his wife, then at their hosts, and then back to his son. He said, "Your mother gave me permission to tell you this. She and I did the same thing the two of you did, before we got married. The only difference is, we were just luckier than the two of you."

Chapter 38

Luther Fischer was walking Lillian Gardner home from the streetcar stop. They'd been to an all-Schubert concert at the university, and both had been entranced with the music. At her front door, he said, "I've been trying to get you to go to a concert with me ever since I came to Minnesota. What made you agree to go this time?"

"I love Schubert," she said, matter-of-factly.

"Well, so do I. But I've asked you to Schubert concerts before."

"I've been busy. This time I wasn't."

"Well, it was perfectly delightful."

"Thank you. I enjoyed it."

"So, does this mean we're an item now?"

She flashed a look of mock disdain. "I should say *not!*"

"Oh. Well. All right then. Just checking." He sounded crestfallen.

She said, "But don't be afraid to check back with me about that from time to time. I suppose it's possible it could happen. Sometime."

"When?"

"Sometime. I don't know. You can't rush these things."

You can say that again, he thought.

AS SEPTEMBER GAVE WAY to October, the pace of parish life at St. Michael and All Angels Church became frenetic. Lillian Gardner busied herself with three choirs, adding a high school-age ensemble to her children's and adult vocal groups. With church council approval, she began offering lessons on the Reuter pipe organ for those of her music students who seemed ready to advance to the king of instruments. Her list of piano students expanded to nearly 40, to the point that Wilma Shaughnessy jokingly told her she might have to reimburse her for new carpeting on the stairway leading to the upstairs parlor.

And, still basking in the accolades she'd received the previous spring, she decided to add a second Mendelssohn oratorio to her choir's repertoire. Next year they would perform *Paul*. Her rationale had been simple. People loved what they'd heard, the choir now had the confidence to do a complex oratorio, and, in spite of the harassment she'd received the previous spring, Lillian loved Mendelssohn's music. She thought she might just offer the two ambitious compositions in alternate years, making them her signature at St. Michael Church.

Or, at least *one* of her signatures. Worshipers continued to arrive for Sunday morning Eucharist, partly to hear the pastor's sermons, but partly to hear the hymn improvisations, preludes and postludes the organist with the growing reputation continued to provide.

It was a matter of some concern to Lillian that the man who had berated her the previous spring, about her readiness to perform music by "that Jew," was sometimes seen lingering in the hallways, both on choir rehearsal nights and on Sunday mornings. It was as if he would wait to be certain that she had seen him before he would disappear each time. On one occasion, Pastor Jonas came into the hallway, just in time for her to point the stranger out to him. Daniel told her he didn't know him, and that he'd never seen him at worship. But, he promised, he'd speak to him if he got the opportunity.

Daniel found himself busied with a full schedule of sermon preparation, worship planning, home visits, hospital calls and committee and board meetings. As little Hannah Ruth and baby Joshua Daniel grew bigger, day by day, he feared he might miss seeing their growing up. But, in spite of his best efforts, he found it impossible to uncomplicate his schedule.

Part of the difficulty for Daniel was the fact that his ministry was bringing such positive results. New members continued to stream into the congregation. One Sunday in October it finally happened: there were no more seats available at morning Eucharist. The church council quickly agreed to add a second worship service. That step, of course, complicated Daniel's schedule even further.

ON THE MONDAY MORNING after Reformation Sunday, Luise Mensing walked into the pastor's office and announced that, if her arithmetic was correct, the congregation had finally reached a total of one-thousand baptized members. The parish was still not five years old.

That evening, after she went home to check on Frieda, slowly but steadily recuperating from her hospitalization, she went out to dinner with Dr. Mason. As they sat enjoying their meal, the physician asked her, "What do you hear from Waverly, Iowa?"

"Nothing in particular. Why?"

"Because my uncle just got back from the American Lutheran Church convention in Fond du Lac, Wisconsin. He reported on it to my father, who just wrote to me."

"What does any of this have to do with Waverly?"

"Well, with the Depression and all, everybody is short of money. Evidently there are five colleges here in the Midwest, and the church can only afford to support one."

There was apprehension in her eyes.

"But they decided to keep two open. They closed the other three."

She said, "Oh, *no*. They closed St. Paul Luther. This is going to kill Frieda!"

"No. St. Paul Luther is still open." He hesitated. "Although just the college department. They decided to close down the seminary and move the students and faculty to Wartburg in Dubuque."

"Well, that's lucky for Wartburg Seminary," she said.

There was a long pause. He said, "They also closed Wartburg in Waverly. They're moving the faculty and students to Clinton."

She was so stunned she tipped over her water glass. It slowly soaked the tablecloth.

He added, "If it's any comfort, it's only temporary. They're going to vote again in two years. The trouble is, then they have to get it down from two colleges to one. Of course, it's possible they might pick Waverly."

"Or, they could move everything to Clinton. Which would leave both Frieda Stellhorn and me feeling betrayed."

"What's Frieda's stake in all of this?"

"She's been a St. Paul Luther booster for the past fifteen years."

"Sorry to ruin your dinner," the doctor said.

"Well, the next letter from home would have brought the news," she said. She studied the soaked tablecloth in silence. Suddenly she looked at John and muttered, "Church politics. It *stinks*."

"Don't be too hard on the church leaders. Under the circumstances, they're doing the best they can. There's just not enough money to go around."

"And *that* stinks, too."

ON THE FIRST TUESDAY in November, Americans went to the polls and turned Herbert Hoover out. Franklin Delano Roosevelt, the Democrat, won in a landslide. Within days, members of St. Michael Church, including Jens Jorgensen, were listening to the new president deliver "fireside chats" on the radio. Jens had mixed feelings. He himself was financially well off. But, he knew there were millions in the country who had no steady employment and no savings. He hoped the new administration would be able to figure something out.

Andy Scheidt worked six days a week to frame in the banker's new lake home. Jens had decided to have it winterized, in case he wanted to retire there some day. So Andy busied himself, enclosing the structure from the elements before the first snow flew. He'd previously closed up the leaks in the walls of one of the counselor's cabins at the defunct youth camp, adding some insulation and paneling. He made it his winter residence while he continued to work at the construction site on the other side of the lake. Every now and then, Tom Pavelka drove up from the city and spent a Saturday helping Andy with the project.

Sonja Jorgensen dropped out of high school and stayed home for her senior year. Jens brought in tutors to guarantee she would get all the instruction she would need in order to graduate on schedule. As the baby began to show, he and Ingrid found it impossible to get their daughter to leave their Kenwood home, even to go to worship with them.

The Luther League at St. Michael Church staged another fall play, just before Thanksgiving. People whispered about how much better it might have been, had Sonja and Tom been in the cast. But Tom, out of loyalty to his pregnant girlfriend, refused to try out. At his father's insistence, however, he continued to serve as president of the youth group. In his presence, both at church and at high school, nobody ever mentioned his "situation," even though everybody knew about it.

JONATHAN ENGELHARDT brought Susan Schmidt with him to Minneapolis, on the train, for Thanksgiving. He had written the previous summer that they were engaged. With David out of the house, he got his old room back, and put Susan up where David had once slept. He announced, to everyone's surprise, that they intended to be married at Christmastime, in Columbus. Elsa, who had thought they would surely wait until spring, was caught completely off guard. She was positive it couldn't happen that quickly. But Jonathan assured his mother that the details were being handled by the bride's family, and all she would have to do would be to show up.

A month later, with Adam, Elsa, David, Molly and little Paul David in the large congregation, Jonathan and Susan were married. The ceremony was held at Trinity Lutheran Church in downtown Columbus, just blocks from the building that housed the Wartburg Press. Elsa's brother, Adolph, and his wife,

Louisa, had somehow found the space to put up all their Minnesota relatives during their visit. Once the bride and groom had left for Philadelphia on their wedding trip, Elsa and her family got reacquainted with her Ohio family, and made certain that Molly felt a part of it.

While in Columbus, Adam took David and Molly on a tour of Capital University and the Lutheran seminary, across the street. When the clerk in the university recruitment office learned Adam was an alumnus, he was more than cordial. But, when he discovered David had graduated from St. Paul Luther, he casually remarked, "Of course, that place is about ready to close down, right?" Without saying it to his father, David vowed he would never send his children to Capital University.

After nearly a week in Elsa's brother's home, the visitors drove north, to Galion, to visit Adam's family, after which they made the long trip back to Minnesota. Fortunately the weather held, and they were safely home in time to celebrate the arrival of the new year.

IN LATE JANUARY, a bedraggled looking man appeared at Daniel's study door at St. Michael Church. The pastor recognized him as the elusive stranger whom Lillian Gardner had once pointed out to him in the church hallway. The man pushed his way in, past Luise Mensing, and announced defiantly, "Well, they finally have Adolph Hitler running Germany. Now watch those Jews run!" He left as quickly as he had come. Daniel sat pondering the comment for a full fifteen minutes. He wondered how anybody could be so sure about what the new German chancellor might be planning to do.

On the fifteenth day of March, Sonja Jorgensen delivered a healthy nine and one-half pound baby girl. Her parents, and Tom Pavelka, were in the waiting room when the doctor came with the news. Sonja named her Greta Ingrid. Two weeks later, on a Sunday afternoon, the child was baptized, in a private service at St. Michael Church.

ON PALM SUNDAY AFTERNOON, while Daniel was napping, as was his custom after worship and the mid-day meal, Rosetta took one-year-old Joshua Daniel out onto the screened front porch and put him in the wooden playpen which was normally kept in the dining room. She had decided to sit on the porch swing and read the Sunday newspaper, while enjoying the sun and the air.

As she sat, barely moving in the swing, she read with interest a feature story describing the coming Century of Progress Exposition, planned for Chicago during the summer. According to the article, the large Illinois city was constructing the pavilions on artificial islands in Lake Michigan, which would provide a view of the city skyline never visible to most citizens.

She heard the teakettle begin to whistle. She looked at the sleeping child in the playpen, and then looked out through the screen, toward the street. Seeing no activity of any kind, she decided not to awaken Joshua Daniel. Instead, she went into the house, past her still-sleeping husband on the couch, and through the dining room, following the whistling sound. She took the kettle from the kitchen stove, poured the water into her cup, and lowered the metal tea ball into it. She left it to steep as she went back to check on Joshua Daniel.

When she stepped out onto the front porch, the playpen was empty. Her heart leaped into her throat. She turned and looked back, into the living room. Daniel was no longer on the couch. "Oh! Thank God!" she said, calming herself. She went to find her husband. He was sitting in his study, scanning a copy of *The Christian Century* magazine.

"Where's Joshua Daniel?" she asked.

He looked up in surprise. "With you. Isn't he?"

Her heart leaped a second time. "Daniel, I left him on the porch, in the playpen. He's not there!"

"*What?*" he exclaimed, jumping up. "Where could he be?"

"I don't know," she responded, panic in her voice.

He raced to the front door, Rosetta close behind. There was no way the infant could have climbed out of the playpen. Then he noticed the screen door.

"Rosetta, did you leave the porch door unhooked?

There was a wild, confused look in her eyes. "I ... I never do ... I wouldn't have ... I don't know. Maybe this once I forgot."

"*God in heaven!*" he shouted. "Somebody has taken our baby!"

Chapter 39

The young policeman sat across the dining room table from Daniel and Rosetta. As never before, the pastor was thankful that one of the pillars of his congregation was on the Minneapolis police force.

Sam Warner said, "The department is on this. Believe me, they are. We have officers looking everywhere. The bulletins are out. Of course, it would be easier if we could describe possible suspects." He looked at Rosetta. She was soaking her handkerchief with her tears. "I don't mean to imply anything, Rosetta. You didn't see anyone. I'm not blaming you or anything."

"Well, maybe you should," she said. She had a miserable expression on her face. "I didn't hook the screen door. I always hook the screen door. But this time I didn't." She covered her face in her hands and sobbed pathetically.

Sam looked at Daniel. The pastor pursed his lips and shook his head slowly from side to side. His eyes were red.

"We'll do everything we can," the young policeman said. He hesitated to say the next thing. "Unfortunately, it's a big city. And, since we don't know who we're looking for, they might even try leaving town. I hope to God not."

Daniel did not feel reassured. "That's not very hopeful, is it?"

"Just keep the faith," Sam said. "And hope. And pray. We'll all pray."

DANIEL COULD NOT SLEEP. At three o'clock in the morning, he went downstairs, out onto the front porch, and sat in the swing. He rocked slowly back and forth, looking at the playpen, still sitting where it had been when Joshua Daniel disappeared. He began talking to himself, then to God. *This is my punishment. I've become too confident, too pleased with myself. That's it, isn't it, Lord? I'm being punished. I'm guilty of the sin of pride. Like Abraham, you gave me a child and now you're taking him away again.*

He stopped to think. It was not good Lutheran theology to talk this way. He knew that many people had evil times visit them through no fault of their own. He had never preached or taught that there was some sort of connection between what people do and what they receive.

It also occurred to him that, in the Bible story, Abraham was asked to give up his child, not because of a lack of faith or because of pride. Abraham had trusted God without hesitation, yet he was asked to give his child back to God. On the other hand, it turned out only to have been a test. Abraham got his son back.

Daniel took hope from that. But then he remembered the story of the slaughter of the babies in Bethlehem, not long after Jesus was born. Was that what was going to happen to his son?

He heard the handle turn and the front door open. Rosetta came out, wearing her nightgown, looking disheveled. She sat down next to him and leaned on his shoulder. She began to shudder. At first he thought it was from the coolness of the night. But quickly, he realized she was silently crying. Then her sobs became audible, and soon they were deep and loud, the awful heartrending sounds of a grief-stricken parent, who fears the worst.

He held her, letting her weep. She cried and cried and cried. He wondered how either of them would ever survive, should the unthinkable happen to Joshua Daniel. He wondered how they had been so lucky, to be so happy and untroubled, so far in their married life together. He wondered why in God's name this was happening to them.

Rosetta said, "This is all my fault."

"Please, Rosetta."

"I left the screen door unhooked. I left Joshua Daniel alone on the porch. I'm a horrid mother. What kind of mother leaves her own child alone on the front porch?"

"We have to pray and wait and hope," Daniel said. His own words sounded lame to him.

"What good is praying going to do?" she demanded, in a tone so sharp it cut through him. He wondered whether anyone else was outdoors at this hour, to hear Rosetta's angry words. He was certain they could have been heard a block away.

"Let's go in," he said. But she made no move to do so. "Rosetta, let's go back to bed."

She sat up straight and looked at him. "Why aren't you upset like I am? Aren't you even the tiniest bit sorry about any of this?"

He felt guilt and anger wash over him. Didn't he have to be strong for both of them? What made her think he wasn't grieving? What was the matter with her, to accuse him of such a thing?

She said, "I'm sorry. I'm sorry. It's not your fault. It's my fault."

"It's nobody's fault. It's the fault of whoever came onto the porch."

"I should have listened to you."

"What do you mean, Rosetta?"

"You told me you wanted to give your name to the district president. Maybe by now we would have been living somewhere else."

"Rosetta, it could have happened there, too."

"I'm a horrid mother. Our baby could be dead!"

"Rosetta, Joshua Daniel is going to be found. Alive and healthy."

"It's happening again, Daniel. Don't you see?"

"What is?"

"The Lindbergh baby. Those awful people stole him last year. In New Jersey."

Daniel hadn't thought of connecting their son's abduction to that of the child of the famous airplane pilot. The story had gripped the nation, but New Jersey was a long way from Minnesota, and it had seemed no more than a sad and tragic — but distant — story.

"They killed that little boy," she said, sobbing. "They're going to kill Joshua Daniel." She began to weep uncontrollably once more. He held her close, trying without success to calm her.

ON MONDAY MORNING, Daniel delayed as long as possible going to the church office. When Molly Engelhardt came by, he felt less guilty leaving Rosetta. As he moved toward the front door, he heard his wife say to her best friend, "Now I know how you felt, losing your child."

When he arrived at his office, Luise Mensing looked up from her typewriter, an uncertain expression on her face. She said, "I'm so sorry. Everyone is so sorry. People have been calling. They want to help. They don't know what to do. I've told everyone you and Rosetta need their prayers. They're all praying for you."

He nodded but said nothing. As he turned to go into his office, she said, "Oh, and this was under my door when I came in this morning." She handed a white, sealed envelope to him. On it was written, in pencil, "For the pastor. Personal."

He went into his office, sat at his desk, and broke the envelope's seal. He pulled out a folded piece of paper. As he opened it, a thick chunk of dark brown hair fell out. On the page were penciled, in block letters, the words: "On Good Friday, tell your congregation that the Jews killed Christ. Or else your little boy will die."

He stared at the paper, uncomprehending. Then there crept back into his memory the vision of the defiant stranger who'd shown up at his office door and railed against the Jews. Angrily, he crushed the paper and threw it across the room. "You sad, pathetic little man!" He shouted. "You sad, sad, *sick, pathetic man!*"

Luise came to the office door and stared at him in bewilderment.

He calmed himself, then said, "Call Sam Warner. Tell him I need to see him, right now. And then call Lillian Gardner. Tell her I need to see her, too."

WITH THE DOOR to Daniel's office closed, the three of them sat talking urgently. "It has to be this man that Lillian kept encountering here in the building," the pastor said. "He hates Jews. Somehow, he blames me for allowing Lillian to perform music by Felix Mendelssohn. Now he's getting his revenge."

Sam said, "It's only a guess. It might be possible. But we still don't know who he is. You've given me an excellent description, Lillian. But we don't have a name."

The director of music said, "I recall he once told me he used to own a small business over on Chicago Avenue. He said he lost it after the stock market crashed, and that a Jewish family bought it and is prospering there now."

Sam brightened. "Now we're getting somewhere. I'll put the department on that right away. How many Jewish families could there be, operating businesses on Chicago Avenue?"

Lillian replied, "Well, to hear this fellow talk, you'd think most all of them."

DANIEL found himself in a spiritual desert. He could not think about preparing for the busy week of worship. How would he ever get through Maundy Thursday, Good Friday and Easter morning? Every time he began to think about it, he felt paralyzed.

He opened the *American Lutheran Hymnal*, and began turning the pages. His eyes came to rest on a familiar hymn. A chill ran down his spine as he realized it had been one played on the Titanic as the ship was going down. Still, he scanned the verses, driving himself more deeply than ever into a state of gloom as he did so:

Nearer my God, to thee, nearer to thee.
E'en though it be a cross that raiseth me ...
Though like the wanderer, the sun gone down,
Darkness be over me, my rest a stone ...

All that thou sendest me, in mercy giv'n,
Angels to beckon me nearer my God to thee ...

If ever there was a time he needed to feel the presence of angels, it was now. Instead, he was feeling bitterness in his heart and ashes in his mouth.

He prayed, "Lord, I know all things work together for good, for those who love you. But right now I'm feeling forsaken and nothing seems good to me. I don't blame you for what has happened, but I need your help for getting through all of this. Watch over Rosetta. And send your angels to guard and keep Joshua Daniel. He's so small and helpless. Please watch over him. And please, *please* bring him back to us."

He paused. He felt drained of energy, and of hope. But he remembered something he'd learned in confirmation class, back in Fremont, Ohio. To his prayer he added the phrase, "According to your will."

THE SEMINARY STUDENT sat opposite the pastor in the church office. Daniel felt fortunate to have reached him so quickly after his personal crisis had begun. Joshua Daniel had disappeared on Sunday afternoon. Now it was Tuesday morning.

With two years at St. Paul Luther Seminary, just blocks from his St. Paul home, Carl Jech had been a second-year student when the seminary was closed the previous spring. Now in his final months at Wartburg Seminary, he was home from Dubuque, Iowa, for Holy Week and Easter. Daniel had met him at St. Paul Luther the year before, and had been impressed with his theology, his self-confidence, and his affable nature.

Daniel felt guilty asking the seminary senior what he was about to ask. But he felt the need to do so.

"This is extremely short notice, and probably not even fair, so I apologize in advance. But I need someone to preach on Maundy Thursday, Good Friday and Easter Day. We have Holy Communion on Thursday and Sunday. I know you're not ordained yet, so I'll preside at the Sacrament for those two services."

Jech had assured him that he'd done extensive preaching during his course of study, some of it on short notice. He said he was confident he could manage preaching at the coming three worship services. In fact, he admitted, he rather relished the idea of preaching from the ornate pulpit in the big stone church.

Daniel said, "I truly appreciate your helping out. I'm ... I'm going through a faith crisis right now. A sort of dry season of the soul."

Jech replied, "Look, just do what you think you have to do. I don't think anyone will think less of you. Who knows? Maybe some day I'll be in your shoes, and will want someone to show me the same consideration." He paused, then said, "I realize it must feel a little risky for you, not knowing what I might say to the congregation."

Daniel was thinking about the penciled message he'd received the day before. He said, "Well, since you brought up the subject of sermon content, there's one thing I must insist on."

"What's that?"

"On Good Friday, under no circumstances are you to imply that the Jews bear guilt for killing Jesus. That's bad theology, and I don't want it preached here."

"I hadn't thought of saying anything like that," Jech said. "For one thing, I don't believe it. For another, I understand Minneapolis has a dirty little secret when it comes to its treatment of the Jewish people. I'd be the last one to want to feed anti-Semitism. What's going on in Germany right now is bad enough. We don't need to give encouragement to any of that over here."

"Thank you," Daniel said, feeling reassured. But he wondered whether, with his request to the substitute preacher, he might not have sealed his infant son's doom.

Chapter 40

To Daniel's surprise, Rosetta insisted on going to all three services — on Thursday, Friday and Sunday. As he thought about it, he realized she would probably get more sustenance for her shaken faith by going to worship than he himself had been able to provide her.

Since Good Friday was one of the few days in the entire church year when the Sacrament was not part of the liturgy, he found himself in the unusual situation of being able to sit next to his wife at worship. It seemed strangely comforting, not having to take responsibility for what went on in the chancel.

The seminary senior preached an exemplary Good Friday homily. He said, "We are in grief. All of us suffer from something. Everybody here has a story of tragedy, if not their own, then that of someone near to them. The question is, what will we allow God to do with our tragedies?"

He said, "It's tempting to believe that it was easy for God to send his Son to the cross. But if we believe the story, as it's told in the Gospels, especially Mark, then we know it was hard as hell for God to watch his Son die."

At that last phrase, Daniel sat up straight. This young man, he decided, wasn't going to pull any punches.

"When tragedy strikes," he continued, "the worst thing we can do is look for someone to blame. Some people blame bad luck. Other's blame fate. Some blame God — which, when you think about it, is pretty insulting to God." He paused. "We even have people ready to blame the Jews for whatever we don't like. Don't fall for that foolishness. If it wasn't for the Jews, one of whom was Jesus' mother, we wouldn't have had a Savior. Think about that."

Daniel didn't hear anything else. His mind was wandering, to Molly's tragedy, to the death of young Michael Morgan-Houseman, and the suicide death of the child's father, to Jens Jorgensen's daughter, just having given birth out of wedlock, to the elusive stranger who had tormented Lillian Gardner for nearly a year. And, he thought of his own missing son.

Yes, he thought, there's plenty of tragedy to go around. He remembered his own seminary training, and the assurance he'd taken from the promise of Paul the Apostle to the Christians in Corinth — Jesus' death on the cross is either foolishness, or else the power of God, depending on who Christ is for you.

But, as he left the service in silence, as was the Good Friday custom, he still felt barrenness in his soul.

AS THE SUN was going down on Saturday evening, Sam Warner came to the front door of the parsonage. "I have some news," he said. "May I come in?"

When they were seated in the parlor, he said, "We've found a baby boy. We don't know who he is."

Rosetta's eyes were as large as saucers.

Sam said, "I don't want you to get your hopes up. It's a big city. We find babies sometimes. It could be somebody else's."

"Where did you find him? Where is he now?" Daniel asked urgently.

"Someone left him wrapped in a dirty baby blanket, in a trash basket at the bus station downtown. They took him to Swedish Hospital. He hadn't had his diapers changed lately. And he was pretty badly dehydrated. I don't think he'd been fed for a while."

The pastor and his wife stared at the policeman in disbelief.

He said, "One other thing. He has a chunk of his hair missing. About as much, I'd guess, as you got delivered to you in that envelope, Pastor."

ROSETTA stayed overnight at the hospital with Joshua Daniel. It was only with great difficulty that the nurses succeeded in getting her to relinquish the child so that they could put him down for the night. On Easter morning, it was clear that they were not ready to release the infant, so Rosetta spent Sunday at the hospital as well.

Daniel went to both liturgies and sat in the chancel, waiting to preside at the sacrament. During the sermon, he heard everything but remembered nothing. He focused, however, on a stanza from one of the hymns which the congregation sang.

The strife is o'er, the battle done!
The victory of life is won!
The song of triumph has begun! Alleluia!

He knew the reference was to Christ, but he couldn't help also applying the words to Rosetta and himself.

At the church door, following both services, the outpouring of good wishes for the parsonage family was almost more than he could absorb. He found himself wondering whether Eldon Sanderson, the sad and angry anti-Semite whom the police had finally identified, and named a suspect, had actually been the one who had taken their child. He wondered whether anyone would ever know for sure. If Eldon had been the one to write the threatening note, then had he actually shown up at Good Friday worship, to hear what the sermon would say? And, if he had, why hadn't anyone spotted him there?

He also wondered what had become of the profoundly troubled Jew-hater. In spite of everything that had happened, he found himself praying for him, even as he sent prayer after prayer of thanksgiving to the throne of heaven for the safe return of Joshua Daniel.

IN EARLY JUNE, Tom Pavelka graduated from high school. Two weeks later, he and Sonja Jorgensen were married in a quiet Sunday afternoon service in the Chapel of the Victors at St. Michael Church. There was no music, and the only ones present besides the bride and the groom were their parents and the pastor.

Tom's father tried to hire him as a car salesman at the dealership where he was now co-owner, but the young groom declined. Selling vehicles held little interest for him. Jens had offered to try to find a bank teller position for him, another option he'd rejected.

What he really wanted to do, he explained, was to help Andy Scheidt build houses. But Andy's work on the lake home had come to an end in late May. Instead, Jens persuaded the council to create a position for Tom, supervising the volunteers who had signed up to run the first season of Saint Michael Church Camp. The newlyweds moved into the lake house Andy had just completed.

With the vacation home he'd planned to use himself now occupied, Jens set Andy to work building another just like it, a distance down the shoreline.

Tom's performance running the summer camping program was so exemplary that, at their August meeting, the members of the church council voted to make the position a permanent one, on the condition that Tom spend the winter months in Minneapolis, directing the congregation's youth program. Jens invited his daughter and her family to live during the school year in the empty servant's apartment above the carriage house behind his Kenwood home. Later he'd help them find something more satisfactory.

The auto dealer's son thought he'd died and gone to heaven.

ONE DAY IN SEPTEMBER, Dr. John Mason took Luise Mensing for a walk in an urban park not far from Fairview Hospital. They sat on a park bench overlooking the Mississippi River and watched the boats floating far below them. He handed her a diamond ring and asked her if she'd be willing to wear it.

The following June, they were married at St. Paul Lutheran Church in Waverly, Iowa, six blocks from the deserted campus of the Lutheran college that had been closed for an entire school year. Following a wedding trip to Canada, they settled into a comfortable two-story home in a tree-lined Cedar Rapids neighborhood.

St. Michael Church hired a forty-year-old unemployed executive secretary to fill its newly-created vacancy. Janet Fenstermacher, portly, efficient and garrulous, would hold the position for twenty years.

With Luise Mensing's departure, Frieda Stellhorn gave up her apartment and moved into the Ebenezer Home, a south Minnesota care center operated by Norwegian Lutherans.

THE FOLLOWING SUMMER a series of strikes crippled the city, as truck drivers demonstrated in the streets for better wages. Several of St. Michael Church's members were involved in the conflict, some employed by firms impacted by the protests, others marching on the picket lines. At one point, an angry exchange at the men's breakfast meeting at church resulted in sympathizers of the strikers walking out without finishing their meal. Daniel was so troubled by the incident, he launched a series of sermons on the topic of justice and reconciliation.

When someone surreptitiously mailed a copy of notes he'd taken during the preaching series to the governor of Minnesota, Floyd B. Olson sent the pastor a letter of commendation. Daniel tried in vain to discover who might have sent the notes to the state capitol. Janet Fenstermacher took it upon herself to frame the letter and hang it in the Reformation Room.

IN OCTOBER, Daniel drove down to Waverly, Iowa, as a non-voting observer at the national convention of the American Lutheran Church. He was fully aware that the question of what to do about St. Paul Luther College was on the agenda, along with the question of which — if either — of the two Wartburg Colleges the cash-strapped church body might keep open.

It struck him, listening to the impassioned debate, that, no matter how the vote came out, there were bound to be a lot of embittered church members.

Faculty, alumni and community boosters from all three schools had drawn lines in the sand. There was no talk of compromise. Clearly, with so few resources available to the denomination, it was going to be a winner-take-all situation.

It seemed remarkable to Daniel that the national church had agreed to meet on one of the three campuses involved in the dispute. How, he wondered, would voting delegates avoid undue pressure from those who favored consolidating all three schools in Waverly?

As he walked around the compact campus, he realized there was far more to it than tiny St. Paul Luther. And, while he'd never been to Clinton, he knew that the two buildings there were adequate enough, but simply too few for a coeducational school. Waverly had dormitories for men and women. There was no women's dormitory in Clinton.

The tension was high when debate began. Impassioned speeches on behalf of each of the three schools came in rotation. Dr. Proehl, the president of Wartburg at Clinton, spoke eloquently and persuasively. So did the Waverly partisans.

Daniel was thunderstruck when Oswald Hardwig, a member of the board of directors at St. Paul Luther, but a resident of Waverly, took the floor to argue that the Minnesota school had outlived its usefulness and should be closed. He was vilified by Twin Citians who saw his comments as an unconscionable betrayal. It seemed to Daniel that Hardwig's speech had put the final nail in St. Paul Luther's coffin.

The debate continued so long that Clinton supporters began to depart for home. Late in the day on which the vote had been scheduled, the question was finally called. The delegates decided to close both the Clinton and St. Paul schools, and move the displaced faculty members to the Waverly campus.

A delegate was heard to declare, walking out of the assembly room, "You could certainly feel the Spirit of God at work here today." But, nearby, a member of the Clinton faculty muttered, "There are spirits and there are spirits. Some of them are evil." And a member of Zion Lutheran Church, the large Clinton congregation which had given forty years' worth of support to the college on its city's outskirts, snarled, "We will never, *ever* send our sons and daughters to this godforsaken mudhole of a campus!"

Daniel had a deep sense of sadness as he drove home to Minneapolis. The college where both his sons had attended for two years had just been voted out of existence. The result had not exactly surprised him. The school had been on life support ever since the Great Depression had begun. Still, it seemed tragic the church had not been able to find a way to save it.

Adding to his melancholy was a gnawing sense of dread. Someone, he realized, was going to have to break the news to Frieda Stellhorn.

THE NEWS about the closing of St. Paul Luther College traveled faster than Daniel's Chevrolet. A resident of the Ebenezer Home, also a member of the American Lutheran Church, had heard about the decision in a phone conversation from a relative who had attended the convention. She made mention of it to Frieda as they sat next to one another in the community room.

Distraught, the octogenarian got out of her chair, took four steps toward the doorway, staggered and then fell to the floor. Efforts to revive her were in vain.

She was pronounced dead at the hospital emergency room.

DANIEL CONDUCTED Frieda's funeral four days later. A great number of her friends came to pay tribute to her, including many from the now-doomed college.

Her casket was loaded onto a passenger train for the long journey east, to Canton, Ohio. She had purchased a cemetery plot there in 1885. At last, she was going home.

Chapter 41

By early 1935, it had become obvious to everyone at St. Michael Church that one pastor was not enough. There were now nearly 1,500 members in the congregation, and almost 900 at Sunday worship. Daniel brought a request to the annual meeting of the congregation that funds be authorized for a second clergyman. There was little discussion and no opposition.

In February he sent a letter to the president of the Minnesota District, asking whether there might be candidates available. He received a peculiar reply. At the moment, he was informed, there was an ordained pastor, one of the last graduates from the St. Paul Luther seminary program, who was without call and living in St. Paul. The young man had served two congregations, one year in each, and had departed from both for unspecified reasons. He was now selling suits and neckties in a local clothing store, waiting for another opportunity.

The district president admitted he was eager to find another location for the gentleman, since he was now receiving almost weekly queries from him, and it was beginning to wear him down.

Daniel was dubious, but agreed to interview the young man. He invited him to the church office for a conversation. When Matthew Scharlemann walked into his office, he was polite, deferential, and immaculately dressed. His hair was parted neatly in the middle, and he wore a cordial smile.

"Thank you for letting me come," he said, sitting down across from Daniel. "I haven't had an interview for almost a year. I'd hate to think I completed seminary, only to end up working in a clothing store."

"Tell me about your first two calls," Daniel said, cutting to the chase.

"Well, the first was in North Dakota. A dreary, little town a long way from St. Paul, Minnesota, my hometown. I was desperately lonely out there."

"People in North Dakota need pastoral care, too."

"Oh, of course they do. But it's hard for a city boy to get used to such isolation. I was miserable, and they knew it."

"So you just resigned and left?"

"Well, there was one other thing. One of the members got it into his head

I should be getting serious about marrying his daughter. I had the old-fashioned idea it should be at least partly my choice whom I might marry. Unfortunately, he was a person of some influence. So I decided I should leave."

"Without another call?"

"The district helped find another one for me, after about six months. Over in Wisconsin. Another small town. That wasn't so bad, because I'd already experienced North Dakota by then. But I got into a conflict there, after I preached a sermon series about the Ten Commandments."

"What did you say in your sermons?"

"Well, mainly, that legalism isn't Christian. Laws are important, I told them, but not if they get in the way of loving your neighbor. I quoted Paul, where he says that all things are lawful, but not all things are helpful."

"And how was that received?"

"They lied about me. They spread the word all over town that I didn't believe in following the Ten Commandments. I hadn't said that." He sighed. "I wonder how the Apostle Paul dealt with his critics. After all, he said almost the same thing I did."

Daniel realized the younger pastor actually had it backwards. "How would you feel about working under another pastor?" Daniel asked.

"In this congregation? It would be an honor. I don't know if you realize it, but St. Michael Church's reputation is very positive. People are talking about the preaching here, and the music, and the social ministry you're doing for the hungry, and the fact that you have your own church camp. You're to be commended. And, I'd be honored to be asked to serve with you."

DANIEL SAT in the parlor, on the couch beside his wife. On the floor, in front of them, two-year-old Joshua Daniel played contentedly. Nearby, four-year-old Hannah Ruth read picture books to her dolls. Daniel said, "You were a gracious host for our dinner guest this evening, Rosetta. But, now, tell me. What do you think of Matthew Scharlemann?"

She said, "He says all the right things. He's polite … thoughtful … almost too complimentary. He seemed to love what I fed him."

"He's trying really hard to be accepted," Daniel said. "Two failed calls. He wants to fit in and make something work."

"Well, that's fine. I guess."

"Do you have misgivings?"

"I don't know. I have an uncomfortable feeling about him. And I hope I'm wrong. But … he almost seems too charming for his own good."

THE FIRST TIME Lillian Gardner sensed there might be a problem with Wilma Shaughnessy was the day her landlady called her 'Evelyn.' Lillian had been so surprised, she'd ignored it. But over the period of a month, she became 'Evelyn' more often than 'Lillian.'

One day in April, while she was on her knees, planting bulbs in a backyard flower bed, one of several plots which Wilma had encouraged her to make her own, Lillian heard the familiar sound of the hand-pushed rotary mower. She looked up to see nineteen-year-old Tony Murphy, shirtless, wiping perspiration from his muscular frame.

He grinned at her and said, "Front's done. Okay if I do the back now?"

"Sure," she said, getting up. She had gotten well-acquainted with the youngest of the four Irish lads who had once hauled a piano upstairs to her music room. Tony had been mowing Wilma's lawns for the past two seasons, and was just starting a third.

"Looks like you need to take a break," she said, watching him mop sweat from his forehead.

"Naaah. I like hard work," he said, cheerfully.

"Well, take a break anyway," she said, gesturing toward two lawn chairs. "I need to ask you something."

When they were seated, she said, "Tony, does your aunt Wilma know anybody named Evelyn?"

"Evelyn? Sure. That was her older sister."

"*Was*?"

"Evelyn's been dead for ten years. Why?"

"Well, Wilma's started calling me by that name. I'm a little worried about her. She's starting to forget things. Three times in the last month, music students of mine have called to cancel a lesson and Wilma took the messages, but never passed any of them along. I have a policy of charging for lessons if the student doesn't arrive, or phone in a cancellation. I almost overcharged all three."

"What did Aunt Wilma say?"

"She didn't remember any of the calls." She hesitated, then said, "That's not all. One day last week your aunt left the flame burning on the stove and then walked out of the kitchen. An hour later she discovered it and came storming upstairs, interrupting one of my lessons, to accuse me of having done it. I hadn't been in the kitchen at all."

"Jesus, Joseph and Mary!" exclaimed Tony. "Maybe that explains why she tried paying me *twice* last week. I told her I already had my money. She said that wasn't possible, so I didn't argue. But she really did pay me twice."

Lillian said, "Does Wilma have anybody … you know … to watch out for her if she'd need help?"

"My folks. She and my ma are sisters."

"Well, if you don't mind, you might want to mention this to your parents."

A MONTH LATER, Wilma took the streetcar to her favorite market, then boarded the wrong one and ended up in North Minneapolis. When she didn't come home in time for supper, Lillian called her sister in St. Paul. When they finally located her, she had no idea how she'd gotten there, much less how to get home again.

Shortly thereafter, Wilma was "invited" to spend the weekend in her sister's home. She never came back to Minneapolis. Agnes Murphy informed Lillian the house would have to be put up for sale, but assured her she would be allowed to stay, and that a guaranteed right of occupancy, if she wanted it, would be a condition of the sale.

Agnes also asked Lillian if she wanted to make an offer on the house. The musician declined, saying, "I love the house, and the flowerbeds, but I'm not prepared to take on property ownership and all the headaches that go with it."

MATTHEW SCHARLEMANN proved to be an energetic member of the pastoral team at St. Michael Church. He was eager to visit members in their homes — although, Daniel soon discovered, less so with elderly members. He was assigned to preach once a month, which he did credibly, and to work with the Sunday school teachers and the confirmation program.

Within a month of his arrival, he was also beginning to accumulate a list of appointments for counseling. While not exclusively so, it appeared to Daniel that a substantial number of them were with young women.

LUTHER FISCHER came by the day the movers carried all of Wilma's furniture out of the first level of the house on Caldwell Street. When they had gone, he walked through the parlor and the dining room, listening to the sound of his shoes echo off the hardwood floors and plaster walls. Overhead, the upright piano could be heard, as one of Lillian Gardner's students played the final chords of a piece.

Shortly thereafter, the young musician descended the stairs, followed by Lillian herself. She looked at Luther with uncertainty. "Here to welcome my new landlord?" she asked, trying not to sound bitter. "I'd certainly have liked to have interviewed this mystery buyer before he bought the place. But, I guess that's not the way it works."

"More likely, the buyer would want to interview *you*," he said.

"Agnes Murphy told me explicitly I could stay on, and that would be a condition of the sale."

"Well, once the sale's final, how could she guarantee that?"

"It's a contract. It's on paper."

Luther nodded, then sent a look her way she could absolutely not interpret. "What do you know about all of this?" she demanded.

"I know the next owner's going to have a devil of a time furnishing all these empty rooms," he replied, scanning the emptiness.

"And just why is that?"

"Well, because you're looking at him. And I don't own a stick of furniture."

"You? *You*! What business do *you* have buying this place?" She was almost sputtering.

"Well, I understand you had right of first refusal. And you refused."

"Just what in tarnation do you want with a big barn of a house like this?"

He shrugged. "It's the Depression. They were offering it at a fire sale price. I think they wanted to unload it before it sat empty for six months or more. And, just in case I find someone to marry me, I'd be all set. I'd have the house we'd need."

"Luther Fischer, you have no intention of marrying anyone and you know it."

"Oh, you don't know any such thing."

"And, besides, you're just starting to teach at the university. On a salary like yours, how can you afford a house like this?"

"I had the down payment. I can swing the monthly payments. The bank said I was a good credit risk. That's all it takes."

She took a deep breath. "So, just when were you and the elusive Mrs. Fischer planning to move in?"

"That all depends."

"On if you ever find her, right?"

"Well, I'd like to think I already have."

"Are you going to tell me who she is, or not?"

"I'd like to think I'm looking at her."

"*What*!"

"Lillian, I've courted you for ten years. I can never get a straight answer out of you."

"You've done no such thing. You can't call our relationship courting, not by any stretch of the imagination."

"Well, let's not get technical about it. I'll just ask you straight out: will you marry me, Lillian Gardner?"

"And what if I don't? Am I out of the apartment?"

"No. Stay as long as you like. Your rent will probably be enough to make my monthly mortgage payments."

She glowered at him. Why did she find him, and this whole ridiculous turn of events, to be so exasperating? She didn't know. But she did know one thing for certain. Luther Fischer wasn't getting an answer to his impertinent proposal.

She wheeled and marched back up the stairs.

Chapter 42

Molly Engelhardt came to Daniel's office on an afternoon when she knew it was Pastor Scharlemann's turn to make hospital visits. She wanted to be sure he wouldn't be in the building. Seated in Daniel's office, she skipped the small talk. "My younger brother, Martin, is attending Gustavus Adolphus College this year. Maybe you knew that."

Daniel didn't.

"Anyway, he wrote to me last week. He says there's a young woman in his class, from a small town in North Dakota. Somehow they got talking about Minneapolis, and she found out I was a member here. She also seemed to know that Pastor Scharlemann was serving at St. Michael Church now."

"What's her interest in Pastor Scharlemann?" Daniel asked.

"Well, as it turns out, Pastor Scharlemann was *her* pastor, in North Dakota, for one year. She told my brother that, while he was serving there, Pastor Scharlemann got extra friendly with some of the older girls in the Luther League, and with her in particular. Evidently she told her father about one counseling session the pastor had talked her into having, in the church office. It got pretty intimate. Her father told the pastor that he'd either better marry his daughter or plan to resign. About a week later, he resigned."

Daniel felt his blood running cold.

Later that day he asked Janet Fenstermacher to write a letter for him to sign, to the president of the church council of the small Wisconsin parish where Matthew had previously served.

LILLIAN GARDNER sat at the second-hand table Luther Fischer had brought into what used to be Wilma Shaughnessy's kitchen. Luther sat across from her. It seemed odd, having a conversation of what she considered to be such great importance at a kitchen table, but so far it was the only furniture on the lower level — except for the bed and chest of drawers Luther had brought into the downstairs bedroom when he'd moved in three months before. He'd been willing to divide the space in the icebox, and was always gone to the university before she wanted breakfast. He rarely came home until after eating supper in a cafeteria near the campus, so sharing the kitchen hadn't been a problem.

Since Lillian had called the meeting, she decided it was her place to begin. "I've been thinking about this new situation, and about your proposal."

He smiled serenely. She felt like slapping him, but wanted to keep things dignified. "I could move out, but I haven't found a suitable place to go. I need a piano, and I have one here. And, my students are used to coming here. I hate to disrupt all of that, if I don't have to."

His brow furrowed. Where, he wondered, was she going with all of this?

"And, I've also considered your ..."

"My invitation to you to marry me?"

"Yes. That."

"Well?"

"And, I've decided to accept. With certain conditions."

He began to laugh, softly at first. He said, "Lillian, a marriage proposal isn't something to be negotiated like a contract between labor and management."

"Well, maybe it *should* be. We might get fewer marriages with disappointed people in them."

He grinned. "Okay. State your terms."

"I want to move my music lessons to the downstairs parlor."

"Not a problem."

"I want to put a baby grand piano in there. I'll pay for it."

"Well, when we get married, then we'll share the cost."

"That's another thing. I want to manage my money. You can manage yours."

"Oh, no. None of that. Our money gets combined. If you want to manage all of it for both of us, that's great. But no separate accounts. All that would mean is that we're not completely married."

She mulled it. "All right. That's fair."

He gave her a look of consternation. *What was coming next?*

"Now, about children."

"Surely you want children!"

"Yes. At least one. I want a girl. And I want to name her."

"What if we have a boy?"

"You can name him. But I want at least one girl."

"Why is that?"

"Because I like girls." She hesitated. "And, because I want to train her to become my successor on the organ bench at St. Michael Church."

Luther turned it over in his mind. He suspected the church council might want to have something to say about that, and that a boy could conceivably become a church organist just as well as a girl. But, he decided not to take a detour with the discussion, not now when negotiations seemed to be moving along so well.

"What else?"

"I … I want to get going with this as soon as possible."

"*What*!" He could hardly believe his ears.

"You heard me right. I'm tired of paying rent. And I'll be darned if I'm going to keep paying rent to *you*, Luther Fischer."

He laughed. "Too bad those truck drivers didn't have you and me to bargain for them when they were on strike a couple years ago. They'd have had it settled in fifteen minutes." His face turned thoughtful. "I really do love you, Lillian."

"Well, I would hope so. Why else would we be having this conversation?"

"It just seems to me it would be important for you to say the same thing to me."

She looked at him as though he'd asked her to wear a clown suit. "Oh, piffle."

DANIEL COULDN'T FIND his Greek New Testament. He'd meant to bring it home with him at suppertime, in order to begin sermon preparation for the following Sunday. He liked doing it in his home office, before going to bed. That way, as his seminary preaching professor had suggested, the ideas could "incubate." He'd found that always worked well for him.

He told Rosetta he'd be gone only ten minutes. He was sure the book was in his office at church. As he walked the block and a half along Anderson Avenue, he found himself remembering the spectacular performance on the Reuter pipe organ the previous Sunday by Lillian Gardner's friend, Daniel Schwandt. He had agreed to fill in for Lillian while she and Luther Fischer were in Bucyrus, Ohio. Daniel had heard that their wedding at Good Hope Lutheran Church had been solemnized before an overflow congregation.

Daniel thought back to the first day he'd met Lillian, when he had first heard her play the organ for him, in that historic old building. Hiring her, he was convinced, had been a stroke of genius.

Schwandt would be back on the bench again the following Sunday, while Lillian and Luther were away on their wedding trip. Trying not to be disloyal to Lillian, Daniel realized he was relishing the prospect of hearing the flashy young keyboard artist play a second Sunday at St. Michael Church.

The parish hall was locked, as it should have been. He found his key and let himself in. Walking along the dark hallway, toward his office, he noticed a crack of light beneath Pastor Scharlemann's office door. At such a late hour, he thought, that seemed odd.

Then he heard a woman's voice. She was weeping. He stopped near the door. The sobs grew louder. They seemed to go on and on. He realized it was probably a breach of privacy, but he grasped the door handle and opened it. What he saw paralyzed him.

Matthew Scharlemann was seated in a chair on the visitor's side of his desk, with Amy Miles, one of the congregation's Sunday school teachers, seated on his lap. With one hand Matthew was stroking the young, married woman's long, dark brown hair. His other hand was on her breast.

As the door opened, Matthew looked toward Daniel, a startled look on his face. He demanded angrily, "What ever happened to knocking before entering?"

Amy looked at Daniel with tear-stained eyes, then pulled herself off Matthew's lap. She stumbled out the words, "I know this looks really bad. It's my husband, Gary. He's been unfaithful to me. Pastor Scharlemann was ..."

"I was comforting her," he said, getting up. He tried to reclaim his dignity. It was too late.

Daniel said, "Amy, you need to go home. Right now. I'll come by your house in a day or two." She nodded, wiped her eyes with her handkerchief, and left the room. When the door closed, Daniel said to Matthew, "I'll see you in my office, tomorrow morning."

"This isn't what it looks like," the young pastor protested.

"Nine o'clock. Not one minute later."

DANIEL WAS NOT ONE to pace the floor, but this time he was pacing. Matthew Scharlemann was seated in the senior pastor's office, watching his supervisor walk back and forth on the carpet. Finally, Daniel turned to his associate and asked, "What really happened in Wisconsin?"

"I beg your pardon?"

"Why did you really leave your second call?"

"I told you when I interviewed for this position. I preached about the Ten Commandments, and got a lot of people upset."

"Was that all?"

"I don't understand. What else would there be?"

Daniel pulled a folded newspaper clipping from his pocket. He handed it to Matthew. The younger pastor scanned it and colored. "This is fiction. This never happened."

"You never got snowbound in a retreat center with four high school girls?"

"Yes, that part happened. They were the Luther League program planning team. We were planning for the group's summer activities."

"Why did you find it necessary to do the planning at a remote retreat center?"

"One of the members owned the cabin. It was a good place to go to get away."

"Did you ever stop to think about how all that looked?"

"I preached my sermon about legalism after that. It all started with a discussion at a church council meeting, after we got back, about the eighth commandment. Spreading rumors. Gossip. Things like that. I decided to preach on all ten of the commandments. That's what I did for ten Sundays in a row."

"One of the girls who was at the retreat center with you became pregnant."

"I wasn't responsible for that. She was pregnant when she got there."

"She told you that? This story says she gave birth nine months later."

"It was her boyfriend. She told me." He exhaled heavily. "You see how this all gets blown up into lies and falsehoods?"

"Matthew, there's more. I know what happened in North Dakota."

The younger man leaped from his chair. "What are you, the goddam Inquisition? Are you planning to investigate what I did back in high school, too?"

Daniel walked to the other side of his desk, giving himself time slow the racing of his heart. When he was seated he said, "I could take this to the church council. If I do, they'll back me up. To save you the humiliation, I strongly urge you to consider handing in your resignation. Before suppertime."

Matthew was sputtering. "You can't … I have counseling scheduled all this week … I preach a week from Sunday."

"Not in our pulpit, you don't."

Chapter 43

The used Chevrolet Luther Fischer had purchased from Joe Pavelka's Southside Chevrolet had stopped running on his wedding trip. Twice. He'd found mechanics to fix it both times, once in Toledo, Ohio, and again in Stratford, Ontario, where he and Lillian had spent three days together, watching the swans on the Avon River and arguing about which Shakespeare play was the most inspired.

The day after the newlyweds returned to their home on Caldwell Street, he took the vehicle back to the dealer. When Joe heard Luther's story, he said, "That should not have happened. I don't care if it *was* a used car. And to think you were on your wedding trip."

For a second, Luther thought Joe was just being melodramatic. But then the car dealer said, "I'll tell you what. Since you don't trust this car, then I don't either. So, here's what I'm going to do. I'll swap it for any other used car on my lot." He noticed the dubious look on Luther's face. "Okay, even better. Any new Chevy on the showroom floor. Half price. Just for you."

Forty minutes later, Luther pulled up in front of the Caldwell Street house in a brand-new sedan. He honked the horn four times. When Lillian appeared on the front steps, the look of consternation on her face made his euphoria evaporate. But he waved her out to the curb.

"You wouldn't believe the deal I got on this car."

"I thought you were going to get the other one fixed."

"Joe Pavelka says it's not worth fixing."

"Then why did he sell it to you?"

Luther was in no mood for an argument, especially so soon after the honeymoon. "Come on. Get in. Let's take a spin around the lakes."

"I've got a piano student coming in half an hour."

"Okay. Across the Hennepin Avenue Bridge and back, then. We can do it in twenty minutes."

She rolled her eyes, sighed dramatically, and went to lock the front door. On the way toward downtown, he said to her, "So, you have a name yet?"

"For what? Your impulsive behavior?"

"No. Our little girl. The one you're planning to have."

"You goon, we've been married less than two weeks. Isn't this conversation just a little previous?"

"You're probably pregnant already and don't even know it."

"Did your conversation become inappropriate just since the wedding, or have you always been this way?"

"What's to be embarrassed about? We're married. Pregnancy should be something we can talk about."

"Not in polite company."

"There is no company. It's just us."

"For all I know, you've already told Joe Pavelka, and half your faculty cronies, that you think I'm pregnant already."

She was a lot more sensitive about delicate subjects than he'd realized. He decided to switch gears. "I think Ruth is a nice name. Straight out of the Old Testament."

"In the first place," she said, still irritated, "there are already five Ruths in my cherub choir. I don't think this congregation needs still another. And, in the second place, I thought we agreed before the wedding, that I would be the one to pick a girl's name, not you."

"Just trying to be helpful."

"Well save your helpfulness for scraping and repainting the garage. You can't park this thing in a shed that looks like it's only fit for rusty tools and trash containers."

He took the comment as Lillian's backdoor way of accepting the fact that he intended keeping the new car.

AFTER THE FIASCO with Matthew Scharlemann, Daniel was back to where he had started. The church council was pressuring him to find another associate to work with him, and his own heavy schedule was pressuring him even more. But he was feeling gun-shy. He'd put off reopening a search for three months, but now realized it was something he simply needed to do.

In his circle of clergy colleagues he began to ask for suggestions. All recommended he consider a new seminary graduate. That way, he wouldn't be getting a dubious track record, and he could shape the young man himself. Daniel decided that was pretty good advice.

With St. Paul Luther Seminary closed, he was torn. Its students and faculty were now a part of Wartburg Seminary, but he had many colleagues who had attended the theological school attached to Capital University. Still, he thought he should at least give Wartburg some consideration. Besides, Dubuque, Iowa, was a lot closer to Minneapolis than was Columbus, Ohio.

The Minnesota District president provided him with the name of a senior student on the Dubuque campus, one who was assigned to Minnesota for placement. He encouraged Daniel to get acquainted with him.

ADAM AND DAVID ENGELHARDT walked through the empty building, their steps echoing on the cement floor. Adam said, "This place is just one more casualty of the Depression. The fellow was running an auto parts store in here. He finally just had to call it quits."

"It's more than twice as big as the print shop," David said, admiring the roomy interior. "And it seems to be a solid structure." He turned to his father. "Dad, are you sure we can afford to expand the business this way?"

"We've been careful. We've continued to grow — a lot less rapidly than I'd once hoped we would, I'll admit, but we're doing quite well. You've been watching our financial situation as closely as I have. Do you think the numbers add up?"

"Well, yes, I suppose," David said. "I just worry about the economy having another reversal."

"There's not going to be another 1929," said Adam.

"How can you be so sure?"

"I can't. I'm just confident, that's all. That's why Engelhardt Printing has done so well. Confidence — along with some business savvy, and a great junior partner, of course."

David grinned. "Okay, so we move the operation to this building. What happens to the print shop?"

"Well, eventually, we could turn it into a retail store. You know, maybe books and stationery, things like that. Or, we could just sell it."

"Sell the print shop?"

"Are you going to get sentimental on me?"

"Well, a lot has happened there. Molly gave birth to our first child up there. You also could say it was our first parsonage."

"Yes, I guess you could. But the Jonas' haven't looked back on it with too much nostalgia, as far as I can tell."

"Dad, the building is pictured in one of the stained glass windows at church! I don't think we should sell it."

That argument seemed to resonate with Adam. He grinned. " Okay, you win. What's your idea for the building?"

281

"We should start a neighborhood newspaper and run it from there."

"A newspaper!"

"Sure. The neighborhood needs one. And think of the advertising we could sell."

DANIEL CIRCLED the quad, keeping pace with the senior seminarian. He was astonished with the beauty and situation of the castle-like seminary campus perched on a ridge, above the city of Dubuque. James Darnauer, his light brown hair blowing in the breeze, chatted amiably as they continued their tour of the impressive complex of limestone buildings.

"This gentleman here is Dr. Martin Luther," he announced soberly, gesturing toward the bronze statue in the center of the yard. "I understand you've already made his acquaintance."

"Yes. A few times," said Daniel. "There's one just like him at Concordia College in St. Paul."

"Well, we actually do have a few things in common with our Missouri Synod brethren. Copies of this statue is one of them."

Daniel was impressed. Unlike Frieda Stellhorn, God rest her soul, this young man was not inclined to put other Lutheran groups in a negative light without giving them their due.

James said, "Old Doctor Reu, the theological giant on our faculty, made sure this bronze statue got paid for and put up here in the quad. He concocted a surefire way of getting the job done."

"What was that?"

"He started a campaign all over the Iowa Synod. Challenged all the young people to send in their pennies and nickels. Those kids — and my father was one of them — they actually paid for Martin Luther to be here at the seminary."

"I'm impressed," said Daniel. "Dr. Reu is obviously a persuasive individual."

"*Persuasive*! That's not the half of it. 'Intimidating' is more like it. Just try skipping one of his lectures, or showing up unprepared for class, and you'll find out just how intimidating he can be."

"What's his theological discipline?"

"Everything."

"I beg your pardon?"

"He's taught every subject in the curriculum. The man seems to know everything about every branch of theology. He also writes and edits our theological magazine. Of course, it helps if you can read German."

"What about you, James? Can you?"

"*Have* to. Can't understand the man's lectures if you don't." He dropped his voice to a half-whisper. "We've lost some really good ministry candidates to Columbus because of that. The new students can read Greek, but they can't understand German!"

They'd reached the heavy front doors of Grossmann Tower. James opened one of them and let Daniel go in before him. In the chapel, with its arched windows and traditional elevated wooden pulpit, they sat together in one of the pews.

James said, "The chapel is named for our founder, Wilhelm Loehe. He never came to America, but he sent pastors from Germany, to take care of the Lutheran congregations out here in Iowa and Illinois and Wisconsin."

"Not so much in Minnesota?"

"Oh. Of course. Minnesota, too. And quite a few more in the Dakotas as well."

Daniel said, "How much do you know about St. Michael and All Angels Church?"

"I know you started in somebody's living room. Just like the New Testament! And look where you are now!" There was fire in his eyes and excitement in his voice.

"You've done your homework."

"I researched St. Michael and All Angels Church after I learned you wanted to come down and talk with me."

"Which would you more have preferred? To serve a living room church, or one with 1,700 members, a big building and a wonderful pipe organ?"

"Either. Neither. Both. I don't really know. The main thing is to be doing mission work. That's what you're doing. That's what made your congregation grow so fast. Everybody says so."

"Everybody?"

"Well, I've started asking around about your congregation. People say you're a legend."

Daniel tried to keep a modest face.

"My passion is to do mission," James said. "Back in northern Illinois, where I grew up, we talked about it all the time. Especially the New Guinea mission field. Our congregation really supports the work there. So I went looking for a seminary that would get me ready for that. I came to Wartburg because it's a mission school."

Chapter 44

Daniel was curious about what James Darnauer had just said. "Why do you call Wartburg Seminary a mission school?"

"Well, for one thing, it was founded as a missionary outpost. Pastor Loehe wanted the men who graduated from this place to be missionaries. He expected them to start new congregations. He also wanted them to try to reach the American Indians. That hasn't worked too well, but it was tried."

"So, what do you hope to do, James? After graduation, in another month."

"Well, since I was about five years old, I've heard about the Lutheran mission in New Guinea. I've always thought God might want me to go there."

"But you've been assigned to the Minnesota District. That's a long way from New Guinea."

James Darnauer seemed not to have heard Daniel's comment. It was clear he wanted to talk about overseas work. He said, "Loehe got the New Guinea mission started. The American Lutheran Church and the Missouri Synod both have pastors serving there. That's another thing our two churches have in common, by the way."

"So you're hoping to go to New Guinea."

"God willing. But not right away. I want to get three years' experience in a congregation first."

"Would you consider *five* years? At St. Michael Church, you might need at least that long to get to know the members of our large congregation."

"Are you inviting me to join your ministry in Minneapolis?"

"I'm asking you to consider it. But I have a few questions I really need to ask you first."

"Ask away."

"You have to understand," Daniel said, "that there's a context out of which these questions are coming. We had a rather bad experience with a previous staff pastor."

James nodded. He looked curious.

"Would you ever consider going on an overnight retreat, at a remote location, with female members of the Luther League, with no other adults present?"

"No. I can't say I would."

"Would you offer counseling sessions to young women alone in your office, after hours, with the door closed?"

James returned a thoughtful expression. "It sounds as if your previous staff pastor might have had some trouble controlling his sexual appetites."

Daniel didn't respond

"Well, I can sympathize," James continued. "A congregation not far from where I grew up once had a pastor like that. He almost wrecked the place, before they got him to resign. I was only twelve when it happened. Some of those people ended up joining our church. The stories they told were very, very sad."

"Whatever became of him?"

"He started his own congregation. It didn't last very long. After that, I'm not sure. He just sort of disappeared."

Daniel said, "I have a good feeling about you, James. I'd like to invite you to come to Minneapolis and meet with the members of our church council. They're serving as the call committee for this candidate search. Would you be interested?"

"Well, as I said, I can't guarantee you I'd consider staying longer than three … well, all right, five years."

Daniel smiled. "We could do a lot of good work together in five years."

TWENTY MINUTES after the Friday evening Sabbath service had begun at a south Minneapolis synagogue, a latecomer drove past the front door of the building, looking in vain for on-street parking. He turned the corner, but found the spaces already taken there as well. Thinking there might be something on the other end of the block, he took a shortcut by turning into the alley behind the temple.

As he approached the back wall of the synagogue, he saw a shadowy figure, with a gasoline container, vigorously sloshing the fuel onto the building's wooden doors and window frames. The child of a family whose grandfather had fled a Jewish pogrom in Russia, the driver of the car felt animal instinct kicking in. He floored the accelerator, heading directly toward the would-be-arsonist.

The man dropped the gas container and began running down the alley. The automobile quickly overtook him and ran him down. The driver kept on going.

The following morning a vagrant, looking for discarded clothing in a trash bin, discovered the body. When the police came, they found the dead man's coat pockets stuffed with matches.

Two days later he was positively identified as Eldon Sanderson, a man once suspected of kidnaping the infant son of a local Lutheran pastor and his wife. While he had been interrogated at length about the abduction, there had never been sufficient evidence to convict him.

ON THE MONDAY OF HIS FIRST WEEK as associate pastor at St. Michael Church, young pastor James Darnauer resolved to continue a practice he'd learned at seminary — the daily discipline of morning prayer. He went into the silent nave and looked for a quiet place to sit, read and meditate. He'd been impressed, when touring the magnificent facility, to discover that there were kneelers attached to all the pews, something not common in Lutheran church buildings. He headed for a pew toward the front.

As he neared the transept, where the two side chapels came into view, he became aware that he was not alone. Seated in the Children's Chapel, studying the large stained-glass window of Jesus, was a woman, perhaps forty. He thought for a moment he should leave. But then he heard her almost inaudible sobs. "Forgive me," he thought he heard her say. "Can you ever forgive me?"

He felt like an intruder. But his pastoral sense told him not to abandon her. He waited for what he thought was a decent interval, then approached the woman. She heard his footsteps and quickly stood up, as if to leave.

"I'm Pastor Darnauer," he said, as kindly as he knew how. "Can I help you?"

She was drying her eyes. "No. I should be going. I don't belong here."

"Perhaps you do. If you have something troubling you, a church may be the very best place to be."

She sighed heavily. "I'm just so, so very weary. So tired. So sorry."

He said, "Please. Sit down for a moment." As she did, he turned one of the chapel chairs around, to face her. Seated across from her, he said, "I'm brand new here. I don't know any of the members, so I don't know anything about you. But if there's anything you want to share, I promise you, it won't go beyond the two of us."

She said, "I really don't belong here."

He wasn't sure what she meant.

"I'm not a member of this congregation. I'm an Episcopalian. Not a very good one, I'm afraid."

"I overheard you crying. Do you want to talk about that?"

"I've been running. For nine years. I'm so tired of running. I just can't do it anymore."

"What are you running from?"

"From my past. From my own guilty conscience."

"Do you want to tell me about that?"

"I killed a little boy. A long time ago."

James was speechless.

"He's there. In that window. Do you see him? That beautiful little boy, sitting at Jesus' feet. I promised to protect him. But I didn't keep my promise. If only I could have him back, just for an hour. So I could ask him to forgive me."

James had been told the story of the window, and the circumstances that led to the construction of the church building. He said, "I'm so sorry. It must have been a terrible day when he ran out in front of that truck."

"I killed little Michael," she wailed. Her voice echoed through the empty building.

James remembered his conversation with Daniel in the seminary chapel, about meeting alone with vulnerable women. He considered his options, then decided to follow his instincts. He moved to the chair next to the woman and took both her hands in his. "Please. Tell me your name."

"Annabelle. Sorensen." She gazed at him, looking miserable.

"You were his ... his mother?"

"His mother was dead. I was his nanny. His father trusted me to watch over little Michael. Mr. Morgan-Houseman is a very wealthy man. Some day he'll find me. I know he will."

James was thunderstruck. This woman had no idea what had transpired since the boy's death. "Where did you go after the accident, Annabelle?"

"I took a bus to Sioux Falls. I knew that wasn't far enough away. So I went to Omaha. And then to Kansas City. I became a housekeeper there. For a wealthy businessman and his wife. He died four years ago. I stayed on and worked for her."

"You've been in Kansas City all these years?"

"Until a month ago. She finally died. After that I no longer had a job. I could have looked for another, but Minneapolis was always my home. I wanted to come back. Over the years, I always thought of coming back. But I was afraid. Well, I'm not afraid any more. Mr. Morgan-Houseman can send me to prison if he chooses. I'm just not going to go on running, and hiding, and concealing my past."

"Annabelle, Michael Morgan-Houseman, your former employer, took his own life. In 1929."

She seemed stunned. "Were you here when it happened?"

"No. I was in Illinois. I was only a sophomore in high school. But everybody around here knows the story. It was in the newspapers."

She dried her eyes. There was a look of confusion on her face. She said, "Well, I'm still guilty." She nodded toward the window. "He should be alive — little Michael. I've kept track, every year. This year he would have been fourteen. A beautiful fourteen-year-old boy." She began to sob again.

James said, "Annabelle, you're being too hard on yourself. You didn't actually kill little Michael."

"Don't try to excuse my carelessness!" she said sharply. "I should have kept him safe. I didn't do that. What's wrong is wrong."

James pulled a hymnal from the rack on the back of a nearby chapel chair. He opened it and began turning the pages. He came to the Liturgy for Absolution. He looked at Annabelle and said, "Are you ready to have your sins forgiven? Because I'm an ordained minister, and I'm prepared to declare you absolved of them."

She looked at him as if it was an idea she had not considered. She nodded her head and folded her hands.

James began to read words he had heard from his own pastor, every Sunday morning in a German Lutheran congregation in rural Illinois, for more years than he could remember: "Almighty God, our Heavenly Father, has had mercy upon us, and his given his only Son to die for us, and for his sake forgives us all our sins ..."

Chapter 45

Jens Jorgensen had been in his winterized lake home for two years when the idea came to him. Sitting on the front porch, enjoying his morning coffee one vacation Monday, he studied the four "Gospel Islands" screening his view from the church camp on the other side of Lake Saint Michael. It was so peaceful, and so beautiful, he began to feel guilty.

That's when he decided it would be a good idea to sell lots to members of the congregation.

At first he'd thought it would be a fine situation, having only one cabin — his own — in seclusion, where no signs of civilization disturbed his peace and quiet. But then he'd agreed to give his original lake home, an all-weather structure he'd never had the opportunity to live in, to his daughter and son-in-law. They were just down the shore from him. Except when one of their three active youngsters let out a joyful shriek, he could hardly tell they were there.

So, he decided, it wouldn't be a problem to sell off, say, a dozen lots on his side of the lake, to good friends at St. Michael Church. He'd be certain none of the properties could be seen from the camp. And, he'd donate the proceeds from the lot sales to the recently-established endowment fund created to support Camp St. Michael.

He began by offering a lot to his son-in-law's parents. Joe and Mary Pavelka were delighted to have a place to build on Lake Saint Michael. Up until now, they'd stayed with Tom and Sonja at their lake home whenever they would come to visit in the summertime. But it had gotten crowded since the second and third children had arrived.

Jens approached Luther Fischer, instructing him to consult with Lillian. By now, even Jens knew about Luther's legendary impulsive spending habits. When the university professor broached the subject to his wife, she said, "If you promise not to go out and buy another new car next year, I might consider it." Luther promised, although a year after they bought a lot from Jens, he was out looking, again, for still another new automobile.

Both Adam and David Engelhardt bought lots, as did the other five families who first helped organize the congregation, eleven years before, in Adam's living room.

Jens deliberately held back two lots, which he did not intend to sell. He stopped by the church offices one day in February and unceremoniously dropped an envelope on each of the pastors' desks. "Don't open it until I'm out the door," was his instruction to both clergymen, each in turn.

When James Darnauer walked into Daniel's office, the opened envelope in his hand, he said, "This is a really fine gesture on Jens' part. But what am I going to do with a chunk of lakefront property when I'm in New Guinea?"

Daniel said, "Well, there's always a possibility you won't end up going."

"No. There's absolutely no chance of that. Don't even *think* like that."

The senior pastor smiled. "I guess I shouldn't let my selfish desire to keep an excellent young pastor on my staff deter him from doing what he feels his calling is."

"Well, for now, my calling is to St. Michael Church," said James. "Thanks for the compliment, by the way."

"Are you ever planning to come back from New Guinea?"

"Pardon me?"

"You're not going to stay over there forever, are you?"

"The church expects seven-year commitments. They also hope I'll renew for at least a second term of service. That would stretch it to fourteen."

"Well," said Daniel, "in that case, you might want to hang onto your lake property. Your children might like a place to go swimming some day — about eighteen years from now."

MAGGIE WASHINGTON pulled up to the curb in front of the bakery. Climbing down from the driver's seat of the beat-up delivery van, she slammed the door, and wondered how many more times she could do that before the hinges would fall right off. St. Michael Church had authorized her purchase of the tired, old vehicle for her social ministry work, so it wasn't actually her truck. But she hoped it would last a few more years, at least.

In the shop she got the usual shouted welcome from Hans Doermann. The short, pudgy proprietor brushed flour dust from his apron. To Maggie, he always looked as if he ate too much of what he was trying to sell. But if it contributed to his always-pleasant disposition, she decided, maybe it wasn't worth worrying about.

"What have you got for me today, Hans?" Maggie demanded cheerfully. She brushed her unkempt red hair back from her eyes.

"The usual. Lots of day-olds," he said, leading the way to the kitchen. "Sure glad you church people can use this stuff. I can't sell it when it's not fresh, and it's a sin to throw it all away."

"Hans, you'll never know how many starving people you're helping to keep alive. I thank you, the Community Kitchen at St. Michael Church thanks you, and all those hungry people thank you."

"I guess it's a good deal for both of us then," he said, pushing three overflowing sacks of bread across the table. "You sure you can carry all that at once?"

"I can handle it," the diminutive woman replied. "Just load me up. I can make it to the curb if you steer me in the right direction. But get the front door for me, okay?"

He led the way through the deserted bakery. It was closing time, and he was ready to lock up. He opened the door and held it for Maggie. With difficulty, but stubbornly persistent, she struggled out onto the sidewalk, up to her ears with baked goods. Hans closed the door behind her, pulled down the shade, turned the key from the inside, and disappeared into the bakery kitchen.

The sacks were filled higher than usual this time. Maggie was having difficulty seeing where she was walking. Her shoe hit an uneven edge in the sidewalk, sending her and her three bags of bread sprawling. "Oh, crap!" she exclaimed, looking at the torn sacks and the mess she'd created.

"Here, let me help you, honey," came a husky voice from somewhere. Maggie pulled herself up onto her knees and looked around. The woman who was bending down to assist her appeared to be in her mid-thirties, but the make-up she wore suggested she was trying to look mid-twenties.

"Thanks for helping a clumsy old lady," Maggie said, stacking the loaves.

"Glad to help," the stranger said. She carried an armful of bread to the truck. Opening the door, she piled the loaves behind the driver's seat. "We all need to help each other, every way we can."

"You live around here?" Maggie asked, depositing the rest of the bread in the back of the van.

"Right next door," she said.

"Next door's a liquor store."

"Upstairs."

"There's an apartment up there?"

"Yeah. It's also my place of business."

"You live where you work?"

"It's actually kind of nice, having the customers come to me."

"But what sort of work do you actually do?"

"Honey, do I have to spell it out for you?"

Maggie felt foolish. She should have figured it out. "Lucky for me, you were standing there when I stumbled," she said.

"I stand out here a lot," the woman said dryly. She added, "You wouldn't have a loaf of bread to spare, would you? I haven't eaten all day."

Maggie looked more carefully at the stranger. Her eyes looked tired. Everything about her looked tired. "My name's Maggie. What's yours?"

The stranger hesitated before answering. "Merrybelle. Merrybelle Mansfield."

"Listen, Merrybelle, why don't you let me get you a decent meal?"

"Naah. Save your money. A loaf of bread would be fine."

"It's not costing me a nickel. It's what I do. I feed people. We're having a hot meal over at the Community Kitchen in about two hours."

"No, thanks. I don't take charity."

"Fine. Then come along and help me prepare the meal. I need help in the kitchen tonight."

The woman looked at her and offered a wry smile. "You're not takin' no for an answer, are you, honey?"

"You got that right. Come on. Let's take a ride."

AS MERRYBELLE stirred the soup in the big kettle, she said, "Didn't there used to be a cute, little white wooden church around here someplace? I used to go to it."

"What was the name of it?" Maggie asked, opening a bag of day-old bread.

"I don't know. Saint Somethin'-or-other. Saint Gabriel, maybe?"

"Saint Michael and All Angels?"

"Oh, god, yes. That was it."

Maggie wondered if Merrybelle had any idea where she was. "So, you used to go there then, huh?"

"Yeah. For a while."

"Why'd you stop?"

"Well, I wanted the minister to come to my place and help me out, once upon a time."

"Personal stuff?"

"Yeah. *Very* personal. But when he showed up, he brought the sex police along with him."

"Beg pardon?"

"He brought some lady. I'm convinced she was from the morals squad at the police department. He claimed she was his wife. That was creative, I thought."

"Why would he bring along somebody like that?"

"Beats me. Fits a pattern, though."

"Yeah? How's that?"

"Men. They never give me any respect. Never have. Not even my old man. That's probably where it all started, in fact."

"Your father didn't respect you?"

"Let's just say he was a king-sized jackass."

"In my experience, respect has to flow in both directions."

"What's that supposed to mean?"

"Well, Henry and me — Henry's my husband — the two of us had to learn some give and take. When I didn't respect Henry, he didn't respect me back."

"Don't start with me about men, honey. I know more about 'em than you wanna know."

"Well, all I know is, the dining room's going to be full of hungry people in about ten minutes, and most of them will be men. You going to have a problem with that?"

Marybelle gave her a curious look. Maggie said, "Don't even *think* about it. None of these guys have any money. That's why they're coming here."

"Did I say anything?"

"You didn't need to."

DURING THE NEXT TWO WEEKS, Marybelle started coming to the Community Kitchen with Maggie on a regular basis. She'd wait for the old van to pull up at the bakery and then offer to help carry out the bread. Maggie always invited her to come back with her. Marybelle never turned her down.

One night, as they were preparing the community meal, Pastor James Darnauer walked into the kitchen. Maggie said, "Pastor, this is Marybelle Mansfield."

"I'm sorry. She got that wrong," Marybelle said, shaking the pastor's hand. "My name's Maureen. Maureen Rawlins."

Maggie had a huge look of surprise on her face. "*Maureen?*"

"Yeah. I don't use Marybelle in polite company."

"Well, what does that make *me* then?" Maggie demanded.

"Sorry. No offense intended. It's just that, Merrybelle is my business name."

Maggie rolled her eyes. She began again. "Pastor, this is Maureen."

Chapter 46

On September 1, 1939, the German army rolled into Poland. A few days later, England and France declared war on Germany and Italy. Conflict also broke out in the pages of the Minneapolis newspapers. Letters from readers appeared, urging the United States to join the war quickly, on the side of England and France, while equally-impassioned epistles denounced militarism and called for Americans to "let Europe fight its own battles." They were the opening salvos in a rancorous debate that would divide the nation for the next two years.

SHORTLY AFTER Reformation Sunday, Lillian Fischer went on maternity leave. Both she and the pastors were delighted to learn that the accomplished young musician, Daniel Schwandt, was once again available to fill in on the organ bench, through the end of the year.

In December, Lillian gave birth to her first child, a baby boy. She tried bravely not to let Luther see the disappointment she was feeling. Expecting him to choose a biblical name for the infant, she was surprised when he suggested "Christopher." He argued, "It's a Christian name. It means 'one who bears Christ.'"

She didn't challenge his logic.

THE FOLLOWING SPRING AND SUMMER, a curious phenomenon occurred on the shores of Lake Saint Michael. The six families which had founded the congregation, twelve years before, along with David Engelhardt, created a consortium of sorts. They agreed to pool their resources and purchase lumber, at a quantity discount, enough to build eight lake homes — one for each of them, and one for Pastor and Rosetta Jonas.

That wasn't the end of it. The men committed themselves to invest all of their weekends at the lake, working as a team of seven builders, putting up all the houses at one time.

When Daniel learned of it, he volunteered to do his part. His skills as a carpenter had been honed under the tutelage of Andy Scheidt, a dozen years earlier. He spent most of his Saturdays helping with the project, returning to Minneapolis for worship on Sundays.

The others took turns leading Sunday morning worship in the chapel at the church camp. The little congregation of around 40 consisted of the builders, their wives, and their growing families of young children. Tom and Sonja Pavelka also showed up at worship, along with their three children.

By late August, the entire village was completed. On Labor Day weekend, Daniel and Rosetta came to the lake. The pastor ceremoniously blessed each dwelling. Afterwards, on the grounds of the church camp, the two of them, along with Pastor Darnauer, hosted a picnic meal for the entire "south shore community." It was intended to be what Daniel called "our poor response" to the generosity their friends had shown by giving them handsome winterized homes on the edge of Lake Saint Michael.

IN MARCH OF 1940, Joe Pavelka's business partner suffered a stroke while traveling from South Side Motors to his home in Hopkins. The vehicle he was driving careened from the pavement and crashed into a telephone pole. With his body slumped over the steering wheel, the car's horn wailed a mournful dirge to passersby. He was dead before they got him to the hospital.

The partners had written their business agreement in such a way that one could buy out the other before his half interest would be offered to anyone else. Joe went back to the bank and, with creative financing and a good deal of leveraging of his personal assets, bought the business outright. For the first time in more than a decade, he was once again sole proprietor of a Twin Cities auto dealership.

When he and the bank had finished the paperwork, he went home to his wife and told her they were going out to celebrate. He took her to a restaurant on Marquette Avenue, and then to see the new color motion picture, *Gone with the Wind.*

JUST NINE MONTHS after the birth of her first child, Lillian Fischer gave birth to another. Since Luther didn't want another challenge from Lillian, he made sure their second son got a distinctively biblical name. For good measure, John Mark was given a pair of them.

THE FIRST ISSUE of *The Bloomington Avenue News* rolled off the press on the last day of April, 1941. David Engelhardt had worked like a beaver for two weeks, trying to sell advertising to businessmen up and down the street.

In spite of his best efforts, the first edition of the weekly was a money-loser. It was a four-page broadsheet, the size of which Molly charitably described as "modest."

David was undaunted. He recruited all the fourth graders from his Sunday school class at St. Michael Church to deliver 2,000 copies, free, to all the homes within twenty blocks of the print shop, in all directions. The youngsters were paid fifty cents apiece for their efforts, and were promised another half dollar for each additional week's effort.

Within a month, people were beginning to take the newspaper seriously. David wrote an editorial urging readers to write and tell him what story they most appreciated seeing in print; what, if anything, they didn't like about the publication; and what they most hoped would be added. Almost eighty letters came in. He printed a representative number of the responses in the following issue. But that had not been the real purpose for his having issued the invitation.

He printed a box on the front page of the fourth issue, in which he trumpeted the fact that "nearly eighty readers" had already responded to the paper's content, and that "they surely represent a great number more who have simply not found the time to put pen to paper." Then he took copies and made a new series of visits to all the merchants he'd identified as potential advertisers. He pointed out the boxed story to each and said, "You see, people are reading this paper. And if you want to get your message in front of them, you'd better think about taking out some advertising with *The News*."

The ploy worked. A month later, the paper was turning a profit.

DANIEL HESITATED to bring up the subject, but he felt the need to do so. Less than a year after he'd last talked to Rosetta about putting his name in for possible call, something disastrous had befallen his family. He knew, rationally, that the one had no logical connection to the other. Still, an unspecified dread chewed at him when he thought about reopening the discussion.

On a cool Monday evening in September, after the fall schedule had begun once more at St. Michael and All Angels Church, he brought it up, during the evening meal.

"Are we still liking what we're doing here?" he asked.

Rosetta's expression indicated she was baffled by the question.

"The ministry here. Are you still feeling good about being in this parish?"

"You're ready to move, aren't you?"

"We promised to let James Darnauer go overseas after five years with us.

The five years are up next June. That might be a good time to simply clear the decks and let the congregation start with new pastoral leaders."

Rosetta said, "I'm surprised you waited so long to say it. " She buttered a half piece of bread and laid down her knife. "You've been here thirteen years. I wouldn't blame you for wanting to think about leaving."

"Janet Fenstermacher told me this morning that we've reached 2,000 baptized members. We're becoming one of the largest congregations in the church."

Rosetta sighed. "I understand. The work is getting to be a lot, even for two pastors." She took a bite of her bread. "I have a lot of friends here now. But I can't let that stand in the way of what you want to do."

"I'm not necessarily saying it's what I want to do. I love this place. If I go somewhere else, I'll find they're worshiping in some other way, and I'll have to re-educate everybody. Which may not even work. Here we did it with a new congregation. There wasn't much to unlearn."

She nodded. She knew how he loved the liturgy, the powerful organ music, and the rituals which he'd introduced at St. Michael and All Angels. And, for some reason, it occurred to her she would miss those glorious stained-glass windows.

They ate in silence. Then she said, "We could still come back to the lake house, couldn't we? Or wouldn't that be a good idea? What is it they say? Once you leave a parish, you should leave it completely."

What to do about the lake home troubled Daniel. They'd gone there for Labor Day weekend. That was the only time. Still, he realized, he couldn't let his love for the new property, and his appreciation for those who made it possible, shape his decision. Besides, there would be other lakes on which to build. If they stayed in Minnesota.

On the other hand, it wouldn't be Lake Saint Michael.

"So, are you going to send your name to the district office?"

He furrowed his brow. "After the first of the year. I think I'll do it then."

JOE AND MARY PAVELKA hosted Tom and Sonja, and their three adorable children, for Thanksgiving dinner in their Park Avenue home. After the meal, Joe took Tom into the parlor and pulled the sliding privacy door closed. When they were seated, he said, "The dealership's doing better and better. Lots of Chevies going out the door. And get this, Tom. Starting next month, I'm back to selling Oldsmobiles. You remember how long it's been since I sold one of those?"

His older son, tanned and fit from his summer running the church camp, nodded. "Nineteen-twenty-nine. I was in the eighth grade."

"It really feels good, running the whole show again." He paused significantly, then added, "I think I need a partner."

"Dad, you just bought out your partner's share. Why would you want to go half with somebody again?"

"I was thinking of a junior partner. Maybe somebody I could groom to take over the business."

It took Tom a few seconds for the meaning of his father's words to register. He shook his head, smiled in protest, and said, "Oh, no. No, you don't. I'm not signing on with you at the car dealership, Dad."

"We're going to start selling Cadillacs one of these years."

"That's supposed to tempt me, right?"

"Tom, do you really want to spend the rest of your life working with kids?"

"You have a problem with me doing that? Somebody had better do it, Dad."

"No. I didn't mean to ridicule your work. It's really important. But you're twenty-seven years old. One of these days you're going to hit thirty. Your salary is …"

"It's adequate," he said defensively.

"Okay. I'm pushing you. I'm sorry."

"Dad, these kids are my life. I love working with them. And being up at the lake all summer long … my God, I'd do that for *free*, if I didn't have a wife and kids to support!"

"That's my point. You've got three kids. They're getting older. Maybe you'll want to send them off to college some day."

"You never went to college."

"I know. But I'd love it if my grandchildren did. And I have it on pretty good authority that you keep encouraging the Luther Leaguers to plan on going to that Waterbury College down in Iowa."

"*Wartburg*, Dad."

"Okay. Whatever it is. So, don't you think that pretty little eleven-year-old Greta Ingrid might want to go to Waterbury in another six years?"

"Wartburg."

"You know, Tom, just because you and I didn't go to college, doesn't mean the next generation shouldn't. I'd be mighty proud if your kids went."

"Well, Dad, you're making pretty good money once again. Maybe *you* could pay their way."

Joe looked at his son with a mixture of disappointment and admiration. He said, "You're not going to become my junior partner, are you?"

"Not a chance of a rat in a cat house."

Joe sighed. "So you wouldn't be offended if I made the offer to your younger brother then?"

"No. Go ahead."

"All right," the older man said with resignation. "I guess I probably will, then." He paused and looked with affection at Tom. "But, just between you and me, I still wish you'd be the one."

Chapter 47

Lillian Fischer was relaxing on the living room couch, on a Sunday morning. She felt strange, staying home from worship. But she was one month shy of her due date and she'd taken two months away from the organ bench. She was more confident than ever that her third child would be her last. As far as she was concerned, once she had a baby girl, that would be the end of it.

She turned the pages of *Etude Magazine*, looking for new piano solos for her advanced students to learn for the annual spring recital. In spite of her growing family, she had managed to juggle the duties of playing the organ at St. Michael Church, directing all the choirs, staging the annual Mendelssohn oratorio, and teaching piano and organ students. Parents of budding young musicians had beaten a path to her door ever since she'd come to Minneapolis, and she had always had difficulty saying "no" to any of them.

Consequently, she now had over sixty-five students. As soon as the older ones went away to college, a new batch of young prodigies would appear in her music room.

But there weren't any music lessons now. It was December, and she was simply too far along to comfortably continue teaching. She'd given everyone a two month break, warning them that, come February, they'd better not give evidence of having slacked off practicing their musical scales.

She heard a commotion on the front porch. It sounded as if someone had taken a stumble coming up the steps and gone sprawling on the porch floor. As it turned out, that was exactly what had happened. When the door opened, Luther staggered in, looking sheepish. "Should have known I couldn't take three steps in one leap," he said, brushing himself off.

"Well, was that exactly necessary?" she asked, not hiding her irritation. She, after all, would be the one expected to get the stains out of his clothing.

"Yes, it just might have been," he replied, sliding out of his overcoat and dropping it onto a chair. "Big news."

She waited, a skeptical look on her face. The last big news Luther had brought home was that Joe Pavelka was offering deep discounts on used Oldsmobiles.

"The Japanese have bombed Honolulu," he said grimly. "They've sunk a battleship."

THE NEXT DAY, President Roosevelt went to Congress. In a speech broadcast to the nation, he described the catastrophic Sunday and its events as "a day that will live in infamy." He promptly declared the United States to be at war with both Germany and Japan.

BY CHRISTMAS, young men in families belonging to St. Michael Church were being called up for military service. It was the beginning of a process that would result in eighty-five from the congregation heading to the European theater of war, and seventy-one more to the Pacific. Fewer than half would come back alive.

ON THE FESTIVAL OF THE EPIPHANY, January 6, 1942, Lillian went into labor. When she delivered another boy, it was all Luther could do to keep his lips sealed. He was running out of hopeful things to say to his increasingly frustrated wife.

She seemed especially pleased, however, when he borrowed the name of their congregation — and one of the biblical archangels — when naming their third child Michael.

JAMES DARNAUER sat at the reading table in the Reformation Room at Saint Michael and All Angels Church. Daniel was due to arrive momentarily. James turned the pages of his clergy calendar book, reminding himself when Lent would start. The two pastors had scheduled the meeting in order to plan the worship and preaching schedule for the season soon to begin.

Daniel came into the room. He studied the wonderful wall of stained glass, with its Martin Luther geography impressively displayed. The five colorful panels never failed to inspire him.

Before the senior pastor had an opportunity to say anything, James took charge. "I have something I need to tell you."

Daniel looked across the table, expectantly.

"I won't be going to New Guinea next summer. With the war, it's not going to be possible." There was clear disappointment in his voice.

Daniel hadn't even considered that problem.

James said, "I realize I promised to leave after five years. So, I suppose I should put my name in for call somewhere else."

Daniel said, "Wait a minute! We don't hire and fire pastors in the Lutheran Church. As long as you feel called to serve here, and you haven't done something to cause offense, you should consider that this is where God wants you."

The younger pastor nodded. He said, "There's another thing."

"What's that?"

"I had always thought I'd go back to Illinois and marry my high school sweetheart, and then take her to the mission field with me."

"Is your high school sweetheart still waiting for you?"

He nodded. "Esther Staudermann. She's a school teacher. We had talked about marrying this June."

"What's stopping you?"

"Well, I'm not going overseas now."

"Good heavens, James, was that the deal you made with her? She won't marry you if you don't take her to New Guinea?"

"Well, no, not exactly. But it's just that ... I'm still living upstairs over the newspaper office. It's not much of a place to bring a new bride."

The senior pastor offered a wry smile. "It was good enough for Rosetta and me when we were first married."

James looked surprised. He'd never heard that story. He grinned. "So, it's okay with you, then, if I take some time off in June, and marry Esther, and bring her to Minneapolis?"

"I don't think it's my approval you need to get, James, so much as Esther Staudermann's."

TOM PAVELKA drove to Camp Saint Michael one Saturday in March. The new camping season was still three months away, but it was finally decent weather, so he decided to take advantage. He didn't want to go another season with a leak in the dining hall roof. The previous summer, water had started dripping down into campers' breakfast bowls on rainy summer mornings.

As he propped the ladder against the side of the building and then scrambled up to the roof, he caught sight of the sun's reflection on the lake. The beauty and solitude of Lake Saint Michael never failed to captivate him, especially when there were no noisy young campers — all of whom he loved dearly — to interrupt the calm.

He took three steps onto the roof and immediately lost his footing. With nothing to grab onto, he slid backwards, off the building, onto the still-half-frozen grassy surface below. When he tried to get up, he felt excruciating pain in his left leg. There was no one there to assist him. He managed to limp back to his camp truck, where he dragged himself up onto the driver's seat, and then drove himself all the way back to Minneapolis, enduring an increasingly fierce throbbing in his ankle the entire way back.

ON THE FIRST TUESDAY in April, twenty-two-year-old John Pavelka was called up. With his broken ankle, the draft board showed no interest in Tom, a consequence which filled the camp manager with mixed feelings. Watching his younger brother board a train for the east coast made him feel apprehensive about the young soldier's safety. And it gave him a twinge of guilt, realizing he would not be able to serve his country in the war effort. But, he also felt relief, knowing he'd be able to stay in Minnesota, with his wife and three growing children.

ONE YEAR LATER, on the Wednesday before Mother's Day, Sonja Pavelka's favorite maiden aunt died quietly in her sleep. Jens and Ingrid took Sonja and Tom to Des Moines with them for the funeral. Not wanting to pull their children out of school, Sonja arranged to have them stay with school friends whose parents were members of St. Michael Church. With a Saturday funeral, they expected to be home again by Sunday evening.

Eleven-year-old Greta Ingrid was assigned to the Scheidt family. She and Freddie Scheidt were the same age and had gone through Sunday school together. Both at church and at school, their classmates were convinced they were sweet on each other. Freddie thought he might have a crush on Greta. She wasn't sure what she thought of him, except that he was cute, and she liked cute boys.

At Friday supper, Lorene Scheidt said, "Andy wants to go to the lake and open up the summer house tomorrow. Does anybody want to go along?"

The Scheidt children exploded in excited chatter. They hadn't been to Lake Saint Michael since the previous September. "Let's go tonight!" exclaimed eight-year-old Peter Scheidt. His mother scowled good-naturedly at him.

Freddie sent Greta a look of excitement. "Dad can get the canoe out. We can paddle across to the camp."

"Absolutely not," Andy replied. "That's too far for an eleven-year-old to paddle alone."

"*Two* eleven-year-olds," Freddie corrected.

"It's still too far."

"Dad, at camp last summer I canoed all the way across and back."

"You had a counselor in the canoe with you."

Freddie sighed with resignation.

"You can paddle around the Gospel Islands and back. No farther. Otherwise, no canoeing. Okay?"

"Yeah," Freddie groused.

LILLIAN FISCHER came to bed after checking on five-month-old Michael. As she climbed in, Luther said, "Three boys. No girls. Think we should give up? Time to stop?"

She lay staring at the ceiling. "No. One more. The fourth one will be a girl."

BAREFOOT, wearing his swimming trunks, Freddie Scheidt sat in the back of the canoe, patterning his strokes with Greta Pavelka's. He studied the beautiful, long blonde braid that circled the back of her head. He admired Greta so much, it worried him. He figured eleven was too young to actually fall in love with anybody. But he wondered if she'd still be available when he was seventeen. He'd just have to keep an eye on her for the next six years, that was all.

They reached the Isle of John and paddled smoothly around its far side, heading for the other three in the chain. Andy said, "You ever been on one of these islands?"

Greta replied, "No. Of course not. They're off-limits. Nobody's supposed to go on them."

"Yeah, I know. Your grampa's private property." Every church camper got the same lecture from Tom Pavelka on the first day of camp. Freddie had it memorized: *The islands are off-limits. If you set foot on one of them, you'll be sent home and not invited back to camp.* He wondered what the big deal was about staying off the four small islands. Was there hidden treasure on them or what?

They passed the Isle of Luke. It looked mysterious and inviting to Freddie, with its stand of trees and no sign of life. "You think anybody has ever been on any of these islands?" he asked.

"Probably Indians," said Greta.

"S'pose there's any Indian bones on any of them?"

"Freddie, we're not going to find out. My parents have never let me go on the islands. They said Grampa would *really* be upset. And if I can't go on them, you can't either."

They approached the Isle of Mark. "Why do you suppose that is? That your grampa doesn't want anybody going on them, I mean."

"Well, I don't know, but I have an idea."

"What's your idea?"

"The camp's on one side, and all these lake homes are on the other side. There's nothing left that's unspoiled, except the islands. Grampa wants to keep them that way."

They approached the Isle of Matthew, and then began circling it. "My dad says David Engelhardt named these islands, a long time ago. It was sort of a joke."

"Naming the islands was a joke?"

"Naming them Matthew, Mark, Luke and John was a joke."

"I think it was an inspired idea," Greta said.

Freddie thought about it. *Maybe she was right,* he thought. One thing was for sure. Just looking at the Gospel Islands was inspiring to him.

Chapter 48

The canoe was coming up on the other side of the Isle of Mark. They could see what looked like a small beach, about two canoe-lengths long. It was the only place on any of the islands that appeared to have such a landing place.

Suddenly Freddie exclaimed, "We gotta stop! We gotta stop!"

"Why?" demanded Greta.

"Because I gotta go."

"Can't you wait until we get back?"

"You want me to do it right here in the canoe?"

"Oh, all right," she said. "Just don't tell anybody we did this. If Grampa finds out, I'm going to be in big trouble."

"Nobody will ever know," said Freddie. The canoe came to rest on the tiny beach. He scrambled out and hurried, barefoot, into the trees.

Greta saw no point in sitting in a beached canoe while Freddie was off doing his business. She climbed out and stepped onto the forbidden shore. She was keenly aware that it was the first time ever for her to set foot on one of the Gospel Islands. She wondered whether she and Freddie were the first ones to do it — at least the first since her grandfather had bought the lake.

The sun felt good warming her swimming suit and bare legs. She was anxious to get back to the boat landing, so they could go swimming.

Freddie emerged from the woods. There was a sheepish grin on his face. "I guess the Indians had to do it that way," he said.

"Wash your hands in the lake," she said, trying not to sound like his mother.

"Why don't I just wash all of me?" he said, taking off at a run. Leaping into the air and curling himself into a ball, he landed in the lake, creating an enormous splash that doused Greta.

"You little rascal!" she exclaimed. "I'll get you for that!" She jumped in after him. Both were excellent swimmers and had no fear of deep water.

Freddie disappeared beneath the surface, then suddenly reappeared behind her. He grasped her shoulders and playfully shoved her under the water. She came up sputtering. He chortled with laugher and swam away from her.

When she caught up, he was looking contrite. "Okay. Dunk me. Get it over with."

"Forget it," she said. "You'll just come up behind me again, and we'll be back where we started."

"I have an idea," he said. "Let's see who can stay down the longest."

"What for?"

"Just to find out. I have this theory that girls always run out of breath before boys do."

"Nonsense. You have no way of knowing that."

"Let's find out," he chided. "One, two, three." He plunged under the water. She quickly followed. She opened her eyes and saw him nearby, doing his best not to rise to the surface. She waited as long as she could. Finally, when she thought her lungs would burst, she surfaced again. A split second later, Freddie reappeared. He roared with laughter. "I saw you going up," he said. "I could have stayed down ten more seconds."

She looked disgusted. "One more time. Just to show you how stupid your theory really is."

"Okay," he said. "One, two, three!" Down they went together.

She swam lower and lower, until the lake water began to look murky. She saw a root mass extending from the shore and grabbed onto it. That, she decided, would keep her from surfacing too quickly.

Her lungs were beginning to hurt. It was time. She turned, braced her foot on the root mass, and pushed off. But suddenly, something went dreadfully wrong. Her foot had become ensnared. She tried desperately to pull free. But she could not. She reached down, trying to untangle the roots from her foot.

And then her world went dark.

ANDY SCHEIDT bent over Greta's limp body, trying to breathe life back into it. Freddie stood next to the rowboat, now resting where the canoe had been a quarter hour before, a look of horror on his face. This was impossible. This was not happening. This was his fault. This was the end of the world.

His father looked up at him with a defeated look. Freddie had never seen him cry before, but the forty-year-old carpenter, now on his hands and knees, on the compact island beach, was sobbing large, manly, heart-wrenching sobs. Then came the anguished moans, the wailing, and finally the pathetic whimpering of one who had cried for help, for mercy, for a miracle from all the angels who might hear.

But no miracle had come.

Freddie covered his face with his hands and wept, his body shaking in the warm afternoon sunlight, as if it were November and he had caught a lethal chill. He wished it had been him. He wished he could be dead.

He felt as though he were.

ST. MICHAEL AND ALL ANGELS CHURCH was full. The funeral was a somber affair, at which Daniel found it impossible to preach. He deferred to James, who spoke eloquently about the promises of God and the sure and certain hope of the resurrection unto everlasting life. Even so, his voice broke several times before he finished.

Lillian Fischer played an interlude, J.S. Bach's "Come Soothing Death," the English text for which was printed, at Ingrid Jorgensen's request, in the worship folder. As she sat reading the words, matching them to the quiet tones of the great Reuter pipe organ, Ingrid shook with silent grief.

Beside her, Jens sat stoically, wondering whether God was somehow punishing him. If so, he had no idea exactly what his transgression might have been.

From the balcony, under Lillian's direction, a hastily organized chamber choir sang "In Paradise" from Gabriel Faure's poignant *Requiem*.

At the cemetery, Daniel had composed himself sufficiently to read the committal service. As the family turned to leave, Tom Pavelka took his father-in-law aside and said, "Jens, we can't do this."

"What do you mean?"

"She shouldn't be here. I don't want her buried here."

In urgent whispers, Jens replied, "Tom, the grave's been dug. The casket is ready to be lowered."

"This isn't right."

"Tom, why didn't you say something before?"

"I had a dream. Last night. Everything became clear to me. Her grave shouldn't be here, in this cemetery. I want her buried on the Isle of Mark."

Jens looked at Tom with a stupefied expression. But Tom's face was set, like steel.

FREDDIE told his father, "I don't want to go back to the lake. I don't want to go to camp any more. I don't want to go back up there. *Ever.*"

Four months later, at the end of summer, Tom took Freddie out across Lake Saint Michael, in the camp's rowboat, to the Isle of Mark. Together they walked through the woods, to a clearing, where a stone had been set. Freddie read the inscription:

GRETA INGRID PAVELKA
1933 - 1944
Now she is with the angels

They stood together for a long time, looking at the stone. Then Freddie said, "I have to get back out where the sun is."

"I'll be there in a minute," Tom said, patting Freddie on the shoulder. As the youngster walked back through the trees, toward the rowboat, Tom looked at his daughter's grave and said, "Now you're back where you started, Greta." He had thought he'd keep his emotions in check this time. But he could not hold back the flood rising inside. His soulful tears watered the forest grave.

As he turned to leave, he saw a fading inscription on a nearby tree. He walked toward it and smoothed his hands across the crudely cut heart and words, an inscription he seemed to remember having carved about a century ago:

Tom + Sonja
July 4, 1932

As if sensing God's mocking presence, he muttered, "You're making me pay for what I did. I *know* you are." Immediately he repented of having said the words. It was something his father might have said, but it was not what he himself actually believed.

Still, a part of him was convinced of the rightness of the words.

WHEN THE CAMPING SEASON was finished, Tom went to see Pastor Jonas. As they sat in Daniel's office, Tom rehearsed in his mind what he wanted to say. The words did not come out as he'd planned.

"I came here to tell you that I have to give up running Saint Michael Camp. And the youth program at church." He took a breath. "I hope you'll accept my resignation. I really need to have you do that for me." He hesitated, but only for an instant. "But that's not all I think I need to say to you right now."

Daniel had learned a long time ago not to interject a comment prematurely. So, he waited.

Tom continued, "I miss my daughter terribly." He wrinkled his forehead and sighed heavily. "She was such a beautiful little girl. I still don't understand why in hell she had to die." He stopped, trying to regain his composure. His eyes were pooling. "And that damned camp ... I'm sorry, Pastor ... that ...

that camp just holds too many painful memories for me now." He sighed again, more heavily than before. A lone tear ran down his face. "I'm not handling any of this very well. I can't sleep. I feel guilty. I feel angry. I feel sad. I feel hopeless. I feel like I've let down my wife and my in-laws." He paused. "I feel like I don't know what I should do. About anything."

He looked at the pastor with a sad, distant expression. He sighed still again. "Sometimes I wake up in the middle of the night and wonder why I didn't take Greta to Des Moines with us. She might still be alive today. That makes me angry. And frustrated. And sad."

He paused. "I know it's completely ridiculous, thinking like that. It isn't logical. But I feel that way." He sniffed miserably, then pulled a handkerchief from his pocket and dried his eyes. "I also wonder if God is as angry with me as I am with myself."

Daniel was tempted to comment, but held back.

Tom said, "I feel like I don't want to do anything. But I know I have to support my wife and kids somehow. I guess I'm going to go to work for my dad. At least until my brother comes home from the war. But I hate like hell doing it."

"Why do you hate it?" Daniel finally interjected.

"Because I feel disloyal to my brother, taking his job, even for a while. And because I think my dad secretly blames me for what happened, even though he'll never say so." He paused. "And because I really don't like selling cars." For the first time he showed a faint smile.

Daniel said, "Give yourself a chance, Tom. Try it for a little while. Just see how it goes. If it doesn't work out, come back and talk to me again. We'll figure something out. You and I together."

Tom nodded. "Thanks," he said. "Mostly, thanks for listening."

Chapter 49

Joe Pavelka burst into Daniel's office, interrupting a counseling session. The look on the car dealer's face persuaded the astonished counselee to excuse himself and beat a hasty retreat.

Before Daniel had a chance to scold him for his inappropriate behavior, Joe exploded. "I'm goddam mad as *hell* — at you, at God, at *everybody!*"

Daniel gestured to Joe to sit down. He said, "I'll *stand*! I'm too goddam mad to sit!"

He yanked a folded piece of paper out of his suit jacket and threw it on the desk in front of Daniel. The pastor opened it and immediately saw the sentence:

" *... regrets to inform you of the death of your son, John ...* "

Daniel dropped the letter onto the desk. He felt weak. He pursed his lips and tried to calm his racing heart. *How much hell does one family have to endure?* he wondered. When he looked up at Joe, his own eyes were pooling. He shook his head, unable to find words to speak.

That seemed to knock the car dealer off-balance. He'd never seen the pastor so vulnerable. "Oh, Mother of God," he whispered, a tone of genuine contrition in his voice. "I'm sorry. I didn't mean to unload it on you like that." But then his own eyes began to mist. "It's just all been so damn hard. So damn, damn, damn *difficult!*" He fisted one hand and smashed it into the palm of the other. "Dammit, Pastor! Why is God *doing* this to me?"

Daniel did something he'd never done with another man. He walked around the desk, opened his arms wide and embraced Joe in a solid hug. As he held onto him, he heard the car dealer sobbing, and felt him shuddering.

"Joe, you're such a good friend. You don't deserve all this."

"I know I don't, Pastor. I know. I know. I know."

TOM DIDN'T LEARN of his brother John's death until his father came by the dealership in late afternoon. He'd been having a lousy sales day. Ever since the government had issued a mandate requiring auto factories to retool, and start making war equipment instead of automobiles, new cars were no longer available. From Tom's perspective, it didn't make much difference, since the inventory already in the showroom wasn't moving. And, with his disdain of selling cars, his heart hadn't been in it anyway.

When he came into the showroom, his father looked as if his eyes were irritated, but Tom couldn't be sure. Joe Pavelka pulled the letter from the pocket of his suit jacket and handed it to his son. Immediately, he went into his office and closed the door.

After he read the message, Tom felt his body going numb. He felt as if he was floating, out of touch with reality. His head was spinning.

Without saying anything to anybody, he walked out the front door and started heading down Lake Street, to nowhere in particular. As he walked, he looked aimlessly into store windows, into the faces of strangers, at everything and nothing. He crossed four intersections, then stopped. His head was pounding. He wasn't thinking straight. Nothing was making sense to him.

He peered into a business establishment, through the plate glass window. It was a liquor store. A child of the Prohibition Era, Tom had never been a drinker. But Prohibition had been repealed, and this might be a good day to start, he decided. He pushed through the door and began searching for something to dull his senses.

Ten minutes later, standing in front of the store, he opened the flask of whiskey he'd just purchased and began to empty it, gulping the harsh liquid until it burned his throat.

A woman in her mid-thirties approached. She said, "You look like you need comforting. Can I help?"

Her voice was raspy, but had a note of genuine concern. He looked at her uncomprehending. What was she suggesting?

"I live upstairs," she said. "Come on. I'll offer you some comfort."

He looked at her painted face. She'd been around the block a few times, he decided. He took another swallow. The flask was now half empty.

She took him by the hand and led him, through the door between the liquor store and the bakery, and up the dark stairway. As she opened her apartment to him, he took another swallow. He staggered inside after her, and drained the flask.

Then the room began to spin.

SONJA PAVELKA WAITED until the meal on the table began to turn cold. It was not like Tom to be late for supper, but she decided he might have gotten lucky with a customer. She and her children ate in silence, after which she called South Side Motors. There was no answer. She called Tom's parents. Mary answered. Joe was not home yet. She said she'd have him call when he came in.

The reason Joe had not gone home after work was that, on the way to his car, he'd noticed Tom's still parked next to his. He'd begun a personal search of the neighborhood, but failed to find any sign of him. And then he'd called the police.

MAUREEN RAWLINS had not shown up to help with the Community Meal as she usually did, but it wasn't the first time it had happened. So, Maggie Washington had struggled along without her, muttering under her breath about the woman's inconsiderate behavior. After all, Maggie had set her up in a bartender's job, the result of which had been to get her out of the soliciting trade.

She knew Maureen usually went from the Community Kitchen to her late shift at work. So, when the diners were mostly gone, Maggie called the tavern. Maureen had not arrived. That seemed puzzling to her. Maureen had no phone in her apartment, so there was no way Maggie was going to reach her without driving down Lake Street.

She decided, if her delinquent assistant didn't show up at the curb the following afternoon, when she went back to the bakery for day-olds, she'd go up to her apartment and find out what was what.

WHEN THE POLICE hammered on Maureen's upstairs apartment door, at nine-thirty in the evening, she hesitated before opening up to them. She demanded they tell her what they wanted. They demanded she let them in.

When she finally did, they found Tom Pavelka in her bed, his clothing strewn about her bedroom floor. He was wearing nothing but his briefs. And he stank of alcohol. When they informed her that he was the subject of a neighborhood search, she told them they could do what they wanted to with him. But, as far as she was concerned, he was in no shape to be going anywhere.

TOM SAT SLUMPED in a chair in the front parlor. The police had brought him home. The throbbing in his head was intense. He looked at his angry wife, staring at him, and said, "Sonja, I need to sleep. This headache is killing me. Can't we talk in the morning?"

"I'm trying to decide if I still want to *be here* in the morning."

"I'm sorry. For everything," he said, holding his head in his hands.

"What were you doing in that woman's apartment? And since when have you taken to drinking?" she demanded crossly. "And what's all this stink on your clothes?"

"I can't remember anything. Honestly. I can't. Just let me sleep."

"You can sleep, all right," she said fiercely, getting up. "But not in *our* bed. You can stay right here, and sleep in your own filth." She marched out of the room and up the stairs. With difficulty, he moved himself from the chair to the couch, where he collapsed and quickly sank into unconsciousness.

THERE WAS A NOTE waiting for Tom when, at mid-morning he finally stumbled into the kitchen. It was Sonja's handwriting, but it was not signed. The terse message read, "We have an appointment with Pastor Jonas at four. Be on time."

He discovered there was still coffee in the pot. He started the stove and began to heat it up. He found a cup and sat, watching the flame beneath the coffeepot, and tried to think. He remembered walking down Lake Street. He remembered buying a flask of whiskey. He didn't remember much more than that.

He massaged his temples with his thumbs and wondered if the throbbing would ever stop. He looked at the note again. For the first time reality hit him. Sonja might be planning to leave him. That was probably why she'd scheduled a session with the pastor.

If she left him, and got the children, what would he do then?

SONJA WAS ALREADY SEATED when Tom arrived at the pastor's office. She stared stonily at him. She, or someone, had moved the only empty chair away from hers. He sat down in it. Pastor Jonas said, "You haven't missed anything, Tom. I told Sonja we'd wait until you got here."

Tom nodded with appreciation.

The pastor said, "Sonja, this has to be hard for both of you."

She looked defiantly at Tom, then at the floor.

He continued, "First you lose your daughter, and then Tom loses his brother. That's seems so cruel."

She looked up with a shocked expression. "What did you say? Something's happened to John?"

"Didn't Tom tell you?"

"He's been too busy whoring around with loose women to have time to tell me *anything*," she snapped. But then she softened. "What about Tom's brother?"

"The word came yesterday afternoon. John was killed, fighting the Germans, somewhere in France."

"Oh, my God," she said softly. She looked at Tom. "But it's still no excuse for what he did." She said it as if he were not there.

"It probably explains why he started drinking," Daniel said, looking at Sonja. He turned to Tom. "But it doesn't really excuse it."

Tom nodded miserably, and then looked at the carpet.

"What about that …" She hesitated before saying it. " … that *woman*? She's a known prostitute. Everybody knows that apartment is a house of ill repute. It always has been." Her voice was taking on an edge.

"Well, you're right," Daniel said. "Maureen was a streetwalker for a long, long time. But she's given it up. She hasn't solicited men for over a year."

"Who says so?" Sonja demanded.

"Well, Maggie Washington, for one. She got Maureen back on the straight and narrow. The two of them have been working side by side in our Community Kitchen for many months now."

Sonja had never paid attention to what Maggie Washington did, in the church or anywhere else. "It still doesn't explain what Tom was doing in her bed. With practically nothing on."

"Well, it's complicated," Daniel said. "Maureen was on her way from her apartment to the bakery, to wait for Maggie to show up. They were going to bring day-old bread here, to our Community Kitchen. But when she got to the sidewalk, Tom was there, looking pretty pathetic. She admitted to me, when we talked this morning, that she almost relapsed. He was young and good-looking and … do you really want to hear this?"

"I want to hear every disgusting detail," she snapped.

"She took him upstairs. But Tom was so drunk, he vomited all over his clothes. Maureen took them off and got him into bed. He was unconscious before he hit the mattress. That was all that happened. She decided to let him sleep it off. That's what he was doing when the police came."

Sonja was silent. Tom was looking ashamed. Here he was, listening to the pastor describe his own behavior, the details of which even he had been unaware.

Daniel said, "Sonja, Tom's behavior is disappointing. Maybe even disgusting. But there's a reason why it happened. And it wasn't as you thought it was." She was beginning to look contrite. The pastor continued, "The two of you have been through rough times. But you're a really fine couple. I don't think you want to let all that come to an end. Certainly not like this."

She glanced at Tom. He was looking dejected.

Daniel said, "I think some compassion would be in order."

She said, in a quiet voice, "Tom, I'm sorry about your brother. I didn't know. I suppose your father thought you'd tell me yourself." She continued, "And I apologize for being so angry. That probably wasn't fair. Will you forgive me?"

Tom got out of his chair and walked to hers. He pulled her up. "I love you, Sonja," he said. "I'll never love anyone else." He circled his arms around her and said, "I'm sorry. For everything. Please forgive me. If you can." By now, all the anger was gone from her face. Looking at her with beseeching eyes, he said, "Can we go home now?"

Sonja looked at Pastor Jonas. He smiled at them and said, "Go home."

Chapter 50

The war in Europe was over. On the heels of President Roosevelt's sudden death, the Nazi dictator put a pistol to his head and obviated the collapse of the Third Reich. The armistice was quickly signed, and soon the American troops were streaming home again.

It took four more months for the war in the Pacific to end. When it finally came, soon after the detonation of two horribly destructive bombs over Japanese cities, a debate broke out in the country, and also among the members of St. Michael Church, over whether President Truman had been justified, ending the fighting as he did.

On the Sunday following Japan's surrender, Daniel preached a sermon in which he voiced thankfulness for the coming of peace, as well as a hope that healing could now begin, all over the world.

"The victims of war, especially in Europe, will need our help," he said. "Many of us come from German stock. Regardless what we may have believed about Hitler and the National Socialists, our hearts should go out to the people of Germany. Those who supported the Nazi movement, we must learn to forgive. Those who lived in heroic opposition, we need to thank. Those who will now be in need, we will want to assist. And, we Lutherans should be the first to step up to help."

Members of St. Michael and All Angels Church had already been seeing posters on the church's bulletin boards, encouraging their financial support of a church-sponsored program called Lutheran World Action. Within six months, over $14,000 was pledged at St. Michael Church.

On Veterans' Day, a special Eucharist of Remembrance and Thanksgiving was held. Pastor Darnauer conducted the service, during which there was no sermon. Instead, two lists of names were solemnly read. The first remembered the fallen heroes who had gone out from St. Michael Church and not returned. Tom Pavelka had asked permission to read the list, which included the name of his younger brother, John.

Then Adam Engelhardt went to the lectern and began to read the names of those who had served with distinction in both theaters of the war, both the wounded and those who had returned without injury. The list was long, but worshipers hung on every name.

First he recognized those who had shown valor and patriotism in battle. There were nearly thirty. He was in no hurry to get through the list, pausing significantly after each: "Gerald Staehling ... John Thorson ... David Andreae ... James Buenting ... Thomas Lentz ... Terry Peterson ... Duane Waterman ... Albert Harms ... James Oscarson ... " The names went on and on.

Daniel sat in the chancel, listening. He wondered what scars, mental and emotional, these soldiers had brought back home with them. He wondered if they themselves really knew.

At the end, Adam read the names of those who had served with special distinction, including men who'd been cited for bravery. There was Philip Borleske, who helped derail a German train full of munitions ... Vern Harman, who dragged three wounded comrades, one after the other, out of harm's way, at great risk to himself ... Allan Bostelmann, a conscientious objector who had spent the war in England and helped crack the secret codes that crippled the Nazi advance.

Bostelmann's principled opposition to enlistment had caused considerable controversy in the congregation, especially among veterans of the First World War. But when his accomplishment was read publicly, spontaneous applause broke out and echoed through the cavernous nave. It was a significant moment of healing.

IN JUNE of 1946, James Darnauer and his wife, Esther, were commissioned as missionaries. James finally had his call to serve the American Lutheran Church in New Guinea. A week later, the couple boarded a train in Minneapolis for the long journey, first to Los Angeles, and then, by ship, to the Australian protectorate on the other side of the Pacific Ocean. They had committed to a seven-year term of service.

DANIEL AND ROSETTA sat on the front porch of their lake home. Across Lake Saint Michael, interrupting the mid-summer silence, they could hear the sounds of Luther Leaguers, singing around the evening campfire. The sun was disappearing. In the afterglow, a silver sheen cast the lake in ethereal light. To Daniel, the moment seemed magical.

It was Rosetta who brought up the subject he had avoided. "The Darnauers are probably in New Guinea by now. We're a pastor short again." He waited for her next sentence. "So, are you going to put your name in for call?"

"How long has it been?"

"How long has *what* been?"

"How long have we been here?"

"Eighteen years."

The number seemed incredible to him. "But who's counting?"

"So, you're not sure what you want to do?"

"This certainly is a wonderful lake home, don't you think?"

"Daniel, you always told me things like that shouldn't be allowed to stifle the Spirit's call."

"The kids really love Minneapolis."

"So do I. So do you, obviously. But it's been eighteen years, Daniel."

He watched a loon come in for a landing, out near the Isle of Matthew. It created ripples that spread slowly across the smooth surface of the lake. He thought about his ministry at St. Michael Church, and how what he had shared with the members of his ever-growing congregation had been a lot like that.

He watched the ripples disappear. It made him wonder how much of his work would also fade.

He sighed. "Another possibility would be to get another associate pastor. That would take some of the pressure off."

"So, you're planning to stay, then?"

"It sure would be hard, giving up Lillian Fischer's organ playing."

"You're definitely staying. I can tell."

"I don't know. I should pray about it." He watched the loon take off again.

"I'll bet I know what Lillian is praying for this summer," Rosetta said.

"What's that?"

"That she won't need a boy's name for her fifth baby."

"Four boys. Did people just make all that up, about her holding out for a girl?"

"No. Luther's told everybody who asks."

"Christopher, John, Michael, Timothy," the pastor muttered. "They're going to use up all the good names." He chuckled.

The sun was now nearly gone. Daniel said, "Do you know what's really amazing, Rosetta?"

"What's that?"

"Those camp songs the kids sing today. A lot of them are the same ones you and I sang at Bible camp, back in Ohio." He paused. "Lillian would never allow us to sing any of them at worship, and I guess I wouldn't either. But I still like them."

From across the lake, familiar words, sung to a familiar tune, wafted toward them, and they found themselves singing softly, along with the Luther Leaguers, far across Lake Saint Michael, on the opposite shore:

Living for Jesus a life that is true,
Striving to please him in all that I do,
Yielding allegiance, glad-hearted and free,
This is the pathway to blessing for me.
Oh Jesus, Lord and Saviour,
I give my life to thee;
For thou, in thy atonement,
Didst give thyself for me;
I own no other master,
My heart shall be thy throne.
My life I give, henceforth to live,
O Christ, for thee alone.

The last of the sun had disappeared. Although they could not see the glow of the campfire, on the other side of the Gospel Islands, Daniel could visualize the scene. He imagined it, as he listened with appreciation. The exquisite harmonies of the Luther Leaguers from St. Michael Church were rising heavenward.

Somewhere, a million miles from Earth, he thought, their song must surely be combining with that of all the angels.

Gentle Reader,

In The Presence of Angels is the first in what is intended to be three consecutive novels in "The Saint Michael Trilogy." The story will trace the life and ministry of the members of The Lutheran Church of St. Michael and All Angels over the span of 75 years, from 1927 until 2002.

A significant portion of the royalties realized from the sale of this book and the others, when published, will be contributed to *Metro Lutheran*, America's only independent pan-Lutheran newspaper.

If you enjoyed and appreciated reading this book, and especially if you are a friend of *Metro Lutheran* and would like to help assure its future financial success, please encourage your friends to purchase their own copies of this book. They are available from the publisher, who can be reached by calling (301) 695-1707.

Copies are also available for purchase online. Go to www.bn.com and use the search function to find either the title or the name of the author of this book. You may make an online purchase with a major credit card.

Or, copies may be ordered through a neighborhood bookseller.

Thank you for purchasing and reading this book. I hope it has been a blessing to you as you seek purpose, meaning and direction on your daily path.

Michael L. Sherer
The Feast of St. Michael and All Angels
29 September 2004